LIMITED EDITION

DIVINE BLOOD

THE GUARDIANS OF THE MAIDEN

BECK MICHAELS

PLUMA PRESS

PLUMA PRESS
P.O. BOX 341
Camby, IN 46113
Visit Us at PlumaPress.com

Second printing 2023

Author: Michaels, Beck

Title: Divine Blood / Beck Michaels

Series: The Guardians of the Maiden; 1

Genre: YA Fantasy Fiction

Summary: Dyna travels across the Kingdom of Azure, gaining friends and enemies while searching for the magical treasure island of Mount Ida that contains unimaginable power they each seek.

Identifiers:
ISBN 978-1-7347639-2-8 (hardcover) | ISBN 978-1-7347639-1-1 (softcover)
ISBN 978-1-7347639-0-4 (ebook) | ISBN 978-1-7347639-4-2 (Limited Edition softcover)

www.BeckMichaels.com

Printed in the United States of America

For my sister,

who never stopped believing in me.

JERASH
GLACIAL OCEAN
SKATH
UNITED CROWN
THE THREE RIVERS
EDYM
XIAN JING
HARROMAG MODOS
DRAGON CANYON
LEDO
RED HIGHLANDS
LANGSHAN
THE VALE C
SUN GUILD
LEVIATHAN OCEAN
MAGC
MOUNT IDA
LUNAR GUILD

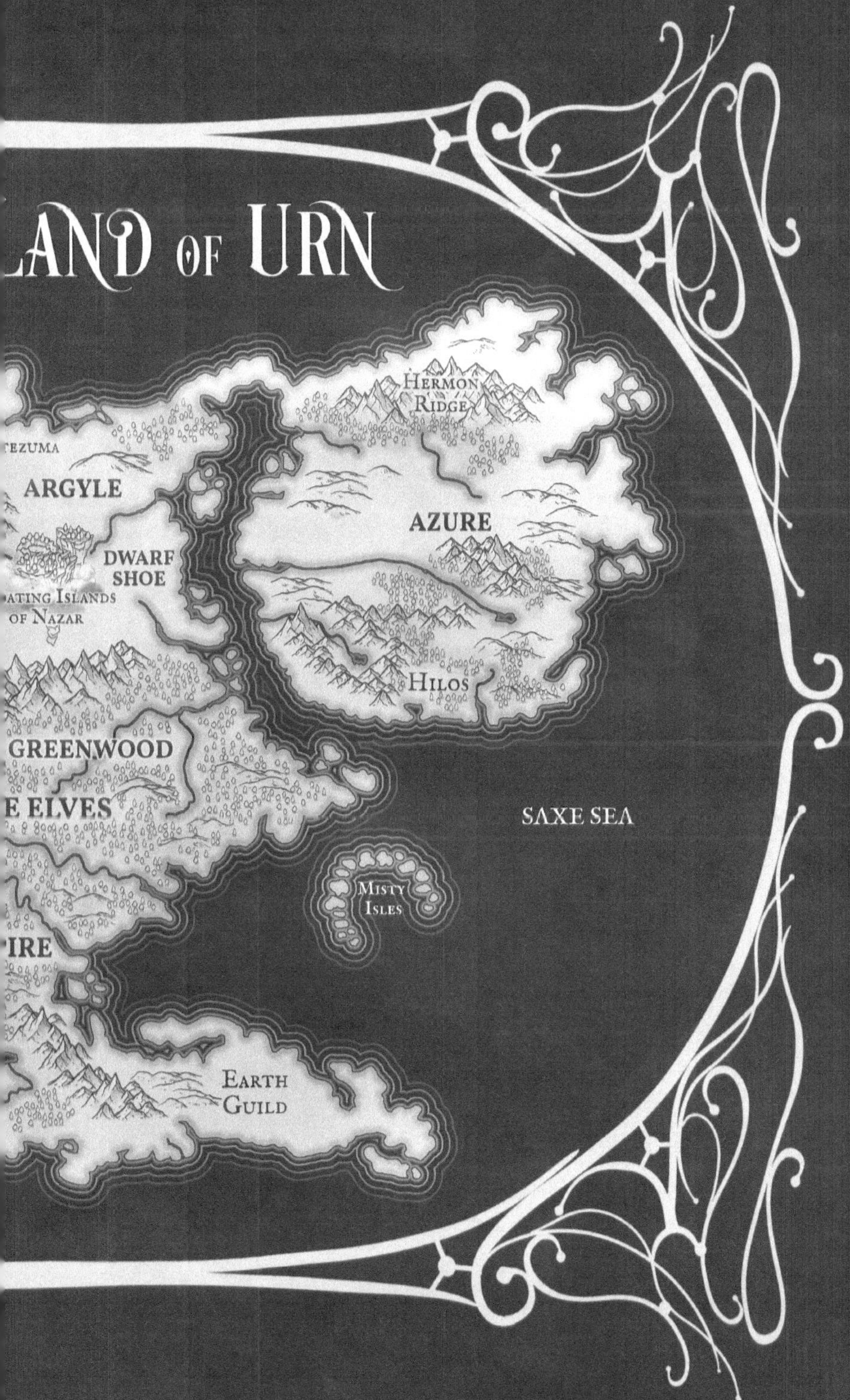

LAND OF URN
TEZUMA
ARGYLE
DWARF SHOE
ATING ISLANDS OF NAZAR
HERMON RIDGE
AZURE
HILOS
GREENWOOD
E ELVES
IRE
SAXE SEA
MISTY ISLES
EARTH GUILD

KINGDOM OF AZURE

The Seven Gates

Each soul passes through the gates at their beginning and their end.

HEAVEN'S GATE

LIFE'S GATE

SPATIAL GATE

TIME GATE

MORTAL GATE

NETHERWORLD GATE

DEATH'S GATE

PROLOGUE

Dynalya

The snowstorm howled and rattled the window, wailing a warning to run, hide, and pray to the Gods, but there was no hope of escaping what had arrived with the night. Dyna turned in place in her bedroom—this dreaded room she couldn't escape.

At the familiar creak of old wood, Dyna glanced at the nine-year-old version of herself sitting in the rocking chair by the fireplace. She held a bundle of blankets wrapped around her baby sister. Her wide green eyes stared out the window, watching the storm. The evergreen trees thrashed in the violent wind, threatening to snap in half and wrench free from the earth. In the moon's gleam, snow whipped like diamond dust; its beauty lost to the darkness surrounding her family's cottage.

Dread crept up Dyna's back.

Her younger counterpart clutched baby Lyra as she rocked, her feet pushing off the floorboards at a nervous pace. She knew they both sensed something sinister hiding within the darkness. Instinct prickled Dyna's skin in warning, tightening her limbs.

The Shadow was watching.

The thought came unbidden. A familiar call. A warning of what was to come.

"Get up!" she shouted at her child-self. *"Run!"*

Younger Dyna didn't hear her.

They both flinched at the spark of embers that burst from the logs in the fireplace. The fire struggled to heat the small space of the bedroom, smothered by the cold clinging to the air. The flames cast an array of disturbing shapes on the walls, which stretched and writhed, creeping toward the ceiling.

Thane, her younger brother, slept in his small bed beneath the windowsill. His mouth was propped open in a slight pout with his chubby cheeks pressed against his pillow. He was so small and precious. Her eyes welled with tears, wishing she could hold him close and brush back the curtain of red ringlets dangling over his forehead.

The sound of her parents' voices slipped through the crack beneath the door like a draft whispering secrets.

"Cease to argue with me on this, Ayla. We are leaving. This instant."

Dyna gasped at the sound of his voice. *"Father!"* She rushed to the door, but it wouldn't open. She couldn't reach them. She banged her fists against it, crying out to them. *"Mother! Father!"*

A clatter of movement beyond the door was followed by a rustle of fabric. "Pack as many provisions as you can carry and dress warmly."

"The council deemed the village safe, Baden," her mother insisted. "We needn't leave."

"The council knows nothing. I've tried to tell them, but they refuse to listen. The winter solstice has arrived, and the third Shadow Winter has come with it."

The definitive tone of his claim sent a chill down Dyna's back. She glanced at her younger self, who also listened, her wide eyes fixed on the door.

"I don't understand. Your father already defeated the Shadow at its last coming."

"Aye, as did my grandfather *ten years* before him. It always returns."

Trepidation skulked into the house, filling the heavy pause. Having been born two years after the Shadow's last coming, Dyna's younger self had only heard tales of the demon—dark tales of it swallowing children whole in the dead of night.

She rose from the rocking chair and tip-toed to the door to peek out through the crack. Dyna peeked with her, but the foyer limited their view of the apothecary. They could only see the small round dining table covered in glass bottles and dried herbs. Her parents were in the kitchen.

She strained to push the door open. She needed to see them, to embrace them, to warn them.

But this was only a dream.

"I've made my decision, Ayla."

"You will have us leave in the middle of this storm? Where are we to go?"

He sighed. "Belzev offered us shelter in Lykos Peak until winter's end."

Her mother sucked in a breath. "God of Urn, are you mad? We can't take the children there."

"It will be much safer than here. He has sent Zev to meet us."

Dyna closed her eyes at the mention of her cousin. He would arrive too late.

"We need to leave the village," her father continued. "Don't you understand? It's coming. *Tonight.*"

"You think we will fare any better out there?" her mother asked incredulously. "To reach Lykos Peak, we must pass through the Forbidden Woods. Do you mean to take us to our death?"

"Enough! I have spoken, and I'll not suffer you to argue with me on this matter!" The booming command vibrated through their small cottage before settling with a dreadful silence. Soft weeping soon followed.

Dyna's younger self gasped, stunned. Father had always been a soft-spoken man.

"Forgive me."

Her mother sniffled. "I'm frightened."

"As am I," he admitted, his voice trembling in a way it never had before. "I watched, helpless, as the Shadow took my sister at its last coming."

"Oh, Baden."

"I don't fear death. I fear what may befall my family. I have been plagued by nightmares of that night for the past year. Now I fear my past will repeat itself, and that is a future I cannot bear."

Dyna looked over her shoulder at the window. The time had come. The Shadow was coming.

She yelled at her younger self to move, to go to her parents—to do *something*. But she didn't. As a child, she knew better than to interrupt them when she should have been asleep.

"Please, we must go," her father begged.

"I will follow you," her mother said at last. He released a long exhale of relief. "But if what you say is true, then the Shadow must be out there."

"For that, I have prepared. I've made cloaking amulets for us all."

Dyna heard a faint clink. She pictured him removing the lid from the ceramic bowl he kept on his cluttered desk among the dusty magic books.

"Luna reeds," her mother gasped. "Where did you get these? They only grow in Magos."

"Aye, and they were difficult to acquire," he said. "Here, take two. It masks everything but sound. As long as you're quiet, you'll be safe. Go for Leyla while I wake the children."

Her mother's thudding footsteps ran out the front door, off to collect Grandmother Leyla. *No, we shouldn't separate!* Dyna shouted. *"Come back!"*

Her younger self backed away, tucking baby Lyra in the woven shawl wrapped around her shoulders.

The door swung open, and her father entered. Dyna inhaled a breath at the sight of him, stifling a sob. She reached out her shaking hands, calling him. *"Father, see me. Hear me, please."*

Dressed in furs and thick wool, he carried a large canvas pack strapped to his back. He brushed his unruly red hair aside, his face set with calm determination. Her father was not tall or strapping, but he was a man of repute in North Star, among the rare few who wielded magic. He would keep them safe. Her younger self had believed it so thoroughly she smiled.

Foolish girl.

"You need to run!" But Dyna's screams went unheard.

His astute green eyes swept around the room as he accounted for all his children. "Dynalya, are you ready?" He smiled, but she read the urgency in his gaze.

"Yes, Father." Her younger self pointed at the two small travel bags packed and perched by the bedroom door.

"Good lass." He held up three necklaces of dried white reeds. From each hung a circular pendant made of polished wood. "These are Waning Amulets infused with the magic of the moon. It will cloak you from the demon."

It was a spell he must have found within his many magic books. The rune for concealment marked each amulet: a single line connected with an inverted triangle on both ends. It matched the one he already wore.

He handed her two of them. "Be sure to wear it."

Young Dyna nodded, stroking the smooth grooves of the carving with her thumb. She placed the smaller amulet over Lyra's head to rest on her chest.

"Dress warm," he ordered. "I'll wake Thane."

Dyna backed up against the wall, knowing what was coming. Her father turned toward her brother and a frigid chill blasted through the room. It extinguished the fire, leaving behind mere wisps of smoke. Her rapid breaths shot visible puffs into the air as it grew frightfully cold.

Silver moonlight slipped in through the window, stretching wide across the wooden floorboards. It offered a brief solace in the dark—until a shape moved into its place.

Dyna was suddenly her younger self again, impossibly small, and terrified. "Father ..." she whimpered. "The Shadow is coming."

"Quiet!" he whispered.

They kept still, but she dragged her gaze to the window. A black form filled the frame, akin to a man's but large and misshapen. Tendrils of smoke and shadow swelled around its translucent profile. From its shapeless face were two eyes glowing molten red, flickering with flame. The amulet slipped through her shaking fingers and clattered to the floor.

The demon's eyes found her. They cut into her with an enthrallment, freezing her limbs in place. She was stone, and she was ice, locked within the walls of her consciousness. The frozen air crushed her lungs, barring her screams. She drowned in desperation to escape. There was nowhere to go but to her death. The chilling grasp on her mind squeezed tighter and tighter.

Her father snatched up the fallen amulet and dropped it around her neck. Its magic cut through the trance and released her. She sucked in a deep breath, air searing down her throat.

The Shadow's furious roar shook the foundation of the house to her bones.

Dyna shrieked, stumbling into the rocking chair in a panic to run away. Her father took her face in his calloused hands and made her focus on him. "Hush now, Dynalya, you are safe," he whispered. "As long as you have the amulet, it cannot see you."

She shook her head. It was too late.

"Papa?" Thane sat upon his bed, rubbing the sleep from his face.

The demon's molten eyes snapped to the boy left unprotected. Thane's expression dulled, mouth slacking as he fell under the Shadow's trance.

"No!" Her father's cry raised the hair on Dyna's neck.

Time paused. The events around her slowed into a cruel rendition out of her control. No matter how many times she had relived this moment, or how many times she willed another outcome, nothing changed. She screamed Thane's name as her father lunged to save him.

But the window shattered—and the Shadow came.

CHAPTER 1

Dynalya

Shrill screams tore through Dyna's throat. Terror wrenched her racing heart, threatening to tear it from her chest. Adrenaline spiked through her veins, and blood rushed in her roaring ears. Hands grabbed her, holding her down. She thrashed and fought against them, screaming and screaming.

"Hush, hush, sister! It's me! I'm here!" The familiar voice slipped through the manacles of Dyna's nightmare, snicked into the lock, and broke her free. "I'm here. You're safe."

Small, gentle hands came over Dyna's cheeks. She looked up at her little sister's face, the delicate features etched in concern. Lyra's presence banished all shadows the way the sun banished the night.

But even the sun had to set by the end of the day.

Dyna broke into gasping sobs. She clutched her sister in a crushing embrace, but Lyra didn't complain.

If only she could stop time and keep Lyra safe where no putrid darkness could reach her. But wishing would not amount to anything—a lesson learned long ago.

Dyna inhaled a shaky breath as her cries eventually quieted. She loosened her grasp on her sister and let her numb arms drop onto their bed.

"Are you all right?"

Dyna nodded and rubbed her swollen eyes. Sweat-matted strands of hair stuck to her temples, mounds of blankets tangled around her legs.

Lyra sat back on her heels. Her red tresses, braided in two coils on her head, were coming undone at the seams. She was every inch their mother, with the same cluster of freckles adorning her cheeks, the same heart-shaped face, and tawny brown eyes.

Grief swelled in Dyna's throat as she fought the urge to weep again. Her sister was all she had left of her mother. She held out her arms, and Lyra readily fell into them.

Dyna held her as she surveyed their bedroom. It was the same one of her dream, but the window was clear of any shadows that didn't belong. Beyond it, the dark sky lightened as dawn kissed the skyline of the Zafiro Mountains. No fire burned in the fireplace, save for a few cindering logs. Several melted candles peppered the ledges in the room. Trails of wax hardened where they had pooled in candleholders, thick runnels leaking over the edge of shelves, end tables, and any available flat surface. Anything to keep the darkness and the past at bay.

Not much had changed in her bedroom. A small empty bed remained under the windowsill.

Dyna looked away, swallowing the wave of emotion dragging through her. She could never bring herself to get rid of the bed. On the days she was exhausted or distracted, a mirage of her little brother's sleeping form filled its space. Sometimes Thane's laughter echoed on the hills outside, his cheerful voice calling out to his friends. It always sounded so real.

"Was it the dark that frightened you?" Lyra asked, her small voice too laden to belong to a child of nine.

Dyna didn't know what frightened her more. The dark? The past? Or the future?

Lyra slipped out of her tight hug and hopped off the bed. She hurried to the desk covered in a disarray of books and scrolls, where one lit candle remained. With it, she relit the others one at a time until the room filled with a warm hue. Lyra beamed in satisfaction. She was a small gangly thing, in a white chemise falling past her knees. At her sweet smile, Dyna offered a small one back.

"'And then there was light,'" Lyra said, quoting the archaic teachings of the Sacred Scrolls. A saying their grandmother used to tell Dyna when her fear of the dark first started.

The light lifted something heavy off her and she could breathe a bit easier.

"Thank you," Dyna murmured. Eighteen was much too old to have such a childish fear, but whenever she found herself alone in the dark, those red eyes always found her.

Lyra tilted her head. "Was it the same nightmare again? About Mother, Father, and Thane? Of the night they died?"

Shards of memories cut through Dyna's eyes, mouth, and ears, gathering into a broken pile on her lap. "Yes."

Lyra returned to the bed, curled up beside her, and covered them with a blanket. She yawned, eyes falling heavy. The dawn's morning light filtered in through the window and graced her cherubic face; her lashes cast faint patterns on her soft cheeks. "Will you tell me about it?"

Dyna shook her head. The past had not reached her sister and she would keep it that way.

"Please?"

"Perhaps one day."

Lyra mumbled a complaint. She nestled closer and soon drifted off to sleep again. Dyna rested her back against the headboard. She watched the candlelight flicker on the exposed rafters constructing the sloped ceiling, attempting to quiet her mind.

Not all of her dreams were of shadows. Sometimes she dreamed of flying with the warm wind carrying her over a gleaming sea. Invisible wings wove her through the wisps of clouds, where the endless sky waited.

The bedroom door creaked open and Grandmother Leyla peeked inside. Long gray hair cascaded down her shoulders, framing her round timeworn face and soft brown eyes full of worry.

"I heard the screams. Oh blossom, look at the state of you. You're as pale as cream. Are you all right?"

Dyna smiled sadly. "It's nothing, Grandmother. I'm fine." She reached out for her soft hand, catching the comforting trace of clove and lavender. It was a miracle her grandmother had survived that night. Dyna may not have been able to recover without her.

Grandmother Leyla glanced around the room at the many candles and the disorderly desk. "It's been quite a while since you have had those dreams, but this is the fifth occurrence within a fortnight. It has stemmed from your relentless study of The Seven Gates and the dark things we have no business delving into." Her petite frame settled on the end of the bed. "Which dream was it this time? The Shadow pursuing you up the mountain? Or the Glass Tree?"

"No." Dyna glanced at Thane's bed. "The moment before."

The creases of her grandmother's face deepened with sorrow. "Perhaps it is time to store the wee thing away. It only serves to remind you of memories best forgotten."

Her grandmother had lost many loved ones in her life, and Dyna wondered who she thought of now.

"If I had been taken that night, would you have forgotten me?"

"Oh, no, I would never." Grandmother gently squeezed her hand. "I thank the God of Urn every day for Zev. No one else could have found you in that snowstorm."

Beyond the window, the sparse forest climbed up the base of the mountains. A tree stood taller from all the rest; its knotted pewter trunk and gossamer leaves catching the morning light. The Glass Tree, the villagers called it. *Hyalus* was its proper species name. Its magic had shielded her from the Shadow, but the ice would have claimed her if not for her werewolf cousin. It was his keen sense of smell that tracked her down on the mountain. Although Zev had recovered her body, her mind had been gone for some time.

Grief was a peculiar thing. It knocked her to the ground, pinned her under its weight, and carved a hole in her chest. It smothered her in a bitterness that fed off her cries until she had no more to give.

Dyna stared blankly out the window. "I was lost when he found me."

"But you returned," her grandmother said.

She had to return when her emotions gave away to fear. Grief crippled her body, but fear seized her mind. It lived in the corners of her consciousness, a sardonic voice that murmured in her ear each night. It laughed at her failure to protect her family and reveled in her pain.

Fear promised the Shadow would return for her sister next.

Dyna looked down at Lyra, and a tear spilled down her cheek.

"Nothing will happen to Lyra," Grandmother Leyla reassured her, wiping it away. "The village council is preparing for the next coming. They have not stopped attempting to replicate your father's cloaking amulets, though the reeds he used are native to Magos. Who knows how he found them? The council hopes the leaves of the Glass Tree will be of some use. And there is talk of bringing demon hunters."

Dyna sat up straight. "They will allow outsiders to come here?"

Their secluded village rested within the Zafiro mountain range on the southern edge of the Azure Kingdom. Centuries ago, the Mages of Old perpetually spelled North Star to remain hidden. The village paid no taxes to lords, nor did they pay fealty to the Azure King. No one knew they were there—with good reason.

"Well, the decision is being debated, but I believe they will see reason. North Star needs help, or we will not survive the fourth Shadow Winter next year."

But demon hunters would be useless.

Of all the books Dyna had read on Netherworld lore, she found little on shadow demons. There were no documented weaknesses or methods to fight them. The Shadow was an intangible wraith, transient like smoke. Neither traps nor weapons would be effective against it.

Not that the village council would grant her the audience to tell them so. When her father said the Shadow would return, he was ridiculed and removed from the council. It took the deaths of children to convince them he wasn't raving mad about the Netherworld Gate opening every decade. What hope did she have of convincing them?

It didn't matter. This time she would not stand by helpless.

"My dear," Grandmother Leyla frowned at her, "I found the pack you hid in the barn. It had enough clothing and food for a week's travel."

Dyna stuttered in reply, unsure of how to explain herself.

"Did you plan to leave without saying a word? Did you think I would allow it?" Her grandmother's mouth thinned in a stern line. "You will not go to Magos. I forbid it."

Magos?

Her grandmother looked to the desk where an open tome rested. The encyclopedia listed the flora found in the Magos Empire—the territory of the mages.

"You were thinking of going in search of the Luna Reeds, weren't you?"

Dyna lowered her gaze and nodded. She hated lying. She had planned a journey, but not *there*.

"Please, stop reading those books. It's time to let it be and trust the council to keep the village safe."

"The council knows nothing," Dyna said, echoing her father.

Her grandmother pursed her lips. "Dynalya Astron, I'll not have you fret over this any longer, you hear?"

Dyna dropped her head in her hands. Nine years ago, she had been too young to understand her father's anguish and paranoia, but they now clung to her like the sweat on her skin. This curse had to end. "It won't work. None of it will work. Even if the council replicates the Luna Reeds, it is not a permanent solution. The amulets will only cloak them under the moonlight. It does not banish the Shadow."

"The Glass Tree—"

She shook her head in exasperation. "The light of the *Hyalus* leaves only appears at night. We need an absolute solution or the Shadow will continue to return."

"I know you are worried, blossom. I am as well." Grandmother Leyla tucked a lock of Dyna's hair behind an ear. "There is a village council meeting at midday. You can voice your concerns there."

"No one will listen to me."

"Lady Samira may listen. She is the least arrogant of them. Occasionally."

Dyna stiffened at the mention of that name and tried to ignore the sour twist in her stomach. "Why is there a meeting today?"

"Lady Samira is stepping down and is to announce her replacement."

Dyna watched her grandmother, reading the touch of resignation on her face. "Is she unwell?"

"She needs all of her strength now. There is not much of it left."

Then Dyna understood. Lady Samira's Essence was not replenishing. It happened in old age. Essence was not only the energy source of all magic itself, it was also the enchanted life force for mages and sorceresses. They could not survive without it.

"Well, the sun isn't up quite yet. Rest a bit more." Grandmother Leyla stood. "Autumn has arrived and we have much work to do in the garden before the frost sets in."

"Yes, Grandmother."

She shuffled out of the room, closing the door behind her.

Dyna settled down on her bed again, eyeing the cabinet lining the wall above her desk. Organized within the many squared drawers were several glass jars containing a variety of dried herbs, extracts, and powders. A small replica of the apothecary in the main room of the cottage.

For years, she studied all the ancient tomes of medicine that belonged to her father to fill in his place as Herb Master. She read all the magic books in his study, hoping to find the casting spell he had used to send the demon back through the Netherworld Gate.

She never found it.

Even if she had, the books contained spells far beyond her ability. But magic lived in her blood, as it had in the many generations before her.

Dyna reached under her pillow, finding a familiar rectangular shape, and pulled it out. The journal was hefty, its cover made of smooth black leather, the corners cracked with age. Two gold clasps kept it locked tight. The journal was one of many others stacked inside an old wooden coffer beneath her desk.

The journal's magic hummed through her in welcome, and her palms glowed a faint green with the awakening of her Essence. She traced the heraldic sigil embossed on the cover: a crescent moon with a swirl of vines. It was the sigil of House Astron, one of the oldest mage families hailing from the Magos Empire.

The journal contained the answer she needed—a way to obliterate the Shadow.

Dyna checked to make sure Lyra still slept before waving a hand over the cover. The light emitting from her palm grew brighter. The enchanted journal recognized her as kin, and the golden clasps unlocked. She opened the cover, admiring the faded, elegant penmanship and sketches of ancient plants and relics as the yellow pages crinkled between her fingers.

A single blank page emerged in the middle of the journal. It had taken her months to realize it was blank on purpose, and a few months more to decipher the phrase needed to unveil the secret hidden there.

She brought the journal close to her lips and whispered, *"Tellūs, lūnam, sōlis."*

Her hands flared brilliant green, triggering the embedded spell on the page. Fine gold dust whirled across the surface, radiating with a swirl of purple magic and a hint of green from her own. Black ink appeared in the center and snaked outward in calligraphic strokes, twisting and curving as it formed a beautiful, detailed map of a continent in the shape of a stout chalice—the country of Urn.

She would need to cross its entire width to get what she needed, and the journey would take many moons. A little over a year remained before the Shadow returned. One meager year to find the weapon she needed to vanquish it.

Dyna slipped out of the bed, wincing when her feet landed on the icy floor. She moved to the window layered in frost and peered out. Her home sat on a knoll overlooking the valley below. A light fog hovered over the sleepy village, smoke swirling from chimneys. Beyond it glimmered a lake, the rolling hills spotted with sheep and grazing cows. North Star was peaceful and beautiful.

But it was no longer safe.

Dyna looked down at her little sister, and the desperate determination to protect all she had left tangled itself tighter around her heart. She would make the council listen.

One way or another.

CHAPTER 2

Dynalya

Morning sunlight shone brightly over the valley, its idle warmth brushing Dyna's cold cheeks as she took the dirt road into the village. Her thoughts were in knots as she tried to prepare a speech to present before the council. The plan of facing Lady Samira filled her mind with the last image of her father's face, stained by the crimson trails dripping down his cheeks. Dyna squeezed her eyes shut against the memory. She focused on Grandmother Leyla's voice, who was giving Lyra a lesson on commonly found plants and their uses.

"It's important you learn this, Lyra. You will become a Healer's Apprentice in the coming spring, and you must have the basics committed to memory. Every plant has a purpose, be it—"

"Sustenance, remedy, or toxin," Lyra recited in a flat tone. "Yes, I know, Gran."

"Oh, do you? Then what is the name of this plant?"

Dyna glanced over her shoulder at where they had stopped. Among the colorful carpet of flowers growing on the edge of the path, Grandmother pointed to a weed with broad hairy leaves.

Lyra scrunched her lip as she studied it. "Foxglove?"

Grandmother crossed her arms, and Lyra squirmed under her disapproval.

"Comfrey," Dyna whispered to her, winking.

"It's comfrey!"

Grandmother Leyla gave them a stern frown. "Learn their differences, Lyra, or you will have grave results should you mistake the two. Foxglove is poisonous."

Lyra winced. "Oh."

"She's learning," Dyna murmured. "It took me some time to learn the difference, Grandmother."

Grandmother Leyla arched a brow and Dyna smiled sheepishly. "Comfrey is medicinal. Do you know its use?"

Her little sister dithered on the answer. Dyna caught her eye and subtly rubbed the scar on her elbow. She had earned it three seasons ago when she fell on a sharp rock and cut her elbow straight to the bone.

"Skin and bone repair," Lyra replied with a victorious smile as she bounced on her toes, her cloak and dress flaring. Dyna stifled a giggle.

"Yes, it is also known as knitbone, which makes it easier to remember." Grandmother Leyla pointed to another tall spindly plant with dark purple petals. "And this one?"

"That one is easy," Lyra piped up. "It's wolfsbane. Very poisonous."

"But it can also treat fevers if you're careful," Dyna said with a frown. "It shouldn't be left out here to cause trouble."

Seeing it reminded her she needed more wolfsbane extract for Zev. She prayed he managed well until they could meet again.

She pulled the poisonous plant from its roots and wrapped it in a cloth taken from the pocket of her olive cloak. A gentle whoosh of energy settled over her as its magic worked to keep her warm despite the brisk breeze. The cloak was old; the fabric frayed and faded, but the runes embroidered onto the ornamental hem maintained their power even after two centuries. Dyna brushed a finger over the rune with an inverted triangle. The last time her father had worn the cloak, he pointed to each rune, testing how many she and Thane had memorized.

The squelch of wagon wheels in the mud and the bustle of people drew her attention back to the road. More villagers had joined them, and the crowd only grew as they passed an intersection splitting from the north and south of the village.

Farmer Wendell marched down the road with his family, his face set in a stern glower. The large and burly man towered over his petite wife, Fleur. Her feet moved swiftly beneath her muddled brown dress to keep up with his long stride as she carried their baby daughter in her arms. Their eldest child, Wren playfully tugged on Lyra's braid. She snatched his cap, and they ran off together into the fields alongside the path, laughing and chasing each other.

"Don't go too far," Dyna called after them, watching as Lyra and Wren joined the other playing children. They were so bright and innocent.

A filling meal.

She banished the horrid thought to the pits of her mind, burying it beneath the mountain of fears and nightmares where churning black clouds and lightning shrouded the precipice. Dyna often climbed the mountain in her dreams, digging her fingers in the wet earth, toes pushing off stacked skulls for the top. But she always fell before she reached it.

"Good day to you." Grandmother Leyla nodded to Wendell and his wife as they approached.

The glowering farmer merely grunted in response.

Fleur offered a kind smile and brushed the loose locks of blonde hair from her face. "Good day, Leyla, Miss Dynalya."

Dyna smiled. "Good day."

"Are you off to see the council as well?"

"Along with every other villager, it seems," her grandmother replied.

Wendell grated, "The only way to set a fire under their arses is if we all beat down on their door."

"I am sure they are doing their best, love," Fleur told him, giving Leyla and Dyna an apologetic grimace.

It mildly comforted Dyna to know others at last worried about the Shadow. Her father had not been so fortunate.

Once Wendell had marched ahead out of hearing range, Fleur whispered, "He has been holding meetings in our home with the other farmers. They want to leave North Star."

"Leave?" Leyla gasped. "Foolish man. Leaving would be dangerous for you and little Finnie."

Dyna looked down at the sleeping baby in Fleur's arms. She had assisted with the birth and it'd been clear Finnie had been born with more Essence than her mother. Because of it, she couldn't leave the village without attracting a mage—none of the women could. Essence was highly prized and sought. No mage would resist stealing it from them.

Her grandmother laid a hand over Finnie's forehead. "How is she feeling?"

"Much better. Her cough vanished as soon as I gave her the tonic. Thank you, Leyla."

"Of course. Bring her to me later so I can make sure she is fully recovered." Her grandmother subtly tugged on Dyna's sleeve. They slowed their pace, leaving Fleur to catch up to her husband. "I have a feeling this meeting will not go well."

Dyna glanced around at the many grim faces of the villagers. Most were tense and angry, sharing grumbling conversations of their own. The villagers had grown tired of the council's inaction of the incoming Shadow Winter. Answers were needed, and they planned to demand them. It gave her the courage she needed to face the council.

"Be careful in there, blossom. Where there is unrest, there is trouble."

"Yes, Grandmother."

The path narrowed as they reached the village, and everyone headed toward the town hall building—a one-story structure of stacked stone walls and a thatched roof. A line formed as people filed inside in pairs, and by the time Dyna entered, they had filled all the wooden benches. Many remained on their feet, arguing and shouting among themselves. Dyna took her grandmother's arm and led her to the back.

Councilor Lorian, in his crimson robes, stood at the front on a wooden dais with all his self-importance. He lazily held up his hands against their growing anger. "I must ask you for silence. We have gathered here to appoint a new council member. There will be an opportunity to discuss other issues at the meeting's conclusion."

The uproar swallowed his orders. Seeing the senseless arguing showed no signs of ending, Lorian gave up trying to get their attention. He may have gained her father's seat on the council, but he failed to command authority like the other five grim council members sitting at the table behind him.

Lady Samira sat at her position in the middle. The thin, wizened woman bared a stern glower, her body arched beneath mauve robes, with her white hair pulled back in a plait. Dyna and the councilwoman locked eyes across the room. Dyna quickly looked away to the other council members.

On the left sat Councilor Pavin, a plump, bald man in light blue robes. Next to him sat Mathis, a thin and tall councilman with dark hair and a sharp, hooked nose. To Lady Samira's right sat councilman Xibil with a long gray beard that matched the shades of his robes. His son, Cario, sat beside him. He was a handsome man with a mane of orange curls who drew the attention of half the women in the village.

And they each had turned their backs on Dyna's father when he'd pleaded with them to listen. She had planned to plead the same, but by their disengaged expressions, they were no more inclined to listen now than they were nine years ago.

"Why are we here discussing trivial matters?" Wendell barked at them. "The Shadow is coming."

Lorian's mouth thinned into a tight line. "Yes, we know it's coming. Do you think us fools?"

"One could argue," the farmer growled, earning chuckles from the crowd. "The demon will be here next winter. It is coming to take our children and all you care about is who will sit on the council."

The councilman flushed. "The Shadow will not take any more children."

"And how do you plan to stop it? By offering it your bony neck?"

Dyna shook her head. As unappealing as Lorian was, shouting insults at the council would not be in their favor.

"We are well aware you have no children of your own," said Duren, a furrier with a family of six. "If you did, perhaps you'd be more concerned."

"We have been assembling a few plans," Lorian snapped.

"What plans?" another man in the crowd hollered.

The villagers hurled their questions. A litany of voices all expressing the same essential concern: how would the council keep them safe?

"Well, we believe demon hunters will be of use."

Duren repeated in angry disbelief, "Demon hunters?"

The room erupted in shouts, everyone fighting to be heard.

"That is your plan?"

"Nothing can kill the Shadow!"

Councilor Lorian stepped back from their anger. It boiled, beginning to spill over the brim. Shouts blended into one mass roar as fear infected the atmosphere. Dyna felt it fall over her, growing and growing until she couldn't breathe.

"This is madness!" Wendell shouted. "We are leaving this place. It's cursed, and I will not leave my family here for the demon to devour. Come with us if you want to survive!" He grabbed Fleur and dragged her toward the exit.

The men followed suit, hauling their wives and children in a rush to escape the impending shadows at their backs. People fed into the panic, pushing to get to the door. Fights and screams broke out among the clamor.

"Enough!" Councilor Lorian yelled at them. "Calm yourselves! See reason!"

His pleadings went ignored. Dyna stayed in place, holding onto her grandmother. They pressed their backs into the wall so they wouldn't be dragged into the chaos. This had to stop, or people would be injured.

"Lyra?" Dyna desperately searched the writhing crowd. "Grandmother, where is Lyra? I don't see her!"

"God of Urn, I hope she stayed outside."

Why'd she taken her eyes off her sister? If Lyra was caught in this, she would be trampled!

A crackle of energy prickled against Dyna's skin at the charge in the air. Lady Samira's dark eyes glowed with remnants of gold Essence as it spread throughout her silhouette. She rose from the table, moving slow but steady with the help of her gnarled staff. Her robes trailed behind her small, hunched frame.

She came to stand by Lorian and her thin arms trembled as she raised her staff and slammed it on the floor with unexpected force, sending a crack like thunder through the room. A wave of gold Essence blasted outward, and people dropped like sheared wheat. The stunned villagers laid where they fell, groaning but otherwise unhurt.

Dyna righted herself and helped her grandmother stand where they had fallen against the wall. She searched for a sign of red hair and finally spotted Lyra standing at the doorway with Wren and the other children who had been playing outside. Exhaling in relief, Dyna motioned at her sister to stay away. Lyra nodded and led the others back to play.

"Are we to squawk and cluck like mindless chickens?" Lady Samira demanded, her harsh tone cutting clear through the silence. She regarded the villagers with a severe glare, arching a white brow and daring anyone to defy her.

No one did.

She was one of the last remaining elders with powerful Essence and had earned their respect. But Dyna could see it had taken a great deal out of her. The color leached from her face, and she gripped her staff tightly in her shaking hands to remain upright.

Wendell cleared his throat. "Forgive us, Lady Samira, but we cannot keep biding our time. The Shadow will come again. Do you expect us to sit around and wait to die?"

"We have sent an expedition to gather Luna Reeds," Councilor Cario reminded them, speaking at last. "We are awaiting their return."

Councilor Mathis nodded. "Traveling as far as the Magos Empire will take time."

"They left last summer," another man wearing a leather tanner apron said as he sat up from where he had been thrown. "Either they didn't survive the journey, or they have abandoned us."

Dyna didn't believe it. No one had volunteered to go on the expedition willingly, so the councilors chose a group at random. Well, they insisted it had been a random selection, but she'd noticed those chosen had families—men with the most to lose if they didn't return.

"What if the Archmage discovered who they are?" Duren grunted. "They could be trapped in Magos for all we know. Maybe no one is coming at all."

Five women gathered in a back corner near Dyna silently wept and held onto each other for comfort. The wives of those who had gone on the expedition, she realized. Every day they must watch the road leading out of the village, hoping and waiting for their husbands to come home.

Would they return? Or would this be another loss the council deemed necessary?

Wendell shook his head. "We need to abandon this place. It's cursed."

The villagers agreed in loud calls.

"You are right," Lady Samira said, her brisk tone silencing them. "Go on, then. Leave the only protection that hides your wives and daughters from the mages. Go and die fighting the Archmage's Enforcers when they come for them. You may as well walk through the Forbidden Woods. It would be a much kinder ending."

The villagers gasped and murmured at the mention of the dark, looming forest on the eastern side of North Star—the forest they were warned not to enter. Any who dared go in were never seen again.

Grandmother Leyla's eldest daughter had been one of them.

The surrounding crowd stole glances at her, whispering among themselves. Dyna's grandmother ignored them all, poised and calm as she looked ahead.

"If you wish to survive, then you must make use of your wisdom," Lady Samira said. She held out her glowing palm. "Have you forgotten who we are? The mages can sense Essence, especially in women. Once they sense your power, however little it may be, they *will* come for you."

The room fell silent.

Shoes softly scuffed the floor, and clothing rustled as the villagers settled down on the benches again. Everyone watched the councilwoman with rapt attention. Dyna felt a different fear stir in them, as it did in her. An old fear they had lived by all their lives.

"Yes, the Shadow is coming, but we know it is coming and we are preparing for it. Here you are protected and free. Out there," Lady Samira pointed to the door, "are countless unknown dangers. One we know for sure is lurking. There is only a question of when it will find you—" The councilwoman wobbled, her complexion becoming bone-white as she gripped her staff to stay upright.

Dyna took an instinctive step toward the dais. "Grandmother," she whispered in warning. Something was wrong.

"I see it," Grandmother Leyla whispered back. They began weaving their way through the crowd to the front.

Councilor Lorian reached for Lady Samira's arm, but she shook him off, much too proud for his help.

"Do not be so quick to run in fear," she continued after shooting him a glare. "The Great Azeran faced worse. He and the Mages of Old fought for the freedom you have. They bled for the land you cultivate. We owe it to them to fight for this sanctuary. *We* are the ones who have brought the Shadow's curse, and *we* will be the ones to finish it."

The courage of her speech eased the apprehension in the room. Even Wendell released a heavy sigh and his rigid shoulders slumped. The villagers were still afraid, but the councilwoman's words had offered them hope.

"Have patience and mark my words—the fourth Shadow Winter will be the last."

"How so?" Dyna asked before she thought better of it. All eyes fell on her. She swallowed, holding Lady Samira's intimidating gaze. "How do you plan to stop the Shadow? That has yet to be made clear."

Lorian smirked. "Were you not listening? We await the Luna Reeds."

"You forget where you first learned of them," Dyna replied sharply without looking away from the councilwoman. "As I have explained to you before, the amulet's power only rises under the moonlight. It does nothing against the Shadow. It will still hunt on our land as we cower in our homes. Then when the moon is shrouded, you will once again be responsible for more deaths because you refuse to listen, as you refused to listen to my father."

Lady Samira stumbled back a step, staring at Dyna in dismay. She tried to speak but could only inhale gasping breaths. Her eyes rolled, and she wavered forward, tumbling off the dais.

The villagers cried out, gathering around the fallen councilwoman. Dyna and her grandmother rushed forward, and a path quickly parted for them.

"Samira?" Grandmother Leyla kneeled beside her and gently checked her for injuries, then listened to her heart. "Samira, speak to me."

"Oh, don't fuss over me, you old woman." Lady Samira's eyes weakly fluttered open. She lay splayed on the ground like a broken doll. Dyna felt awful for snapping at her.

"You're the old woman." Leyla smiled feebly. "You fell. Are you feeling faint?"

"I'm fine. Age has gotten the better of me is all," she rasped. The strength she had displayed before was quickly fading away into her pallid complexion.

"Always trying to save face," Leyla grumbled as she turned to Dyna. "I didn't bring my medicine bag. Examine her while I fetch it."

Before Dyna could answer, her grandmother rushed out. She gaped after her, shrinking under the critical stares of everyone.

CHAPTER 3

Dynalya

Once all the fuss had calmed down, the meeting was dismissed. Dyna asked Wendell to carry Lady Samira to the private council room in the back of the town hall building. The councilors were left to wait in the hall as he laid her on a settee.

Wendell's shoulders hunched and he twisted his cap in his hands. "Forgive me for raising my voice, Lady Samira."

"If you think this is because of you, then you think too highly of yourself," she rasped. The farmer flushed beneath his beard.

"I will see to her," Dyna assured him. He ambled out as she sat in a chair beside Lady Samira. Her grandmother had yet to return, so it was up to her to proceed.

Dyna took the councilwoman's knotted hand and pressed two fingers to her wrist. It was cold and frail. Almost weightless. Her pulse was too faint.

"Is this difficult for you?" Lady Samira asked, straining to speak. "Treating the woman who led your father to his death?"

His smiling face filled Dyna's mind again and she steeled herself, focusing on her task at hand. The question didn't warrant an answer. She couldn't trust what would come out of her mouth if she did.

"I didn't believe him. I truly thought the Shadow would not come. I came to your door many times after, but I couldn't bring myself to knock."

Even if the councilwoman had knocked, Dyna may not have opened the door. She had not been in a place to listen. Her hands glowed green as she brandished them above Lady Samira's body in a slow, sweeping motion. Closing her eyes, Dyna let herself drift into the *Essentia Dimensio*—a plane reached only from within.

Glimmering bulbs of light in all colors spanned a world of darkness, stretching into oblivion. They represented the Essence of every living being. Surrounding her were luminous bulbs from the council members nearby and those of the villagers in the distance. But Lady Samira's golden light dimmed in hazy sputters.

"From that night, I questioned each decision I've made…" Lady Samira gasped for a breath between each group of words. "Whether I could judge correctly, whether I have made the correct decision to keep them here."

Dyna reached out with her green Essence and brushed it against the councilwoman's gold Essence. It pulsed brightly and an outline of Lady Samira's body appeared, splintering into thousands of trails.

Essence Channels.

Tunnels of translucent light ran from the crown of her head to her feet. They should have been solid, pumping steady streams of magic as blood does through veins, but Lady Samira's Essence Channels were breaking down, some completely gone. A small dot of light remained at her heart, and it was fading.

"Am I wrong now, Dynalya? Tell me, will I kill them too? I do not know anymore."

Dyna wished Lady Samira would stop talking so she could concentrate. Her hands shook as she tried to revitalize the councilwoman's Essence with her own. No matter how much she gave, the channels wouldn't reconstruct themselves.

"I am dying."

Dyna opened her eyes.

Lady Samira nodded at whatever she saw on her face. Dyna couldn't find the right words to reply. As much pain as the woman had caused her, she didn't want this.

"I'm sorry."

"Your sympathy is wasted on me. I had sensed my time to walk through The Seven Gates had neared. I only accelerated the inevitable by using my last remaining Essence to stop them from leaving. You have nothing to be sorry for. It is I who must speak those words."

Lady Samira had never been so docile. Perhaps death had left her rueful, or perhaps it was guilt, but this was not the harsh woman who had addressed the village.

Dyna fought to stay focused. The use of Essence had drained her energy, leaving her limp. She had come to speak to the council. Now may not be the appropriate time, but she may never have another opportunity to be heard. "Lady Samira, I must seek your audience."

The old woman studied her. "Speak. Quickly now. I have little time left."

"My father told you the truth when he said the Shadow would come. I tell you the truth now—I have found a way to defeat it."

Lady Samira's unfocused eyes hardened with attention. "But?"

Dyna heaved a breath. "But it requires that I leave North Star."

Immediate refusal arose on the councilwoman's scowl before she answered. "Dynalya, you are one of the few remaining in our village who can wield Essence."

"My Essence is minimal—"

"It is useful," she rasped, her words slowing and weakening further as if it pained her to speak. "You are a healer. You have power. You cannot risk venturing outside the village."

"If we could form another expedition, I would not be alone."

"No. If you leave, you will attract an Enforcer and be taken to Magos."

"I know the dangers, but I must go," Dyna insisted. "I don't fear the Archmage."

"You must *always* fear him. The mages will stop at nothing to strip you of all your Essence until you die … Do you understand?" Lady Samira reached out for her. "Forgive me for not saving your father, but I—"

Dyna pulled away.

Lady Samira let her hand fall. "You must stay … After my passing, there will be an empty seat on the council to fill."

She stared at the councilwoman, not sure if she understood the implication correctly.

"Pardon, Lady Samira," Lorian said from the door, his expression barely containing his outrage. "You cannot possibly be suggesting *she* take it. She is too young—"

"As I recall … you were only a few years older than her when you joined the council," Lady Samira hissed, her weakening voice regaining its edge. "If not for her father's death, you would not have his seat now."

Lorian scowled. The voices of the other council members murmured in the hall.

"I don't want a seat on the council," Dyna said. "It gave my father no sway in convincing you of the dangers to come. None of the plans you have sorted will work. But I know how to end the Shadow's curse."

Quiet shock filled the room.

Lorian glared at her. "Explain."

"What I am suggesting is dangerous," she admitted as she stood. "But not impossible."

Dyna didn't expect to capture their rapt attention, but all eyes fixed on her as they hung on her every word, waiting for her to continue. The situation must be more dire than they had let on if they cared to listen to her now.

"There are other sources of powerful magic," she said.

Lorian crossed his arms. "And where is this powerful magic you claim?"

Dyna swallowed the lump in her throat. "The island."

The councilmen gaped at her before bursting into mocking laughter.

"This is no jest. I can save the village!"

They turned away to snicker among themselves, shooting her contemptuous looks. They dismissed her as she had predicted.

Hope had become sand. It slipped through her fingers faster than she could grasp it. They didn't believe her. How could they when they thought of that place as only a story?

"I did not listen to your father when he warned me," Lady Samira muttered, her eyes drooping heavily. "It was to my greatest regret what befell your family. An apology will never be enough, but you have my blessings. And with it, may your father forgive me. Councilor Pavin?"

"Yes?" The heavy-set councilman readily came forward.

"Bring me paper and ink. I have chosen my successor."

All the council members stood straight and confident, righting the front of their robes.

Lady Samira held her gaze. "I will leave my seat to Dynalya."

The councilor's expressions varied from bulging eyes to gaping mouths. Dyna might have found their reactions amusing if she had not been equally speechless. To take Lady Samira's place meant she would have the high seat, and with it, the power to decide on village matters. It gave her the power to save Lyra.

"Hurry, man, I am dying," Lady Samira snapped.

Councilor Pavin balked and hurried out of the room.

Lorian caught Dyna's eye and motioned for her to come out to the hall with him while the others gathered to say their farewells to the councilwoman.

Once they were alone, he cornered her against the wall, leaning over her until his rank breath blew in her face. "You are cruel to fill her head with dreams and fairy tales on her deathbed."

Dyna glared at him and clenched her shaking fists so he wouldn't see how much he intimidated her. "I'm telling the truth. I can help—"

"You will help us by staying here and not exposing us to the Archmage. If we are discovered, all of Magos will descend upon us."

"Lady Samira has given me her blessings."

"Her seat, you mean. A seat that should go to one of us."

"To you, if you had any say in it."

"It's *my* seat. I earned it and I'll not let some girl take it from me."

"I don't care about that seat, I care about saving the children," she exasperated. "The Shadow is coming and I know how to stop it. If you will not help me, then I will do this on my own."

Lorian sneered and leaned down until their noses almost touched. "Go on, leave if you're so brave. But do give your loved ones a farewell. It will be the last time they ever see you, Dynalya. For you will fail."

His words echoed in the cavern of her thoughts. The floor became quicksand, pulling her under, slipping over her mouth and nose until it blinded her in the cold dark.

You will fail.

"What are you doing to my granddaughter?"

Councilor Lorian jumped away. Grandmother Leyla stood at the end of the hall with her bag, glaring daggers at him.

"Come now, madam, you wound me." He chuckled airily. "We were merely discussing Lady Samira's condition."

Her eyes narrowed. She went to Dyna, searching her face. "How is she?"

Dyna shook her head, and her grandmother sighed.

Councilor Pavin rushed past them with a sheet of paper and a well of ink, and they followed him into the hushed room, but it was too late. Councilor Mathis covered Lady Samira's face with a blanket as they approached the settee.

"She's passed," Councilor Xibil announced somberly. Cario laid a comforting hand on his father's shoulder.

"Oh ..." Grandmother Leyla covered her face.

Dyna dropped into the chair beside Lady Samira and lowered her head. Her bitterness against this woman had been with her for so long it had rooted deep within her. But it served no purpose. It would only keep her in the past when it was the future she needed to face.

Dyna gently took Lady Samira's hand and recited the prayer for the dead, "May you leave the Mortal Gate with no burden to bind you. May you cross Death's Gate with all faults forgiven." Her tears came freely, and she felt each one wash away her resentment. "May you pass through the Time Gate with the wisdom of the age. May you pass through the expanse of the Spatial Gate's wonder. May you pass through Life's Gate as you did at the beginning. May you arrive at Heaven's Gate at the end. May the God of Urn receive your soul." In a whisper, she added, "I will save them. I promise you."

"Lady Samira departed before she could officially leave a successor," Lorian said coolly. "The laws are clear on this. We must vote for a new Head Councilor. Who shall it be? Someone among us? Or will the fate of North Star rest on the whims of an inexperienced girl?"

Unsure, the council members looked at her as Lorian sneered. Dyna didn't bother staying to hear the obvious result of the vote. She took her confused grandmother's arm and walked out of the room with as much dignity as she could muster.

When first discovering the map, Dyna knew she would have to leave, but she had put the journey off, lacking the courage to take the first step away from the comforts of her home. The small sliver of hope that the council would be of any help died with Lady Samira. She had no choice but to do this herself.

The thought was as frightening as jumping into a pitch-black pit, not knowing when she would hit the ground. There was no telling what awaited her out in the world, and there was the danger of attracting a mage. Substantial risk outweighed her success.

Dyna looked up from the letter she had been writing at her desk to the window. The dark sky was lightening. She had stayed awake into the late hour, thinking and planning, but soon it would be morning. She groaned, dropping her head into her hands.

Winter was coming, and soon the gorge entrance to the village would fill with snow until late spring. If she didn't leave now, she would not have enough time to cross Urn and return home before the fourth coming.

Time slipped past her, drawing the Shadow nearer.

She had to go. There was no question. She had to leave today, at this moment, before it was too late. Fear caught her in a snare, reminding her she couldn't sleep by herself, let alone in the dark. She also had dire responsibilities. Zev needed her help, or he would …

Her spiral of thoughts stopped and she broke into a grin. Zev could come with her. She didn't have to do this alone.

Dyna peeked at Lyra, who slept soundly on the bed under a mound of blankets. She picked up the journal where it had been resting behind a stack of books, opened it to the blank page, and whispered the passphrase. Once the map appeared, she tapped on the Kingdom of Azure, and magic rippled across the surface. The continent swirled and expanded until the eastern quadrant filled the page.

She studied the land past the Zafiro Mountains. Zev lived in Lykos Peak—werewolf territory. It was located in a dense region of woods, bordered by coastline cliffs. It lay about thirty miles east of her village, but a thick forest separated them. The villagers called it the Forbidden Woods. On the map, it was identified as Hilos.

Wander in there about and you will never come out, as the saying went. A dire rhyme they were all made to learn as children. No one outside of the council knew what lurked in there. But how dangerous could it be if Zev trekked through those woods when he came to visit her each month? He never spoke of anything frightening prowling within. That couldn't mean much as most found him to be equally frightening, considering his origin. Regardless, Dyna was curious.

"What's in there?" she had often asked him. *"What's it like?"*

Zev would always shrug as though it was a silly question. *"It's a forest."*

"Then why is it forbidden?"

"You must obey the rules, even if you don't understand them."

Her cousin was not of North Star, so the rules didn't apply to him, but the forest mustn't be so terrible if he went in. The rumors had to be mere superstition.

Or perhaps not.

Her aunt had gone through those woods years ago and she didn't return. Dyna shook off the ominous feeling the reminder brought. She had no choice but to go through the Forbidden Woods if she was to reach Lykos Peak before nightfall. If she went around it, the detour would deviate her by three days. She wasn't capable of withstanding so many nights—alone—in the dark. Nor could she stomach it.

Dyna glanced at her father's enchanted cloak draped on her chair. Among the many runes was the rune for concealment. If the magic was strong, it would hide her well enough from whatever made the Forbidden Woods ... forbidden.

Lyra mumbled in her sleep, smiling from what could only be a pleasant dream. Her sister was all she had left of her mother and father, so innocent and sweet, without a care in the world. Dyna would march through any darkness to protect that.

She rushed to her wardrobe and chose a simple kirtle dress in the color of sage with long bell sleeves. Pulling it on over her chemise, she cinched the laces of the bodice from her bosom to her waist until it hugged her slim frame.

Dyna tossed the journal inside the leather satchel hanging from an iron hook on her bedroom door. She slung it on her shoulder and went for the rucksack hidden beneath her bed. It already carried food and water. She added a few more articles of clothing before securing it on her shoulders.

The floorboards creaked as she flitted to her desk. She slipped on her cloak, then grabbed the sheathed, three-inch knife beside a pile of dried stalks, and tucked it into her corset.

In a clay bowl set on top of a pile of books, lay the five Waning Amulets her father had made. Dyna ran her fingers over the smooth wooden pendants. Four would go with the letter she had addressed to her grandmother. It explained where she had gone and why. In the case she didn't return, Grandmother Leyla would need to decide which children would receive the amulets. It was unfair to leave such a burden behind, but it was a last resort.

Dyna placed the fifth amulet in Lyra's palm and closed her small fingers around it. No matter what happened on this journey, she would leave knowing her sister was safe.

Dyna kissed Lyra's forehead and whispered a prayer to the God of Urn to watch over her. After carefully pushing open the window, she slinked outside and frost-coated grass crunched beneath her shoes. Her breath clouded in the air, the early morning chill prickling her cheeks. The darkness above tinged a pale blue and pink as dawn approached.

She took in her home, wanting to memorize its worn stone walls, the thatch roof, and the wooden door with a small round window. She could almost hear her mother humming as she tended to the garden, Thane's laughter as he ran through the yard, and an echo of her father's voice. A dull ache filled her chest. He did all he could to save North Star. That duty fell to her now.

With one last glance at her bedroom window, Dyna said goodbye. She walked away, forcing herself not to look back. She crossed the rickety fence bordered by the stonewalling surrounding her land. Her direction was due east for the valley gorge and the dark stretch of trees that lay beyond it. With each step taking her further and further away, her apprehension grew.

Dyna laid a shaking hand over the journal in her satchel and its gentle energy responded, filling her with strength.

CHAPTER 4

Dynalya

Dyna hiked through the day, her steady pace taking her deep into the Forbidden Woods. Nothing slinked out from the trees to confront her. All was still and quiet. Evening had arrived if the low light was any sign, and apprehension crept over her nerves. The thought of finding herself in the dark terrified her, especially in the forest—and this forest was *strange*. Zev had not been honest with her.

The trees were peculiar, ancient giants. Their thick, white trunks bore massive indigo leaf canopies that cast a wide blanket of shade. The undergrowth of massive iridescent flowers in vibrant purple, teal, and pink coated her surroundings in an eerie hue. There were no roads or trails of any kind to walk on in the dense woodland.

No other but she dared come here.

Dyna shivered, unsure if the chilly air or the notion caused it. She adjusted her hood against the cold and tightened the cloak around her shoulders, letting its enchantments reassure her. The runes did well to conceal her presence as long as she didn't make a sound. And she had the odd sense to be quiet.

Hilos. She turned the land's name in her head, trying to recall where she had heard it. It must have surfaced in her studies. Her aching feet begged for rest, but Lykos Peak shouldn't be too far now. Dyna stopped mid-step, hearing a new sound not belonging to nature. She strained to listen past the rustling of the leaves in the breeze.

Music.

It was such a beautiful and heartrending melody that could only have come from a flute. Something about the tune was familiar, drawing from her a memory of her mother singing a similar song. The tune became clearer as she followed it, forming a deep calling she had to answer. But then the melody reached its end and faded among the trees.

She paused, waiting for another song, but no other melody followed. The longer she stood there, the more she wondered if she had truly heard it. Was this a trick of the forest? Dyna backed up a step at the thought. What would have happened if she had located the minstrel?

She turned to go back the way she had come, only to realize she didn't know which way that was. She spun in place, trying to retrace her steps. The forest floor was too thick to leave behind any footprints. Every course looked the same. The identical trees offered no direction. There were no visible hills, rivers, or trails to guide her.

She was lost.

The long shadows grew as the sun lowered. Dyna's heart raced, her breathing growing erratic. The darkening forest spun in a blur, and the feeling left her legs. She fell to her knees and wrapped her shaking arms around herself. Air wouldn't enter her lungs as the trees closed in around her. She was falling through the cracks of the earth, turning to rubble and dust.

Lyra.

Dyna gasped for air. Her sister's name was a rope, and she used it to scale up the walls of her panic. She forced a mouthful of cold air down her throat over and over until she could think. Once the world stopped spinning, Dyna closed her eyes. As her breathing quieted, she heard distant waves beating against what must be the cliffs separating Hilos and Lykos Peak.

She picked herself up off the ground and ran toward it. Her footfalls carried through the forest, the shrubs rattling in her wake as she barreled past. After a quarter of a mile, Dyna stopped in a pocket of buttery light and listened for the sea again, but unnatural silence hung in the air. The wind halted, the birds no longer sang, and every chatter of life disappeared as though the forest itself held its breath. A reminder that she should not have made a sound came too late. Goosebumps raced over her skin at the sensation of being watched. She whirled around, anxiously searching the greenery.

No one was there.

It stirred memories of the past, of molten red eyes hunting her in the darkness. Dyna inhaled several deep breaths and leaned against a tree, reining in her fear. She gazed up at the delicate rays of sunlight slipping in through the tree's long swooping branches, shimmering on wide gossamer leaves that looked like glass. There was another *Hyalus* tree in these woods.

Dyna stepped back to admire the tranquil giant. The tree stood taller than the rest, reigning overall in its wake. It was much bigger than the one outside of her village. The girth of the silver trunk was as large as her cottage. The peculiarity of the tree was not the beauty of its transparent leaves, but that they glowed a luminous white once night fell.

A passage from the journal came to mind: *Magic is in all life. It is within the sun, the moon, and the earth. Reverence is due, for such a majestic entity has been here since the dawn of the beginning and it will be here long after our end.*

Dyna smiled and patted the tree. If night fell before she found Zev, she'd return to the *Hyalus* for shelter. It would keep her safe. For now, if she could find a fresh leaf, it would provide light without her having to make it herself.

She searched through the plush bed of fallen leaves scattered over the roots when she spotted a long black feather. It was glossy, almost glimmering in the shade. What kind of bird did this belong to?

She picked it up, and abrupt energy collided against her Essence. Gold light sparked at the tip of the feather and spread throughout its profile as a flourish of unexpected power filled her, pumping heat through her veins.

Awed, she brandished the feather around, creating glowing streaks of light. This was magic unknown to her. She'd have to study it later.

Turning to go, she heard a snap. Rope lashed out of the leaves, snatching her ankle out from under her. Dyna screamed as it wrenched her into the air and she lost hold of the world again. She swung erratically from her leg, trapped in a pendulum above the ground.

Once the movement slowed, she found herself hanging upside down with her cloak and dress draped over her face, leaving her legs bare. She tucked her hem between her thighs and inspected her surroundings. The rope fastened around her ankle was fixed to a branch of the *Hyalus*.

Coming through here must have triggered a hunting trap, but she had met no one else in the forest. What kind of animal were they hunting? A large one by the makes of it.

Grunting, Dyna reached to take the rope when the leaves rustled. She whipped her head around to see a man step out onto a thick branch from another tree across from her. Long, blond hair framed the planes of his striking face. More like him emerged from the surrounding trees. They were all men, all golden-haired, and unbelievably stunning—but it was their pure-white wings that caught her breath.

Her mother's faraway voice whispered in her thoughts, tales of old she used to tell her before bed, *"Long ago, during the First Age, the Seraphim roamed Urn. They lived in the Kingdom of Hilos and were kind gentle beings."*

But these winged men didn't look kind or gentle. Harshness cut their features; their glares as sharp as a blade's edge. Fine, dark-green leather armor matching the color of the leaves molded their deft frames. A golden sigil of expanded wings embossed their chest plates, each one of them well-armed with sword and bow.

A nervous pulse beat in Dyna's chest. Recalling how evasive her cousin had been, Zev must have known about the Seraphim. Why hadn't he told her about them?

"How do you do … my lord?" Dyna said to the one who had stepped out of the trees first. She didn't know how to properly address him, regardless of hanging upside down. He must be the leader by the manner the others looked to him. She tugged on her skirts, assuring it covered her. "I'm sorry to disturb your hunting grounds. I, uh, was passing through to Lykos Peak."

His eyes narrowed on the glowing, black feather she still held. Dyna quickly let it go, and they watched it float to the ground.

"Pardon me, I meant no offense. I'll be on my way." She reached into her corset for her small knife and worked on sawing through the rope.

"You will not." The leader's voice was low and rigid. "You have trespassed into our land, *human*," he spat the word. "And for that, you must be executed."

Dyna's heart lurched, and everything in her chilled. Executed? The word rang in her mind like a horrible echo carrying out her sentence. Wander in there about and you will never come out.

He glanced at another holding a gilded bow, giving a silent command. The archer nocked an arrow and aimed at her.

"I only meant to pass through!" Her claim made no difference.

With a slight nod, he signaled the archer and she sliced through the rope, plunging as the arrow whizzed past. She landed heavily on an exposed root, leaving her winded.

The Seraphim flew down. Dyna scrambled backward, pine needles stabbing her palms. The knife in her trembling grip was meant for cutting through stalks, but it was all she had. A Seraph twisted her arm and she cried out, releasing the knife. They tore away her satchel and rucksack to rifle through.

"Don't!" She tried to reach for it, but they kicked in her knees and shoved her down to kneel.

The leader approached, his long strides graceful and soundless. They passed him the satchel, and he dumped the contents onto the ground. There wasn't much: the journal, a small bound notebook, the small jars of medicine, and a handful of copper coins. He emptied her rucksack next and her clothes and food hit the dirt.

"Unhand my things." Dyna scowled at him, trying to appear brave, but it fell away when his withering gaze snapped to her.

The blade of his sword sang as he drew it free. Dazzling white flames burst along the length, and its staggering heat wafted against her face. She recoiled with a gasp, then screamed when they dragged her closer to the fire. Her tears evaporated on her cheeks from the unbearable temperature, all of her hopes and dreams disappearing with them.

"No, stop," she begged. "Please don't do this. My family is waiting for me. My sister needs me!" Nothing Dyna said softened his cold sneer. He meant to send her soul through The Seven Gates—and Death's Gate would be the first.

"To whom do you pray?"

She looked up at him through her blurry vision, wishing to have the answer that would save her life. There were many Gods. She believed in only one, but the world had erased his name.

"The God of Urn." It was a soft prayer and a plea.

His stony expression didn't change, save for the slight satisfaction in his glare. "Good. May He receive your soul."

Dyna buckled and kicked to free herself. They twisted her arms behind her back, forcing her to fold forward into submission. Was this how her aunt had died, prostrated in the dirt?

She wept, begging them over and over. The sword's heat drafted against her exposed neck as it lifted above her head. She squeezed her eyes shut. *Please!*

"Captain Gareel," a new male voice said. "Do not kill this one."

Dyna peeked through her lashes. The Seraphim looked up at the *Hyalus* in angry disbelief. At first, she thought the tree had spoken, but another perched there on a branch. The glass leaves hid most of him from sight, except for an arm hanging lazily over a bent knee covered in white silk. A thin beam of sunlight caught on the flute he spun loosely in his fingers.

The leader, whom she assumed was the captain, tightened his fist around the hilt of his weapon. "You know the law of this land, Your Highness."

"I gave you an order," the other replied, his tone bored. "Release the human."

Captain Gareel glared at Dyna with enough hate to send her through Death's Gate by will alone. She held her breath, awaiting his decision.

After a brief pause, he thrust the sword in its sheath, extinguishing the flames. "As you command."

She wilted in relief. The others removed their vice grip on her and she tumbled to the ground. Once the feeling returned to her numb limbs, Dyna dove for the journal, shoving it into her satchel and holding it close to her chest. She didn't dare reach for her clothes by Captain Gareel's feet.

He crouched in front of her and leaned in until the abhorrence in his blue gaze transfixed her in place. He spoke low for only her to hear, "The Nephilim may pity humans, but hundreds of Watchers lay in wait in this forest. You will perish here before the sun sets." His promise hung over her head as his sword once had.

Clutching her shaking fists, Dyna lifted her chin. "Only if the God of Urn wills it."

The captain sneered and reached for the knife holstered on his calf. She threw up her hands, calling on her Essence out of instinct, even if she had no real magic to defend herself. But an unexpected current of scorching power surged from within her, coursing through her body with an uncontrollable force so painful she screamed.

Green fire exploded from her palms and hit the captain, hurling him across the forest. He crashed into the *Hyalus* tree and collapsed as a charred heap over its roots. Dyna stared at the smoke billowing from the broken wings on his still form, then at her shaking hands.

The Seraphs gawked at her in horrified silence.

What had she done? Had ... she killed him?

Captain Gareel groaned and twitched. He wasn't dead yet. Dyna launched to her feet and bolted for the trees.

No one stopped her.

Thorny brambles slashed at Dyna's cloak and arms as she tore through the forest. Her heavy breaths clouded in the air, a heavy chill embedding in her bones. She had never produced such power before. The blast of Essence left her weak, but she kept running. She had to escape this place.

The forest was thinning. Beyond the branches, the sky merged into shades of blue, orange, and red with the sunset. Hope flooded through her. She burst through a wall of bushes but came onto the boundary of a cliff and her toes teetered on the edge. She shrieked, arms flailing. Thrusting herself backward, Dyna fell on solid ground with a grunt.

Her wild heartbeat drummed in her ears and she gasped for air, placing a hand over her heaving chest. Her lungs screamed for respite, but there was no stopping. Dyna staggered up and peered over the cliff. It rose hundreds of feet high, ending in a strip of sea. Roaring waves rammed into the serrated rocks below. Falling to her death would have been worse than the quick strike of a sword.

Fifty feet across from her was another cliff with the ongoing dense woodland of Lykos Peak. She had made it.

Dyna dragged her pulsing feet north along the cliff's edge, searching for a way to the other side. She came upon a wretched old bridge swaying in the breeze, moss, and vines coating the rotted planks. The rope had wasted away and was missing in a few places. It couldn't have held Zev's weight, but she moved closer to investigate further.

"Stop!"

Dyna jumped at the unexpected shout. The Seraphs had found her!

She dashed to the bridge and ran across the creaking planks. It teetered with each rapid step. She reached the midpoint when a violent crack sounded beneath her feet. She stilled, but it made no difference. The rope unraveled under her fingers.

"No, please no," she begged.

A shadow fell over her and she looked up at the winged silhouette flying against the sun's glare. "Take my hand!"

She ducked out of his reach. "Get away from me!"

"Take it or you will fall!"

The bridge lurched, and wood splintered. It would not hold her much longer. Dyna whirled for the Seraph and reached out to him. Their fingers nearly brushed when the planks beneath her feet snapped. She dropped through the bridge. Her earth-shattering scream rang within the cliffs as she plummeted for Death's Gate.

The winged man watched her go, still holding out the hand too late to save her. Dyna closed her eyes and let herself fall.

All she could see was Lyra sitting on their front step, waiting for her to return, not knowing she would never come back. She would die knowing one dreadful truth: she had failed.

Her descent came to an abrupt stop and the force knocked the breath out of her. The raging sea, inches below, splashed icy water on her battered legs. She stared down at the waves, finding herself floating in mid-air. A rhythmic whoosh filled her ears at the same time she realized strong, warm arms cradled her. The blaze of the setting sun masked her savior's face except for the graceful black wings flowing behind him.

The wind bustled against them as they soared back up the precipice. Dyna gripped his silken clothing, hiding against his chest, inadvertently inhaling his scent. It was unlike anything she had come across before. Otherworldly. Indescribable. But if she had to try, she would say it was almost ambrosial.

Together they flew high in the sky, and the Zafiro Mountains rose in the distance. A sprinkle of red, orange and yellow treetops dotted the forest among the endless pine trees and the rare indigo canopies.

But Dyna couldn't admire the sight when she was highly aware of the stranger carrying her. What did he plan to do with her? He wouldn't have rescued her if he planned to harm her. Would he?

With steady flaps of his wings, he flew them to a small clearing by the cliff. Neither of them spoke, and he didn't put her down. Instinct warned her to be afraid, but she wasn't.

Dyna took a deep breath in preparation before she dared to look at him, sensing she would need it. The moment she met his eyes, gray like a raging storm, the air was once again stolen from her lips.

The low rays of the sunset fell around him in a red, golden hue, accenting his silk black wings and striking features framed by hair so black it looked like spilled ink against his face. His pale skin held a subtle glow, as if he harbored a light from within.

He wasn't real.

How could he be? His kind no longer existed in the world.

Not sure if she was dreaming, Dyna reached out to touch him, needing to prove he was truly there. The moment her fingertips brushed his cool cheek, a gentle electric current pulsed between them. He flinched, inhaling a sharp breath. His ethereal features tightened into a scowl, and he withdrew his arms, leaving her to fall.

She hit the ground ungracefully. Wincing, she rolled onto her knees, inches from touching his toes nestled in the grass. The light caught on the silver trim of his silk robes as a cool breeze fluttered them over his legs; the hem brushing his bare feet. Sunlight gleamed on the sapphire ring dangling on a thin chain around his neck. But nothing compared to the magnificence of his black wings. She could not help but marvel at how the light caught on the sleek feathers.

He was beautiful.

His gaze swept over her, and his mouth twisted. She felt his disgust as much as she saw it. "You are an incredibly stupid human," he said.

Dyna barely registered the insult, for she was too stunned by his voice. It was smooth, lilting, carrying a faint accent slightly different than one spoken in the eastern quadrants of Urn—and it was the same voice in the forest who had spared her life.

CHAPTER 5

Cassiel

Every curse known to man rang in Cassiel's head. He groaned and kneaded his temples. He hadn't expected much to happen when he'd been ordered to accompany the Watchers to the border.

"It is time you learn the governance of our kingdom," the High King had announced, *"including the ways we protect our people from intruders."*

But no one ventured into Hilos. Not anymore. The bones of those who had rested beneath the roots of the trees. Yet Cassiel now glowered at an intruder who gaped at him like a dead fish.

She remained unmoving where she kneeled. Her dress was dirty and torn, cuts marking her ankles and hands. Tiny freckles speckled her flushed cheeks and the bridge of her perked nose. Her full lips were cracked and dry from thirst. She was young, younger than him, possibly. Her wavy tresses were the color of flames, the ends curling past her shoulders. His gaze fell on her eyes, and stayed there, bewildered by the stunning color. They were a deep green, rivaling the purest of emeralds.

Gods, who cared about her eyes? By sparing her life, he had broken laws that had been in place for half a millennium. He could lose his wings.

Damn.

What had overcome him? Why did he save her? Cassiel glared at the dainty human and rubbed his cheek to rid himself of the tingling sensation she left behind. It felt as if her touch had imprinted on his skin.

The moment she touched him, it triggered a second sight, and he had seen through the blaze of her life force to her soul. It was a quick flash, but he didn't perceive any ill intentions in her heart, only the sorrow clouding it.

He looked her over, searching for any hidden weapons. She didn't appear to be armed or trained in any sense.

She still hadn't stopped gawking at him.

"Have you lost the means to speak?"

Awareness returned to her face, and she smiled. "You were the Seraph in the *Hyalus* tree."

"I am *not* a Seraph."

She frowned and tilted her head. "Oh ... are you the Nephilim?"

By asking such a question, she may as well have spat in his face. He had to tolerate the slur hissed at him by his brothers and other Celestials, but he would not tolerate it from a human.

"Call me that again and I will kill you myself," he snapped.

She shrunk back from his dark promise. "I-I'm sorry. I meant no offense. The captain, he ..."

Cassiel scowled at the trees. He had wondered what Captain Gareel whispered to her.

Her brow furrowed as she glanced between him and the forest. Did she not understand what she had said?

"Never speak that word again."

The human nodded fervently. She studied him again, her eyes widening further when she took notice of the circlet resting on his brow. Standing, she bobbed in a clumsy curtsy. "It's a great pleasure to meet you, Your Majesty. I'm Dynalya—"

Cassiel raised a hand, cutting her off. This would be the last he would see her, so there was no purpose in the acquaintance. Her name repeated in his head anyhow. Dynalya. It was the name of an Elvish flower, oddly enough.

"I am not the king. Nor do I care to know who you are."

Her cheeks bloomed pink, and she fidgeted with her fingers. "Oh, well. Is the captain all right?"

He frowned, surprised the human cared to ask. She had appeared helpless against the Watchers until she hit Captain Gareel with green fire. If Cassiel had not borne witness to it himself, he would have thought it impossible. Humans didn't have magic. They were weak, pitiable beings. She too had appeared shocked it came from her.

His feather.

She must have absorbed its magic somehow. It was the only explanation, but how did she manage to wield it?

"His injuries may be fatal if not treated," she said. "He needs tending."

Though Cassiel had enjoyed seeing him thrown clear across the forest, the only injury Captain Gareel sustained was to his pride. Their kind was not so easily killed.

"He will live."

"Why did he want to hurt me?" Her wide eyes searched his, awaiting an answer. Did she truly not know? Well, five centuries had passed since they had any contact with the outside world.

"You should not be here."

She hesitated before asking, "Why?"

He crossed his arms, contemplating how much to reveal. She was not a poacher, that much was clear. Regardless, Captain Gareel had been ready to take her head.

Cassiel had not witnessed an execution before, but it had reminded him of the last trespasser who came through these woods two decades ago. The reminder elicited a wispy image of a woman with black hair, calling his name. He quickly pushed the memory aside.

"This is Hilos, the high court of the Celestials," he said.

The girl canted her head. "In our tales of old, we refer to your kind as the Seraphim."

"Celestials and Seraphim are not one and the same. You will do well to remember that."

Her mouth opened, possibly to ask more about it, but at his glower, she bit her lip.

"How did you cross the Realm as far as you did? You're fortunate the Watchers have grown careless."

"The Watchers?"

"The Celestials who guard our borders."

She lifted one corner of her cloak to show him the faded archaic runes sown on the hem. "I was not sure if the concealment spell weaved through it would still work. I tried to be quiet and not disturb the forest."

He hadn't memorized all the runes and their meanings, but he knew a magic cloak protected the wearer. The tattered fabric seemed to be one color only to change when she moved, camouflaging her from anyone looking too closely. Only the elves or the mages could make such cloaks, and they cost a small fortune. It was not something this human could possibly afford, even in its poor condition.

"But then I heard the music," she said, glancing at his flute.

Cassiel tightened his hand around the cool metal. He had not intended to draw her with it. He had played the flute merely to pass the time and because it irritated Captain Gareel.

"That song, I have heard it before."

"I doubt that, stupid human." The song was his. No one outside of the castle had heard it.

She frowned. "I beg your pardon?"

"It is a befitting name, as you nearly lost your life twice in preventable circumstances."

"Thank you for saving me," she replied stiffly, pursing her mouth. "I am within your debt. How may I repay your kindness?"

"I want nothing from you."

Her mouth fell open. "Bu—but you must ask for something. The God of Urn's Holy Law demands I repay my debt or I surrender my life in service to you. Please, I don't wish to become a life-servant."

The entire concept of the *holy* life-debt was sickening. Humans had invented such a foul belief. Save the life of another and they became indentured for the rest of their life if they didn't have the means to repay the debt with a suitable offering. People owning people and branding them like cattle.

He would never keep a slave, much less a human one. Nonetheless, Hilos didn't allow life-debts. But she didn't know that.

The longer Cassiel glared at her, the more she squirmed. She pushed the worn satchel hanging on her shoulder behind her and shifted her stance to hide it. Not that he cared. She was a peasant and wouldn't have anything of value.

"I relieve you of your debt, Dynalya," he said, acknowledging her name at last. It surprised him how easily it rolled off his tongue and the pleasing sound of it.

She sighed in visible relief. The phrase released her of any obligation to him and once said, he couldn't retract his decision. She was free.

"Thank you, and please call me Dyna, if you will. May I know your name?"

"No."

Dyna huffed in slight indignation. "Very well. If you have relieved me, then I must be on my way. Good day to you." She gave him another curtsy and turned to leave.

"I have not dismissed you. Explain why you have intruded on our lands."

"I'm searching for my cousin, Zev. He lives in Lykos Peak." She pointed at the overgrown thicket beyond the cliff.

She must be joking. Cassiel was about to say so, but she was already walking away. "You cannot go there," he sputtered.

Dyna called over her shoulder. "But I must."

She continued her brisk walk along the perimeter of the cliff and disappeared past a tall hedge. Cassiel stared in the direction she went. Well, that was it then. It was time he returned to the castle and provided an explanation. The High King was surely waiting for one.

But Cassiel couldn't make himself go, indecision and confusion keeping him there. This had nothing to do with him. He did his part in saving her life already. The human was nothing to him.

He muttered a curse and flew after her.

Dyna lingered ahead in the dusk, standing by a fallen tree lying across the two cliffs. It was massive, with exposed, desiccated roots as sharp as talons. He circled over the unexpected tree-bridge. Who placed it here? The Watchers avoided patrolling close to the Lykos border, so this had happened unbeknownst to them.

She tested the roots, then began climbing. "This must be how Zev ventures across."

Cassiel crossed his arms. "Should you fall again, do not expect me to catch you."

"I'll be fine, Your Highness," she said as she reached the top.

He scoffed. "Is that so?"

Dyna stopped in the twilight and gave him a soft smile. "My good fortune truly came with our meeting. I wouldn't have survived this day if not for you, and I believe the fates are not finished with us yet."

Cassiel was too dumbfounded to respond. Who was this girl that she thought his presence meant something?

Her light laughter followed his reaction, and the delightful sound vibrated through him in a way it shouldn't have. She looked at him with such undeserved reverence that for a moment her smile gave worth to his crime of sparing her life.

Dyna crossed the wide width of the tree, arms held out for balance. He jolted, instinctively reaching out to catch her again, but she made it to the other end without incident and hopped down.

Walking to the dense try line, she paused. "Will you accompany me?" Traces of fear lingered beneath her inquiring expression.

Cassiel arched an eyebrow. "No."

"All right…" She took a deep breath and faced the woods of Lykos Peak.

Surely, she wouldn't risk going there on her own—

Dyna ran inside.

If he wasn't sure before, this convinced him he had indeed saved a stupid human. She went in after he warned her. It wasn't his responsibility to see to her survival, but he couldn't make himself leave.

Was it because she willingly trusted him? Or because he knew she would be killed if he didn't go after her?

Cassiel groaned. Damn the fates, and damn him for being the fool.

He flew across the chasm and landed by the boundary of the cliff. His knowledge of Lykos Peak made him hesitate. He had to retrieve her before *they* took notice.

Cassiel rushed through the trees and bumped into Dyna. Her startled shriek rang in his ears.

"Quiet!" he hissed.

A shaky smile rose from her lips. "You came."

"Against my better judgment, which you apparently lack." He held out an arm to keep her from going any further while he observed their shadowed surroundings. They stood in a dark glade enclosed in thick foliage. Sweat sprouted on the nape of his neck, and his heart raced with the receding light. "We must go. This territory belongs to the were-beasts."

"Were-beasts?"

"Yes, also called shapeshifters, wolf-men, or whatever you know them as from where you are from."

She frowned. "We call them werewolves."

"Then you know what they are." So as not to touch Dyna directly, Cassiel grabbed her hood and pulled her back the way they came.

"I'm not leaving." She slipped out of her cloak.

"Bloody hell, I should have let you fall over the cursed cliff." He pitched the cloak on the ground.

She huffed. "I cannot leave without Zev."

"Be quiet or you will draw the beasts right to us," he snapped. What was so important to risk her life to find this cousin? If he came here, he was surely dead. "Night is falling and I do not have a weapon." He gripped the flute, remembering it was made of silver. It would do some damage to a were-beast—in close range. No, he wouldn't risk that. "We are leaving."

She stood firm and crossed her arms. "I need to find my cousin."

Cassiel was finished with this nonsense. "Listen, stupid human, either you come with me or I will leave you here alone."

Dyna's complexion paled, her breathing growing quick and heavy. "Please don't leave me in this dark place," she begged. "You don't understand. I must find him."

A brisk breeze caressed the beads of perspiration on his nape, continuing east. Dread sank in Cassiel's stomach. That wind carried their scent.

The trees were so still, Dyna's hitched breathing sounded loud in the quiet. There was no mistaking the threat creeping into the chilly air as the last of the light washed out with the night's arrival. Thin shafts of moonlight trickled through the branches, and in the far reaches of the woods, a howl broke the deafening silence.

Cassiel snatched Dyna's sleeve and hauled her away.

"My cloak!"

"Leave it."

"No!"

"We cannot stop—" A low, menacing growl halted him in place. A chill skittered down Cassiel's spine. Slowly, he inched his head and glanced over his shoulder.

There, from within the depths of the bushes, were two yellow eyes watching them in the dark.

CHAPTER 6

Cassiel

oosebumps rushed down Cassiel's arms and a curse caught on his tongue. His limbs were locked in place by those predatory eyes as thoughts raced through his mind. He wasn't armed. The trees were too dense to fly through. He couldn't fight a beast. *Run*.

They had to run!

"Zev?" Dyna called to it, her voice quivering.

Cassiel's attention snapped to her. "Your cousin is a were-beast?"

She nodded without looking away from it.

The creature snarled and moved into the moonlight, revealing a huge gray wolf. It was three times bigger than an ordinary wolf, but thin with bald patches in its fur. Foam lined its mouth and drool seeped through its sharp teeth as it stalked forward.

She stumbled back. "That's not him!"

Cassiel grabbed her elbow, and they ran. In one leap, the wolf took Dyna down, wrenching her from his grasp as they crashed to the ground. Her terrible scream rang in his ears. He gathered the force in his wings and spun, whipping them against the beast. The blow threw it across the glade, but it quickly rolled back to its feet.

Cassiel held his flute as he would a knife and braced his legs. Silver would kill it as long as he struck a piercing blow.

The wolf prowled toward them as a young man came tearing through the bushes. He ripped off his shirt and leaped into the air, shifting mid-arc into a black wolf, and tackled the other wolf off its path. The monstrous beasts tussled on the ground—a snarling mass of fur and teeth.

Cassiel yanked Dyna to her feet and shoved her toward the cliffs. "Go!"

But she stayed in place, staring at the creatures, hands covering her mouth.

The two wolves circled the clearing, their reflective yellow eyes glowing in the night. The black wolf was massive and much stronger. That didn't deter the gray wolf from challenging it. They charged at each other, tearing into flesh.

Watching their attacks, Cassiel determined the fight would not last much longer. The black wolf was winning, though it didn't aim to kill. It attempted repeatedly to herd its opponent to the woods, but the beast was relentless. It kept trying to reach Dyna. The black wolf slammed into the gray, throwing the massive beast across the clearing. It collided into a tree with a loud *thwack*, sending a scatter of leaves raining down. It didn't get up.

A low growl rumbled from the black wolf. It circled the tree warily, eyeing the fallen beast. When it didn't move, the black wolf approached and the gray lunged for its throat.

"No!" Dyna cried.

The gray wolf's attention locked on her at the shout. The black wolf tackled it, and they rolled into the underbrush out of sight. Vicious growls and snarls filled the glade. A sharp whine sliced through the night air, coming to an abrupt end. After a brief quiet, a chorus of mournful howls resonated beyond the woods. The haunting sound turned every muscle in Cassiel's back rigid.

The bushes rustled and the massive black wolf ambled out with a glistening muzzle.

"Zev!" Dyna ran to the wolf and wrapped her arms around its neck, burying her face in the thick fur. It whined softly and nuzzled her cheek, leaving behind smears of blood.

"That *thing* is your kin?" Cassiel asked. Perhaps she called it cousin as a term of endearment.

The wolf growled, baring its fangs.

"This is Zev." Dyna stood and brushed herself off. She hurried to the bushes to gather the strewn clothes and boots and laid them by the beast.

When she turned her back, the wolf's form shifted and its fur receded, revealing a crouched, naked young man. Zev rose to his full height. He stood significantly taller than Dyna, with a broad body layered in corded muscle. In the moonlight, Cassiel could barely distinguish the warped scars all over him. Zev's eyes no longer shone yellow. They were a different shade, not perceptible in the night, but his wayward dark hair and scruffy face hardly hid the wild, sharp features that hinted what he truly was.

Cassiel struggled to explain what he was seeing. He glanced back and forth between Zev and the moon peeking through the branches. This werewolf somehow shifted to his human form at night. How?

Zev quickly yanked on his trousers and slipped on a dirty white tunic, then his boots. "Dyna, are you all right?" he asked, his gruff voice full of concern.

"Yes." She turned around with a smile, but it faltered at the sight of blood soaking through his tunic from his ribs. "You're hurt."

"It's nothing." He rested his hands on her shoulders. "I feared the worst when I caught your scent and realized Faolan hunted you."

"Faolan?" She glanced at the bushes. "He's of the Lykos Pack?"

"He was."

Dyna's face crumbled. "I'm sorry."

"It had to be done. He was feral and wouldn't have stopped."

Feral? Cassiel frowned. He would assume all of Zev's kind to be feral.

Dyna's eyes widened. "He had gone mad?"

At the question, the were-beast looked away from her. What did she mean by mad?

"Did he hurt you?" Zev asked instead. He held her back, examining her scratched arms and legs.

"I'm fine. Let me tend to your wounds. It will only take a moment." Dyna reached for the bite on his shoulder, but he lowered her hand carefully, as though aware he could harm her with his sharp nails.

"There's no need. They will scar by tomorrow."

She sighed. "Take a salve at the very least or those bites could become infected."

He didn't dispute further. Perplexed, Cassiel watched as Zev let her smear a waxy substance on his wounds from a jar she produced out of her satchel. Dyna truly didn't fear the were-beast, and he made no move to attack her either.

"How did you find your way here?" Zev asked as she worked. "I was to see you in North Star within a week. You shouldn't have come here. Lykos Peak is no place for humans."

"Which is precisely what I told her," Cassiel muttered to himself.

The were-beast turned to him, his brow furrowing. Elongated canines flashed in the corners of his mouth when he spoke. "Good evening."

Cassiel chose not to respond.

Zev frowned at Dyna. "Care to explain?"

She fiddled with the jar, returning it to her satchel. "Well, I—"

Zev spun toward the woods, his eyes flaring yellow.

Cassiel stilled as another chorus of howls echoed in the distance—sounding much closer than they had before.

"We must go." Zev rushed to the bushes and pulled out a frayed rucksack. He slung it on his shoulder, its bulky contents clanking inside.

Dyna eyed it. "Were you planning to leave? You gave me your word we would discuss it first."

"This isn't the time to argue." Zev hauled her toward the cliffs. Cassiel followed behind. As soon as they cleared the woods, he returned to the sky.

The were-beast and Dyna sprinted to the tree-bridge connecting the two cliffs. Zev tossed her up on the tree's trunk before leaping up himself and picking her up again. He rushed across, moving in a swift and agile stride. Reaching the other side, he bound off the bridge and set her down to take hold of the tree roots. Cassiel watched in speechless amazement as the wood creaked and groaned, slowly breaking away from its deep groove in the earth. Zev's back strained as he pushed the tree-bridge with impossible strength, shoving it off the edge. The tree plunged down the precipice and smashed on the rocks below.

He stared across the cliff at the woods of Lykos Peak. Cassiel followed his line of sight to the several, yellow eyes gleaming in the dark.

The Lykos Pack.

Zev didn't look away until they withdrew. "They'll not follow us here," he said. "The Pack has a treaty with Hilos that prevents them from crossing territory lines."

That was knowledge Cassiel should have known, but he often ignored his government studies or anything else of non-interest. He had assumed the were-beasts didn't enter their Realm because a chasm separated their territories. If the treaty was true, why was Zev on Celestial land?

Zev released a long breath and rubbed his face. "What a night it's been."

"Yes, it's been quite eventful," Dyna agreed.

His wary gaze bounced between her and Cassiel hovering above them, then he groaned. "You entered the Forbidden Woods, didn't you? They forbid it for a reason, Dyna."

She kicked at a small pebble, scuffing her shoe in the dirt. "Why didn't you tell me?"

The were-beast clamped his mouth shut and his eyes slid up to Cassiel again. They both knew he could never have told her about the Celestials.

Cassiel flew to a nearby tree, landing on a branch. "She encountered the Watchers. Nearly lost her head."

Zev gaped at her.

Dyna nodded sheepishly. "He saved my life."

Cassiel crossed his arms and sat against the trunk. "I have saved your life three times now, stupid human."

Zev growled at him. "Pardon?"

"I believe I spoke clearly." Her antics until this point had only proved the moniker befitting.

"You have my thanks, Your Highness," Zev grated, "but if you expect to collect a debt, know this: I will never allow my cousin to become your life-servant."

"I am not a slave keeper."

"Then why have you followed her?"

Cassiel glanced at the human, so small compared to her large cousin. As much as she annoyed him, he couldn't leave her behind to die.

"Don't worry. He relieved me of my debt," she said, and Zev's shoulders relaxed. "He is much kinder than the other Seraphim."

"He is a Celestial, Dyna."

"Oh right, he said that." But by her frown, she didn't understand the difference.

Cassiel leaned his head back against the truck. "The Seraphim are of Heaven's Gate. They are not earthbound."

That was all he would bother to say. He was not in the mood to give them a history lesson.

"Forgive me," Dyna said. "So as not to keep referring to you as such, may I please know your name?"

He didn't want to answer, but her soft eyes pinned him. He flew down and landed on a patch of grass at a careful distance. "I am Cassiel Soaraway, third prince of Hilos."

The were-beast gave him a nod. "I am Zev Astron of Lykos Peak."

Dyna smiled. "I am Dynalya Astron of North Star."

He almost laughed. They couldn't expect him to believe that a human and a beast were of House Astron, one of the most powerful mage families in the Magos Empire. The mages were pureblood elitists. They didn't make unions outside of their race. But Cassiel ignored the lie because he had other pressing questions.

"What *are* you?" he asked Zev. "Were-beasts are to remain as beasts under the moonlight until dawn. How can you assume your human form?"

Zev cocked his head, gaze narrowing at him in return. "For a Celestial, you are also unique, Your Highness."

Anger rushed through Cassiel's head. Dyna looked at him questioningly, and his face heated. If she realized what he was, she wouldn't mistake him for a Seraph or even a Celestial. She would call him that other word he hated so much. Why should it matter what she thought?

"Dyna, the Holy Law calls for you to compensate the prince for saving your life," Zev reminded her.

"Yes, of course." She turned her smile to Cassiel again. "Please allow me to gift you a token of my gratitude."

"As I said, I want nothing from you," Cassiel said. "You clearly have no wealth or stature or an ounce of intelligence for that matter. Anything you would gift would be rubbish." He walked past her, ignoring the small twinge of guilt at the flash of hurt crossing her face.

A frightening growl vibrated through the forest, jerking him to a stop.

Zev stalked toward him, primal eyes flashing yellow. The threat in the beast's low, menacing growl sent a cold wash through him. Not in a position to fly out of reach, Cassiel readied his flute. He would not go down without a fight.

"No, Zev!" Dyna leaped between them, placing her hands on his heaving chest.

Gods, what was the stupid human doing? He expected the beast to tear through her, but to his amazement, it halted in place.

"I'm at fault," she said. "I have offended him. Peace now. Breathe."

Zev inhaled a deep shuddering breath and continued until his eyes returned to normal, the fur along his arms receding. Dyna whispered something, and he locked his gaze on the silver flute. Cassiel had been ready to shove it through Zev's chest if he had gotten any closer.

"I'm sorry, Your Highness," Dyna told him. "It's safe."

Cassiel didn't believe her. There was no such thing as safe around *that*. "You cannot tame a beast."

She bit her lip, looking away. "He won't hurt me. Nor you," she added, giving Zev a stern look. "Sometimes werewolves can be provoked when it comes to protecting their families. If he feels I am being threatened or harmed, his wolf surfaces."

Had he harmed her? Verbally, Cassiel supposed. He should apologize, but pride pushed such a notion away.

Zev backed away from them, rubbing his face. "Darkness has fallen. If we don't leave, soon we will become the hunted."

CHAPTER 7

Zev

Zev knew he had made a mistake when he saw the wild look on Dyna's face. He heard her rapid quivering breaths as she whipped around, searching the silent forest for the presence that haunted her whenever darkness fell. She crouched over her knees, shrinking herself as small as the day he found her in the burrow beneath the *Hyalus* tree in the mountains.

He pushed past the confused Celestial prince and caged her in his arms. It was the quickest way to ward off Dyna's terror. She needed to feel the physical presence of another person to remember she wasn't alone.

"You have nothing to fear," Zev soothed. "I'm with you."

He could hear her heart thrashing erratically. Her shaking hands clutched his tunic, clinging to him like driftwood in the storm of her panic. Zev tasted her terror, her skin ice cold against his. He contained her in an embrace, willing her all of his warmth, and remained that way until her stiff body slowly relaxed, and her trembling eased.

"Thank you," she mumbled. "I'm all right now."

Cassiel eyed them strangely, no doubt confused about what had happened. Before Zev could explain, he was interrupted by the flutter of approaching wings. The treetops rustled in a gust as a flock of Celestials flew down to meet them, their flaming swords blazing in the night.

Dyna scrambled to her feet and backed away, pulling on his tunic. "They must have come for me."

They would not have her. Fur rippled along Zev's arms and his claws extended as he prepared to fight them all. The Watchers readied their weapons in response. He followed their movements, deciding who to take down first.

"Do not be a fool," Prince Cassiel said under his breath. "The archer has you in his sights."

Zev spotted the Celestial who had a loaded bow aimed at him, the arrowhead glinting in the moonlight. He was confident in his abilities, but the archer was too close to avoid Dyna being hit.

The prince addressed the Watcher in the center. "Why are you here, Captain Gareel?"

Zev had seen the captain before during the many times he had trekked through Hilos to reach North Star. The Celestials had never noticed him when he passed. He always slinked by under the cover of darkness as his wolf, but *they* were easy to detect in the foliage.

Celestials glowed.

Their light was muted to others, but to his wolf's eyes, they emitted a flare of golden light. A sign they were not of this world.

Nor did they usually reek. Zev's nose curled at the stench of burned leather. Captain Gareel's shredded clothing and armor were scorched. Soot stained his long hair and wings. He appeared to have walked through fire but was otherwise uninjured. Although the prince had spoken to him, the captain's attention remained on Dyna, his face contorted in fury.

"I'm sorry," she said meekly. "I didn't mean to hurt you ..."

Captain Gareel's glare wavered at the apology. Zev glanced between them. She was responsible for his appearance?

"Ah, so it is true," an amused voice called out at the tail of the flock.

The Watchers bowed as another slipped through their ranks. This Celestial was notable with power and elegance that matched the deep blue silk of his robes. Age didn't defy the splendor of his face, framed in golden hair and a short beard. Even in the dark, he emitted a light far more brilliant than the others. A regal crown of gold and sapphires adorned his head.

Prince Cassiel gave him an austere bow.

The Celestial acknowledged him with a nod before he fixed his deep-blue gaze on Zev and Dyna.

"Intruders," Captain Gareel said through his teeth. "You are in the presence of His Royal Majesty, Yoel Soaraway. A divine son of the Heavens, the High King of Hilos, and the Four Celestial Realms. You. Will. *Kneel.*"

Zev took Dyna's elbow and tugged her to the ground. He tensed, keeping his head bowed as the king circled them.

"Cassiel," King Yoel said conversationally, his voice idle and smooth. "Imagine my surprise when the captain came to inform me of your encounter with a human in my forest, and that you deemed it suitable to dismiss the Watchers from their post."

"I had little trust they would abide by my command not to harm her, sire," the prince said indifferently.

"You defied our laws when you spared her." The High King sounded curious rather than angry. "Why?"

Cassiel kept his gaze respectfully lowered as he rose stiffly from his bow. "She is not a poacher."

Zev clenched his fists to control his wolf pacing inside of him. They spoke of Dyna as though she wasn't listening to them debate her life. He sensed her confusion, but she did well to remain demure and quiet.

Zev bated a breath before slightly lifting his head. King Yoel stood with his arms crossed, the edges of his mouth curled in disapproval at the prince. They didn't resemble each other, except around the nose and jaw. Their colored features were stark opposites. The prince blended in the dark, whereas the king was the light.

"You have broken a momentous law, son."

Cassiel lifted his head, a flash of defiance in his eyes. "I am *not* the first."

That must have held meaning, for something crossed the High King's face before it slipped away. "This is a grave matter. The court adheres strictly to Rael's Laws."

"This human is innocent. She means us no harm. I have proven it."

King Yoel looked to Dyna. "Have you?"

"Yes." Cassiel crossed his arms. "Therefore, I am granting her royal immunity and amnesty. It is my right, and the court has no say against it."

His father and the Watchers gawked at him.

"Such absolution places a perpetual liability over you both," King Yoel said. "It requires her fealty and silence. The repercussions are grave if she is ever found in contempt. Are you certain you wish to grant her this?"

Cassiel sighed as though the whole subject was of no consequence. Zev knew little of Celestial law, but what the prince offered was protection at his own expense. If Dyna revealed to anyone that they existed, her life would be forfeit as well as his.

"Yes," Cassiel said, "it is granted."

The High King raised his brows and glanced back and forth between his son and Dyna. "Very well, I have no choice but to release her into your care. You are responsible for her discretion."

"What of the were-beast, Your Majesty?" Captain Gareel asked.

The High King observed Zev thoughtfully. "We have shared our borders with the Lykos Pack for centuries. We have had no qualms with them and we will not start now," he said, motioning at the Watchers to stand down.

A grating whisper stirred in Zev's thoughts, dragging through him like claws. *Would their decision change should they discover you have no Pack? What would they think if they knew what you have done?*

"Zev?" Dyna called faintly. She looked at his arms where fur sprouted, his fingers digging into the earth.

If he didn't silence the Madness, he would shift. He closed his eyes and focused on the scents of damp soil, pine, and old fallen leaves until the whispers faded. The Madness could condemn him later.

The Watchers sheathed their swords except for the captain, the white flame of his weapon glowing brightly in the dark forest. The archer lowered his loaded bow but kept it at the ready. Zev felt him tracking his every move.

"Rise," the High King said. "No harm shall befall you."

Zev helped Dyna stand, and they both met his penetrating gaze. "Thank you, Your Majesty."

"And with whom do I have the pleasure of acquainting?"

"I am Zev, and this is Dynalya of North Star."

Dyna pinched the corners of her dress and curtsied.

The High King canted his head. "It truly is a pleasure to meet you, my dear, for you must be a wonder to have stirred the favor of my son. At the news of his transgression, I came to see for myself what could have possessed him to do such a thing." He hesitated before reaching out and cupping her cheek. His eyes slid closed, and he smiled. "I see."

Zev growled. The king was Soul Searching. The Celestial ability to see another's soul was a rather intimate thing, and he didn't care for that intrusion on his cousin. Without thinking, he reached for Dyna and the archer immediately released his arrow. Zev tackled her out of the way, bracing for the blow.

A drop of blood splashed on his cheek instead.

The Watchers drew their blazing swords, flooding the forest with light once again. Zev looked at the prince's hand splayed out above him with the bloody arrow point pierced through his palm. Red rivulets trailed down his pale arm, glistening against the white of his silk robes.

"You were ordered to stand down," Cassiel hissed through his clenched teeth.

Dyna gaped at the prince. Zev stared at him too, bewildered that he would intervene. The prince glanced past him to Dyna and his gaze flittered over her as though checking that she wasn't harmed. Had he done it for her?

Zev slowly rose to his knees, remaining crouched by Dyna as a precaution.

King Yoel chuckled. "What happened? He moved so rapidly I nearly missed it."

"Be cautious, sire." Cassiel grimaced as he pulled the arrow from his palm, tossing it away. "It seems their kind have a tendency for belligerence."

The prince dropped his wounded hand to his side. Scarlet trails trickled down his fingers, collecting into a puddle by his feet. *Drip, drip, drip* echoed in Zev's ears. The sweet metallic scent of Celestial blood flooded his senses.

"Why is no one helping him?" Dyna demanded.

No one cared that Cassiel bled. No one moved to help him, not even his father, but it wasn't indifference. Before Zev could explain, she rushed to the prince. She tore the edge of her wool dress and pressed it into his wound. He tried to pull away, but she held firm.

"Please be still. I'll give you laudanum for the pain and stitch this closed."

"That is unnecessary," he said, his eyes becoming lidded. "I am fine."

"You're not."

Cassiel's tight scowl smoothed out, his eyes falling closed as his fingers wrapped around hers. Zev glanced at the others, wondering how they would react to this. But the Celestials watched silently, the High King wearing a slight smile.

This was what the prince must have meant when he said he proved Dyna's innocence. He had seen her soul.

"Prince Cassiel?" she called worriedly. "Are you feeling faint? You've lost a lot of blood."

His eyes sprung open and he yanked his hand away. "Your concern is needless. I'm no longer bleeding."

"That's ridiculous. An arrow went through your—"

Cassiel removed the soaked cloth to reveal he indeed no longer bled. Zev watched in amazement as muscle and skin stitched themselves together on an invisible loom until it left his hand without a hint of a scar. The crimson stains on his clothing were the only evidence of the injury.

Zev knew about the regenerative abilities of the Celestials, but to witness it was nothing short of miraculous.

"God of Urn," Dyna whispered.

"Forgive the Watchers for their impulsiveness, my dear," the king said. "We do not receive many visitors around here."

The captain's glare trained on the archer. "You spilled the blood of a prince. Others have been exiled for less!"

The archer dropped to his knees before King Yoel, lowering his forehead to the ground. "Forgive me, sire."

"I am sure you did not intend to harm my son. However, I said our guests would not be harmed. What value does my word have if it is not honored?" The king glanced at Cassiel. "Though, I would say the slight is yours. Do you wish for his exile?"

The prince gave him a look of barely restrained annoyance. "I will shear no one of their wings."

Dyna's eyes widened and she looked at Zev. He gave her a subtle nod. Exile called for the removal of the wings. The Celestials couldn't go out into the human world with them visible. They were a secretly hidden race after all.

"My son has shown you grace. May you not take it for granted," the king said.

The archer bowed again in gratitude.

"Tend to the mess you have caused," Captain Gareel barked.

Cassiel dropped the bloodied cloth and moved Dyna aside as the archer approached. He offered the prince a waterskin he unhooked from his belt. While Cassiel cleaned his hands, the archer nudged the cloth into the puddle of blood and snapped the bloody arrow shaft in half before tossing it on top with a handful of kindling. Then he set it afire.

Zev watched the flames devour it all. They couldn't allow any trace of their existence for anyone to discover—especially divine blood.

Cassiel shook his head, the fire turning his silhouette orange. "As thrilling as this day has been, we must return to the castle, sire."

Yoel's smile broadened. "Yes, you are quite right. Master Wolf, Fair Maiden, it would be my honor if you would join us for dinner tonight."

Dinner?

The alarm that crossed every Celestial's face was not lost on Zev.

CHAPTER 8

Zev

The Hilos castle rested on a summit. Its sharp-pointed towers rose high in the sky, poking through a veil of stars. Torches blazed in the night, but it was the bioluminescent plant life that highlighted the kingdom embedded in the slope. The summit rested on the edge of a cove, a half-moon shimmering on the surface of the sea. The soft whoosh of the waves lapped against the coast, carrying the scent of brine in the air. The beauty of this place appeared as though a piece of the Heavens had descended to the land of Urn.

Zev kept Dyna close as the Watchers marched them up the summit, bringing them to cross a narrow stone bridge leading to the castle. They passed by boisterous cascades that sprayed a fine mist over them. The High King and the prince flew overhead out of Zev's earshot, having a private conversation, no doubt about them. The Watchers led them to lofty wrought-iron gates wrapped in rusted chains that hadn't been opened in centuries.

Yoel and his son flew ahead with Captain Gareel, landing on one of many balconies of the castle, heading inside. Another Watcher took out an old set of keys and unlocked the chains. Two others took hold of the thick bars and pulled with the force of their wings. Zev winced at the sound of the corroded hinges screeching in his ears as they opened.

Prince Cassiel soon returned and landed beside Dyna in clean robes. It was clear he hadn't wanted them to come, but his father insisted and there was no gainsaying a king. "Keep close," he said.

Zev tried not to gape at the castle's grandeur as their footsteps echoed through the quiet courtyard. They followed the prince to the grand entry and he guided them into the main hall. Inside, all surfaces were constructed of polished marble; gilded vines and leaves adorned the pillars, every detail meticulous and pristine. Chandeliers hung from the soaring cathedral ceilings, casting lambent light in the quiet halls.

Royal Guards stood in every corner, stiff and almost lifeless in their gold-plated armor that glinted under the candlelight. Their cold blue gazes followed them as they passed. The atmosphere didn't feel right here. His wolf paced inside of him, restless and bristling.

Cassiel brought them before a set of massive gold doors and he glanced over his shoulder at them, his jaw tightening. "Do well to mind yourselves while you are here," he said curtly. "Do not go anywhere alone. Do not speak to anyone." His cool eyes narrowed pointedly on Dyna. "And do not *touch* anyone. Above all, do not address Her Majesty unless spoken to. The High King may have invited you here but you are not safe from the queen if you offend her. Do you understand?"

Zev nodded, wishing he had declined the invitation, but it was too late to turn back now.

Cassiel dismissed the Watchers, and the Royal Guards marched forward to take their place. They pushed open the doors to reveal an enormous dining room. Much like the rest of the castle, it was adorned in more polished stone and gold. Zev heard the prince's heart rate spike, but his outward poise remained indifferent as he led them inside.

Several servants in silk gray robes carried decanters of gold and platters of food. A massive hearth with a roaring fire made up the west corner. On the walls hung tapestries with the sigil of wings expanding from a crowned sword lit aflame.

Set in the middle of the room was an extensive table with the reflective surface of a mirror. The High King sat at the head of the table in a throne of glass. To his left sat a gorgeous woman with a mane of sun-spun locks and an ornate crown. The queen, Zev presumed.

On the king's right was the royal family by the take of their similar features. Two males and a young female. They wore silk white robes with shimmering embroidery; the fine garments flowing to their bare feet. Their hair was golden, eyes deep sapphire, each possessing pearlescent wings.

The room was a resonance of racing hearts. Only the king's heartbeat was steady, but Zev tasted the anger and apprehension in the air. They should not have come.

"Welcome!" King Yoel's voice echoed in the silence. "Please, come join us."

Cassiel left them to take his seat at the far end of the table, opposite of the others.

"It's very kind of you to invite us this evening," Zev said as he and Dyna bowed. "This is truly an honor."

Decorum required the response, though it felt false on his lips. He had been curious to see the hidden kingdom of the Celestials, but now that he had arrived, Zev wanted nothing more than to leave.

"The pleasure is all mine." High King beckoned them to sit in the two glass chairs the servants placed at the center of the table. Once they settled, he said, "It pleases me to present my family. My wife, Mirah." He indicated the queen, then to the others one by one. "My sons, Malakel and Tzuriel, and my daughter, Ariel. I have shared with them how you came to be here, and the story rather intrigued them."

Of that, Zev had no doubt.

The queen didn't bother acknowledging them. The princes and princess sat in identical stiff postures with their heads lowered as if their crowns weighed too heavy.

The king leaned toward Malakel and whispered, "Where is Princess Briel?"

"I will not have my wife near the beast," the eldest prince replied. "She is to dine in her chambers tonight."

No one outside of their proximity heard the exchange, but Zev's sharp hearing missed nothing. Not the grinding of King Yoel's teeth at his son's insolent tone, nor Princess Ariel's soft gasp or Prince Tzuriel's stifled cough.

The High King straightened in his seat and smiled at Zev and Dyna. "Quite an adventure you've had today. You must be famished."

The servants came forward and set the table with heaping trays of raw fruit and vegetables, bowls of nuts and seeds, and plates of dates and figs. Within golden goblets, they poured a white substance, sweet rice milk by the smell of it. Zev's stomach rumbled with hunger, but he was disappointed at the lack of meat. It was against the Celestial faith to eat the flesh of animals and to drink anything fermented. They believed it would taint their sanctity.

Regardless, the variety of food was perfect for his cousin because she too abstained from eating meat. She smiled when the servants set a plate of fruit before her. They served Zev the same, along with a second plate containing light brown crumbles.

"That is called manna," the High King told him. "You will find it delectable."

Zev waited for the king to eat first before he reached for anything. The manna was like bread. The outside was a soft, crumbly texture while the inside tasted as sweet as honey. Heavenly was the easiest way to describe the strange food. But he was too uncomfortable to stomach another bite. The tension in the dining room was too palpable to ignore.

Utensils clinked against dishes as the royals picked at their food. Prince Malakel's face remained pinched while Princess Ariel stared down at her lap. Only Prince Tzuriel ate as he listened to his father's conversation with Dyna.

King Yoel's laughter filled the room when she told him about her meeting with the Watchers and what she first thought was a talking tree. To which he said talking trees existed but not in Urn. He carried on with the conversation; either ignoring or oblivious to the temperament of the room. Servants and the Royal Guard watched with stern eyes, their scorn digging into the back of Zev's skull.

But he and Dyna were not the only unwanted guests.

Cassiel sat with his chin resting on a fist, pushing a lump of food back and forth on his plate with a fork. Like his father, he didn't notice or care about the sporadic glares shot his way by the servants and Prince Malakel. Queen Mirah glanced at the dark prince next, and her features twisted with revulsion.

How could his mother look at him that way? Unless ... she wasn't his mother.

Cassiel was an obvious contrast to his family and to the entire Celestial population, Zev mulled. A stain on a white sheet, judging by the contempt simmering in the faces of anyone who looked at him.

It could only mean one thing.

Crossbred, the Madness whispered. *As are you.*

King Yoel let out another burst of laughter, silencing the whispers in Zev's thoughts. "You sure are a lively girl. I find I haven't been this well entertained in years!"

Zev forced a smile as he tried to straighten his thoughts. "She is wonderful, isn't she?"

"As wonderful as her name. Dynalya, was it?"

"Yes, like the flower, sire," she said. "Are you familiar with it?"

The High King leaned on the armrest of his glass throne. "Oh yes, I'm familiar with the flower. It only grows within the Vale of the Elves. In the Elvish language, *Dynalya* means 'great healing'. Who named you?"

Dyna's smile faltered. "My mother."

It must still pain her to think of them, a sorrow Zev knew all too well.

He cleared his throat, drawing the High King's attention. "Dyna's parents were Herb Masters and once owned an apothecary, sire. They taught her the ways of botany healing from childhood. She has already completed her training and now holds to the trade herself."

The expressions of King Yoel and the other Celestials who had been listening switched to amazement. Herb Mastery was a highly respected title given to accomplished healers. It meant she possessed an in-depth knowledge of anatomy and the skills to use each medicinal plant in the region.

"You have become an Herb Master this young?" King Yoel said with great approval. "May I ask your age, Dynalya?"

"I have lived for eighteen-spring-seasons, Your Majesty."

"Many are double your age before they have attained such an accomplishment. You're quite the extraordinary human."

Human.

The word had such a powerful effect in the room, it was as though everyone sucked in a breath at once.

Prince Malakel lifted his burning gaze to the High King. "So, you do realize *it* is, in fact, *human*. I was beginning to question your sanity, Father."

King Yoel's expression hardened at the blatant disrespect. "I am aware," he said tightly.

"Then why bring it into the castle?" Prince Malakel shot to his feet, launching his glass chair across the sleek floor. The servants scurried out of the way before it shattered against the wall. Zev winced at the sound stabbing his ears, and Dyna yelped.

Malakel whirled on Cassiel next. "How dare you risk all our lives by sparing it? Then you see fit to grant it *immunity*? You have spat in the face of our kinsmen and everything they died for. You are a traitor!"

The taut muscles in Cassiel's jaw flexed. His indifferent expression didn't falter, but his fists set on either side of his plate, curled so tightly his knuckles turned white.

Malakel continued to berate him, his words reverberating against the walls. "You have defiled the kingdom and dishonored the Soaraway family! You are not fit to bear the name! You disgust me, you filthy, vile Neph—"

"Silence!" King Yoel cut him off. "You will not speak *that* word in my presence."

Malakel sneered at his father. "And I will not sit here to dine with a human and a beast. It is intolerable. When I succeed the throne, all those who show mercy to humans will be sentenced to death."

The queen smiled at her son's proclamation. Ariel and Tzuriel gawked at him.

The High King's eyes boiled with rage, but his words were nothing short of calm. "Tell me, Malakel, when have I said the throne would go to you?" He stood, never looking away from his son. "That human girl has accomplished more in her life than you have in all your years in this world. You have yet to prove to me you would make a wise ruler. Of your brothers, you are the least deserving to rule *my* kingdom."

Queen Mirah glared at him through narrow slits. "He is the heir apparent. By the law of succession—"

"I *make* the law!" They all cowed at King Yoel's deafening bellow. He loomed over the stunned prince, his expanded wings casting menacing shadows. Prince Malakel shrank back. "I am the High King and I am your father. Conduct yourself to that esteem. One more word out of your mouth and I will have you exiled with the removal of your wings. Then you will resemble the very humans you loathe so much."

The color drained from the prince's face. He flinched when the queen's utensils clashed on her plate, the sound echoing within the hushed room.

The king reined his fury and evened his expression like he had not threatened his son. "This is the last time you ever show me such disrespect, Malakel. Now remove yourself from my sight."

The eldest prince lowered in a stiff bow, then pivoted on his heel and headed for another golden door. No one stirred for a long stretch once he left. Zev didn't move a muscle or raise his gaze, and Dyna followed his example.

The queen was the first to speak, her faint hiss reaching Zev's ears. "You would be so barbaric as to exile your son, Yoel? Shearing of the wings is worse than death."

The High King's glare cut to her. "Question me again and I will show you the same favor, Mirah."

The queen gasped in outrage. Her chair screeched as she stood and pinned her eyes on Prince Tzuriel and Princess Ariel. They rose at the silent command. The whisper of their footsteps crossed the room before vanishing with the slam of the heavy door closing behind them.

After another drag of silence, the servants began clearing the dishes. The movement slowly dispelled some tension trapped in the confines of the air.

King Yoel exhaled a long breath and ran his hand down the length of his face. "Please disregard that unfortunate display of theatrics. Perhaps I was too hasty in this gathering."

"I'm sorry for any offense our presence may have caused, Your Majesty," Dyna said.

He waved her apology away. "Do not pay Malakel any mind. He is my eldest and the most foolish."

Zev caught Cassiel's barely audible scoff. Prince Malakel's reaction had not been meaningless.

"It's not your fault," Zev told Dyna. "There is an unfortunate history between humans and Celestials."

The servants paused and the room once again filled with heavy quiet and the scent of nervous sweat.

"Why?"

He hesitated to answer. She had seen enough horrors without him burdening her with the ones of others, and this was not the place to speak of it either.

The High King was studying her again, his expression indiscernible. He turned away and headed for a westward entryway. "It is best we move the remainder of this evening to my study. Come, my son will escort you."

Then he strode out of the dining room without another word.

Zev and Dyna rose uncertainly from their seats. Did the king plan to answer her question?

Cassiel came around the table, staring after his father as though he too couldn't believe it. He nodded for them to follow. Zev took a deep breath, Dyna linked her arm through his, and they trailed after the dark prince.

CHAPTER 9

Dynalya

Dyna kept close to Zev, wary of the castle's dark corridors, although torches lined the polished walls. Two Royal Guards marched behind while Prince Cassiel led them through the west wing. She was not a "stupid human" as he had called her. It was clear even to her that their presence in Hilos was wrong. Prince Malakel's outburst and the abhorrence from each Celestial that met her eyes more than proved it.

Why had the High King invited them here?

Among the many questions circling in her head, the one she asked aloud had brought the dining room to a standstill. It appeared breaks in conversation was a common thing among the Celestials, and it spoke much louder than words. Whatever the answer to her question, the subject was so ominous they were being ushered somewhere else, deeper into the castle, away from other ears.

They followed Cassiel down several more corridors, leaving her disoriented. She tried to keep track of how many turns they made, but the halls were a maze. The walls melded together in endless marble and finery. It would be impossible to find her way out without guidance.

Zev sniffed the air of each hall they entered, his eyes constantly studying. His head was canted as he listened beyond the thumps of their footsteps. It must be a lot for his senses to take in. She felt overwhelmed herself. The view coming into the kingdom was breathtaking, the lavish castle equally magnificent. All of it felt surreal—and daunting.

They passed by massive portraits of who she assumed were the past rulers of Hilos. The most recent was of King Yoel, with Queen Mirah at his side. The one before that bore one Celestial alone. Dyna almost didn't recognize King Yoel's soft and youthful face. At the crest of becoming a man. The painter had captured the High King's vacant expression, detailed brush strokes shaping his withdrawn, glassy eyes. She recognized that look, for she had worn it as well when she lost her family.

Dread hung over her. Heavy and suffocating as a blanket during the humid heat of summer. If the events during dinner were any sign, the history of this place was grim, but her curiosity begged to uncover it. A part of her identified with the darkness here. After all, her village had a sinister past of its own.

They came before a strip of orange light slicing through the dark corridor from a door left ajar. The Royal Guards took their posts outside the study and opened the door for them to enter. Zev hesitated, then led her in after Prince Cassiel. Dyna jumped at the sound of the heavy door shutting behind them and Zev stiffened; his apprehension at being trapped in an unknown place mixing with her own.

Dyna peeked past Cassiel's shoulder and took in the opulent study. Burning wood crackled in a great hearth encased in polished white stone that twinkled in the firelight. Encircling it was an arrangement of velvet settees and leather chaises positioned atop a plush blue rug. An ornate desk of dark wood and an empty wingback chair sat upon a raised platform on the other side of the room.

Iron candle stands set throughout the room cast flickering candlelight over the several bookshelves constructing the soaring walls. Innumerable books and scrolls lined the shelves. Some were so old they had gathered a layer of thick dust. Gilded pillars held up the curved ceiling painted with golden lined clouds so detailed, they almost seemed to glow as though it was a window of the Heavens.

Prince Cassiel moved to stand by the massive windows with a broad view of Hilos below. Winged figures in the distance flew against the light of the moon.

Being here, seeing such incredible things, solidified her reality and skewed it.

"Please, make yourselves comfortable," King Yoel said. He searched through the tomes at the top of a bookshelf, his graceful wings keeping him in the air.

Cassiel motioned to the seating area. Dyna chose a tufted sofa and Zev settled next to her.

"I believe Miss Dynalya asked a rather important question," the High King said to a book he was considering. "Care to share the answer, Master Wolf?"

Zev shifted in his seat. Tension creased his brow and his throat flexed. Several times he attempted to speak, but no words came. At his stalled silence, the High King and the prince glanced at him, then at each other. There was a nuance in their silent exchange that Dyna didn't quite follow.

The king flew down with a large book and handed it to her before taking a seat in an armchair across from them. The book was large and heavy; fastened shut by thick metal clasps colored by oxidation. The brittle leather cover had seen more wear than her journal, the edges peeled and worn to the core. *The Fall of Gamor* was stamped on the center in old Urnian.

"Dynalya, are you familiar with the city of Gamor?" King Yoel asked.

"It used to lie not too far from here," she answered, "in the southern boundary of the Azure Kingdom. Gamor perished in a great fire five centuries ago and it is now a ruin."

The High King and his son shared another look. What did Gamor have to do with them? Zev picked at a frayed hole in his trousers, avoiding her gaze.

Dyna crossed her arms. "You know what happened and you knew Celestials lived within miles of North Star. Grandmother always coddled me with half-truths, but why would you keep this from me?"

Zev exhaled a heavy breath. "Your Majesty?"

King Yoel nodded. "For tonight, I grant you leave to speak on this matter."

"Thank you." Zev turned to her. "I couldn't reveal the existence of Celestials because I am sworn to never speak of it. All mystical creatures are bound to secrecy set by the Accords. They are held between Celestials and the Pack Alphas, the Elven Kings, the Fae Gentry, and the sovereign of every mystical creature in this world. The Accords were created because of Celestial history and they are gravely enforced."

Dyna searched his troubled green eyes. It was the only feature they had in common, but his were expressive like her father's, displaying his thoughts and emotions like his worry.

"You need not protect me from the past, Zev," she said. "Ignorance does no one any good and I nearly died because of it."

He cringed at the reminder. "There is no happy ending to this story, Dyna."

That was something she was familiar with.

She caressed the beveled lettering of the book on her lap, the edges silken against the pad of her fingers. "Please, I would like to hear it."

Zev relented with another heavy sigh and stared off into the fire. "Gamor was a small unremarkable city, but Celestials would visit often due to the short flight from Hilos. Humans were in awe of them, for their beauty was unrivaled. They never fell ill, and they lived for centuries. Humans believed the God of Urn sent these sacred beings to defend them from the demons that once roamed the Mortal Realm."

Dyna straightened in her seat. Demons?

"They healed humans on the brink of death from fatal wounds and sickness with mere drops of their divine blood."

She glanced at Cassiel's hand, recalling how the wound had so seamlessly healed. The ability to self-mend was incredible and much more advanced than anything she could do.

"And their feathers? They hold magic too, don't they?" The black plume she had found must have pertained to the prince. Its power had enhanced her Essence, giving her strength she hadn't developed herself.

Zev nodded. "Their feathers carry innate magic capable of heightening the most delicate spells. People traveled to Azure from all corners of the world as word of Celestial power spread. They came seeking miracles for themselves, and to find a cure for their dying loved ones, or for the magic they could gain.

"Most traveled to Gamor knowing Celestials congregated there, and it brought commerce to their economy. The Lords of Gamor saw an opportunity in this. They convinced High King Rael, the ruler of Hilos during that time, to form an exclusive trade deal with the Azure Kingdom and to sell only in their city. It didn't take much to convince him. The Celestials gave their blood out of compassion and kindness, but as the city grew in size and wealth, the humans grew in their greed." Zev paused and Dyna stilled, sensing the tale had reached its dark turn.

Quiet sadness gathered in his next words. "Once humans killed the first Celestial for blood, King Rael ended the trades. But the Lords refused to surrender the source of their riches. They employed poachers to hunt them, and so—The Decimation of the Celestials began."

A coldness crept over Dyna. She glanced down at the book on her lap, heavy dread weighing on her again. She opened the cover and turned the frail, yellow pages full of faded script until she came upon a section of illustrations. Each one displayed the horror that had taken place in Gamor. Celestials trapped in nets, bound by their hands and legs, some screaming in pain as humans sawed off their wings.

Her vision blurred with each turn of the page. A tear rolled down her cheek and splashed on the illustration of a Celestial hanging by his feet from a tree branch, blood pouring out of his jugular into a barrel beneath him. This was why the Watchers wanted to kill her, and why Prince Malakel detested the sight of her.

Humans had murdered their people.

The next illustrations that followed were of Celestial women with child. They were kept in small cages, sobbing with their hands outstretched through the bars, begging. Men pinned them down to tear the newborns from their arms. But these babies didn't have wings. Written beneath the frame in thick, harsh letters was the word HALF-BREEDS.

"Dyna." Zev stopped her from turning another page, but she yanked her hand away. She needed to see what her people had done.

The next picture was so horrible, her stomach heaved as bile surged to the back of her throat. Zev quickly closed the book and took it away. She closed her eyes, but it didn't erase the image burned in her mind.

Dyna covered her mouth, afraid she would scream, or sob, or do both at what they had done to those children. Her stomach churned with bitter grief.

"They took our females to sire Celestials of their own," King Yoel said softly. "Most of them did not survive."

"Your Majesty, please. She need not learn this," Zev pleaded.

But the High King continued despite her obvious horror. "They bled many of the younglings dry before realizing they could not heal. Their blood was useless. Not because they were half-breeds, but because Celestials do not develop divine blood until their wings sprout at three-years-of-age. That is where our power centers. Without our wings, we are essentially human."

Dyna's vision blurred. How many had died for greed? Why had it reached such a wretched point?

She must have spoken aloud because King Yoel answered, "The Decimation went on for many years, for we feared perhaps this was the will of *Elyōn*."

"Ehl-*youn*?" she repeated the foreign word.

"You call him the God of Urn. To us, he is *Elyōn*, the maker of The Seven Gates that each soul passes through at their beginning and their end."

Goosebumps prickled down her arms to hear the God of Urn's true name.

"We do not live in the Mortal Realm out of our own volition," he said. "Our ancestors were the Seraphim, but they were also the Forsaken. They were cast out of Heaven's Gate, and they fell to this world in the First Age to serve a penance. As their descendants, it was our purpose to aid humans in the hope it would one day redeem us so we may return to Heaven's Gate.

"*Elyōn* had forged us weapons of divine fire meant to cut down demons while protecting his making. Taking a human life would go against his order and eternally damn our souls. Therefore, when humans hunted us, we did not fight back. We hid."

King Yoel sighed and looked out the window to his kingdom, seeing something she could not see. "Humans reveled in their wickedness and greed. The Decimation spread to the Four Celestial Realms, and King Rael left Hilos to aid them. In his absence, his wife, Queen Sapphira, met with the Lords of Gamor to beg for peace. She believed words of reason would turn them from their ways." Sorrow flooded his gaze like an overflowed stream after a storm. "She was wrong."

Dyna held her breath.

He linked his hands together and leaned his forehead against them. "Our blood gave them wealth and power. Invincibility. That was something they would never surrender. King Rael was thousands of miles away when he experienced every depravity the Lords unleashed upon his wife. Felt every torture and violation as her screams echoed in his mind."

Dyna's heart sank through her, then through the many floors of the castle and into the earth, falling.

Falling.

And falling.

"He tried to fly to her." The King's voice was a sad whisper, weighted by the tale of what once was. "Even as he withstood the agony of their bond breaking."

"Bond?" she asked faintly.

"Once a Celestial chooses a life-mate, they are wed with a binding of blood," he said without looking up. "It connects their souls eternally until they are torn from each other at death. King Rael and Queen Sapphira went beyond Blood Bonded. They were True Bonded. It is difficult to explain other than to say they were one: mind, body, and soul. Losing a True Bonded is the worst agony a Celestial can endure, for when the bond breaks, they are losing half of themselves."

"Did ... did he reach her in time?"

"No."

An ache burned in Dyna's chest and stung her eyes, welling them with unshed tears. She couldn't imagine King Rael's pain, but she knew the pain of loss and feeling powerless to stop it.

King Yoel exhaled a shaky breath. "Once the lords drained the queen of her blood, they hacked off her wings and dumped her naked body in the street. They had mutilated her so far beyond recognition ... I nearly did not recognize her."

He had found her?

She puzzled over how he fit the timeline, for he didn't look a day over fifty years, but Zev said Celestials had prolonged lives.

"I am much older than I appear. I was about your age during The Decimation." King Yoel unveiled his laden eyes and met hers. "Queen Sapphira was my mother."

A sob lodged in Dyna's throat. She bit her lip to keep it in, trapping it behind a dam she struggled to build. They killed his mother, and he had seen what they had done to her. Dismay hovered on the prince's features, too raw and surprised to have heard this story before.

"When my father lost her, he lost all reverence for *Elyōn*. He no longer cared to return to Heaven's Gate. Nor did I." The High King's quiet tone smoldered with a rage that sent a tremble down Dyna's back. He straightened and lowered his hands, curling them over his knees. "We gathered the armies of Hilos and the Four Celestial Realms and descended upon Gamor with swift retribution. We were not kind, nor merciful. We laid waste to the city—and everyone in it."

Everyone.

The guilty and the innocent. She knew it to be true by the sharp edge of his sapphire gaze.

"The Celestial children as well?" The question slipped out before she thought better of it.

King Yoel's stare bore into her, holding her in place. "They were misbegotten half-breeds born from sin. We could not allow them to live."

Dyna closed her eyes and looked away, no longer able to stop the tears from spilling down her face.

CHAPTER 10

Dynalya

er cousin had been right about Celestial history, Dyna thought. It was dark, much like her own. The men remained quiet, allowing her a moment to lament. The only sounds were the crackle of burning wood and the muffled sniffling she tried to hide. Prince Cassiel fidgeted with his flute, twirling it in his fingers as he looked at anything else but her.

"Your pardon," Dyna said, wiping her eyes. "What happened next?"

"King Rael isolated his people for their safety," Zev said carefully, watching her face. "He made new laws to avoid this from happening again, and the Watchers were posted at the borders of the Realms. They executed all who trespassed on their land, and King Rael threatened war against the Azure Kingdom should humans continue to hunt them.

"The destruction of Gamor was enough warning. The Azure King who ruled at the time was young, and Azure was not the prominent kingdom it is today. He didn't desire warfare, so he commanded his citizens not to venture past the Zafiro Mountains under penalty of death."

Dyna wondered if that was why her village was founded within those mountains. The decree indirectly protected North Star.

Zev continued, "Eventually, the poachers stopped hunting them, and no one searched for miracles any longer. Once the humans who lived during the Decimation passed on, Celestials formed the Accords with those who rule the mystical to maintain the secrecy of their existence. After five-hundred years, most of the world has forgotten them."

"We have not forgotten nor will we ever," King Yoel said. "We are not the peaceful beings we once were."

Another shiver passed through her. Captain Gareel would have killed her if Prince Cassiel hadn't stopped him. Sparing her life and granting her immunity had gone against the security of his people.

"It was a long time ago," Zev said, patting her hand.

"It weighs on my heart all the same." Dyna blinked her watery eyes. "Forgive me, but I ...." She had to pause so she would not cry again. "I find what befell the children was such undeserved cruelty. No one deserves hatred or death for their birth. Coming from two species doesn't make them or you any less valuable."

She needed her cousin to remember that.

Zev sighed. "I know."

Dyna sensed a change in the room and met the stares of the royal Celestials.

"He is a half-breed?" King Yoel asked.

She winced.

"I have upset you, Dynalya." He canted his head when she hesitated to respond. "This is not the royal court, my dear. You are free to speak what comes to mind."

"Zev is my cousin, Your Majesty," she said, cautious. "He's half-human, but I'm not fond of that distinction. To be called half of anything suggests one is incomplete or a mistake."

"You do not see it that way?"

"We exist because the God of Urn willed it. He is the God of Life, and he created life in all varieties. To be of mixed lineage doesn't revoke one's right to exist and their right to live."

A slight curve tugged on the corners of the king's mouth, but she wasn't sure if he agreed or if he found her belief amusing. The prince's brow furrowed as though her answer was strange.

Dyna bowed her head. "It may be of little value coming from me, but on behalf of humans, I'm sorry this was done to your people."

"You carry no blame, but I am honored by your apology," King Yoel said.

She met Cassiel's gaze. "You had no reason to spare me, but by some grace you did. Forever will you have my gratitude. I owe you an eternal debt."

The prince finally spoke since they arrived in the study. "As I have said, I relieve you of your debt. This is the last we speak of it."

Dyna smiled. "As you say."

The High King raised his brows in bemusement, but he made no comment. He focused on Zev instead. "On lighter matters, Master Wolf, I have been told you can shapeshift at will. That is unusual for your kind."

She glanced at Cassiel, who avoided her gaze. He was the only one to witness Zev's shift.

"Might it have to do with your ... pedigree?" King Yoel asked him, giving her a wink. She flushed, embarrassed that a king felt the need to accommodate her.

"Perhaps, sire," Zev said. "I'm uncertain. There are no others like me in the Lykos Pack."

"In your pack, you mean."

Something flitted across Zev's expression before he hid it behind an impassive shrug. "I have no pack."

He hadn't been part of the Lykos Pack for many years. Werewolves were social beings, and they thrived in a group setting. It was a great shame to be a lone wolf. Often it was the death of them.

"*We* are a pack," she said.

Zev gave her a faint smile. "Aye."

"Is that so?" King Yoel asked her. "But you do not live in Lykos Peak. You are of a small remote village that lies within the Zafiro Mountains, about a day's walk south-west of Hilos."

"You have heard of it?" Dyna asked, surprised he knew its location.

He looked away for a moment, then back at her, his blue eyes now guarded. "Tell me, what brought you here? It must be important enough to risk your life."

She shifted her ankles around her satchel where she had placed it. He didn't press, but he waited for an answer, as did the others. She had planned to tell Zev when they were alone, but something about the High King and prince told Dyna she could trust them with her secret. They had trusted her with theirs.

She brought the satchel to her lap. "I came because I needed to see you, Zev. To tell you I found the answer."

His eyes widened. "Do you mean …"

"I found a way to defeat the Shadow."

"The Shadow?" King Yoel interjected.

"I'm referring to a shadow demon." Dyna looked to the grand windows in the study, seeing the demon's profile that had once filled the frame of her small bedroom window. "North Star is cursed, sire. Each decade on the night of the winter solstice, the Netherworld Gate opens in our village, and the Shadow comes through to hunt …"

She couldn't bring herself to say it.

"Children," Zev finished under his breath.

Cassiel's eyes narrowed. "Impossible. Shadow demons cannot leave the Netherworld. Their forms are insubstantial. If they passed through the Mortal Gate, they would dissipate."

King Yoel frowned at him. "I see you have been neglecting your studies. If you had read the demon dissertations, you would know it is very possible." He turned his frown to Dyna. "A shadow demon may cross both the Netherworld and Mortal Gates if it is summoned. Then it would be quick to possess a body so it can remain in this world."

Dyna nodded. The Shadow came to North Star because a villager had meddled with dark magic.

The prince crossed his arms. "Then you have brought it upon yourselves."

She lowered her head. He was right.

Zev growled. "We had nothing to do with it. The shadow demon was summoned before either of us was born. Yet our generation is suffering the repercussions. During its last attack nine years ago, it took Dyna's brother and her parents perished in their attempt to fight it. Don't you dare say it's her fault."

"Zev." Dyna laid a hand on his taut arm. His claws retracted from the upholstery.

"You have my sympathies, Dynalya," the High King said after a short pause.

She nodded, not knowing what else to say.

Prince Cassiel turned to his father. "If the demon has possessed a body, it can be destroyed."

King Yoel shook his head. "This is no simple matter, son. Possession gives the shadow demon a solid form to walk the Mortal Realm, but it does not lose its vitality or its abilities. They are smoke, spawned from the fires of the Netherworld. Quick and vicious. Humans cannot stand against them."

"It was not for our family's lack of trying," Dyna said. "My grandfather and my father lost their lives trying to stop the Shadow. Now, it is up to me. I have dedicated my life to preparing for its next coming. I have read all the books in the village about demons, possessions, and The Seven Gates. I believed there had to be a way to end the ten-year cycle or some manner to defeat the demon, and I was right." She smiled at her cousin, blinking back her misty vision. "I know how to destroy the Shadow once and for all."

His mouth fell open. "You do?"

Dyna took out the journal. She caressed the embossed sigil of House Astron on the aged leather. It responded with a gentle, warm energy that seeped into her as it connected with her Essence.

She had been angry for a long time after the brutal massacre of her family. Their absence left a void inside of her, but the world remained and life had continued in the wake of her loss. There was nothing she could do about the past, but the future she could change.

"This journal belonged to *him*," Dyna told Zev. She opened it to a page with detailed drawings of two medallions. One was the Lūna Medallion plated in silver and diamonds, a moonstone at its heart. But it was the other medallion made of gold with a large red gem in the center that held her hope. "This is the Sōl Medallion. The Head of the Sun Guild created it three-hundred-years ago. See this here?" She pointed at the gem. "It's a Sunstone, and it contains the power of a single sunray. Tell me, what extinguishes the dark, Zev?"

"Light," he whispered in awe. "This is real? You found the answer?"

"Yes!" She laughed breathlessly. "The journal confirms the Sunstone kills demons. All I have left to do is find it."

Zev squeezed her in a bone-crushing hug. They celebrated together, at last allowing themselves a small semblance of happiness.

"Hold a moment," King Yoel interrupted. "Does your journal mention where to find this medallion?"

"Yes, sire." Dyna sat straight and prepared herself for what she was about to reveal, bracing for humiliation and reproach. Whatever his reaction may be, she had waited years for this discovery and she knew deep in her bones it was true. No one would take that from her. "The Sōl Medallion was stolen from the Magos Empire centuries ago during the War of the Guilds and hidden ... on the island of Mount Ida."

No one laughed.

The prince's flute slipped through his fingers, and he floundered to catch it. "Did you say Mount Ida?"

"I did."

King Yoel studied her. "Are you familiar with the tale of that island?"

"Yes, sire," she said. "Most say it is impossible to find—"

"Correct, my dear. Mount Ida is impossible to find because it is not real. It is simply a grand tale of adventure and lost treasure."

The High King glanced at his son, pausing before he strode to his ornate desk. With an iron key, he unlocked a drawer and returned with a stack of books, placing them on an end table beside her.

They were much more modern than the history book he'd given her first, at least created within the century. Dyna picked one up with a detailed painted cover of a volcano island masked in clouds. Before she could admire it, Cassiel snatched the book from her. His hands gripped it so tightly they shook. He shifted through the others, knocking them to the ground in his haste as he read the titles. His furious glare pinned on his father, who ignored him.

She glanced back and forth between them. The books held some meaning to the prince. "I'm familiar with the legend of Mount Ida, sire, but it's not just a story. It's true."

"Dynalya," the High King spoke her name as though she were a child he needed to reason with. "It is easy to let our imaginations run rampant and believe such fairy tales. Relic Hunters pursue the legend hoping to find its fabled treasures and enchanted relics only to return years later empty-handed or not at all. I am sorry, my dear. I am afraid your Sunstone is not there, for Mount Ida is a myth and nothing more."

Most didn't believe the legendary island to be real, and she had never thought it was until she discovered the journals. King Yoel was attempting to convince her it was all a lie, but he knew it wasn't. She could see it on his face. He was hoping his words would make her see reason.

That was impossible.

Dyna smiled. "Mount Ida is real, sire. I have a map."

CHAPTER 11

Cassiel

The room was as quiet as a crypt, but Cassiel's heartbeat roared in his ears. A part of him denied what Dyna had revealed, even if the stunned reactions of the others proved they had heard the same thing. Mount Ida was a mystery that had plagued him for most of his wretched life. While that cursed place was real, it was lost to the world, yet this human claimed to have the means to find it.

Lies.

"This journal once belonged to a renowned mage," Dyna said. "On his many ventures, he discovered the location of Mount Ida."

The sigil on the journal's cover looked familiar, but Cassiel couldn't quite remember which House it represented while his mind was reeling. He watched her slender fingers divide the pages to a glowing section. He inched closer, marveling at a detailed map of the country of Urn lit up with a swirl of purple magic tinted green.

To the southwest, within the Leviathan Ocean, the light pulsed the brightest over an island, as though the enchanted journal itself indicated what he so desperately searched for all these years.

Dyna tapped the island with her finger and the image expanded until it filled the page. Accompanying it in elegant script, were the words *Mons Idaeus.*

Language of Magos. It's Urnian translation: Mount Ida.

Cassiel stared at the image until his vision spun, his mind struggling to accept it as real. This had to be the only map in existence to that place.

The myth, the island, finding it—all of it was impossible, but how did she?

He leaned against the fireplace column, needing something solid to support him. His father's wide, astonished stare fixed on the glowing journal.

Zev's mouth opened and closed repeatedly before he managed to speak. "You truly have a map to that place. Dyna, you mustn't tell people about this. It can get you killed."

"Merely attempting to go there will get you killed," Cassiel said, forcing a dull tone. "You would have already died if not for me. How do you expect to survive traveling across the country?"

She sighed. "I appreciate your concern, Prince Cassiel, but I must go."

Zev shook his head. "It's not that simple. You've never left the village before. The journey will be far more dangerous than crossing Hilos."

"That's why I came searching for you," she told him. "I hoped you would accompany me on this quest. I need your guidance out there, and you need me to keep my promise."

Shadows crossed Zev's face, a profound misery filling his distant gaze. Cassiel watched, wondering what promise could make him respond that way.

"If you had the means to save others, would you not do it?" Dyna asked them. "That demon has taken so many lives, so many *children.* I wasn't able to stop it from taking my brother, but I won't stand by again. I'll stop the Shadow before it takes anyone else."

Cassiel clenched his flute in his fist. That look, he had seen it before. On another human with the same determination, with the same stupid stubbornness.

Zev rubbed his neck. "Is Grandmother aware of this?"

"I left her a letter."

"You left without saying goodbye?"

"I had to or she would have stopped me."

"With good reason," he exasperated.

Dyna closed the journal, cutting off its light. "Grandmother will understand."

"Dynalya, might you be too rash in this?" the High King asked. "There could be other means to defeat the Shadow that do not require such a treacherous journey."

"It is the only answer I found, but tonight you mentioned Celestials can fight demons," she said, hope filling her voice.

His responding smile was rueful. "We did, once upon a time. The Seraphim slay demons, but that is not who we are. Not anymore. Once we stained our hands with human blood, we lost the sanctity needed to extinguish evil."

Cassiel frowned. That was not completely true. Loss of sanctity applied to Celestials who had killed humans. Not to those who had been born since The Decimation—like him.

His father gave him an inquiring look, offering him the chance to volunteer, but Cassiel looked away. He wouldn't get involved in her matters. It had nothing to do with him. Besides, his impure blood may lack the true divinity needed to slay demons. He could heal himself, but certainly that was where it ended.

"Then I have no other choice," Dyna said.

The king's brow pinched. "If you do this, survival is unlikely, my dear."

"The fourth Shadow Winter arrives next year, sire. My sister is a child, and there are hundreds more in my village. I won't fail in my quest. I can't. I will find the Sunstone or die trying."

Her words invited something foreboding, weighing with a warning on Cassiel's bones. "If by some miracle you survive the journey to that island, there you will meet your end," he said quietly. "You will never come back."

Alarm flickered across her face, but her mouth set with stubbornness. "Never is a strong word. I indeed have much to lose, but I will *never* give up. I'm going to Mount Ida."

Cassiel stared at the stupid human, the fire in her eyes burning hotter than any forge.

"That is enough, son," his father cut him off before he disputed further. "She has made her decision."

Cassiel clenched his teeth to keep from saying what he wanted to say. *You most of all know she mustn't go there.*

His father's expression grew stern. "Need I remind you that you have given up your right to make demands of her?"

An angry flush rose to his head. Slavery may not be practiced in Hilos, but he could have requested an offering. If he knew Dyna had the map, he would have taken it as payment for the life-debt and forbidden her from going. His arrogance in believing there was nothing of value in her satchel had cost him.

King Yoel stood. Dyna and Zev did as well. He looked upon her with a mixture of approval and worry. "Nothing I say will change your mind?"

"No, sire."

"I understand why you must go, but this is not a quest you should risk alone."

"She won't be alone," her cousin said. "It's a dangerous world out there, Dyna. I'll not leave you to face it without me."

She beamed with relief. "Thank you, Zev."

"There it is then. You have your heading and your guardian." King Yoel placed his hands on their shoulders. "I pray *Elyōn* will safeguard your steps. If your heart is true, so will be your course. You are welcome to stay for the night to rest before beginning your noble quest. Provisions will be prepared for you in the morning, and the Watchers will escort you to the end of our Realm."

"Thank you, Your Majesty," Dyna exclaimed.

Cassiel couldn't believe this. They were fools, the lot of them.

"If you will excuse me, sire, I bid you good evening." He gave a quick bow and walked out of the study, leaving the heavy door to slam shut behind him.

The corridor of the south wing may as well have been a pitch-black cave. It had no windows, and the servants hadn't come to light the torches. They never came to this part of the castle.

Blind but not lost, Cassiel ran his fingers along the wall, absentmindedly counting the gilded moldings as he had many times before. It was quiet, the faint swish of his footsteps on the cold floor keeping him company.

He battled against his will to not sprint back to the study, wrench the journal away from Dyna, and destroy it.

Or keep it for himself.

Cassiel had spent years pointlessly studying every book in the castle library about Mount Ida, searching for a clue on its location only to learn certain books had been hidden. His father must have enjoyed making a fool out of him.

Cassiel's fingers landed on the familiar embellished designs on a door, and he pushed it open to enter his dark chambers. The sheer white curtains framing the open balcony floated in the breeze, and he shivered at the brisk change in temperature. Moonlight gleamed on the polished floors, casting enough light to distinguish the few pieces of furniture in the vast room. A massive four-poster bed stood at the far end, a lounge chair paired the wardrobe beside it—and two winged forms waiting for him in the dark.

One lunged forward and propelled him backward. The back of his head collided against the wall and his flute clattered to the floor.

Searing pain jolted through his wings lodged behind him. He was slow to make out the outline of Malakel's sneer in the minimal light, but he had already guessed who pinned him.

"Release me." Cassiel attempted to straighten, but Malakel slammed him into the wall again.

His left wing snapped beneath him. He bit down on his tongue until it bled so he wouldn't cry out. He refused to give Malakel the satisfaction of hearing it. Blood coated the inside of his mouth before his injuries numbed, a sign he was healing.

"Your miscreant deeds brought a human and a beast to our door," Malakel snarled in his face, "to sit at our table, to eat our food. You have sullied our halls with the stench of their presence."

Tzuriel chuckled. "You must admit, it is quite amusing, Mal. The servants have not stopped tittering about it. This is the most scandalous occurrence that has happened in Hilos since our dear little brother was born."

"No, it is repulsive and so is he." Malakel gave him another shove and stepped back, his lip curled in disgust. "You are an abomination, Cassiel. You should never have been allowed to live. If you were not the High King's bastard, your mother would have been executed before she birthed you. That would have been a mercy."

Cassiel straightened his robes, brushing off non-existent dust. It was best not to respond. This was nothing he hadn't heard before.

"I want to know why he spared the human." Tzuriel strode into view. Moonlight shimmered over the pearl sheen of his wings, the feather tips brushing the floor. "I'm curious."

"No Celestial females will look your way, so you are itching for a filthy tryst with a human, is that it?" Malakel demanded. "You are besotted with her."

"Spare me your assumptions," Cassiel retorted.

"Then why is she alive?"

"I do not answer to you."

Malakel's glare sharpened. "Do not be mistaken. History will not repeat itself. I will geld you myself before I allow you to spawn more half-breed bastards with the Soaraway name."

Cassiel rolled his eyes. He had never considered doing anything of the sort.

Tzuriel chuckled and leaned his shoulder against the wall, crossing his ankles. "You need not be concerned, Mal. Father has repeatedly failed to acquire a life-mate for our dear little brother. Despite that marriage would provide his bride with the title, Princess Consort of Hilos."

Cassiel stilled at the unexpected news. Why would his father do such a thing?

Malakel laughed at his confusion, misreading it as disappointment. "That's right. Becoming a part of the royal family is not enough to bribe the nobles into giving their daughters to the likes of you. No one would ever form a Blood Bond with a *creature*."

Composure unruffled, Cassiel flicked the twinge aside as he would a speck of dirt. He had long known it wasn't possible to marry, nor was he interested. It was for the best, in any sense. If he took a life-mate, she would be reviled like his mother, and any children he sired would be subjected to the same censure he received. No, his soiled bloodline would end with him.

Dyna's voice drifted in his mind, *"To be of mixed lineage does not revoke one's right to exist and their right to live."*

Malakel yanked Cassiel forward by his robes, tearing the delicate silk in his grasp. "Do you think your actions will be pardoned because Father spared your mother from the Watchers? You may have protected that human with immunity, but you are not immune to the law. The queen will have the court sanction you for this. If somehow you slither your way free, remember one day I will be High King, and my first command will be to exile you."

Cassiel couldn't help but release a snide remark. "Unless father exiles you first."

He knew the blow was coming, but Cassiel wasn't prepared for the loss of air when Malakel's fist smashed into his abdomen. He folded over his aching gut and his circlet clanged on the floor, glinting in the moonlight. The gaudy thing was a ridiculous piece of metal that had no more value on his head than it had on a boar. At the thought, Cassiel's coughs turned into a chuckle, then full-blown laughter.

"Why are you laughing?" Malakel shouted.

Cassiel didn't know what was so amusing. Perhaps he was tired of being angry, or he had lost his bloody mind. He shook his head, snickering. "Tell me, brother, are you still the heir? Father was not quite clear after he reprimanded you like a child in front of the servants."

Malakel lunged for him again, but Tzuriel pulled him back. "Pay him no heed, Mal. You are the heir apparent. There is no question."

Cassiel strangely enjoyed his elder brother's rage, and it made him foolish. Thoughts that had festered inside of him all these years poured off his tongue like poison. "You hate me because we share blood. Because Father spurned your mother when he chose mine. I may be a bastard, but he legitimized me at my birth. I am a prince of Hilos. I am of the Soaraway line. History will always remember you as the High King with a Nephilim brother, and that stain will mar your legacy. Forever."

Malakel thrust out his wings with a furious roar, throwing Tzuriel back, and attacked Cassiel with an onslaught of blows. He dropped to his knees, not able to stand any longer, but he never stopped laughing. He laughed and laughed as the punches burst stars in his vision and his ears rang.

Tzuriel was shouting. Cassiel couldn't tell if he was goading their elder brother or telling him to stop. Another bash slammed into his jaw, and his head cracked against the wall. Pain speared through his skull. Needles jabbed into the back of his eyes, light flashing in a void meant to pull him under.

"Cease!" Tzuriel yanked Malakel back. "That is enough. We must leave before Father gets word of this."

Malakel shoved him off. His fists clenched and unclenched, his ire filling the room. When he spoke again, he was poised, his tone detached. "You are irrelevant. A blight. When you are gone, no one will ever care to remember you."

Cassiel no longer laughed.

His elder brother strode out the door, footsteps fading down the corridor. Cassiel spat a clot of blood on the floor and leaned against the wall, closing his eyes. The icy breeze brushed over his throbbing face, but the pain dulled and tingled as his blood worked to heal him.

"You are full of surprises today, little brother," Tzuriel said from the door. He wore an expression of confusion and something that seemed like respect. "Why provoke him only to let him give you a thrashing? Lord Jophiel has trained you well during your time in Hermon Ridge. You can hold your own."

Why would Tzuriel care? He never had before.

It wouldn't serve him to fight Malakel. He should have remained subdued on principle. When he was old enough to speak, Queen Mirah made it clear not to challenge any of her children. *"They are purebloods, heirs to the Realms. You are nothing."*

Tzuriel took a step toward him. "Cassiel—"

"Get out."

Tzuriel paused as though to say more, but he sighed and slipped into the dark corridor, his wings the last to disappear.

Malakel was many things, but Cassiel had to agree it was stupid to bring the human and her werewolf cousin to the castle.

Why tell Dyna about The Decimation and The Fall of Gamor? He knew his father had been involved in destroying that city, but it was not spoken of until this day—and he chose to share it with a human.

Cassiel picked up his flute and walked out onto the balcony. A thick blanket of clouds crept across the stars, filling the crisp air with the taste of imminent rain. He climbed onto the broad stone banister to sit facing outward, leaving his legs to dangle above the castle gardens hundreds of feet below. Beyond the summit descended the skyline of the Hilos Kingdom, outlined in bioluminescent flora glowing in the night.

His mother's spirit lingered in this spot. She had often come to this balcony to play music or to read him fairy tales when he was a child. Her soft voice came to him then, carried by a current of memory.

"A pirate named Captain Rozin Ida ruled the seas centuries ago, little one. He ravaged and thieved as he collected gold and jewels. He favored artifacts infused with magic for their power made him unrivaled on the land and sea. One day, Captain Ida stole a Sacred Scroll containing a terrible secret, and it led him to a great volcanic island in a perilous region of the ocean. There he gained the Unending. Because of it, no one could ever oppose him. He dubbed the island Mount Ida, turning it into his fortress as he plundered to his heart's content.

"He polluted the island with so much magic it became alive and served him in all he desired. Even the desires that were hidden in his heart. Captain Ida feared others would try to steal his treasures, and he soon grew suspicious of his crew. The island, wanting to please its master, did away with them and marooned his ship. It cloaked itself in magic to protect the treasures, trapping the pirate for all eternity. Mount Ida has since never been found, but I promise you, little one, I will find it."

Cassiel wondered if his mother ever did.

Was Mount Ida as beautiful and treacherous as the legends say? He quickly pushed the question out of his mind.

He had to.

If he gave it too much thought, all he could imagine was the island swallowing her whole.

CHAPTER 12

Not sure how long he had idled on the balcony, Cassiel tensed at the sound of soft knocking at his door. He didn't answer, but approaching footsteps followed, regardless. By not waiting for admission, it could only be his father. He altered his position on the banister to hide the dried blood on his nose and his torn clothing.

King Yoel stepped outside, his breath swirling in the air. "The nights are beginning to chill."

Cassiel frowned, confused as to why his father had come to discuss the weather. They hardly ever spoke, so any conversation outside of formal matters was unusual. This entire day was unusual.

The High King leaned on the banister and looked out at the kingdom. The lack of his obnoxious crown took away the regality that made him appear younger than he was. "Our guests have settled for the night."

Wherein, Cassiel assumed, trusted guards must have been placed outside their door. How safe could they be in a castle full of Celestials that would rather see them dead?

"Zev's ability to shapeshift at will is astonishing," his father commented.

The were-beast was unusual. Once Cassiel got a good look at him, he had tried not to stare at the many scars that snaked over every inch of him in haphazard lines. Bracelets of scarred flesh circled his wrists, and the skin pulled around them, appearing as though he'd been cleaved in pieces and stitched back together.

"Half-breed werewolves are called Lycans. Once they mature, they develop two forms: the wolf and the Other. They are rare, for the mothers often will not rear them."

Other?

Cassiel sighed. He didn't want to think about the beast or anything else for that matter. He wanted to be alone.

"And Dynalya, she has a brilliant soul. You saw it for yourself, did you not?"

Of course he did. But what was the purpose of having the ability to see and feel the souls of humans?

The first time Dyna touched his cheek was brief, but when she held his injured hand, he had seen everything. Her soul was a luminous, blazing green with the light of a thousand thunderstorms. The entirety of it was beautiful. The sense of it almost familiar, like returning to a place he once knew. It was her soul that convinced him he made the right choice to save her, but it carried tremendous grief that left a burden on him. After hearing about her past tonight, he had learned why.

The High King tilted his head, a wistful expression on his face. "Soul Searching can be overwhelming. To see and touch something so phenomenal leaves one almost at a loss for words."

Yes, Cassiel would put it that way. At that moment he had willingly surrendered himself to Dyna's soul, basking in the glorious sensation.

"You do not have experience with this, and I imagine your first time was unsettling. Seeing a soul comes immediately upon any physical contact with humans, but it is easy to control. Simply decide not to see."

That was a rather vague explanation.

His father broke out into a playful grin. "I have almost forgotten the feeling of Soul Searching. It has been quite some time since a lovely human has passed through my forest."

Irritation ignited Cassiel's nerves. "How can you jest of such things?"

The High King's smile fell. "Forgive me, I did not intend to slight your mother's memory." He nodded to the flute. "Is that hers?"

Why ask questions he knows the answers to?

"Elia was never more beautiful than when she played it."

The sound of his mother's name slammed into Cassiel like a chilling ocean wave.

"I was there the day she crossed into our territory playing her flute," his father said, his voice as far away as his dreamlike stare. "Her melody filled the forest with something akin to magic. I had to find the source, and when I laid eyes on her, all rationality left me. I granted her immunity and escorted her home to North Star."

Cassiel straightened. North Star was Dyna's village.

"She was a novelty, your mother. Her features. Her voice. The fragility of her life. All of it allured me. I should not have had anything to do with a human, but I was inexplicably drawn to her. I often flew to her village, and she was always waiting, as though she sensed I would come. She knew from the beginning that I was hers, and she was mine."

This was the most Cassiel's father had spoken to him in years about anything, and he chose this moment to speak about *her*.

"You should have let her be," Cassiel seethed. "You stole her life when you had the audacity to think you loved her."

His father stuttered, taken aback by his outburst. "I did—"

"If you did, you would never have brought her here as your consort when you already had a queen!" His shout echoed over the summit, and the words kept rushing out of his throat. "You assumed Hilos would accept a human because their High King willed it so. You assumed she could ever have such a thing as happiness here. Her life had been insufferable, and it drove her mad. Your meeting spelled her end!"

Cassiel turned away as the last of his words faded into the night, bracing himself for the repercussions of his disrespect. His mother's suffering was the deepest resentment he held against his father. But it was pointless to reveal it now.

"Perhaps I should have let her die," his father said, surprisingly tranquil. "But I could not turn my back on her, as you could not turn your back on Dynalya. Why did you save her?"

"I have no answer," Cassiel mumbled the lie.

It had angered him that the Watchers would kill her for being human. She had trespassed, but it wasn't to do any wrong against them. Listening to her cry and beg had filled him with an insatiable need to protect her. So he did. That infuriating need followed him every moment after. Granting her immunity had been done on impulse and spite when his father had questioned him, but he struggled to understand why he was so compelled to save her.

"You do," his father insisted, searching his face.

If they were to have a conversation, Cassiel didn't want to be impeded by royal propriety. "May I speak freely?"

"Have you not been doing so?" he responded with a chuckle.

Cassiel looked out to the cove, watching the waves crashing on the shore. "I ask you not to patronize me, Father. That human is a foolish peasant who found her way here unknowing of our laws. I saved her out of pity."

"Peasant? She is well-spoken and literate. Deny it if you must, but I believe you care what becomes of her."

"Not in the slightest."

His father shrugged and continued smiling. "Say what you will."

Cassiel scowled. "Are you mocking me?"

"I am not."

"Then I do not pretend to know what you are insinuating."

"I touched her soul as well, son. It is too much like yours to deny that your fates are not intertwined."

Cassiel narrowed his eyes as he absorbed his father's meaning. A new suspicion arose about the purpose of tonight. "I feared you may be mad to bring a human and a beast here, but I should have known it was with intention. You assumed I had taken a liking to her."

"Why else would you save her life and grant her immunity?"

"Because it was right, nothing more," he replied tersely. "Is it so questionable that I spared someone that did not need to die?"

"I said the same when I spared your mother, but there was a reason for our meeting as I believe there is a reason you met Dynalya. She has not once questioned why you are unique."

That was true. Did she not realize he wasn't a pureblood? It was clear that he wasn't like the others, but she didn't treat him any differently.

"You told her of The Decimation and about the half-breeds of Gamor. Misbegotten sin, was it?"

"That is not how I see you, son. I said it to provoke her, and she reacted unexpectedly."

Cassiel frowned, recalling the tears glimmering on Dyna's cheeks. Tears for the loss of those she never knew. "Yes, well, you misled her to believe they were put to death."

"I will leave it to you to tell her the truth if you wish." His father shrugged. "She would be glad to hear it, I'm sure."

"Why lie at all?"

"I wanted to know her opinion on the matter."

Cassiel scowled, something hot rising in his chest. "You wanted to know what she thought of me, you mean."

"I believe she would not judge you for being different."

"I do not care what she thinks, nor do I want anything to do with that human," he snapped. "I will not repeat your mistakes."

His father turned to him, tone hardening. "I have made many mistakes in my life, but your mother was not one of them. You will *never* refer to her as a mistake again."

Cassiel grimaced and looked away to the kingdom below. He hated this place. Her memory was embedded everywhere and he couldn't stand it any longer. "I'm leaving tomorrow."

"When have I dismissed you? Less than a month has passed since you have returned home from Hermon Ridge."

"Hilos is not my home. I would not have returned if you had not commanded Lord Jophiel to send me back." Cassiel turned on the banister to face him.

His father's wide eyes roamed over his battered appearance. "Who has done this to you?"

"I do not belong here. I choose to live in Hermon Ridge. No one there despises me for being half-human."

His father sighed. "I understand that life here has been difficult, but you are a prince of Hilos. You must fulfill your duties to the Realms. At nearly twenty-winters old, you have come of age to be bonded."

He clenched his jaw. "I have *no* need of a wife."

"Our lives are long. We are not meant to be alone, and I will see to it that you will not be."

Cassiel leaped off the banister, clenching his fists. "I will not be forced into a marriage I do not want. You may be miserable with your wife, but I will not endure the same."

He knew he misspoke when his father's expression darkened.

"You forget who you are speaking to!" the High King thundered. "I am allowing you to air your grievances, but do not disregard your manner of respect."

Cassiel reeled back a step, bowing his head. "Forgive me, sire. I have forgotten my place."

His father turned away, muttering to *Elyōn* to give him patience for his impudent sons. He exhaled heavily before speaking again. "It is the responsibility of the High King to choose the life-mates of his children. Strong unions ensure strong Blood Bonds, which provides measured strength to guide the Realms."

Cassiel held his tongue before he misspoke again. Blood Bonds were a perpetual promise, but it never instilled love. That was something that couldn't be forged. Proven by how much his father and Queen Mirah loathed each other.

"My father was rash in his choice for me, given the circumstances," King Yoel said, as if he read Cassiel's mind. "I will not be. I have taken great care in choosing Malakel's life-mate, and he is pleased with her, as is Tzuriel with his intended. You have my word it will be no different for you."

"Please." Cassiel hated the pleading tone he could not keep out of the single word. Whoever became his bonded would suffer. Why couldn't his father see that?

"You will do as you are bid." It was a command. The matter was closed. "Meanwhile, continue to accompany the Watchers to the border."

"You trust me to guard the borders after I spared an intruder?"

His father leaned on the banister as a soft mist fell. "Dynalya posed no threat. You were right to spare her. Humans of the past have wronged us, but those of the present are not to blame. That is something our people do not understand. Our misguided beliefs have put us on a path from which we may not return if we do not change. Jophiel predicted that after the Fall of Gamor and wanted no part in it."

At the mention of his uncle, Cassiel glanced north, to the Realm too far to see.

"I did not agree with my brother's ideals at the time. I was too invested in my anger and hate. It took half a millennium to see what Jophiel saw in humans. The answer lies in acceptance. It is the foundation of his Realm, and I wish to have the same here."

Cassiel didn't understand how that could happen. Hermon Ridge was the opposite of Hilos in everything from its citizens to its politics.

King Yoel raised a hand to the sky as if to grasp something out of reach. "'There is a time for everything under the Heavens; a time to love and a time to hate; a time for war and a time for peace.' One day, this kingdom will accept humans again."

Cassiel squinted at the ludicrous speech. His father had been acting strange since meeting Dyna, and now he was quoting consecrated parables from the Sacred Scrolls written in the First Age. Of the thousands of scrolls that once existed, there were three in the castle kept locked in a chest.

His father motioned at his black plumage. "Who you are, and what you are is exactly what the kingdom needs. Your hands are clean. You have not killed a human, nor do you hate them. That alone makes you worthy."

"Of what?"

"My reign is ending, son. I must think of what is good for our people and leave a much wiser ruler in my stead. One who will be the epitome of change in our future. I believe that is you."

Cassiel stared at him in disbelief. The idea was so bizarre he wanted to laugh. His father truly was mad. He pointed to the kingdom below. "*Their* hate is rooted in their bones. Celestials hate humans for what they have done, and they hate me for reminding them of that. They would never accept me as the High King. I'm a half-breed bastard."

His father scowled. "Do not call yourself that. You are my son, and I have proclaimed you as such."

"It matters not. Malakel is a pureblood and your first trueborn son. He is the rightful heir."

"I decide who takes my throne."

Cassiel shook his head and backed away, searching the shadows for spies. Queen Mirah would have him killed in his sleep if she received word of this. The king may desire change for Hilos, but it won't happen. Not during his lifetime. "This place sent Mother to her death, and it will be the death of me if I stay."

"Cass—"

"Why did you hide the books from me?" he demanded.

His father grew pained. "You know why. If I had let you have them, that island would have taken you from me as well. I had to protect you."

He reached out, but Cassiel jerked away. "You turned your back on me when she left. Where were you then?"

His father lowered his gaze.

Cassiel clenched his shaking fists, furious with himself for divulging his resentments again. He was so angry with them and the life they gave him. The anger suffocated him. It was far too late to protect him from anything.

His father's shoulders sank under an invisible weight. "I was mourning your mother. You have her likeness and I … couldn't be near you because of it. That was not fair to you. I see that now, and I will always carry the guilt of the grief I have caused you. I am so very sorry, son."

As a child, he had craved to hear those words. Craved for some sliver of hope his father hadn't abandoned him. But he didn't care for it now. His heart was a cold rock in his chest. It may as well have been dead inside of him.

"What can I do to earn your forgiveness?"

The question was a kindle to his rage. True forgiveness couldn't be bought, but he thought better of it. This was an excellent opportunity to make a request of the High King for whatever he wished.

Dyna's naïve, smiling face came to mind.

It cost him a great deal to keep her alive, but she was headed toward certain death. If she walked out of the castle gates, she wouldn't ever return. As his mother never did.

"Prevent the human from going to Mount Ida," Cassiel replied. He instantly regretted wasting this opportunity on her. He should have requested his freedom.

His father groaned. "Of all the things to ask of me. Did you not see her determination?"

Yes, and it reminded him so much of his mother, it was uncanny.

"The death of her parents weighs on her. She needs to go on this journey for them and for herself. You cannot stop her, even if you were to follow her all the way there."

Follow her?

Cassiel glanced down at the ring hanging from the chain around his neck. He cradled it in his palm, the sapphire glimmering in the moonlight. Perhaps the fates had something to do with him meeting Dyna after all.

"I was not here to stop Elia from leaving," King Yoel said, gazing at the ring. "I will never cease to regret it."

Cassiel let it fall back on his chest. "She made her choice."

His father sighed. "While I cannot interfere with Dynalya's journey, what other favor may I grant you?"

"I wish to return to Hermon Ridge," Cassiel said right away. A plan was forming, but it would only work if he had permission to leave.

"Very well."

That was oddly easy. "I have your leave?"

His father nodded. "For now. You are young and have much to learn before we discuss your future. Meanwhile, you may leave Hilos. I will contact Jophiel tomorrow morning through the water mirror and inform him of your impending arrival." He held up a hand when Cassiel thought to make another request. "I will not allow the use of Stardust. You are to remain unseen during travel between the Realms."

"Yes, sire." Cassiel bowed in compliance, if only to hide his annoyance at being read. The lack of Stardust would be inconvenient.

"Our years are long and plenty," the High King said. "Incomparable to humans. The important thing is not how long we live but *how* we live, son. I only wish for your happiness."

Cassiel had nothing else appropriate to say. He bid his father a good evening and leaped over the balcony. His wings carried him off into the brisk night and out to sea as he rode the wind in idle arcs.

He wholly disregarded the last part of that absurd conversation. It held no meaning to him.

Happiness was an illusion, much like love.

CHAPTER 13

Zev

There was nothing peculiar about the forest outside of Hilos. The flora didn't glow, and the trees were younger. Nor did it carry an eerie cling of danger. Dew beaded on every leaf and blade of grass, gleaming under the morning light streaming in through the treetops. Gentle wind rippled over the muddy puddles left behind after last night's rainfall. Nothing seemed amiss, but Zev remained on high alert.

Castle servants had awoken them before dawn without ceremony or the offer of another meal. They were rushed out of the castle before the rest of the kingdom had risen, and the Watchers left them with a hefty rucksack of promised supplies at the Hilos border without a word. It appeared Celestials weren't much for farewells. Zev didn't complain. He was glad to leave such a splendid place founded in gloom behind.

Zev turned away from studying the trees when he heard Dyna grunt as she tried to lift the rucksack again. He tightened his lips together, fighting a grin. This was her fifth attempt, but she insisted on doing it herself. She swung the rucksack upward, and the weight threw her back into the mud with a splat. He burst out laughing.

"Zev!" She kicked her feet in the air, struggling to get up.

"I told you to leave it to me, Dyna." He took her hand and helped her stand. "I'm the strong one, eh?"

"Oh, I suppose." She sighed and wiped the spattered mud off her ankles.

Zev hauled the rucksack up and slid the thick straps onto his shoulders with no trouble. He added his pack and the chains clinked inside. The sound grated on his ears. He wasn't looking forward to listening to the clink and chime as they counted down the next six days until the full moon.

By some luck, he had been ready to leave Lykos Peak before Dyna's unexpected arrival. He had spent months deliberating whether to go. Although he was an outcast, he'd been free to roam the outskirts, and there'd been plenty of prey. Lacking that security unnerved him, but going back wasn't possible.

He needed to get Dyna far away from here. The Pack couldn't cross into Celestial territory, but they were sure to trek around the ridge to capture him. Once werewolves were on the hunt, they didn't stop.

"Come, we have a long way to go, and it's best we don't linger close to Hilos," Zev told her. Or Lykos Peak.

He marched on, the threat at his back urging his quick pace. Dyna followed him without complaint. They traveled far through the endless forest, crossing through several streams to muddle their scents, but that wouldn't work for long. Werewolves were skilled trackers. The alpha was better than most.

As the clear blue sky leisurely turned orange with the approach of evening, he noticed Dyna's feet drag and her stomach gurgled.

"Let's stop," he said as they entered a glade lined by wild shrubs and trees. "I'll find a secure place to camp."

"I can keep going."

"You did well. We covered plenty of ground, but it's time to rest now." He led her to sit on a large boulder and unhooked the waterskin from his pack, passing it to her.

"Thank you." She drank while he searched the rucksack for food. The autumn wind had her shivering and rubbing her arms for warmth. The cold wasn't something that bothered Zev since his kind was always warm, but the tip of Dyna's nose and cheeks were ruddy.

"Did you bring a coat?"

"No," she admitted.

"Extra clothing at least?"

"I lost them in the Forbidden Woods."

"The nights will only grow colder, and that dress won't be enough to keep you warm," he said, frowning at the thin fabric of her sleeves. "But I have some money. We'll buy you a coat in the next town."

"Thank you, Zev." She sighed. "It's unfortunate I lost my cloak in Lykos."

Her cloak!

That meant the Pack had Dyna's scent. They'd be found no matter how many bodies of water they crossed. Adrenaline spiked through Zev's veins, but he didn't want to frighten her. After this short break, he would carry her on his back and run all night if he had to.

He passed her a burlap pouch filled with dried fruit, forcing a smile on his face. "Here, eat."

"It was kind of King Yoel to provide us with so much," Dyna said, exchanging it for the waterskin.

"Aye, it was," Zev agreed before taking a drink. He tensed when his senses flared in warning of a presence nearby. He slowly lowered the waterskin and wiped his mouth with the back of his arm.

His wolf sight took over. He scanned the growing shadows within the trees and undergrowth for any movement as he inhaled the air. Buried beneath the scent of damp earth and decomposing leaves was a familiar sweet smell. It didn't carry the musk of the Pack, but werewolves weren't the only danger. They were alone with a map to

Mount Ida in their possession, and no one outside of Hilos knew about it.

Would the Watchers defy their High King's orders and come for Dyna? Zev's canines extended at the thought. He searched the branches overhead, but whoever followed them wasn't up there. With another sniff, he pinpointed their exact location. He remained facing her, not wanting to give away he was aware of the presence behind him.

"Dyna." She met his glowing eyes and hurried to his side. His eyes only changed for two reasons: when he was angry, or when he sensed a threat.

"What is it?" she whispered, staring at the darkening forest.

"Wait here." Zev dropped their bags with a loud clanking thud.

Her breath hitched. "I can't."

"You can." He took her shoulders. "Don't worry. I won't be long."

She bit her lip and gave him a brave nod.

Backing away, he tossed his shirt aside, and an ache passed through him as his bones fluidly shifted. The wolf came forward and his trousers slipped off as he dropped on four paws. Everything was clearer and brighter. His sight, hearing, and smell sharpened, heightening the scents of nature and the chatter of the wildlife.

Shaking out his flank, Zev darted into the trees. His muscles rippled under his fur as he picked up speed. His paws pounded into the wet dirt. He raced over fallen logs and through shrubs, the forest passing him in a blur. Revolving around the way they entered the glade, he picked up a mixture of scents past the decomposing leaves. Leather, honey, and divine incense. It told him exactly who it was.

He stalked forward and peered out from the foliage at the winged figure. Prince Cassiel hid behind an old tree layered in vines, frowning at Dyna. She stood visible in the open glade, hugging Zev's clothing to her chest as she stared in the direction he had gone. Cassiel shook his head and took a step toward her. Zev growled and sprung from the bushes, tackling the startled prince. They crashed in a lumbering heap.

Cassiel's heart raced and Zev tasted his panic, but he hid it well behind a glare of steel.

"Off," the prince commanded as if he were a dog. "I will not say it again."

Zev released a rumbling growl. Cassiel produced a knife from his sleeve and pressed the crossguard against Zev's ribs, searing his side with a flash of white-hot pain. He whined, leaping away. The spot where he'd been burned throbbed in a pulsing wave.

The prince rolled to his feet and slid into a lead-fighting stance. He flipped the silver knife in his hand, the edge as sharp as his sneer, using it to beckon Zev forward. "Come on."

Zev snarled and lowered into a crouch, deciding he would bite that hand clean off. But before he could lunge, a patter of running feet burst through the shrubs.

"Prince Cassiel?" Dyna called in surprise, distracting him. Zev dove and slammed him on the ground, knocking the weapon away.

Cassiel cursed. "Call off your beast."

Zev snapped his teeth a hairsbreadth from his nose.

Dyna picked up the knife, her eyes narrowing as she inspected it. "Please don't move, Your Highness. He's not as agreeable in his wolf form, and at the moment, you're a threat. I would agree, bearing in mind you came armed with silver."

The prince glared at Zev pointedly. "I would be a fool to come unprepared this time."

"What brought you this way? We didn't expect company."

"Allow me the dignity of standing before I answer you."

"Zev, it's all right." Dyna signaled. "Let him stand."

Zev ambled off and his muscles rippled as he shifted back. He grabbed the prince's arm and jerked him upright on his feet, leaving behind a litter of black feathers on the ground.

Cassiel scowled, brushing himself off. "Look at what you have done."

He nudged Dyna aside to gather them before she reached for one and plucked the knife from her hands.

Zev ground his teeth. "For a prince, you lack manners."

"And you lack modesty. You are shamelessly exposing yourself in front of a girl. Get dressed at once."

Dyna laughed and handed Zev his clothes. "I have become accustomed to his constant shifts since we were children. I don't pay it any mind, Your Highness."

The prince wrinkled his nose in disgust.

Shapeshifting was a way of life for werewolves. Zev had given little thought to his nudity, but he understood how it would make others uncomfortable. "Why are you here?" Zev asked as he dressed.

While Cassiel still carried an air of arrogance, he no longer wore his silk robes. He'd dressed in cream-colored trousers, a long-sleeved navy brocade jacket fastened with ivory buttons, and black boots. A luxurious sword with an embellished sheath and a golden hilt in the shape of wings hung secured at his waist. The crest of Hilos adorned the pommel.

Dyna spotted a leather rucksack wedged in the bushes. "Are you going on a journey as well?"

The prince grabbed the rucksack and slung it on one shoulder. "I came to join you."

There was no request in that statement.

She raised her brows. "Oh?"

Zev glowered. "You were quite clear in your opinion about this quest."

And he came armed with silver. Why come if he didn't trust them?

Cassiel crossed his arms. "It is dangerous, there is no denying that. However, she may fare better with someone of knowledge to guide her."

"I've had no problems so far, Prince Cassiel."

"Refrain from speaking my title outside of Hilos."

Zev gave him a mocking bow. "As you command, Your Highness."

Cassiel ignored him. His cool eyes flitted over Dyna's appearance in disapproval. "The journey will be long and perilous. I imagine you will be difficult to protect, but I will make sure you survive." His gaze fixed on her face. "Unless my presence displeases you."

She beamed. "No, not at all. You're welcome to join us."

"Good," Cassiel replied in a manner that indicated he expected nothing less. "Now, to be clear, there are caveats with the immunity I have granted you. Never disclose the existence of Celestials. I will be damned if I am the one responsible for poachers returning to hunt my kind because I saved a stupid human."

Her eyes widened. "I would never."

"She'll keep your secret," Zev growled. "And if you're not a prince outside of Hilos, then I won't tolerate your discourtesy. You'll not call her that again."

Cassiel's jaw worked, no doubt with an equally scathing reply, but Dyna quickly moved to stand between them.

"I'm glad you joined us," she told the prince while giving Zev a measured look that warned him to control his temper. "We could use your knowledge of Urn."

Zev supposed she was right. Neither of them had done any traveling.

He looked up at the darkening sky as the sun winked out on the horizon, and he felt the pull of the moon taking its place. It called to his wolf, making his skin itch. The wild part of him craved to give in to his baser instincts and shapeshift, to run through the forest with nothing but the earth beneath his paws.

"The day has ended," he said.

Dyna nodded, seeing the nightfall's effect on him. "We should make camp."

Cassiel's large wings unfurled. The soft hue of twilight shimmered over the glossy feathers. "Not here."

Zev agreed. The open glade left them vulnerable. They needed to keep going. They had traveled through the day, but it was not enough. "We must go. We've wasted too much time here."

"I take it you are unfamiliar with these lands," the prince said to Dyna. "Let us see your map again."

She reached inside her satchel for the journal when a breeze passed over them and the musky scent Zev had been dreading hit his nose. He spotted the large forms lurking within the trees, their yellow eyes glowing. It was too late to run.

They were surrounded.

CHAPTER 14

Zev

Two instincts warred within Zev: attack or take Dyna and run. Neither action would end well for her, nor would he get far. That left only one option.

"Don't move," he warned. Dyna and Cassiel hadn't noticed the Pack, but they immediately alerted at his tone.

The bushes rustled as a group of brawny men crept into view. Not all the werewolves were visible, but by their scent alone, Zev counted over twenty. They snuck up on him from downwind, taking advantage of the distraction. Maybe they had always been close, waiting until dark to invoke their wolves.

The prince reached for his knife.

"*Don't*," Zev growled at him. "If you draw that thing, they'll rip out your throat."

That would most certainly put an end to the peace treaty between Lykos Peak and Hilos. Cassiel must have had the same thought because he stiffened and his fingers slipped from the hilt, but he kept his large wings primed to fly.

The men parted as their alpha came forward. Thick muscle layered Owyn's tall frame. He only wore dark trousers, his feet bare. Long clawed scars marked his chest and arms by those few who had challenged him and lost. He wore his black hair tied back from his hard face and reflective eyes.

Zev didn't find Owyn as intimidating as he used to, but he lowered his gaze so as not to challenge him. His restless wolf paced inside of him, demanding to meet the threat, urging him to shift for his self-preservation. But one instinct prevailed above all else: protect Dyna.

He extended his arms in surrender and lowered to a knee with his head bowed. "My companions have nothing to do with this. Please, allow them to go."

Owyn's loud snarl reverberated through the glade. Dyna drew back a step.

"Alpha, I beg you," Zev said deferentially. He added the title to condone respect, even if he wasn't Pack. Owyn didn't answer, but the growls of the others had softened. Zev took that as permission and motioned for Dyna and Cassiel to leave.

She clung to his shirt with trembling hands, pungent fear oozing from her pores. "I won't leave you."

The thought of harm befalling her terrified Zev more than anything. He couldn't lose any more family, not at his own hands.

"Take her away to the Cyclops," he told Cassiel, hoping the prince knew what that meant. "If I don't return, please see her home."

Dyna yanked her elbow from Cassiel's grasp. "I'm not leaving. It's my fault Zev fought that wolf," she told Owyn.

"Stay out of it," the prince hissed under his breath.

"Forgive her," Zev cut in quickly at the growls surging from the Pack. "She's unaware of our ways."

"I know enough," Dyna replied defiantly, much to his horror. She met Owyn's cold gaze head-on, fists shaking at her sides. "A member of your Pack attacked me. It's against Pack law to hurt the mate or family of another wolf."

The men snarled at her.

"Dyna!" Zev whispered sharply. "You cannot speak here. Please step back."

Prince Cassiel pulled her behind him and snapped open his wings, concealing her from view.

"Zev Astron," the alpha's gruff voice rumbled. "I allowed you to stay on my land to repay my debt to your father. Yet you betrayed me and ran to the Celestials for sanctuary."

"I didn't betray you, Alpha."

"You killed my nephew!" Owyn roared. His power pressed into Zev, forcing his body to prostrate in submission. A hostile growl drew his attention to the man flanking the alpha. The Pack beta—Kenlan, Owyn's brother, and Faolan's father. He was shorter, leaner, but hardened with the same brutality that came with fighting to keep his position.

"I'm sorry," Zev said. "I truly am. But Faolan left me no choice. He was past the Madness and had gone feral." The men abruptly stopped growling, their shock sticking to Zev's skin.

It was the duty of the alpha to put down any wolves fallen into Madness for the safety of the Pack. They became unstable and confused before the feral stage came. A feral wolf was extremely dangerous. By the alpha and beta's expressions, they had suspected Faolan's condition and they couldn't bring themselves to end him. Family was always a werewolf's weakness.

Owyn rubbed his face. "When Faolan wandered off, he hadn't yet gone mad."

"He shouldn't have been left to reach that state."

The alpha's mouth twisted into a snarl, fangs extending. "Are you questioning me, half-breed?"

"No." Zev lowered his head again. "If I may ask, what caused it?"

"He lost his mate."

Yes, loss would do it. Werewolves felt everything so deeply. Joy. Anger. Pain. But grief most of all was a treacherous trigger for Madness. Zev was constantly teetering on the edge of it.

Owyn looked past him to Dyna. "Who is this female with you?"

"She is family. Daughter of my uncle," Zev replied, hoping the fact would hold sway in his case. Owyn sniffed the air to verify the claim. While she wasn't a wolf, there was no denying the scent of kin. "Faolan targeted her as prey. I had to stop him."

Kenlan hovered between both human and wolf as he vibrated with rage. When he spoke, the strained words were more of a growl than speech. "It doesn't bloody matter who the bitch is."

Zev snarled, his wolf nearly surfacing at the insult.

"She's not of the Pack and neither are you. You had no right to take my son's life. Now you will pay with yours!"

"Will you answer the challenge?" Owyn asked him.

Zev inhaled a deep breath to calm himself. He didn't want to kill anymore. He'd done enough of that. "I don't wish to fight."

"Then do you wish to bare your neck?"

The question should have frightened him, but he was numb to it. He looked up at the alpha, reading the verdict there. Kenlan was the second strongest fighter, and the other wolves were Pack warriors. They weren't here as witnesses.

They planned to end him.

With life comes death. There was no chance of avoiding such a definitive end. And no matter what Zev did, death always followed him.

What kind of life was this? Belonging nowhere; shunned for what he was and always struggling to remain sane. Living had become too hard. He had no home to rest in. The home he once had was haunted.

Zev could still picture his old house flanked by ash trees, nestled in a garden of wolfsbane. It was late Autumn when the yellow leaves had floated in through the broken window and stuck to the red-splattered walls. His father's mangled body lay on the floor, entrails torn out, his life seeping through the cracks in the floorboards. There had been so much blood. The stench of carrion filled Zev's nose as his mother's terrible screams echoed in his memories.

"You did this! You killed him!"

Weight compressed on Zev's chest. He couldn't breathe. Darkness clouded his vision, and a piercing ring filled his ears. All sound and surroundings faded. His very being plunged through him, as though the earth was dragging him down. The Madness was attempting to take him again. He fought to claw out of it. He needed to resist, but it enticed him with promises.

Give in to the wolf and rest. The whispered words were a sweet, luring caress—and a sharp whip. *All you touch withers. All those you love die. Forget it. Be unburdened from pain and despair. Forget it all.*

Forgetting. That would be a welcomed peace.

Yes, it hissed greedily. *Forget what you have done. Murderer.*

The accusation struck down Zev's wavering will, and he let go. The Madness took from him, plucking away each fault.

Killer.

Destroyer.

Monster.

Each sin snipped away left him weightless. The ache in his chest eased, and he drifted away. The Madness would take him to a new home. To a place where there was no pain or grief. Where nothing mattered at all. As he faded into the void, he questioned why he had resisted to begin with.

"No, Zev. Come back!" a desperate voice cried out. "Don't give in! Stay with me!"

His consciousness burst back to reality with an abrupt force. His soul barreled into his body, snapping into its rightful place—along with all of his sins. He fell on his hands and knees, gasping heavily as his black fur receded, and his elongated canines shrunk.

"Zev!" Dyna shouted.

He clutched his aching head, groaning at how shrill it sounded in his ears. She called him again, and he waved a limp hand to signal he was fine.

"He almost went mad, did you see?" Kenlan said.

Their disgust and hatred pressed into him. They wanted him gone.

"Rubbish," his father's last words came to him. *"Don't surrender, Zev. When you surrender, the Madness sets in. A mad wolf becomes a feral wolf. And when you become feral—you're dead."*

No alpha would suffer a mad wolf to live.

Zev looked up at Owyn who watched him with cold calculation, clawed hand poised to strike.

"The Madness was always meant to claim him," Kenlan sneered. "He's an *Other*."

The word was like a curse from the Gods. Since Zev had been old enough to understand his mother's scorn, he realized he was different.

Something ... else.

Other, the Pack whispered whenever he passed, eyeing him with fear and disgust. He hadn't understood what they meant until he had his first full moon shift. Werewolves had one form, but he had two: the wolf—and the Other.

"It was a mistake to let him be reared," Kenlan told Owyn. "We bore witness to the outcome. You should have broken his neck that day!"

The Pack agreed in rumbling growls.

Owyn's lip curled over his teeth. "Now *you* question me, brother?" His alpha power demanding subjugation filtered through Zev's senses and he nearly keeled over. The men dropped to one knee all at once.

Kenlan hunched forward, straining under Owyn's might. "No, Alpha," he grunted.

Owyn glowered down his nose at Zev. "You're on the brink of Madness. I may as well kill you now, but my brother seeks that satisfaction. I ask again, do you wish for death?"

Zev glanced over his shoulder at Dyna, her face marred with tears.

Do you wish for death?

Not yet.

She needed him. As long as she did, he would fight to go on. Keeping her safe was all that kept him from sinking into the oblivion of his mind.

"I will fight." He nodded at Cassiel to take her away. She shouldn't witness what was about to happen if Kenlan won.

"No!" Dyna tried to reach him, but the prince yanked her back.

She fought him angrily, kicking and flailing. Cassiel swept her off her feet, struggling to restrain her squirming form in his arms. In their scuffle, the journal fell unnoticed in the mud. The prince crouched, his wings expanding wide, then he shot into the sky.

Zev remained prostrated, listening to the flutter of wings fade with Dyna's cries over the treetops.

Kenlan's mocking laughter rang in the glade. "I'll hang your bloody pelt on my wall, Other. It'll be the last thing she sees before I rip out her pretty neck."

Rage pumped through Zev's veins and he snapped his teeth. That was all he needed to let go of his restraint.

As the last of the twilight vanished, the men tossed aside their clothes and they shapeshifted. The ripple of their change tugged on Zev's wolf. The Pack wolves were massive and powerful, all with variants of dark fur. They stood at about the height of his shoulder, their sharp teeth glistening. Kenlan dropped on all fours, becoming a dark gray wolf with a pale patch on his chest.

"Shift," Owyn ordered, before shapeshifting himself and standing beside his brother. Their sizes were drastically different. While Kenlan was smaller, the alpha was powerful in size and height.

Zev pulled off his tunic, letting it drop over the journal. The ache came as his body reformed itself, and he rose as his wolf.

The wolves backed away as all of them raised their heads to look at him, including the alpha. It had been some time since Zev had shifted with them. He hadn't realized how large he'd grown.

Owyn growled. He motioned with his muzzle for the Pack to move back, and they gathered in a wide ring around Zev and Kenlan.

The beta circled, and Zev did the same, studying him. He had seen a few of Kenlan's challenges before. He was a seasoned fighter. His thin and limber form made him fast. Like the alpha, he didn't lose fights, but Zev didn't care. Kenlan threatened Dyna. He would not leave the glade alive.

They charged into each other in a clash of teeth. Vicious growls reverberated in the glade. Kenlan forced Zev down and aimed for his neck. He dodged, but claws slashed through his shoulder. Whining, Zev twisted and swung at Kenlan's face, tossing him away. Zev rolled back on his feet and pummeled through the beta's defense, pinning him in the mud. Kenlan kicked him off and bounded backward, putting space between them.

Zev snarled, crouching as they circled each other again. Pain smoldered from his wounds, hot blood oozing through his fur. Kenlan exuded smug victory. That arrogance was to Zev's advantage.

The beta ran and leaped into the air for him, leaving his underbody exposed. Zev dove up and clamped his jaws on Kenlan's neck in one swift move, bringing him down. The wolves quieted. Kenlan keened, his paws sloshing through mud, desperate to break free.

It was over.

Zev broke the beta's neck, crushing bone and tendon in his teeth. Hot blood seeped through his mouth and poured down his muzzle. The bitter taste of wolf blood churned his stomach, the sour scent stinging his nose. Kenlan's last breath left him and Zev let go, dropping the body on the ground.

The werewolves howled in mourning, their long wail echoing in the forest. Owyn shuddered and shook out his flank at the loss of another wolf leaving the link of his pack. His fierce yellow eyes trained on Zev. The wolves quieted, shifting on their feet, their tails twitching. He smelled their unease.

They feared him.

He had killed the beta in minutes and stood taller than the alpha.

Owyn growled, low and deep. His fur expanded in a display of dominance. Whether intended or not, Zev was a risk to his position, and it couldn't go unaddressed.

The alpha amplified his power, but Zev's own surged forth and shook off his grasp. A surprised rumble passed through the wolves.

"Are you to challenge me next?"

Zev flinched at the sound of Owyn's harsh voice in his mind. It had been years since another wolf spoke to him through the link. *"No. My place is not in Lykos Peak."*

"Other, there is no place for the likes of you."

The wolves stalked forward, growling and snarling as they surrounded Zev. Clouds crept over the moon, darkening everything around him but the circle of iridescent eyes glowing in the night.

Zev bared his fangs. *"I defeated Kenlan. By Pack law, I am pardoned."*

"Our laws don't protect you anymore," Owyn said, snapping his jaws. *"Nor your cousin. You've taken my family from me. I'll make sure you never see yours again."*

The Pack attacked.

Zev bit and clawed his way through the raging wolves. His ears filled with their growls and snarls. He tore out the jugular of one wolf and broke the neck of another. He struggled to fight the swarm striking from all directions. Blood sprayed in the air, but he didn't know if it was his or theirs. He keened at the bite on his hind leg. It was all they needed to overpower him.

They took him down, their teeth tearing into his flesh, ripping him apart piece by piece. He fell to the ground as his blood poured out beneath him. The onslaught stopped, and the wolves backed away. Owyn came into his view, superiority edging his unfeeling gaze. He would snap his neck, and that would be the end.

At last, Zev would see his father again and beg for forgiveness.

But wrath-fuelled desperation washed through him. His wolf demanded he get up. He couldn't fall. Not yet. If they finished him, they would go after Dyna next.

Family. Must protect family. Those were his last thoughts before he sank so far within himself to think of anything else.

Zev found himself standing nude in the glade, breathing ragged with blood leaking from his many wounds. The Pack was gone. What happened? He had no recollection. No memory would surface from the dark fog of his mind. That only occurred when …

A terrible chill sank through him when he realized he held the severed head of a wolf, its muzzle cracked open. Glass-like eyes frozen in terror stared up at him. The head slipped through his fingers and splashed in the red pool at his feet.

The moon rose above the clouds and bathed the glade in moonlight. Dismembered wolves splayed on the ground like gruesome roses, eviscerated with their innards spilled out, saturating the mud with blood.

The Other had come out to play.

Zev's breath came in quick, his hands shaking. This shouldn't have happened. His beast was only to be freed during one night of the month. Had it grown stronger? He clenched his fists, claws puncturing his palms. Why did it always have to resort to this?

A whimper drew his sights to Owyn, lying a few paces ahead. Bloody stumps cut off at the alpha's knees, where his legs had once been. Zev approached, his slow steps squelching through the sea of the dead.

The alpha watched him come, shivering as he bled out. "Lykos will never accept you as their alpha," he snarled weakly. But the last fight went out of him and his eyes grew pleading. "Don't harm them. Don't you touch her. Tasnia was always kind to you."

"I'll not hurt your mate, Owyn."

"Swear you won't return."

"I swear it."

The alpha nodded and slumped back in the bloody mud, his expression was as broken as his body. He looked up at the sky as his thin breaths rattled in his lungs. "Kill me."

Zev shook his head.

"Do it. You have ravaged me and mine. You owe me a quick death."

Forgive me, Zev wanted to beg, but the only thing he had a right to was completing the task asked of him. He carefully took the alpha's throat in his hands.

"You're no wolf." Owyn's voice was but a faint whisper in the wind, carrying the smell of death. "You're a demon."

"Aye … I believe you're right," Zev said, then he snapped Owyn's neck.

CHAPTER 15

Dynalya

yna wrapped her arms tight around her knees, attempting to contain her trembling as much as it was for warmth. A chill had settled in her bones and sitting close to the campfire did little to help. Cassiel stood guard across from her, arms crossed, silent and irate that she had insisted on building one. A fire would reveal their presence if any of the were-beasts came looking for them, he had said. But she couldn't wait in the dark.

She looked around at the lakeshore he had brought her to. The water rippled in the wind, glistening white under the half-moon. A wall of pine trees surrounded them like quiet sentinels guarding them in the night. Why did they come here? The prince had flown with her for several miles without leaving their scent below. How would Zev find them?

She said, "We need to go back."

Cassiel, who had been studying their surroundings, slid his eyes to her. He returned to surveying the dark.

"How do you know Zev meant us to come here?"

"This is Lake Nayim," he replied, as though it were enough explanation. At her confused frown, he sighed. "It is perfectly round. See the isle?"

At the center of the lake, there was a small isle with trees and shrubs. It had blended so well with the night she had not noticed it at first.

"On a clear day, the lake reflects the color of the sky. From above, it looks like a single blue eye."

"Ah, like the eye of a Cyclops," Dyna concluded. She rested her cheek over her knees, looking out at the lake again. Zev had not told her about this place. He didn't tell her about many things, but she didn't care anymore. She only cared that he would survive.

"What is the Madness?" Cassiel asked after a while, surprising her with the hesitant question.

"At times, the wolf spirit can grow too strong and overcome the consciousness of a werewolf," she said, watching the moon's reflection ripple on the water. "That is the Madness. It reverts them to their wild instincts. They become increasingly more aggressive and more violent until they are nothing more than feral wolves. Who they once were vanishes."

What she didn't say was that the Madness came when a werewolf no longer wished to live. Zev had many reasons to give up, and she feared one day he would. He had almost done so at the glade. As he had struggled to stay conscious, he had shifted between wolf and man, back and forth until he stopped fighting.

If she had not called his name …

Hours had passed since Cassiel took her away, but her hands still shook. Fresh tears trickled down her nose. She couldn't lose him too.

Cassiel tossed a waterskin by her feet, the contents sloshing inside. "Drink," he ordered, then added mildly, "You will feel better."

Once the cool water slid down her throat, some of her anxiety eased. She wiped her cheeks with her dress sleeve and forced the brunt of her distress aside. It wouldn't do to assume the worst yet.

"If your cousin does not return, he instructed you to go home."

"I won't go back."

The prince's mouth thinned. "You will go back."

Dyna glared at the command. The history of her village was founded by those who fought for the right to make their own choices, and she would not let that be taken from her.

"I think you have misunderstood me, Prince Cassiel. I have decided where I am meant to be, and that is here. I won't go back. Not without the stone."

Astonishment settled on his features. It was the first time she had spoken to him so firmly, but he needed to understand that no matter what happened, she would not give up.

"Even if you were to drag me away again, you would not find my village," she said, still upset that he had snatched her into the sky. Fearing he would drop her, Dyna had clung to him desperately. Remembering her sheer panic made her insides drop.

A hint of amusement swam in his cool eyes, as if he also remembered it. His large black wings flexed at his back, the plumage as sleek as oil in the firelight.

"As long as I can see the skyline, I know my heading. Your village lies due west. It will not take much to find it."

Dyna shrugged. "Even then."

Cassiel arched an eyebrow as he gauged whatever he read on her face. She wasn't lying. The Mages of Old had cloaked North Star from any unwanted attention. He would never find it. Not from above, not even if he stood right in front of it.

"Once you see what darkness awaits out there, you will beg me to bring you home," the prince said over the crackle of burning wood.

Dyna rested her palms over the tall grass as she leaned forward, holding his hard gaze. "Be it here or out there, darkness finds its way into every remote corner of the world. I am not a demon hunter, or a warrior, or anyone with experience. Perhaps I should leave this quest to someone else far more qualified, but I won't because it's *mine*."

She curled her hands into fists, tearing up blades of grass. Essence stirred through her, hot and electric, agitated by rare anger. Its invisible energy prickled along her skin and cast static around her. The firewood snapped, and the flames flared, startling the prince.

If she had a significant amount of Essence, she would have expelled uncontrollable magic. Emotions riled up magic in those who hadn't trained in control. Her father had passed before he could train her, but it didn't matter. She didn't have enough Essence to produce any actual power.

But she would not turn back.

Not when she could clearly remember how her family's blood had crystallized in the snow after the Shadow came. It had looked like a hill of crushed rubies glimmering under the sunlight. Beautiful. Devastating. A reminder of what was to come.

"The Shadow took *everything* from me," she said, pinning Cassiel with her stare. "I won't rest until I turn it to ash."

He didn't look away. Nor did she until the moon rose above the clouds like it was called by the ancient powers in her lineage. Whether it was the moonlight or the settling of her Essence, the roiling in her faded away like a passing breeze, sweeping all the bitterness away in her next breath.

Dyna laid her cheek back on her knees, closing her swollen eyes. "Do you believe me so foolish that I don't fear what may happen on this journey? I know what I risk. I know the dangers, but I have to try. The Sunstone is the only way to defeat the shadow demon. So, I will go on this journey, even if it costs me my life."

A heavy silence fell, thickening the space between them. She had not admitted that aloud to herself before, but it was an oath she kept locked within her heart. For Lyra, she would do anything. Her sister would not suffer Thane's fate.

Cassiel fidgeted with the belts of his sheathed sword lying beside him. "If you found another way, would you forget Mount Ida?"

She could not read his expression, and he wouldn't meet her gaze. "I would have no reason to go. Why do you ask?"

He shrugged.

Dyna waited, but he offered no other answer. She glanced around at their belongings and came to a startling realization. "If Zev doesn't arrive by morning, I must return to the glade."

"It would do no good to see his body. If there is anything left of it."

She winced. Zev deserved a proper burial, should it come to that. "I have to return."

"Why?"

"I'm afraid I dropped the journal there."

"What?" Cassiel hissed. "You *dropped* it? How could you drop it?"

Dyna's reply caught on her tongue. For a large, warped figure came out of the tree line and stumbled into the clearing.

CHAPTER 16

Dynalya

P ure relief flooded through Dyna when she saw who it was. Choking back a sob, she leaped to her feet and sprinted across the distance between them. "Zev!"

He let the rucksacks he'd been carrying drop to his feet before plunging to his knees. She threw herself at him, arms wrapping around his broad shoulders. He groaned, his face scrunching in pain.

"God of Urn, what did they do to you?"

Red trails leaked down from the deep gashes all over him. A chunk of skin hung from beneath his left ear where teeth had tried to take his jugular. Gravel and dirt were embedded in his wounds. There was so much blood splattered all over his face and mouth, it couldn't have been all his own.

Mingling with the strong metallic scent was the faint smell of vomit. The back of his forearm was smeared red where he had used it to wipe his mouth.

Dyna's hands hovered around him, not knowing what to tend to first. "I'll stop the bleeding."

"No," he rasped, slumping back on his heels. "Save your strength."

"But your neck—"

"It's nothing vital."

Cassiel lingered at a distance with his arms crossed, trying not to cringe. "Do you have the journal?"

Zev brought out the rectangular bundle wrapped in his dirty tunic he had tucked under his arm. He unwrapped it to reveal the leather-bound book, to Dyna's relief.

"First day on this quest and you have already gained enemies," Cassiel said, his eyes trained on it.

"The matter is settled. We are safe now."

Dyna flipped the tunic inside out to the clean side. She turned Zev's chin to mop the blood from his neck, making note she would need to find proper bandages as soon as she could. She was grossly unprepared for a healer. "We need to wash these wounds."

"How did you escape?" Cassiel asked.

"I didn't." Zev's blank stare focused on something over her shoulder. Lost to horrors she couldn't see. Something dreadful had happened in that glade.

"They let you go?" the prince pressed.

"Aye …"

She searched her cousin's face. "But now you can never go home, can you?"

"That place is not my home anymore, Dyna. It hasn't been for a long time."

They fell quiet, not knowing what to do or say. Prince Cassiel turned away and wandered off to the lake. With a couple of flaps of his wings, he rose easily into the night sky, flying in lazy circles overhead.

Dyna watched Zev stare blankly at nothing. She should have known he wouldn't be able to live in Lykos Peak much longer. They had never accepted him there. She took his face, turning his unfocused gaze on her, and she saw the Madness swimming in it. Speaking to him. Turning him.

"Zev? Zev!"

His glowing eyes blinked, switching back to green, and the growing fur along his forearms receded. He shook his head to rid himself of the whispers she knew he'd been listening to.

"Where were you planning to go?" she asked, her voice cracking.

By Zev's pained expression, he knew what she meant. Where was he letting the Madness take him?

"I had thought to come here." He looked at the lake, his wild hair undulating in the wind. "It's quiet and a day's travel from the village. Without the need to pass through Hilos, I can visit more often."

He must not have fully given up if he made plans for the future. It was a kernel of hope Dyna grasped onto tightly.

She returned to wiping the rest of the blood off him, but there was too much of it. All she managed to do was to push it around. "How did you find this place?"

"It looks much the same since I last came. When I was a child, my father would often travel to Landcaster for work. Lake Nayim is the midway point, so we would camp here. He told me there was once a fishing town past those trees, and that it's believed the isle was the eye of Utgard, the Cyclops giant confined under the mountain ice caps of Skath. They say he cursed the lake when he opened a small rift in the Spatial Gate to look into our world, and it forced the townsfolk to flee. The tale was meant to be frightening, but I don't think the Cyclops intended to scare them away. All he wanted was not to be alone."

There was so much sadness on his face that Dyna wanted to cry. "Come back to North Star when this journey has ended. You'll live with me, Lyra, and Grandmother. You don't have to be alone anymore."

Zev sighed. "You know I can't—"

"I don't care what the village council says." Dyna shook her head. "We are your family. Uncle Belzev would have wanted you to be with us."

"The council was right to banish me, Dyna. It's not safe for a werewolf to live among humans. But this place is safe. Here, I'd hurt no one."

Zev was strong and kind, yet so brittle. Something had broken on the inside, and it was visible on the outside. His body was a testament to his life; covered in scars placed by others and ones he placed himself. His new wounds would add more. She couldn't see him that way any longer.

Dyna placed a hand over his neck wound and called on her Essence, drawing a vivid green light in her palm. She sent it forth to flow through her fingertips, picturing the layers of muscle and skin—

"Dyna!" Zev jerked away. He glowered at her, tentatively touching the wound site. The bleeding had stopped. Its swollen red ridges had reduced significantly, and the skin had fused in a pink line. "I told you it wasn't necessary."

"I can help. Let me!"

"No. Essence Healing is depleting. Look at you."

She tried to appear fine, but her breath came heavy, her limbs trembling. Only a sliver of ancestral power was left in her bloodline, so Essence Healing cost her a great deal of effort. It always left her drained to the point of extreme exhaustion.

"What is the purpose of this ability if I cannot use it to help others?" she asked.

Zev had let her heal him once before, as he'd been too wounded to stop her, but she had fallen unconscious for three days. After that, he wouldn't allow her to heal him again.

"Help those who need it, not me. Werewolves recover quickly. My injuries will scar by morning." He shook his head when she tried to protest. "Please, let's not argue about it. I'm tired and starved."

Dyna huffed and picked up her journal as she stood, but she wobbled and her head spun. Zev reached out to steady her.

"I'm all right," she waved him off. "We'll camp here tonight. Go wash up while I prepare our meal."

Zev staggered to his feet. He dragged their rucksacks to the fire before limping for the lake.

Dyna washed her hands and searched through Zev's pack for a change of clean clothes. Most of his tunics were threadbare with holes. She took out a pair of trousers, and her fingers brushed against the icy links of his thick chains. She snatched her hand back with a shudder.

After leaving his clothes by the shore, Dyna rummaged through the other rucksack for more items. She withdrew rolled-up bedrolls made of treated canvas and wool blankets. Then she worked on gathering more firewood to last the night. Prince Cassiel flew down, taking a seat within a nearby tree. Dyna felt his eyes on her as she worked, but he made no effort to help.

Once she'd set up the camp, Zev returned clean and dressed. Dyna passed him a plate of manna, cheese, and dried fruit. He ate urgently while she applied a salve to his wounds. Cassiel remained seated above them. He produced his own rations from his pack and kept to himself as he warily surveyed their surroundings.

Dyna ate quietly while she studied him in turn. The prince's winged profile cast a long shadow on the balding branches, swaying with the campfire. Even in the dark, he didn't look human. The unearthly beauty, the subtle glow beneath his skin. Cassiel was unreal. It wasn't only the discovery of his kind.

He was distinct.

His black wings and hair were unique among the Seraphim she'd seen. *Celestials*, she corrected herself. What was the difference? The prince said they were earthbound. Was that all it was?

Sensing her stare, Cassiel's silver eyes met hers. They were guarded and as cold as steel in the snow. She sensed so much hidden behind his indifference that she wished, for only a moment, to know what entered his mind when he looked at her.

Well, he had already said what he thought. *Stupid human.*

"Thank you for keeping Dyna safe," Zev called up to him, breaking the silence.

Cassiel leaned back against the tree's trunk, hitching up a leg on the branch to rest his forearm over it. "I would not consider this safe."

Zev followed his line of sight to the shadows enclosing them. "They won't come back."

"They hardly left you alive. They may return to finish the task."

Dyna wondered if that's why the prince wouldn't come down, or if he naturally preferred to be high off the ground, like birds.

Zev looked down at the wounds on his chest, visible through his open tunic. "They won't."

"If he says we're safe, you need not worry," Dyna said at the obvious skepticism on the prince's face.

Cassiel eyed her a moment, then dropped to the ground in one agile leap. He kept one hand resting on the hilt of his sword, the silver knife strapped to his belt within reach of the other. His gaze flickered to Zev. The Pack may not be the only thing he was wary about.

The prince sat on the exposed roots of his tree like it was a throne. It really would be impossible for anyone to mistake him for anything but royalty. He waved her forward. "Bring forth the map."

Dyna retrieved the journal from the top of her bedroll and turned the delicate pages to the section where the map should have been. The page was blank. "It disappeared."

Cassiel jerked to his feet. "What do you mean it disappeared? Where is the map?"

Zev searched around him, rifling through their belongings. "Did it fall out? I must have dropped it in the glade."

Dyna smiled. "The map is enchanted to fade away as a precaution. The mage this journal belonged to secured it with his Essence."

Cassiel's eyes narrowed. "What?"

"Essence is the source energy of magic," Zev explained. "It's found in those trueborn with the ability to wield it, like the fae, the elves—"

"I am quite familiar with the definition," Cassiel cut him off. "She failed to mention last night the map was locked under an enchantment. Only the mage can reveal it."

"Yet I have already shown it to you," Dyna pointed out.

He gave her a dubious look. "How can a *human* reveal an *enchanted* map?"

"Allow me to show you." She was excited to demonstrate this part. They gathered around her and watched as she brought the journal close to her lips and whispered, *"Tellūs, lūnam, sōlis."*

Her hands flared green, and a burst of purple light whirled across the page. Zev and Cassiel's mouths hung open, the mystical glow reflecting on their faces. Their wide eyes followed the stroke of ink moving across the page. An invisible brush seemed to draw each delicate curve as the continent of Urn took form. Then the shining island of Mount Ida appeared to the west.

Their speechlessness only lasted a couple of seconds before Zev laughed. "Aye, I should have known. You never cease to amaze me."

But Cassiel's eyes sharpened on her. "You are a *witch*."

Dyna grimaced. "I beg your pardon?"

"She's not a witch." Zev glowered.

Cassiel backed away from them. "That was clearly a spell."

"Well, yes, but not mine," she told him. "The words were the passphrase to unlock the spell concealing the map. I didn't *cast* a spell."

He backed up another step when she stood, keeping an eye on her hands. Did he expect her to throw a hex on him?

Dyna frowned. She preferred to be called stupid than a witch. Humans weren't born with Essence, but they could be granted black magic by the God of Shadows, ruler of the Netherworld, in so becoming witches.

"I used Essence to trigger the spell," she said. "I know it may be confusing to see a human with power, but I didn't gain it through dark means. I was born with it. Zev and I descend from Lunar Mages, from Azeran himself."

The prince scoffed at the claim, but grew serious when Dyna held her steady expression. She closed the journal and showed him the sigil of House Astron on the cover.

Cassiel's eyes grew wide. "You mean to tell me you come from the bloodline of *the* Azeran Astron; the mage who brought about the War of the Guilds in the Magos Empire, two-hundred-and-fifty-years ago?"

"Yes."

He raised his chin. "I overlooked that claim before, but you cannot be of House Astron."

It was a hard thing to believe. Mages didn't marry outside of their race. Her fiery red hair could portray her as someone of the Sun Guild, but Azeran was of the Lunar Guild. His hair had been as white as starlight, and he had eyes the color of amethyst crystals.

Zev crossed his arms. "She speaks the truth."

"It's an honor to be his descendant," Dyna added.

Cassiel curled his nose. "That is nothing to be proud of. Azeran committed treason."

She sighed, shaking her head. "That is not true."

"You would dispute the hundreds of books and mage biographies that documented the War of the Guilds?"

"Yes," she and Zev answered definitively.

"Azeran's uprising led to countless deaths," he shot back. "By the time the war ended, most of Magos was rubble and ash."

"The mages fabricated their history," she said. "The Archmage of the Orbis Age made sure only his account of the war was known."

The prince glared at her across the fire. It crackled and popped, casting a swirl of embers. "Who told you such *lies*?"

Dyna hugged the journal to her chest, and it responded in a warm current of energy. It was Azeran's Essence, but a part of her believed it held a piece of his spirit. The embedded magic was so gentle there was no denying what kind of person he was.

She had only known a general account of the Lunar Mage and what had led him to defy the Magos Empire. It wasn't until she read his journals that she learned much more about his courage and the cost he paid for freedom.

"I have a coffer full of his journals chronicling his life before and during the war," she said. "Magos is not the place you believe it is,

Prince Cassiel. Perhaps now is not the time to speak of it, but Azeran's deeds were for peace."

He was not convinced. The glint in his gaze was much harsher than it had been in Hilos. Dyna sighed. Nothing she said would change his mind. It was her word against an empire.

"And yet there is a fact that negates your story," Cassiel said after a pause. "Azeran had sired no children, and he died during the war. You cannot be of his bloodline."

Zev said, "You witnessed her use of Essence."

"*That* can be explained."

"She's not a witch," Zev growled. The prince rested a hand on his silver knife, and Zev's eyes flashed yellow at the subtle threat.

"Azeran survived," Dyna said, drawing their attention back to her. "He and a handful of Lunar Guild mages escaped Magos and founded North Star. We are their legacy."

She sat beside Zev, close enough to remind him he could harm her if he shifted. It was enough to calm his wolf, and he settled again.

"How do you suppose the Shadow has not laid waste to our village and made its way to Hilos?" she asked Cassiel. "It's untarnished because a village elder cast the shadow demon back to the Netherworld at its first coming. My grandfather did so at its second coming, and then my father at its … third." The word came out as a breathless utter.

It still hurt to speak of him, to remember him. But she would not let herself forgot what he sacrificed.

Zev gave her shoulder a gentle squeeze. "They did so with magic, but the cost was their lives. Her father passed away before he could share the spell used to access the Gate."

Dyna looked up at the twinkling sky. The night the Shadow came, the village was in chaos as the people ran with their children. Her father told her to run, so she did, but she wished she had stayed. She had gone over it in her mind several times, imagining different scenarios, questioning which one could have ended with the destruction of the Shadow instead of her family.

"The spell would be useless in my hands," she said. "Magic has nearly diminished in North Star. The first generation of Lunar Mages who founded the village were all in close relation, so their children took humans for life-mates when it came time to marry. As did their children, and so on. Within each generation, their magic dwindled."

The scowl faded from Cassiel's face.

"The preservation of magic within bloodlines is a delicate thing," she continued. "Because of this, the Magos Empire forbids mages to marry outside of their race, including outside of their guilds. In my generation, the ability to wield magic and cast spells is nearly gone. However, Essence remains. My family is one of the few remaining in the village who can wield it."

The prince sat against a tree and propped his elbow over his bent knee. "I suppose that is how you revealed the enchanted map?"

Dyna nodded, glad he was listening at least.

"And in the forest…" He stared at her intently, his wings tucking close against his back.

The firelight caught on the plumage at the apex of each one. His feather she'd found had fueled her Essence when she needed to defend herself against Captain Gareel. The green fire was not something she could muster on her own, and not something she would ever experience again by the way Cassiel reacted when she attempted to touch another feather. But it was expected after what his people had suffered.

"Azeran had many secrets and held a vast knowledge of powerful spells," Dyna said, breaking eye contact first. "He encrypted the journals for only his descendants to inherit. They are sired to me now." She patted the journal on her lap. "If I'm separated from this one, the map vanishes. It's the warding spell he put in place."

Cassiel gave Zev a deadpan look. "Am I to believe that you can wield Essence as well?"

Her cousin snorted. "I cannot. There are a few in the village who can and even fewer who can wield it as Dyna. I believe her sister will also have the ability with some training."

The prince glance at her. "Why your family?"

She shrugged. "I suppose it could be because the Astron bloodline contained significant power or because my family continued to practice with it. Azeran had an affinity for healing magic, which he called Essence Healing. The knowledge of how to perform it has been passed down over the generations. We apply it in our trade as Herb Masters."

Zev gave her a half-smile. "Perhaps one day you'll see it, Cassiel. It's a wonder."

The prince didn't dispute their claim to the Astron line any further, but his doubt, however lessened, remained apparent.

"Essence is the extent of my abilities and it's not potent," she said. "This is why I need the Sunstone. My power alone is not enough."

Cassiel looked down at his sword, almost thoughtful. "Well, then we must form a plan." He held out a hand for the journal, beckoning with his fingers.

She went to him readily, excited to learn what he could share. She tucked her dress around her legs and kneeled beside him. Her arm brushed against the edge of his wing and he flinched away from her.

"Your pardon," Dyna mumbled. The silky feathers had left a tingle on her skin. She opened the journal to the section of the map before passing it to him.

The prince's stared at it so intently Dyna knew he studied every detail. "The best way to Mount Ida is through the Xián Jīng Dynasty on the west coast, but not on foot," he said. "We must sail. The only ships that sail directly to Xián Jīng are the merchant ships from Dwarf Shoe."

"Dwarf Shoe?" Dyna asked, intrigued.

"The free state of the dwarves." He traced the outline of the state on the map, his fingertip shimmering where he touched the page. It did indeed have the shape of a shoe, to Dyna's amazement.

Dwarf Shoe laid northwest, separated from the Azure Kingdom by the Saxe Sea, a strip of water that cut through the eastern continent of Urn like a chip in a cup. It's what gave the blue kingdom the moniker Urn's Chip. Azure was connected to the rest of the continent by a thin bridge of land on the north coast.

"Are we to cross the isthmus?" Zev asked.

Cassiel smirked. "Not unless you wish to be devoured alive."

Dyna's eyes widened. "What?"

"It's infested with swamp trolls," the prince informed them. "Fifteen years ago, the Azure King foolishly settled a town on the isthmus in an attempt to claim it, but that did not bode well. The isthmus is now known as the Troll Bridge."

"Oh!" she and Zev replied together. She shuddered at the thought that they wouldn't have discovered it themselves until it was too late.

"We will reach Dwarf Shoe by sailing from the Port of Azure." Cassiel pointed out the seaport city on the map. It lay past the Zafiro Mountains, on the northeast end of the Saxe Sea. "The journey will take a little over a fortnight on foot, should traveling go smoothly. Less if we take a caravan from Corron. There are always traders traveling along the central road to the west ports. If we join a caravan, it will take us directly to the Port of Azure and save us a week of travel."

Dyna nodded eagerly. The quicker they could reach Mount Ida, the better. "I like that plan."

"We will stop in towns along the way to replenish our fares when needed."

"Landcaster is the first town we'll cross," Zev said. "It's a small farm town that lies about ninety miles from here."

Cassiel snapped the journal closed, dissipating the purple glow of the map. "Right, best get our rest. We leave at first light."

He returned to his tree and Zev added more wood to the campfire. Dyna laid out on her bedding with a happy sigh. As much as the prince was guarded, she was glad for his company on this quest. She didn't feel so unprepared now that he was with them.

Perhaps it meant everything would be all right.

CHAPTER 17

Cassiel

Cassiel suppressed a groan when Dyna stopped, once again, to pick another measly plant. Balancing on her heels, she crouched by a patch of dark red grass and pulled out a handful of the long stems with the leaves and roots intact. Her deft fingers quickly tied them together with twine before storing them in a burlap pouch. Then she took out a small bound notebook from her satchel and scribbled something down, tiny creases forming between her brows as she bit her lip in concentration.

Shafts of afternoon light spilled through the branches and shone in a scarlet nimbus around her bowed head. The corners of her mouth lifted in a faint smile, as it always did when she studied the flora. Whenever she shared her knowledge on their uses with him, her voice had spiked an octave with excitement. Plants made her happy for whatever reason.

"If you were not aware, your constant stopping to pick another weed is delaying our journey by the day," Cassiel said. "We need to reach Landcaster soon to replenish our fares."

He'd been too ambitious to estimate it would only take a fortnight to reach the port. They couldn't fly like him, and she couldn't move as fast as her brute of a cousin. This excursion may take twice as long as he thought. And sailing to the island would take weeks, if not months. He most certainly won't return for the better part of a year. His father would be furious.

"Please excuse the inconvenience, Prince Cassiel," Dyna said as she wrote another line in her notebook. "It is necessary for healers to carry adequate medicine."

Medicine for whom? With his regenerative abilities, he never fell ill. The fatal injuries for Celestials were those sustained to the heart or the head.

"And what, pray tell, is the use for grass?" He only asked because she would tell him regardless if he cared to know.

She stood and put away her items. "Phyllon roots are good for pain and steeping the leaves can induce sleep. I'll make a soporific for Zev tonight. He's been having trouble sleeping."

At the reminder, Cassiel searched their surroundings for any streak of black among the greenery. "The beast has wandered off again."

Dyna frowned. "*Zev* is patrolling. He'll find us when it's time to make camp."

Since the night at Lake Nayim, the were-beast had shapeshifted into a wolf and remained that way. He spent most of his time out of sight in the forest as they traveled, coming to check on Dyna throughout the day. At night, Zev waited until she fell asleep before he sauntered off to do whatever animals do. Cassiel hadn't been able to sleep well knowing he roamed free.

The were-beast must be going mad. It would explain the strange behavior, but Cassiel didn't know him well enough to say.

Other, the Pack had called him. They couldn't have been referring to his ability to shapeshift at will during the day. Whatever *Other* meant, the Pack feared him. It was obvious the alpha had planned to have him killed in the glade because of it. But Zev had arrived at Lake Nayim alive with grave wounds and vague answers.

How had he survived against so many werewolves? The creatures were massive. Deadly. Survival should have been impossible, and

Cassiel doubted the alpha let Zev go free. So, after Dyna and Zev fell asleep that night, he had flown back to the glade to investigate.

"He is not right …" Cassiel stopped from saying more. What he had seen was too gruesome to tell Dyna. "Your cousin has been a wolf for two days," Cassiel said instead. "He may have already fallen into the Madness."

Dyna shook her head, expression wistful as she gazed at the tree branches swaying in the gentle breeze. It passed over her, fluttering her tresses and ends of her sage dress. "Zev will shift back when he's ready."

Ready to face what he had done went unsaid.

There was no way for her to know what happened in that glade, but Cassiel suspected she knew. He had thought her a foolish rube with nonsense in her head, but she proved far more intelligent than he assumed. He supposed she had to be intelligent to become a healer.

Dyna continued onward. "How much longer until we reach Landcaster?"

Cassiel took out the enchanted journal from his pack and flipped to the section of the map, but the page was blank. He glowered at her back as she passed through a gathering of ferns. They had tested how far she could be away from the map without it disappearing, and a mere twenty paces were the limit.

When she had first revealed the map in his father's study, he hadn't stopped to think about how she came by it. He had assumed she found it, not that it had been passed down in her family.

Was there any truth to what she said about her lineage? A human wielding trueborn magic was unbelievable. Though that would explain how she could harness it.

Cassiel caught up to Dyna, holding out the journal. She said the passphrase and the blank page flashed with light as the map reappeared. It had occurred to him the other night that those words were of the native language of the mages before they became accustomed to speaking Urnian. *Tellūs, lūnam, sōlis* translated to Earth, moon, and sun—respectively, representing the three Guilds that pillared the Magos Empire.

"We are not far from Landcaster. We should arrive by tomorrow morning," Dyna said, studying the glowing page with a smile. She looked up, and the sunlight graced her eyes, the striking, vibrant green color glimmering with flecks of gold. "Have I astonished you again, Prince Cassiel?"

He quickly looked away, realizing he was staring. "I am not quite convinced you're not a witch."

But he had already accepted that she wasn't. After he had time to think about it, he recalled having already seen her soul, and it was not marred by dark magic. That was proof enough.

Dyna's eyebrows lifted in response. "Are you teasing me?"

He cleared his throat, resuming their hike. "I cannot deny you have use of magic."

"I don't have enough power to do much with it, and it's difficult to use."

Cassiel said nothing else as their footsteps crunched over fallen leaves and forest debris. He sensed her invitation to converse, then heard her sigh when he ignored it.

They reached a steep hill layered in wet moss and stacked rock, which he used to climb up. "From what I have learned, magic can grow with continuous use," he commented. "Is it not similar to training your body and mind?"

Dyna climbed up behind him. "Well, yes. The more it's used, the stronger you become and the more magic you can wield—" She slipped on a patch of moss, and he caught the back of her dress before she landed on her face.

He rolled his eyes and hauled her upright. "Watch your step."

She muttered her thanks and followed him, taking his exact path. "But everyone has a limit and using too much magic can deplete it."

"Essence regenerates itself," he countered.

"True. However, the elves and the fae draw Essence from nature, so their depletion is merely physical, but the mages draw it from themselves. It's their life force. Therefore, using copious amounts of magic all at once and completely expending their Essence is fatal. Without it, they cannot survive."

Cassiel remembered that from his lessons. He didn't care to listen to his teachers when they droned on about boring subjects, but magic had been one of the interesting ones.

"Mages train their Essence to grow in strength and quantity, but that too has its limitations," she said. "Not all can wield endless amounts of Essence."

He leaped up onto another boulder and glanced over his shoulder to check on Dyna's progress. She had fallen behind. Her short legs couldn't make the jump to him, and he wasn't inclined to take her hand when it meant seeing her soul again.

When he didn't offer his help, she grabbed a thick vine and tested to see if it would hold her weight. That made him feel like a lout. He held out his hand, but she ignored it. The vine went taut and held as Dyna hauled herself up the hill, using exposed roots and boulders as footholds. He watched her climb, mildly impressed that she made it to the top without slipping again.

She disappeared from view for a moment, then popped her head over the edge, beaming down at him. "Coming?"

He smirked. With one flap of his wings, he soared the rest of the way up and landed beside her. "Would it be fatal for you should you expend all of your Essence at once?"

She shrugged, biting her lip. "Possibly, but I am not a trueborn sorceress, so I'm not sure."

"Sorceress?"

"A female mage."

Cassiel frowned at the odd term. He had not heard it before. As he thought of it, there was no mention of female mages in his studies of the Magos Empire. They stated that only the men had power. But she could use magic, so how…

Eh, he wasn't in the mood to argue about it. He nodded for them to keep walking. They eventually came upon a brook cutting through the forest. It was shallow, only a couple feet wide.

Dyna stopped to take a drink and refill their waterskins. "Whenever I use too much Essence, I'm left fatigued, and I may faint. I've trained to develop my strength further, but something hinders me. Like I'm running with shackles on my ankles. My power won't ever be as potent because of my human heredity. It is difficult for me to harness Essence, but I'm grateful that I can do anything with it at all."

She held up a hand and her fingertips glowed a faint green before the light faded. From what he remembered, the manifestation of Essence took on the color of auras. It fit perfectly that her aura was green. It was a color that represented healing and a connection to nature.

"Does it tire you to unveil the map?" he asked as they jumped over the brook.

"Not at all," she said, even though fatigue had settled on her features. He doubted it had anything to do with the hike.

"If it tires you, stay close to me." A flush rushed to his face when he realized what he had said. "I mean, stay close to the map. If you should faint, it will delay us further."

Dyna stopped walking, and he drew back when his wing brushed against her. He cringed at the sensation zinging through his wingspan. Celestials never allowed others to touch their wings. It was the source of their divinity and might. A point of vulnerability. The only thing that kept them from becoming human.

Dyna often moved near him, careless or uncaring of subconsciously touching him when he was accustomed to avoidance. No one in Hilos approached him. She didn't seem to mind him though.

Cassiel tried to avoid getting too close to her, in any form. Be it proximity or company, but the map forced him to be near her. The weight of it in his pack and the faint hum of its power was a sense of security. Having it on his person assured they wouldn't run off without him. And he couldn't stop staring at the glowing island. Even after knowing the map existed, seeing it for himself, and holding it in his hands, he still wondered if this reality was a dream.

Dyna studied him as if she could see him in a way he wished she couldn't. "Thank you for your concern, Prince Cassiel. As for the use of Essence, I don't mind it in the least." She strolled on, leaving behind the subtle honeysuckle scent of her hair.

He watched her go, again left wondering who she was. Dyna was such an odd human. Too kind. Too curious. Too confounding. Not someone he expected to be trekking across the world with. Yet here they were, tied together by some chance.

Lost in his thoughts, Cassiel forgot to keep up with her. At twenty paces, her petite form slipped through the trees and the journal's hum faded away.

CHAPTER 18

Cassiel

A rustle in the bushes jolted Cassiel awake. He jerked upright on his branch, almost falling over until he remembered he had been sleeping in a tree. Gripping the bark beneath his fingers, he surveyed the area below, searching for what had disturbed his sleep. The dying fire did little to illuminate their small, dark campsite they had set up in the middle of the forest. Dyna slept on the other side of the campfire—alone.

Where was the beast?

Zev's bedroll was empty, a wool blanket left in a crumpled heap on top.

Cassiel's skin prickled under his damp clothes. A chilly veil of mist hovered between the dense hedges enclosing them. He had chosen this campsite for its seclusion, but the still trees now entrapped him.

At another whisper of rustling in the bushes, he dropped from the tree branch, landing lightly on his feet. From his belt, he unsheathed the silver knife. He slowed his breathing, straining to catch any approaching sounds. A cold draft brushed against the nape of his neck. He spun around, and his heart lurched at the sight of two reflective, yellow eyes watching him in the dark. The massive black wolf sat silently among the foliage, nearly swallowed by the night.

Cassiel tightened his sweaty palm around the slick hilt of his knife. "I suspected you would come after us next. Well, come on then. I am ready for you."

The wolf blinked at him in question.

"I went back to the glade. I saw what you did. You slaughtered them all. Your own kind." Another shiver skittered down Cassiel's spine. "Does she know what you have done?"

Those yellow eyes moved to Dyna's sleeping form, proving Zev remained coherent.

"No. Otherwise, she would fear you as well."

The wolf slinked toward the camp, giving him a wide berth. Cassiel turned, keeping it in his sights. When reaching the campfire, the wolf took firewood within its jaws from the stack beside it and dropped them over the dying flames. The fire rekindled, providing more light. Then it headed for Dyna.

"Stop. Stay away from her."

The wolf chuffed what sounded like a human scoff and laid down, curling beside Dyna.

Cassiel glowered. Was it safe to let the beast near her?

As though to answer, Dyna murmured in her sleep and her arm wrapped around the wolf, nestling into the thick fur. Well, she said Zev would never harm her. Werewolves were protective of their kin.

But was the Pack not kin?

Cassiel took a corner of his bedroll and dragged it to the far end of the campsite at the base of a gnarled tree. He sat with his back against the trunk to watch the beast and shook out his blanket over his legs. The journal tumbled out. Firelight shone on the crescent sigil of House Astron.

The Astron's were an infamous family. Notoriously powerful Lunar Mages that maintained dominion over the Lunar Guild unopposed for the last three-hundred-years. He was to believe that Dyna had descended from them?

Wispy clouds parted overhead, allowing moonlight to shine over Dyna's small form crowned by fog. It made her pale skin milky compared to the large, black beast beside her.

There was one thing she had said that he believed to be true: her pledge to destroy the Shadow. He had to admire her determination. She found the means to defeat her demon so she would never give up this dangerous quest.

But the Sunstone might not be the only option.

Cassiel turned over his hands, studying them. His father had said they were clean. He had taken no human lives. That would mean with his sword he had the power to eliminate the Shadow. *Possibly*. As a half-breed, there was no telling if his blood was pure enough to extinguish evil. However, he had regenerative abilities, so there was a probability that it was.

But if Dyna knew he could slay the demon, she might give up her mission to Mount Ida, and that could not happen. He needed to know if—

Cassiel looked down at his mother's ring and tucked it within his shirt. He needed to reach the island, at any consequence. Besides, why get involved? People weren't made to help each other. It was everyone for themselves. Her secluded village kept her sheltered and naïve. She had no idea how cruel life was. A part of him—a small part not tarnished by pessimism—wanted to slay her demon so she could continue living that way.

Dyna's soul was the last bit of good left. Not that he would admit he liked the colors of its electrical storm. Her soul was uncorrupted, not yet tainted by greed, lust, or even wrath. She was angry, but as much as the demon took from her, her soul wasn't dark with hatred. Though she attempted to hide her sadness under smiles, it hovered on the surface.

What happened the night the Shadow came to her village? They spoke of her father opening the Netherworld Gate, and that surely had killed him, if not the demon. The Seven Gates contain a power that mere mortals cannot touch and expect to survive. And now Dyna searched for another method to fight the Shadow; one that would most likely claim her life as well.

Cassiel sighed and leaned his head back against the tree, tucking the journal under his crossed arms. His eyes grew heavy as the sky lightened. Why was he contemplating this? The stupid human meant nothing to him. He only had one priority.

Reaching Mount Ida.

Morning light filtered in through Cassiel's eyelids. He realized too late he had fallen asleep and left himself defenseless when he sensed Zev looming over him. The camp was quiet. Too quiet.

They were alone.

Forcing himself to keep calm, Cassiel listened for Zev's movements. Slowly, he tightened his grip on the hilt of the silver knife hidden under his crossed arms. A heavy hand fell on his shoulder and Cassiel lashed out, feeling the blade connect with flesh. Zev's startled roar filled the camp. He was in his human form, staggering back, and clutching his bleeding arm to his chest.

His eyes flashed yellow, and he gasped in pain through clenched teeth. Stumbling, Zev dropped to his knees as his complexion quickly turned ashen. His veins blackened beneath his skin and coursed up his forearm like a web, spreading across his shoulder to his neck.

Cassiel rose to his feet, surprised the silver had been immediately debilitating. He hardly cut him. "I warned you."

"I was not going to hurt you," Zev rasped, a sheen of sweat sprouting on his face. Dark blood oozed from his wound.

"No, I suppose now you will not."

Dyna came running through the trees with haphazard clothes and hair dripping wet. She must have been bathing in the nearby stream. "What happened? I heard a shout." She gasped at the sight of Zev's bubbling wound, and her wide eyes flitted from him to Cassiel's knife. "What have you done!"

She snatched a small ceramic vial from her satchel, popped off the cork, and yanked Zev's head back to pour the murky purple liquid down his throat.

Zev heaved and coughed, clutching his stomach as he convulsed on the ground. Dyna patted his back, murmuring soothing words while he vomited. His forearm became so rigid it turned white as more black sludge was dispelled from the wound.

Once Zev stopped convulsing, she stood and spun to Cassiel. "You almost killed him!"

Cassiel looked away, his face growing hot. "It was not without cause."

"What cause?" she hissed.

"The mongrel attacked me."

Zev snarled at him, baring his teeth.

"Oh, have I offended you?"

"You have no right to bloody criticize me, *Nephilim*."

Fury blazed through Cassiel, and he pointed the knife at Zev. "Speak that word again, and I will cut out your tongue."

Zev growled, "You will receive respect when you give it. If you don't wish to be called that, you'll not refer to me as anything other than a werewolf."

"Call yourself what you will. Silver still burns you."

The were-beast staggered to his feet, his expression murderous. Cassiel beckoned him forward with the knife.

"Enough!" Dyna jumped between them. She pushed on Zev's heaving chest, failing to hold him back even in his weakened state. Her shoes dragged through the mud as he advanced. "Stop it, Zev. Stop! If you fight him, you will hurt me!"

He halted mid-step.

She shook her head. "Another cut will kill you. Please, don't do that to me."

Zev closed his bloodshot eyes and heaved a deep breath. He stalked away through the bushes, heading for the stream.

Dyna remained facing the direction he went. "I had sent him to wake you, Prince Cassiel. You slept through the morning and if we delayed any longer, we would not reach Landcaster today as you had demanded."

Cassiel shifted on his feet, taken aback by the anger simmering in her quiet tone.

"You will apologize to him."

He retorted. "Come again?"

She whirled around and fixed him with a furious glare. "You made a mistake. An apology is due."

"I do not owe him one. I was defending myself." Cassiel's scowl faltered at the disgust rising to her face.

"I'll not have you threaten Zev with that knife any longer. If we are to continue traveling together, you will get rid of it here and now."

He seethed, jaw clenching. How dare she make demands of him? "I will not be ridding myself of anything."

Dyna released a long exhale and held out her hand. "Then this is where we part. Now, hand over my journal. Please."

He stared at her in disbelief. "You do not realize how dangerous he is."

"The only danger I see here is you." Dyna wore an expression that left no room for arguing.

Cassiel never imagined that he would bend to the will of a human, but as her eyes bore into his, he retrieved the journal and placed it in her palm. She turned on her heel and went in the direction Zev had gone. With each step she took, Mount Ida slipped further and further away.

"Wait," Cassiel called faintly. Nothing, absolutely nothing, could take precedence over his goal. It was worth defying his father, and it was certainly worth this. He swallowed his pride, and it settled bitterly in his stomach. The knife glinted as he held it out to her, hilt first.

If that surprised Dyna, she didn't show it. "Thank you," she said softly.

Her fingers wrapped around the hilt, brushing against his. It left a tingle on his skin, but he didn't receive a glimpse of her soul. She had closed herself off from him. Dyna retreated, slipping into the bushes out of view.

Grumbling, Cassiel packed up his belongings and rammed them in his pack. That look she wore plagued his mind. He didn't understand why it bothered him. He only knew that her disgust had nothing to do with his lineage.

She had not believed for a single moment that Zev had attacked him.

Well, did he?

As soon as Zev had touched him, Cassiel's reaction was to strike first. He groaned and kneaded the knots in his stiff neck. Had he made a mistake? In any case, Dyna thought the worst of him.

He hiked his pack over his shoulder and looked around the empty camp. They had already packed their belongings. Only the dead campfire was left and a small puddle of a congealed substance. Zev's blood had reacted to the silver, turning black as it had clotted. That would kill anyone.

If Cassiel was being honest, that had not been his intention. He only meant to hurt Zev enough to make him back off, but now he may have made things worse. Dyna had her journal and hadn't specifically said he could remain with them.

If she left him behind, Cassiel supposed he deserved it.

CHAPTER 19

Zev

To keep his mind off the pain, Zev listened to the burble of water and the trill of birds chirping in the surrounding birch trees. He laid by the bank of the stream while Dyna worked on washing out his wound.

If the knife had only touched him, it wouldn't have had such an effect. But the edge of the blade had sliced through his skin, seeping silver into his bloodstream. The poison had blazed through his veins as if he'd dipped his entire arm in flames from his fingertips to his elbow.

How far would the pain have taken him if Dyna hadn't forced another poison down his throat? Swallowing wolfsbane was like swallowing liquid fire, searing his stomach from the inside. Thankfully, most of the burning agony subsided after he spewed.

"Uncle Belzev told me to always carry wolfsbane extract with me in case I needed to restrain your wolf." Dyna placed his injured arm next to him and dried it off with the hem of her dress, careful to avoid the wound. "I also thought if I could put your wolf to sleep, the silver poisoning would have less of an effect."

Zev had struggled with controlling his wolf after his first full moon shift at thirteen, and his father tried to treat its aggression with the poisonous plant.

That worked—until it hadn't.

Zev closed his eyes against the glare of the sun and laid his other arm over his face. He didn't need to search inside of himself to know his wolf was gone. It had fallen dormant from the wolfsbane.

"Forgive me. It was the only thing I thought of at the moment," she murmured. "Uncle Belzev had a theory that its toxic properties would overtake another poison in the bloodstream and push it out of the system. I think he was right."

"You did well," Zev croaked. His stomach ached and the rhythm of his heart was too slow for his kind, but the burning had reduced to only his arm now. Had his father not built his tolerance to poisonous plants against werewolves, the extract might have done more harm than good.

Dyna rifled through her satchel and took out a sprig. "Eat these. They will treat your stomach."

Zev chewed on the sweet leaves as she applied a topical salve to his wound. He winced when she touched the swollen ridges, but soon the wound cooled and the pain lessened further. By tomorrow, it would scar, although it would always be tender, as were most scars on his body. Wounds caused by silver never fully healed.

"There, I think that should do it. Has the burning ceased?"

"Aye, thank you."

Dyna sat with her knees propped up and looked out at the stream. The water lapped up the bog, reaching for the tips of her leather slippers. Azeran's journal and the knife lay in the grass beside her. He didn't need acute hearing to catch her conversation with Cassiel. She had been shouting, unusual for her gentle manner.

Zev sat up at the sound of distant rustling behind them. Cassiel was quiet, but his scent had given him away. He didn't come forward though. The prince briefly paused behind the dense wall of shrubs, then turned away as if he had only come to check on their location.

"What is a Nephilim?" Dyna asked, unaware of his presence.

Zev surreptitiously glanced at the prince's still back through the foliage where he had halted in mid retreat. "I should not have called him that, Dyna. I misspoke in my anger. It's an awful word."

It wasn't his place to explain further, and he sensed Cassiel's unease. As much as the prince held to his air of superiority, he cared what she thought of him.

"He's different, isn't he?"

"He certainly is," Zev smirked. It was a jab at Cassiel's temperament, but he knew what Dyna was referring to. Though, she would never use the word half-breed.

Dyna picked up a stray stick and used it to draw shapes in the mud. "Prince Cassiel does not trust us, but I believe it's more than that. He does not trust anyone. How could he? His family …"

"What about them?"

"I was also present at the king's table, Zev."

He had not forgotten. The repulsed expression Queen Mirah wore when she looked at Cassiel reminded Zev of the way his mother used to look at him.

"Prince Malakel said horrible things," Dyna huffed. "I had half a mind to throw a fig at his pretentious face."

Zev chuckled, imagining the eldest prince's reaction if she had dared to do such a thing. "That would have been the last day we drew breath."

She laughed. "Thank the God of Urn I didn't."

Letting his chuckles fade away, Zev sighed again. Cassiel was listening, so he may as well air his doubts.

"The question is, can we trust him?" Zev asked. "He purposely came armed against me. Why join us if he felt unsafe? He's not here to accompany you across Urn, Dyna. The prince came for your map. I've seen the way he stares at it all hours of the night. If it were not sired to your Essence, he might have taken it for himself. Mount Ida is a place that instills ambition and greed in all who hear its story. We can't assume he'll be any different."

Cassiel held quiet. It had to mean there was some truth to what Zev said.

Dyna drew the rune for humankind in the mud. One straight line and a half-circle crossing upward at the top. It looked like a lone man holding up the world or pleading to it. "People are similar to plants. Neglect will cause them to wither, but with proper care, they will flourish. Prince Cassiel is only in need of a bit of sun and water."

Zev smiled at the analogy. "I take it this means you will allow him to continue traveling with us?"

She stood and picked up the knife, tapping a finger against its pointed end. "Life is a risk, and he risked his life several times for my sake. I'm indebted to him, but I won't put that ahead of your wellbeing, Zev. Whether he is to accompany us, I'll leave that decision to you."

She pitched the knife. It sailed far through the air, further than he had thought she was capable of, before plunging into the deep end of the stream.

Zev rose to his feet and stretched his arms backward, feeling some of his strength returning. It had been a few days since he stood on two feet. His mind was clearer now than when he was a wolf.

"He has reason to think ill of me, but I cannot blame him for it," he said. The prince had seen what he'd done to the Lykos Pack. That would frighten anyone.

Dyna glanced at him, catching the nuance he failed to hide behind his words. Zev couldn't bring himself to confess what he had done. Wolves were predators. She must have known he had to kill to make it out of the glade alive, but she didn't know how far he had gone. As aggravating as Cassiel was, he hadn't told Dyna about what had occurred in the glade, and for that, Zev was grateful.

"We are going on a journey that will take us further than either of us has gone before. I suppose it will take all of us to make it to Mount Ida alive. If he can learn to trust us."

Dyna's responding smile lit up her face and the sunlight danced on her freckles. "Trust is hard to come by. Perhaps we must put effort into earning his."

"Aye." Zev smiled, sensing she was glad. She wanted to give the prince a chance, as she had given him one when no other would. "Shall we go back?"

She picked up the journal and shouldered her satchel while he gathered their packs. The shrubs were clear by the time they passed through them.

"What is the difference between a Seraph and a Celestial?" Dyna asked, ducking past a stray branch.

"A Seraph has six wings, and a Celestial has two," Zev explained as they cleared the forest and entered the small clearing where they had camped.

"It is more than that," the stoic prince said where he leaned up against a tree, his arms and legs crossed. The afternoon sunlight gleamed on his ink-black feathers as he gazed at the sky. "Our ancestors were Seraphim, but *Elyōn* removed four of their wings before they fell here, taking most of their power and their immortality. In Heaven's Gate, there is no marriage, nor the need for procreation. Whence the Forsaken were cast here, they were given the means to form Blood Bonds and have families. However, the children born unto them were not born of the grace of *Elyōn*. They only developed two wings; therefore, they were not Seraphim. They were given the name of Celestials, for they were still descendants of the Heavens even if they were not worthy of it."

Cassiel sighed and brushed his black hair out of his eyes to meet Dyna's. "The difference is simple. I am not from Heaven's Gate. I was born in the Mortal Realm, as were you."

She fixed him with a soft look. "Nonetheless, I would not say you were unworthy of it."

He flushed and looked away with an odd expression Zev couldn't read.

"I understand your need to protect yourself, but you need not do so from us," she said. "Do you mean to harm me?"

He frowned. "No."

"Then believe me when I say that Zev is not a threat to you. I ask that you both get along, and for there not to be another repeat of today."

The prince rubbed his neck. "As you say."

"Thank you, Your Highness."

"You need not be so formal. My name will do fine."

"Cassiel," she said, drawing his eyes to her again. "If we should hurry, we may arrive at Landcaster by tomorrow morning." She turned to Zev excitedly. "And if the inns aren't full, we could stop for lodging."

Zev smiled, infected by her enthusiasm before he noticed the prince's obvious displeasure at the idea. At the sight of his large wings, he remembered why. "We can't. No one is to see him, Dyna."

"I will manage," Cassiel said.

Zev furrowed his brow. "How?"

"I have my ways."

"I will leave it among you both to discuss then," she said. "After you have apologized to each other."

Dyna spoke the passphrase to the journal before handing it to Zev and ambling north to the forest. He and Cassiel stared at each other, then at her in astonishment. When she fell out of sight, they quickly followed.

Zev couldn't think of a reason to apologize when he was the one who had been wounded. Neither he nor the prince offered one as they hiked through the forest after Dyna, and the moment passed, leaving the opportunity to do so behind.

They camped again for the evening near a small pond, lively with the croak of frogs and the fluttering of dragonflies. Once they had eaten and put out their bedrolls, Dyna fell asleep as soon as she lay down. Zev pulled a blanket over her shoulders and tucked it around her. The long days of travel had worn her out.

The prince lounged on a tree branch again, spinning his flute between his fingers. Without Dyna to hold the conversation, an uncomfortable silence dragged between them. Zev sighed. They would always be at odds if they didn't understand one another.

"I did what I had to do to protect Dyna," he said, keeping his voice low. Cassiel glanced at him from his peripherals, then to where she slept. "They planned to come after her. I couldn't let that happen, so I finished them all."

He had almost succumbed to the Madness after seeing what became of the Pack. The reminder to return to Dyna was all that had kept him sane. He had to shapeshift so he wouldn't have to think about it. His thought process and instincts were different as a wolf. But the scent of blood coating his fur stung his nose, no matter how many times he washed.

"You're right to call me a beast," Zev murmured. "For that is what I became to keep her safe."

The Other may have inadvertently protected her, but it was an entity that killed anything in its path. If she had been in the glade, it would have torn through her as well.

You're no wolf. You're a demon.

Something cold dropped in his stomach, twisting through him.

Cassiel's silhouette faded into the dark as night fell, his voice quiet in the cool breeze. "Will any more of the Lykos Pack come for you?"

Zev had patrolled the forest day and night since, but there were no tracks in the mud, no musk of prowling wolves. Would they come for him after seeing the carnage he had left behind?

"Perhaps not."

CHAPTER 20

Zev

The afternoon hike through the woods went without further incident. Zev glanced up at Dyna's humming where she walked ahead, picking leaves here and there. The sparse trees in this part of the forest allowed the prince to fly above them. Buttery sunlight formed patterns over the carpet of fallen leaves, clear blue-sky peeking through the treetops.

Again, they had squandered most of their morning sleeping. This time because of him, Zev thought. As he had yet to recover from yesterday's incident.

His wolf still slumbered somewhere deep within him. It was a strange feeling. Most of his senses had dulled from their usual amplified state and he was weaker, but for once there were no more whisperings. His mind was clearer and lighter—vacant without that extra presence he didn't miss. It would be a miracle if the Madness never returned, but he knew it would. All he could do was enjoy the time he had left without it.

Curious of how much farther they were from Landcaster, Zev opened the journal to the section of the map and studied their current location. Cassiel threw subtle glances down at the map, attempted to peek over his shoulder. Zev stopped and held it out.

After wary hesitation, the prince landed beside him and accepted the journal. His face glowed purple from the embedded magic as he examined the map.

Zev said, "I had always wondered if Mount Ida existed."

"Of course it exists," Cassiel replied evenly. There was a tentative pause before he added, "We should arrive in Landcaster soon. I know a tavern we can lodge in for the night."

"You have walked among humans before?"

"Only when necessary."

Zev stopped short. "But what of your wings? You could be discovered."

The prince smirked. "I have not been so far."

"And this is permitted for your kind? I can't imagine your father approving of that."

"I'm sure he would not."

Zev stared at him incredulously. "Does the High King know that you left Hilos to join us?"

He didn't reply.

"This journey may take many moons, Cassiel. We won't return until next year."

"I'm well aware. I have traveled between Hermon Ridge and Hilos several times. I know what I'm doing."

Zev let the matter go at the prince's defensive tone. From what he had seen, Cassiel shared no relationship with his family other than his royal lineage. He must spend his time traveling Urn alone, pretending he didn't care that he wasn't wanted. What was his reason to leave the protection of the castle this time?

"There's something on Mount Ida that you seek," Zev stated.

Cassiel's eyes, as hard as granite, narrowed. "It has nothing to do with you."

Zev supposed he was right. "What's in Hermon Ridge? I haven't traveled past Landcaster."

The prince dithered on the answer, giving him a sidelong glance. "Another Celestial Realm is hidden there within the mountains. It is under my uncle's rule."

"Oh, I didn't know." The location of the Four Realms was not readily shared.

Cassiel passed him the journal. "No one is to know."

Zev found the Hermon Mountains on the map. They rose on the north end of Azure, about nine-hundred-miles from Hilos. Now that he looked at it, the Azure Kingdom was only a fragment of the country. The rest was unfamiliar to either of them.

"After we leave Urn's Chip, we will travel blind," Zev said. Following a map was not the same as accurately knowing your surroundings based on experience. There was no telling which road was safest or quickest.

"We should use the services of a Guidelander," came Dyna's distant declaration. She was nowhere in sight.

"Dyna?" Zev called, wildly searching their surroundings.

"I'm up here." They followed the sound of her voice to the tree beside them that she had climbed when neither of them had been paying attention. She stood on the tallest branch, looking out past the leaves. "Zev, you must see this. The view is incredible."

"God of Urn."

"What are you doing?" Cassiel asked dully. "Are you attempting to break your neck? Because this is how you break your neck."

"Get down from there." Zev rushed to the tree, holding out his hands to catch her, but Dyna laughed and started climbing down. "Be careful."

"We aren't far from Landcaster," she said as she reached for another branch. "We are less than a mile away."

"You did not need to climb a tree to know that," Cassiel replied. "Now watch your footing."

"I climbed to the top, didn't I? I can manage to climb dow—" Her foot broke through a brittle branch and Zev cried out when she fell, but Cassiel launched into the air in a bustle of wings, catching her with a grunt. "Oh …" She blinked at him. "Thank you."

"Are you all right?" he asked tersely.

Dyna gave him a small nod.

Cassiel landed and thrust her into Zev's arms. He strode away, muttering under his breath, "She is a living calamity, that one. It is no wonder humans do not live long."

Dyna's blush reddened under Zev's frown as he set her down. He sighed, rubbing the center of his chest. "I'm sure I lost a few years."

"I'll give you some of mine," she said sheepishly as they continued. "As I was saying, we should employ a Guidelander to guide us. It's their livelihood to know all there is to know of Urn and the surrounding continents. We can find one in Landcaster."

Cassiel shot her a glower over his shoulder. He opened his mouth, probably to call her "stupid" again, but he gave Zev a pointed look instead.

Not that Dyna was stupid. She was simply unaware. She had lived in a secluded village that was, for the most part, safe. Other than the Shadow, she hadn't been under any other danger and she had grown up with people she had known her entire life. The villagers helped one another, but that couldn't be said for the rest of Urn where most stole and scrounged to survive. Revealing their map to the treasure island would attract Relic Hunters, thieves, and cutthroats, who wouldn't hesitate to take it.

"Look, there it is," she announced.

They came to the end of the forest and it opened to a vast meadow with tall grass rippling in the wind. Beyond were endless rows of crops and fallow fields. Large timber houses and farms spread out among the valley speckled with sheep. A group of foremen on horses led a large herd of cows down the hills, and below the rise appeared Landcaster. It wasn't a large town, but it was full of activity with travelers coming and going on wagons and caravans, taking the dirt roads snaking into the horizon.

Dyna bounced on her toes. "Come, let's find a guide!"

"Hold a moment," Zev said, but she was already rushing down the meadow.

The prince rolled his eyes to the sky as though to ask for mercy from the Heavens. "Go. I will meet you in the market."

Cassiel pulled out a long dark gray coat from his pack. He slipped it on, and his wings immediately disappeared. The coat settled on him like he had none at all.

Zev gawked a moment, not sure what he was looking at. There would be time to ask about it later. He had to go after Dyna. He jogged down the hill and spotted her where she had stopped by the trodden and mired road as a yellow caravan jostled by.

"Dyna, you need to wait for me," he said.

"I did. Where's Cassiel?"

"He'll catch up to us."

They joined the travelers on the road, their steps squelching in the thick mud. The road eventually progressed into cobblestone as they neared the town. The name *Landcaster* was engraved on a large wooden sign by the entrance.

Zev led Dyna past it and they merged into the swarm of people going about their business. The quaint wattle and daub homes with timber frames and steep red-tiled roofs clustered together, lining the streets. Most had overhang second stories, their stone bases adorned with climbing vines and flower gardens.

They came to a commerce section where several of the streets met, circling a stone monument carved in the effigy of an unknown nobleman. Townsfolk swarmed the surrounding shops of clothing and goods. Wagons rattled as they rolled over the uneven cobblestone, paired with the clomp of horse hooves. Children ran past, laughing and playing in the fountain's water.

"Come, Zev." Dyna pulled him eagerly toward the crowded market, beaming with awe.

He chuckled as she flitted from stall to stall, seeing all that she could. They sold everything from grains to spices. Zev took a seat on a nearby bench and let her explore. He remembered how excited he had been when his father first brought him to town.

The memory made him sigh. The town had changed since then. More homes had been built, more businesses had been established, and the population had grown judging by the sight of so many people passing through.

Zev wondered if there were more blacksmiths in town as well. He glanced at the smithy street beside the market, contemplating whether to make a stop to see Ragan. He had not seen the old blacksmith in nearly six months, and it was time to reinforce his chains again. Dyna was well into a conversation with an herbalist, so Zev decided to make a quick errand about it.

He strolled through the street lined in forges, listening to the steady beat of hammers and inhaling the iron-tasting smoke. The stifling heat of the fires pressed against him. Many townsfolk were about making requests or picking up orders.

Zev reached a familiar forge. The old blacksmith there wore a rag around his head, his clothing stained with soot. He used a pair of long tongs to pull out a molten piece of metal from the hearth, and it hissed when he dipped it in a well of water to cool.

"Ragan," Zev called out.

The old blacksmith turned and gave him a broad smile. "Ah, I wondered when you would come about, lad."

"You look well, sir."

Ragan wiped his weathered face with a rag and looked out at the busy street with a frown. "As well as I can be. Business is scarce now that the town has more smithies than available labor, but I can't complain."

"Well, might you have time to tend to my chains today? I'm going on a journey and need them to be secure."

"Aye, I haven't much work. I'll see to them."

Zev took out the cold mound of chains from his pack and they clanked heavily on the service counter. When he pulled out a small pouch of money, Ragan waved him away, looking mildly offended.

"How many times do I have to tell you? Put your coin away. I owe your father a great debt for saving my daughter from the fever. I pay him back by tending to his son now."

Zev bowed his head in gratitude. "Thank you."

"Aye, come back for them tonight."

Zev waited for Ragan to turn before he slipped the money in the blacksmith's pocket and left before it was noticed. He returned to the market in a good mood, but when he reached the herbalist stall, that vanished when he found Dyna was gone.

"Madam," he called to the old woman. "Where has my cousin gone? You spoke to her. Red-haired lass."

The hunched herbalist balked and leaned her head back to look up at him. Her white brows rose high on her forehead. "I—I am not sure, sir. Pardon."

Zev quickly made his way through the crowd, sniffing the air. He caught Dyna's scent and followed it to a small bridge set over a waterway that stank of something terrible. He couldn't breathe without gagging. By the potency of her scent on the balustrade, she had lingered here for a moment. Possibly too lost to find her way back to him.

Endless smells and sounds assaulted Zev's senses, making his head spin. It would be impossible to locate her exact trail without shifting, but his wolf hadn't surfaced yet. He groaned in frustration and hurried through the town square, going off instinct now. The evening was approaching and he prayed he found her before trouble found her first.

Zev inhaled a deep breath, trying to remain calm. By some luck, he caught her scent again. He pursued it, shoving through a passing crowd, and came behind two men walking briskly onward—one in a black leather coat, and his companion in a black hooded cloak. Dyna's scent lingered on them, so they must have encountered her.

As he neared, the hooded man spun around and whipped out a dagger, bringing it under Zev's chin. "Whoa." Zev held up his hands in surrender, preferring not to be stabbed a second time.

The stranger's hood slipped off with the wind, revealing his cropped, dark brown hair and hard face flanked by pointed ears. The elf's brows set low over his amber eyes, which were fixed with disinterest. The confrontation was merely a lazy warning, but Zev had no doubts about how quick his throat could be slit. Elves were a nimble sort, and lethal. The crossguard of the knife gilded in red metal gleamed in the sunlight. On the back of the elf's hand was a perfectly round scar, as if he'd been branded.

The elf's companion in the leather coat half turned, scowling in annoyance. He was human. Tall with chestnut hair slicked back from his face, a strong jaw layered in enough stubble to be considered a short beard. The man was dressed in all black, down to his boots. A series of brass buttons adorned the lapels of his coat, exposing the many knives sheathed on the crossed bandolier strapped to his chest. He noticed Zev looking and adjusted his coat to hide them.

"You're too old to be a pickpocket," he said with the brogue Azure accent of the north, his sea-green glare as sharp as the knife held at Zev's throat. "How unfortunate that you've chosen the wrong man to thieve from."

CHAPTER 21

Von

God of Urn, Von didn't have time for this. The bedraggled young man standing before him looked like he'd rolled out of a cave and smelled like he lived in one too. By the torn clothing, anyone would have guessed him a beggar, but he wasn't starving. He was robust with unsightly scars and a wildness about him that made Von wary.

"Pardon me, sir, that wasn't my intention," the young man said, the edges of his canines flashing into view when he spoke. So not human, then. "My name is Zev, and I'm searching for my cousin. I believe she came this way. She has red hair, about yea high." He motioned to his lower chest to show her height.

Von studied him a moment longer before deciding his worry seemed genuine enough and signaled Elon to stand down. "Aye, I met the lass. She stumbled into me before she meandered on yonder." He motioned in a general direction toward the market.

"Thank you," Zev said profusely, then ran off and slipped into the crowd.

How did he know they had contact with her?

"Wolf," Elon supplied as he tucked his dagger away.

"Aye?" Von arched an eyebrow at his impassive companion.

Elon rarely spoke, so when he did, it was only with good reason. The elf lifted his hood over his head again, giving Von a glimpse of the scar on the back of his hand where his Red Highland tattoo used to be.

"How do you figure?" Von asked.

"Sensed it, Commander," Elon said in his idle tone. "Shifter magic."

"Hmm."

The lass they had bumped into didn't appear to be of any relation to a werewolf. She had an endearing smile that reminded him of Yavi. The thought of returning to her had Von picking up his pace again.

"The young lady strayed that way." Elon motioned in the opposite direction Von had sent Zev.

"Oh." He hadn't paid attention to her after she begged her pardon and scurried off. His mind had been on his purpose in this town. "If he's a werewolf, he'll find her on his own soon enough."

They crossed the town's length to a narrow street that smelled of stale urine and sickly-sweet ale gone rancid. The cobblestone was slick, though it hadn't rained in days. Von curled his nose and avoided walking through any unidentifiable puddles. The timber buildings compacted close together, making the shaded street feel isolated. Muffled voices and music leaked through dark-stained windows and doors left cracked open.

Each entrance had carved wooden signs hanging from corroded chains with the names of their pubs. Von checked each one, looking for the sign that read *Big Valley*. He found it with the last pub that sat parallel to the main road leading out of town. Within the alley between the pub and another were two lads sitting on barrels waiting for him.

The lad, with messy copper hair the same color as his jovial eyes, jumped to his feet, bearing a wide grin. Geon stood proudly in his all-black uniform. It was inconspicuous enough with simple trousers and a leather coat, no livery or emblem as intended. At fifteen-summers-old, he was the youngest Raider recruited. "Commander Von, Captain Elon. You made it," Geon said.

"Why wouldn't he? You sent for him," said the other lad in his smug Magos accent.

The young mage was only a year older than Geon, but carried himself with an arrogance not fit for a slave. Dalton flicked his brown hair out of his dark eyes and stood, resting his staff across his shoulders. On one end of the staff was a jagged, orange crystal, encased in an intricate weaving of carved wood. Brass bangles at his ankles—a clear representation of slavery—glinted beneath his umber robes as he moved.

Von crossed his arms. "The only one who summons me is the master. The Raider you sent back to the camp said you've found a Sacred Scroll. That is why I've come." Otherwise, he wouldn't have risked showing himself in public. There were too many Rangers in these parts, and any of them would gladly turn him in to the Azure Guard. "Where is it?"

Geon gave him a sheepish smile. "Ah, well, we don't have it yet. We met a merchant who told us he had one for sale. He's waiting inside."

"He's here?"

"Aye, in the taproom."

"He's a portly clod in posh garb," Dalton added. "You can't miss him."

"Did you see the scroll?"

Geon winced. "No, Commander."

Von exchanged a look with Elon and gritted his teeth. "Then how did he know to approach you?"

The lad chuckled awkwardly, scratching at his cheek. "Well, funny thing, that ..."

Dalton snickered and poked Geon's head with the end of his staff. "This little twat was bragging about being a Raider. Tossing back ale and jarring about in the pub, acting a bloody fool."

Geon flushed, knocking the staff away. "Bollocks. I was not!"

"I was there, you pillock."

"Piss off!"

Von grabbed Geon's coat and growled in his face, "I should toss you back onto the streets where I found you, lad. If only to save your life. The master would have you killed if he learns of this. No one must know he's in Azure. Being his Raider isn't for pride. It's to serve him and him only, understand?"

Geon went pale. "Aye, Commander. It won't happen again."

Von released him and glared at Dalton's smirking face next. "And where were you when this was happening? Sitting back and enjoying this folly?" The guilty mage avoided his hard gaze. "Brainless hellions the lot of you. Always gallivanting about getting into trouble. I should drag you coofs back to camp by your ears and have you whipped!"

The lads winced and dropped their heads.

Von took a deep breath to ease his irritation. This was most likely a trap, but the chance that he may find another Sacred Scroll was too much to ignore.

"Elon and I will meet the merchant. If this is an ambush, you know what to do."

"Aye, Commander," they replied.

Von nodded to Dalton. "Are you carrying?"

"Always." The mage reached into his robes and pulled out a canvas bundle. He unrolled it and laid it out on a barrel. Several rows of small glass vials were strapped inside. Each contained a different colored elixir or shimmering powder. He picked a vial with iridescent pearls inside and held it out. "Father says these are potent. Each will last you for an hour."

Von snatched the vial. "I'm aware of how truth spells work."

For mages, spells were as easy as waving their hand, but humans relied on potions when in need of magic. He popped the cork and tossed a pearl into his mouth. It quickly dissolved on his tongue, tasting bitter, as was any truth hard to swallow. A tingle spread throughout the inside of his mouth to his lips and down his throat.

For an hour, it would give him the power of extracting information from anyone he spoke to, compelling them to tell him the truth whenever he asked a question. Those weak of mind would be completely unaware of it.

"Both of you wait outside the pub where I can see you," Von commanded, eyeing them sternly. "Keep to yourselves. Don't speak to anyone else."

The lads nodded and moved to stand by the pub's grimy windows. Von and Elon went inside. The taproom was packed with people, the lively music blending in with the chorus of voices. A haze of smoke hung in the air, smelling of sweat and cooking meat. Most of the patrons congregated at the bar. They jeered at the women serving them food and drink as the barkeep collected their coin.

A barmaid, with her fleshy bosom pushed up on display, simpered to them. She balanced a tray of tankards, their frothy contents spilling over the rims. "Take a seat anywhere you fancy. I'll come to service you in a bit." She winked and moved on to serve the drinks.

There were no empty tables available. While searching for the merchant among the faces, Von spotted someone in a dark corner of the room watching them. The lone stranger sat still under the shadow of a tattered cloak the color of the woods. The hood hid most of his face, except for his mouth and loose locks of long blond hair. Elon noticed him too, and while his demeanor didn't change, Von sensed his caution increase.

"Green Elf," Elon informed him.

The stranger wore no livery to prove he was of the Greenwood Kingdom, but Von took his word for it. Whether it meant trouble, Elon didn't say, which meant he hadn't decided yet. The captain was a Red Elf, once in service of the Red Highland Kingdom before he was exiled. Though Elon appeared young, Von guessed he was well over a century old, so there was no telling how long ago that was.

More often than not, the meeting between a Red Elf and Green Elf ended in bloodshed. The fragile peace between the two kingdoms within the Vale of the Elves hung on a thin line of twine, waiting to be snipped. But the Green Elf looked away and continued sipping his drink, apparently uninterested in confrontation.

Von resumed searching for the merchant and met the inquiring gaze of a man in a brocade vest with the buttons straining over his belly. He sat alone in the opposite corner at the back of the room.

"Mind the door," Von told Elon, then weaved his way through the crowd to the table. He pulled out a chair and sat across from the plump man.

"Oh, good. I feared no one would come." The man smiled uneasily as he wiped the sweat from his greasy head, his red scalp shining under the lanterns hanging from the exposed rafters.

"I take it you're the merchant?" Von asked, activating the truth spell, and the man shivered as the magic worked through him.

"Yes." There was no shift in his expression, a good sign he wasn't privy to the spell. "My name is—"

"No names." Von leaned forward, keeping his voice low. "Do you have it?"

"Yes." The merchant reached behind his chair and Von tensed, arming himself with a knife beneath the table. The man brought out a cylindrical case about two feet long made of dark leather. A cap sealed it and attached to both ends was a loose strap made for carrying. He set the case on top of the table, keeping a meaty hand on it. "I have it here."

"Why did you approach the lads?"

"They mentioned their master's name. I heard among the traders he is buying every Sacred Scroll he can find, and I happen to have one for sale."

Von worked his jaw. He was leaving behind too many witnesses for a word of that to have gotten out. He eyed the man, scrutinizing his face for any signs of deception. "Is this a trap?"

"No," the merchant answered without hesitation.

Von nodded and leaned back in his chair. "Where did you find the scroll?"

"In Yamshal. Some decrepit old village in the outskirts of the Mirage Desert. It had belonged to a destitute woman."

"Had?"

"I took it."

"You stole it." Not that Von was one to judge the morality of people. "Why?"

The merchant shrugged. "I have fallen into deep arrears with gambling and spending too much of my time in houses of ill-repute. I need to right myself with the banks, or they'll seize what remains of my assets."

"And what of the woman?"

"She was on her deathbed. The scroll would be of no use to her."

"Did she have a family?"

"Yes."

"And what became of them?"

"I didn't stay to find out."

Von smirked, his lip curling in disgust. "You're the dark end of an arse, aren't you?"

The merchant grinned like it was a compliment. "I care nothing for integrity. I only care about maintaining my wealth."

It was said with such callous arrogance, the truth spell might not have been needed at all.

"The value of Sacred Scrolls is akin to gold," the merchant went on to say, "and I know Tarn has quite a bit of that."

Von stabbed the table with his knife, snarling at him. "Hold your tongue."

The man cowed, shrinking into a lump. "Y—yes, your pardon."

A glance at those around them assured Von no one had heard his master's name spoken aloud. The racket in the room had been enough to drown out the merchant.

"Give it here." He snatched the case. "If I find that you have attempted to swindle me with a forged scroll, you'll no longer be alive to worry about old debts."

"It's real, I swear. I had it appraised myself."

"I'll be the judge of that."

The spell guaranteed he spoke the truth, but who's to say the appraiser didn't lie? The merchant could only give truths that he knew.

Making sure no one was watching, Von tugged on a pair of leather gloves he produced from his coat and removed the lid off the case. He overturned it on the table, and a rolled-up parchment slid out with trickles of sand. Gently, he unfurled the parchment, careful not to disturb the brittle edges. It was smooth, worn with time. Faded script of the ancient language spoken during the First Age filled the delicate weathered page. Von recognized it easily, as he had seen Yavi spend hours translating similar documents.

It was real. Master would be pleased.

Yavi once told him the Sacred Scrolls held several mysteries of the foundations of the world, like the keys to The Seven Gates and the quintessence of life.

How many still existed was unknown. Only that the scrolls were once kept in temples dedicated to the God of Urn all over the country before they were destroyed centuries ago. Von went on excursions across the world to find any that remained.

Two things the master desired above all else: to find the Sacred Scroll with the secret of the Unending, and the foretold Maiden that would lead him to where the Unending was kept.

Mount Ida.

Fortune telling, prophecies, or any divination of the sort was all nonsense to Von. He wouldn't—*couldn't*—put any value on the prophetic words they received from the famous Seer of Faery Hill. But his master believed in them, so they spent years searching for the Maiden. Von had better luck finding Sacred Scrolls. Though, none had the Unending.

This one probably wouldn't either.

He returned the scroll to its case. "I'll take it."

"Marvelous."

"Who else knows about this?"

The merchant leaned back in his chair, propping his linked hands over his belly. "I have a broker in Corron. He was to buy the scroll if our deal fell through."

Von made a mental note to look into this broker. He was not willing to risk others knowing of Tarn's whereabouts. "And how much are you expecting out of our deal?"

A slow, devious grin split the man's round cheeks. "Well, the bounty on your master's head is worth ten-thousand gold pieces. I think that sounds like a fair price, eh?"

The threat went unsaid, but the notion was clear.

Von smiled a tight smile. "See my companion over there?" He shifted in his chair sideways and nodded toward Elon, who watched them under his shadowed hood. Von signaled him over. "He will see that you receive your dues."

"Brilliant." The merchant bumbled to his feet as Elon approached.

"He is to be well paid," Von told him.

The elf nodded once. Von knew he had heard their hushed conversation in the bustling room. Elves had an acute sense of hearing, which made him an excellent spy.

"It was a pleasure. Good day," the merchant said. He followed Elon to a back door exiting into the alleyway behind the pub.

Von sighed and jerked his knife free from the table, tucking it away. They couldn't risk letting the merchant live at the chance of exposing Tarn's presence in Azure. Elon was a swift executioner; the man wouldn't suffer.

The barmaid returned and placed a mug in front of him. "Here you go, handsome. I thought you might need that." She preened and swept her dark locks over a bare shoulder, with an invitation that wasn't so subtle. "You're looking a tad knackered. We have rooms upstairs should you need a place to gather your bearings."

Von propped his feet up on the table, crossing them at the ankles. He flipped a single russet in the air and it landed with a clatter on her tray. Stamped on the copper coin was the sigil of Azure, an interwoven seven-pointed star. "For the drink. Nothing more."

The barmaid huffed and headed for another table with more willing men.

Von sipped the spiced ale, finding it wasn't bad, certainly better than the swig they had at camp. Past the rim of his mug, he noticed the Green Elf watching him again.

It was uncommon to see their kind in Urn's Chip for the Vale of the Elves lay to the west across the Saxe Sea. Most of the elves wandering about Azure were exiled soldiers looking to put their unparalleled skills to work like Elon. They either served as spies or sentinels for wealthy lords or bounty hunters for the Azure Kingdom. Therefore, any attention from this one couldn't be a good sign.

The elf's gaze shifted to the new arrival who had walked in the front door. It was the lass Von had met in the town square—the one the werewolf searched for. She looked around the taproom anxiously, but also with a bit of curiosity.

The patrons immediately noticed her. She had a soft and pretty face, but her dress was dirty and the sleeves were torn. Mud caked the hem of her petticoat, and what seemed like old blood stains spotted her skirts. The din in the room quieted as all eyes followed her approach to the bar.

She addressed the barkeep, her light voice sounding clear through the hushed room. "Good evening, sir. I wonder if you could help me. I got turned around in the market and I'm searching for—"

A lascivious grin spread on the old barkeep's face. "Unless you're searching to serve my patrons, best be off with you, hen."

Her gaze circled the room at the leering men, her cheeks pinking. A man leaned over on his stool and pinched her thigh. She jumped backward only to bump into another drunkard who pulled her into his lap. The lass squealed in horror and rushed outside as the room burst into uproarious laughter.

Von smirked to himself and finished the last of his drink. She mustn't be from around here. The lass lingered outside the windows, looking about her uncertainty like she wasn't sure what to do. Geon and Dalton ogled her with coy grins. They deliberated only a second before making their approach. Von groaned in annoyance. He had told those two idiots not to speak to anyone.

Dalton dipped in a flourishing bow before the lass, most likely giving her the flamboyant introduction he always used to impress girls. *"I am Dalton of House Slater, a mage of the Earth Guild."*

But instead of interest, she blanched. The lass gave a quick answer and bobbed in a quick curtsey before attempting to leave. Dalton blocked her way with his staff. He snapped his fingers and produced a lily in a show of glittering magic, offering it to her. She shook her head, backing away.

Dalton laughed as if she was merely being coy, but as soon as he grabbed her arm, his amusement melted into shocked anger. He yelled something indiscernible and the girl screamed back. Geon tried to pull them apart, but the mage hit him with a blast of orange Essence that tossed him out of sight.

Von jolted to his feet. Careful not to draw attention to himself, he hung the strap of the cylindrical case from his shoulder and quickly made his way to the door. The Green Elf who'd also been watching the occurrence through his window did the same. Von feigned accidentally knocking into him, nearly throwing him against the wall.

"Oh, begging your pardon," he said with measured politeness as he helped steady the elf. "I was in a hurry to beat some sense into my brothers. They see a pretty girl and forget to mind themselves."

Unusual turquoise eyes looked out from beneath the elf's hood. Lantern light caught on the luxurious sword strapped to his hip. On the pommel was the sigil of Greenwood, a *Dynalya* flower in full bloom. The elf nodded stiffly and moved aside, allowing him to pass. Making sure he wouldn't follow, Von left the pub blather for the shrill outside.

"Let go of me!" the girl shrieked, pulling against Dalton.

Geon groaned from where he'd fallen on the ground. "Stop it, Dal, you're hurting her."

Dalton jerked the lass back and forth by her arm. "How did you escape? You're of the Sun Guild, aren't you? To which House do you belong?"

She shook her head. "Unhand me! I'm not of the Magos Empire!"

"Liar! I'm taking you back where you belong!"

"Dalton," Von barked. "What are you doing?"

Geon scrambled to his feet, his smoking hair sticking up at all ends. "He's off his wits, Commander."

"She's a sorceress," Dalton sneered at her. "I sensed her Essence. She belongs in Magos, not roaming about free in Azure."

The lass lifted her chin. "I'm not a sorceress, and you'll not decide anything for me, mage. I was born free and I'll remain so."

With a swift kick to his shin, she broke his hold. Dalton yelped, hopping on one leg while holding the other. Von tried not to smile at her ferocious glare. She had mettle.

"Such drivel," Dalton snapped. "Under the Mage Code, a sorceress is never to step foot outside of Magos."

Von arched a brow. "Why?"

Dalton flushed and squirmed for his mistake. The Magos Empire liked to keep its secrets, but Von knew of their vile culture and the discrimination they had against their women. It appeared so did the dainty redhead.

"You're coming with me." Dalton reached for her again.

Von shoved him back. "Leave her, or I'll tan your hide."

"You have no right to interfere in this," he hissed. The young mage had never defied him before, yet as his eyes glowed with the crystal on his staff, malice crept across his face. "She belongs to us. She's ours."

Von backhanded Dalton so hard it knocked him down. The stunned mage gaped at him, holding his reddened cheek. It was the first time Von had struck him, but it was enough to snap him out of whatever had possessed him. "Get your arses back to camp," he growled.

Geon saluted meekly. "Aye, Commander."

Dalton shot a contemptuous look at the lass, as if he truly felt cheated out of something that should belong to him. It made Von want to smack him again. What rubbish was Magos feeding its people?

"Go on, then!" The lads scurried away. Once they were gone, Von turned to the girl. "So, we meet again, lass. Are you all right?"

She rubbed the welt on her forearm, giving him a tired smile. "Yes, thank you. I don't believe I was given your name last. Commander, they called you?"

"Aye, Von will do." He tipped his head in greeting.

"I'm Dyna," she said, giving him a curtsy. She didn't offer her family name as he had not offered his.

"A pleasure. I met a young man claiming to be your cousin, not shortly after in the square."

She groaned. "That was Zev. He must be worried. I tried to find him myself, but I should have stayed put."

Dyna looked out to the road to the few passing travelers leaving town. The setting sun stained the cobblestone a golden orange, leaving the pub street to darken.

"Aye, well, night will fall soon, and it is best you do not linger here," he told her. "This is not the sort of establishment for a respectable lady."

"Thank you for your kindness, sir, but I must wait here. Roaming about will only confuse Zev further. He'll find me."

Von nodded and turned to leave. "Well, have a good evening."

"Commander." Dyna chewed on her lip as she glanced at the darkening corners of the street and wrapped her arms around herself. "If I may impede you further, would you mind keeping me company while I wait? If it's not too much trouble."

Von glanced down the alley where Elon lurked. They should return to camp. He was a wanted man and risked recognition while in public.

"I should not have asked," she said at his hesitation. "Go on about your evening, if you please."

But he couldn't leave Dyna alone, especially outside a pub. Trouble could be found within the proximity of drunk men, and she already looked scared. If Yavi were here, she would expect him to keep the lass company.

"I'll wait with you." He pretended not to hear her heavy sigh of relief.

"Thank you."

"Think nothing of it. I'm at your service." Von settled against the moldy clapboards of the pub. "So, whereabouts are you from?"

Dyna shivered suddenly and immediately replied, "I'm from North Star, a remote village in the Zafiro Mountains."

Oh. He had forgotten the truth spell was still in effect. He had not intended to use it, but he was curious enough about the girl to want to know more about her.

"Is that so?" Von said. "I wasn't aware there was a village there."

"It's hidden." Dyna frowned and touched her lips, visibly worried about what she revealed. Before he could wonder more about that, she forced a smile. "Commander, I'm unfamiliar with this town. Do you perhaps know where I can inquire about a Guidelander?"

"I don't, sorry. Are you going on a journey?"

"Yes," she promptly answered.

"With only your cousin to accompany you?"

"And one other." The words came forcefully now against her will. Her confusion morphed to suspicion. Dyna was sharper than she looked, and would soon realize he had bespelled her.

Von continued before the ruse was up. "This is the first time you're traveling across Urn?"

"Yes."

"I see. Not a well-equipped plan then, is it?" He chuckled, rather enjoying this silly conversation. "Where are you going that you need a guide?"

"Mount Ida—" Dyna gasped and clapped a hand over her mouth, her eyes widening in dismay.

A jolt of shock went through Von as she stumbled backward to get away from him. He straightened with a dubious smile, for he was sure he hadn't heard right. "What was that, lass?"

She shook her head, stumbling out onto the road. The sunset stretched over her with unearthly grace. It illuminated her red locks like dancing flames in the wind, green eyes shining as bright gemstones.

The Seer's words whispered in his mind, *"Seek the Maiden with emeralds for sight and tresses of fire ..."*

Von stiffened as an icy chill sank through him.

This was it.

The moment he refused to believe was coming.

All the hope he had for the future vanished in his next breath. The world came down, and the floor crumbled beneath him, tossing him into a wretched sea of dread. It dragged him into its dark depths while everything he yearned for floated to the surface out of his reach.

This wasn't supposed to happen. The divination wasn't supposed to be real. It had to be a terrible jest by the fates, so Von did the only thing he could do in that incredulous moment.

He laughed.

CHAPTER 22

Von

on's crazed laughter resonated in the pub street. What else could he do but laugh? His world was slipping through his fingers, replaced with a reality he feared coming true. A strained smile etched on Dyna's face, hands fidgeting with the strap of her satchel. She took another step back, primed to run. If she did, Von debated if he would let her go. Another dark thought suggested he should kill her now.

How could such a small, sweet thing be the end to it all?

He snapped to attention at the sound of running footsteps drawing near, and the lass turned away at the call of her name. Von joined Elon, and they moved to the adjoining alleyway set behind the line of pubs, leading out to the main roads on either end. It reeked of rubbish, pish, and shite. A small rill in the ground carried sewage down the road where it would settle in the canal outside of town.

Von buttoned up his coat and covered his nose. He pressed against the end of the wall, careful not to make a sound as Elon loitered in the shadowy depths of the alleyway. Beside him, the merchant slumped against a stack of barrels, his neck twisted, vacant eyes staring at nothing.

The two male voices arguing with Dyna echoed in the empty alley.

"We have been searching all over this town for you, stupid human," a cool voice snapped.

"I-I'm sorry."

"Don't call her that, Cassiel," another voice chided. This one was familiar. The wolf named Zev. "Dyna, are you all right? Are you hurt?"

"No, but I ... made a mistake."

Von took out a knife and used the flat side as a mirror to see out onto the road. The image was warped and cloudy, but he recognized Zev's tall form as he ushered Dyna away from the pub entrance, moving in his direction. Another huddled close. Von ducked further behind a stack of broken crates, and Elon retreated into the adjacent alley.

Dyna's companions stopped short of the alleyway; their long shadows visible from Von's vantage point. One large, one lean, and the third small.

Zev said, "What happened?"

"I ... told someone about Mount Ida."

"Why?" Cassiel asked incredulously.

"I—I don't know! The words left my lips as if by magic."

"What do you mean?" Zev asked, his tone pitching in frustration and worry. "Who did you tell?"

"A man that goes by Commander Von, but he left. Perhaps he didn't believe me. He laughed."

"I suppose it is laughable, but he may still lurk nearby," Cassiel said. "Can you locate his scent, Zev?"

Von stiffened. A werewolf would easily find him. That was not a creature he'd fought before, but he knew how dangerous they could be. He gripped the knife and braced to spring.

After a pause, Zev gagged and coughed. "I can't smell anything past the rubbish."

Holding in a sigh of relief, Von was grateful for the sewage trickling past him.

"He mentioned you had met," Dyna offered. "He was the man from the town square."

"What man?"

"Someone she met in passing," Zev replied.

"Did you mention the map to him?" Cassiel asked her next.

The breath stalled in Von's lungs. *Map?*

"No, I didn't," she assured them.

Zev exhaled heavily. "We are fortunate that nothing happened. This was my doing. I shouldn't have stepped away. From now on, don't stray from us either."

"We can only hope that man did not believe you, whoever he was."

"The commander didn't seem like a bad man," Dyna told them. "He was kind to me."

"That means nothing," Cassiel said coolly. "We cannot risk lingering here. You better hope our provisions will last until we reach the next city. Corron is not but four days from here."

Zev's shadow moved away from the others. "Take her and wait for me outside of town. I'll find you."

"Where are you going?"

"There is something I must see to." That was all he said before jogging away.

Cassiel grumbled as he moved into Von's view. He had a striking countenance that almost seemed to radiate light. Dyna followed when a group of drunk merrymakers stumbled by. They stopped to heckle her, asking to have a turn after him.

Cassiel shoved her behind him. "I will only say this once," he said to the men in a low, guttural snarl. "Go."

The single word promised violence, but Von doubted he could defend her against so many. Drunk men tended to be bold, sometimes sinking into salacious depravity they wouldn't otherwise resort to while clear of mind. He had seen it happen enough that he prepared to intervene, but the drunks cackled and went on their way.

Cassiel leaned against the coarse bricks of the alley wall and rubbed his face. "Are you cursed to attract trouble?"

Dyna winced. "Please don't be angry, Prince Cassiel."

Von raised his brows at the new revelation. *This one's a prince?*

The young man groaned and pressed on his forehead. "It is one mishap after another. Can you attempt not to be so reckless? *Please.* That is not a word I say often."

"Yes," she said with a smile in her voice. Von had a feeling that wasn't something Dyna could truly promise. If only they knew the trouble the lass had already encountered.

"Zev said this was all his doing, but it was you who wandered off," Cassiel groused.

"Forgive me. When he disappeared, I attempted to find him myself, but then I was enthralled by Landcaster and had gotten ahead of myself."

The prince grunted at that. "There is nothing enthralling about this filthy town. It reeks of chamber pot."

Von had to agree. He'd seen better.

Dyna laughed, and the delighted sound echoed in the alley. "There is a lovely canal that passes right through the square, did you see?"

"That is the sewage system …"

"And there are so many people. I think there were thousands!"

"The local population is hardly a thousand," Cassiel retorted. "I am beginning to wonder what your village must look like."

"One day I will take you, but first, you must show me Urn. The village elders that would leave North Star in the summer always returned with incredible stories of the outside world."

"Is that so?" he said, his tone hovering between mild mocking and disinterest.

"Yes!" She buzzed with excitement. "They spoke of the Azure mines where pulverized sapphires cover the ground, glittering like the ocean. And of the mischievous pixies of the Phantasm Moors who dance and sing if you sew them new clothes. Even of the great train in the west that travels from the Saxe Sea to the Dragon Canyon." A smile rose to Dyna's lips and Von followed her gaze to the blend of rich orange and violet streaking across the evening sky. "There is much I'd like to see," she murmured.

The lass was a vision of innocence and all that was pure in the world. Von swallowed down the sickness in his stomach, knowing she would not hold on to it for long. Not here, and certainly not now that he knew who she was.

"Well, then be sure I am with you before you amble about," the prince replied, his words much softer compared to how he had spoken to her before. He hooked a finger around her satchel's strap and pulled her close, too close. She had to raise her head to look into his eyes. "It is a treacherous world," he murmured, "and if you are not careful it will devour you, Dynalya."

Seeming to catch himself, Cassiel took a step back. They were unmoving and quiet for a moment until Dyna gasped and spun him around, patting all over his back.

He whirled away. "What are you doing?"

"Where are they?" she asked in confusion. "Where did they go?"

"Nowhere." He strode away.

"I don't understand." She rushed after him. "What did you do with them?"

Their voices faded as they made their way down the road leading out of Landcaster. Von left the alley and stared after Dyna, watching her walk away into the twilight with her prince.

Elon appeared from the shadows. "She is the Maiden, Commander."

"Yes, I gathered that. Thank you," Von snapped. The incredulity of it was agitating him. Her existence gave substance to his greatest fear.

"Shall I follow?"

To capture Dyna now would be easy. The werewolf had left and the other would be no match for them. If there was any chance, it was right then.

"No," Von said. "We need to proceed with caution. Return to camp while I report this."

Elon didn't leave and Von tensed. The elf was under his command, but he ultimately served Tarn's best interest and was paid well to do so.

"Commander," Elon warned, looking past him.

Von heard the rapid rhythm of hooves beating on the road before turning to see an assembly of Rangers in navy frock coats racing toward them on horses. Brass badges with the insignia of Azure shone on their lapels.

"Shite." Von slipped back into the dark alleyway, cursing the fates under his breath.

"Search every building and alley!" a Ranger shouted as their horses galloped into the pub street. "Bar the exits! The merchant said he would be here!"

Von glared at the dead merchant at their feet. So, this had been a trap after all. How had he managed to lie?

"Deniability," Elon answered his silent question. "By not being aware of the plans for the ambush, he could deny it."

Von swore again. He used truth spells to avoid unnecessary bloodshed, but he may have to rely on other methods from now on.

He took out another knife and Elon drew his sword, the blade soundless as it left the sheath. Von took point, sprinting down the alleyway. Three Rangers charged through the adjacent alley of the Big Valley pub and immediately spotted them.

"Halt in the name of the King!"

Von flung a knife, impaling a target in the heart. He leaped over the body and stabbed through the stomach of the second. The third Ranger whipped out his rapier. Von ducked under the whizzing edge, coming out behind the Ranger and slashed through his gullet. The man gurgled, blood spurting from his mouth before he crumbled in a heap.

Another five Rangers came running.

Elon shrugged off his cloak. "Go, Commander. You are needed elsewhere."

Von hesitated to leave him behind, but the elf readily faced the men with rare elation. The Rangers took out their rapiers, calling out orders of surrender, but there would be none this day.

Elon streaked between the men like a black spirit, parrying and evading attacks at incredible speed. His sword glittered between bodies in flashes of steel and blood, taking down opponents as quickly as they came. Their cries drew more men, and they swarmed into the alley from all directions.

Von felt more than saw the elf draw Essence from the surrounding atmosphere.

Elon raised his sword straight in alignment with his face and murmured, *"Ogap'maler."*

Wild electricity sparked from his hands and coiled around the blade in spiraling vines. The elf ran to meet the Rangers and launched into the air, bringing his sword downward. It hit the ground with a deafening *boom*. Thunderbolts blasted outward in violent waves.

Von sprinted from the explosions and shaking buildings, ducking low. The remnants of electrical magic crackled at his back. The screams of the dying followed him, even as he exited the alleyway into town.

Von stalked through the dark, avoiding the lanterns lining the deserted roads as he headed for the Smithton Tavern in the posh part of Landcaster. The imposing stone building stood three-stories tall with arching windows. He went through the front doors and found it much quieter than the pub. The sleek wood floors gleamed under the chandeliers overhead, and stairways with iron spindles flanked the tavern walls, leading to lodging on the floors above. Dark wood tables spread throughout the public lounge. There were only a handful of patrons and all had veered off in private corners where servants brought them fine food and drink on polished trays.

The master sat at a table within a shadowy alcove. The sharp planes of Tarn's face were not easily discernible under his white-blond hair. A section of it hid part of the mangled scar that coursed diagonally from his right brow, across the bridge of his nose, curving over the left end of his jaw. An immaculate overcoat, the color of charcoal, with notch lapels and silver buttons contoured his lean frame.

Two other men accompanied him, laughing and drinking while shuffling a deck of cards. A pile of gold coins gleamed in the center of the table. Tarn sipped from a goblet as he tossed in a few more stacks, coins spilling down the mound. The men shared a conspirative grin and added their bets. They saw Tarn for his appearance, as a wealthy lord in his early thirties, untried and careless with his money. If they truly knew who this man was, they wouldn't dare sit at his table, Von thought.

He came up behind them, glancing at their cards. Each had been beautifully painted with a sigil of a kingdom within Urn. The game valued the kingdoms differently based on their size, wealth, and army. Both of the gamblers had matched pairs. Good enough plays to win, not that they would.

Von approached his master's side and bowed. Tarn idly flicked his fingers, permitting him to stand. He glanced at the cylindrical case and Von nodded, confirming they'd gained another Sacred Scroll. But then Tarn noticed the speckles of blood on Von's coat and fixed on him with eyes that were the striking ice blue of a frozen lake, bottomless and frigid. A chill flushed through Von's veins at meeting them.

He leaned down to whisper, "We had trouble with Rangers."

Tarn took another drink. "Cause?"

"It was a trap."

"You shouldn't have lingered."

"I was delayed, Master." Von inhaled and added, "I found the Maiden."

Tarn's responding smile was slight and as cold as the rest of him.

The two players laid down their ten cards. Tarn then tossed his across the table, revealing a matched set representing the five major kingdoms of the country: the seven-pointed star of Azure, the Dynalya flower of Greenwood, the dunes of Harromog Modos, the fire-breathing dragon of Xián Jīng, and the triad symbol displaying the three guilds of the Magos Empire.

The men scowled.

The one with a beard slammed his hand on the table. "It's impossible to get all five. You bloody cheated."

Tarn took another drink. "Did I? Or might it be you're too incompetent to win?"

The man lunged. Tarn kicked out the vacant chair between them, knocking the man's feet out from under him, and he tripped face-first onto the edge of the table with a sickening crunch. He cried out, blood gushing from his broken nose. His friend leaped to his feet as he whipped out a dagger, but Von grabbed the man's arm and twisted it behind his back until there was an audible snap. A keening cry echoed in the quiet parlor, followed by the dull thud of the dagger hitting the floor.

Von slammed him atop of the pile of gold. "He won this round fairly, aye?"

"Aye," the man garbled against a mouthful of coins.

Von tossed him next to his companion. The servants hardly looked over at the commotion. This must be a common occurrence.

"Shall we play another round?" Tarn asked as he shuffled the cards.

The gamblers shrunk back, their pale faces bloody and beaten. Von jerked his head for them to go. They snatched up their belongings and scurried out of the tavern.

Tarn's icy gaze pinned on him again. "Are you sure she is the one? I'm tired of rumors and false leads."

Von lowered his head, keeping his voice low. "She matched the Seer's description: hair like fire and eyes emerald-green." Those were common characteristics, but there was no mistaking how Dyna had looked to him in the sunset—and there were other indications. "She has the key, as foretold. I overheard her companions mention a map to Mount Ida."

Tarn's expression didn't change, but Von sensed his contentment. "And she's accompanied, you say. By the Guardians?"

"Possibly."

"How many?"

"Two. There may be more. The Rangers impeded us from following."

Tarn studied him. Von was careful to keep himself composed, forcing himself not to tense at the partial lie. There had been a chance to go after her.

"Send the spies."

He suppressed his relief. "Yes, Master. Allow me to escort you to camp. After today, the news of your return will spread to all of Azure."

Tarn flagged down a servant for more wine. "How did you escape?"

"The captain."

"Then he will see to any other problems tonight. Go. You know what must be done."

CHAPTER 23

Dynalya

Landcaster's silhouette blended into the night, despite the faint candlelight glinting from the windows and scattered moonlight trickling over the roofs. A nervous sweat sprouted along Dyna's skin. The shiver whispering down her spine had nothing to do with the chilly breeze rustling the leaves.

Zev said to wait for him. Why had he gone? He knew she couldn't stand to be alone in the dark.

Well, she wasn't alone. Beside her, the silent Celestial prince leaned against a tree, arms crossed, frowning in the direction of the town.

"Should we light a fire?" she asked, struggling to hide her unease.

He pulled his gaze from Landcaster to her. "It would be pointless to do so. We will not camp here tonight."

Dyna rubbed her arms, biting her lip. She heard the accusatory hint in his voice. He was annoyed at the mistake she made, but revealing the location of their journey had not been on purpose. The words had been plucked from her somehow. She had no explanation.

But how much longer would Zev take?

The shadows grew and stretched in the forest where they waited. Shapes lurked in the foliage, watching. No, there was no one. It was only her unfounded fear. But the darkness was all-consuming.

Dyna squeezed her eyes shut and crouched down on her heels, wrapping her arms tight around her. *It cannot hurt me. It cannot reach me. I am not alone.*

She pictured herself huddled in the burrow beneath the *Hyalus* tree outside of North Star. The glowing tree was all that had protected her from the Shadow that night.

"Are you cold?"

Dyna flinched at finding Cassiel suddenly in front of her. He canted his head, skimming her face. She gave a stiff nod. Her arms were prickly, and she was trembling.

"Perhaps a small fire?" she managed. Anything to bring the light.

The prince stepped back and drew his sword, white flames bursting to life. Dyna yelped, and she recoiled from the rupture of heat, falling back.

Cassiel raised the blade and thrust it into the dirt. "There."

The wide band of flame cut through the darkness, banishing all creeping shadows.

She sighed in relief and basked in its warmth. "That'll do."

Rummaging through his pack, Cassiel pulled out his enchanted coat he'd used to hide his wings and unexpectedly draped it around her shoulders. He had taken it off as soon as they had left town. She wasn't sure if it was from her constant questions or from the discomfort of having his wings confined. A brocade jacket now rested on his frame. It was as black as his hair and patterned in gold embroidery.

"Thank you," she murmured, wrapping herself in the large coat. The fine material was unfamiliar, smooth, and lined with what felt like velvet. It carried his unearthly scent that Dyna couldn't help but breathe in.

She slid her arms beneath the coat and stretched them behind her. Where she should have felt the back of the coat was instead endless space, as though it was an immense cavern.

Stardust.

It was all Cassiel had offered as an explanation. Dyna had read about Stardust in Azeran's journals. It was a spell in mineral form the mages had created to enchant limitless space where it was needed. It was rather clever of Cassiel to use it on his clothing to conceal his wings. He had looked almost human with the coat on.

The prince took a seat at a careful distance away from her. He didn't like being touched, which she had noticed the first time they met. Did it have any meaning, or did he simply find her repulsive?

A silence settled over them as they watched the petals of fire swivel around the sword. The roots of the flames were the color of cobalt. It didn't affect the blade, though she felt the tremendous heat. A weapon of divine fire meant to strike down demons.

What would it do against humans?

She glanced at the prince, finding his faraway stare fixed on the flames. This firelight differed from the muddled orange glow of a campfire. The white fire lifted all darkness, casting it away. It softened the sharp planes of Cassiel's face, drawing out the hint of luminance that lingered beneath his skin. For a moment she could almost see how he'd looked as a boy: cherubic, soft eyes, mouth curved with a hint of laughter. She blinked, and it vanished.

He caught her staring, and Dyna quickly looked away. "Where do divine weapons come from?"

"I would think the answer obvious."

Right. Such sacred things were not man-made.

"Divine weapons are called *Neshek Hael*," Cassiel said, the lilting words sending a whoosh of warmth through her—the way it had when King Yoel spoke the God of Urn's true name.

She tried and failed to repeat it so eloquently.

A slight twitch of Cassiel's lips gave away his barely reserved amusement. He said it again, slowly sounding each syllable. "Neh-shek Ha-el."

"This is the language of the Celestials?"

"It is the language of the Heavens."

The revelation left her briefly astounded. "What does it mean?"

"To arm with His divinity. A general translation. The first true divine weapons forged by *Elyōn* contained blue fire. Some had been brought down with the first Seraphim, but they are kept locked away. Too valuable and too powerful in their creation to be wielded in the Mortal Realm."

Then where did the white fire blades come from?

"We had to make do without them," Cassiel said, answering her silent question. "When a Celestial child comes of age to train in combat, they choose their weapon, and it will be forged by the Smiths in the blessed fires of—"

He abruptly cut off and his expression grew guarded. Their conversation flowed so easily he must have been about to reveal another location of the Four Realms. Hermon Ridge—the northern mountain she overheard Cassiel mention to Zev—was one. Perhaps he revealed that to her cousin because of the Accords, knowing Zev could never speak of it. Dyna wasn't sure how that differed from her royal immunity, but she didn't press any further. While she knew some Celestial secrets, it was best that she didn't know all of them.

"Does your sword have a name?" she asked to change the topic. "Every great sword has one."

"No," he answered much too quickly. A flush rose to his face.

She smiled mischievously and inched closer to him. "It does! Tell me."

"No."

"Why? Is it a secret?"

He turned redder, looking away. This was the most unruffled she had seen him. She waited, silently begging to know what could make him blush that way.

Cassiel rolled his eyes at her grin and cleared his throat. "*Lahav Esh.*"

"What does it mean?"

The question hung in the awkward silence as the prince picked at the cuff of his jacket. Dyna kept still, waiting.

"Fire Sword," he mumbled so faintly she almost didn't hear it. At her blank stare, the blush sunk down his neck. "I was given my divine weapon at eight years of age. I was not the most creative sort."

A giggle slipped out before she stifled it behind her hand. Cassiel shot her a mild glare.

"Well, I like it. A sword befitting of its name." She smothered another laugh, meaning it only as a gentle tease.

The prince scratched his head, wings twitching. The color remained in his cheeks. Unusual of his cool, stiff manner, she found it rather charming that he would be embarrassed over anything.

"What happened to your arm?" he asked suddenly.

The coat sleeve had slid down her arm, revealing a part of the welt. Before she could reply, Cassiel yanked the sleeve down further and exposed her swollen wrist to the light.

"Ah, there was a bit of trouble—"

His expression darkened with a fury that stalled the words on her tongue. Whatever he was going to say was interrupted by a rustling in the foliage. Cassiel leaped to his feet, simultaneously tearing his weapon free.

"It's me," Zev said as he entered the pool of white firelight. "Though you were easy to find. I could see you from the road. Put that thing away. I'm here now." He said the last bit while looking at Dyna.

She nodded to assure him she was all right. Her conversation with the prince had done well to distract her.

Cassiel sheathed his sword. The darkness engulfed them again and banished all remnants of heat. "What had you deemed so important to return to town for?"

"I had to see an old friend," Zev said, coming quickly to her side, but his answer momentarily diverted her fear of the dark.

What friend? He didn't have any friends in town that she knew of, other than … oh.

The rattling coming from his pack as he guided her further into the woods was answer enough. Zev had gone to see Ragan.

"What is this about trouble?" he asked, removing the attention from himself.

Cassiel looked at her expectantly. Zev waited for an answer as well. Dyna tried to hide her hand, but he noticed and pulled back her sleeve. He growled, his eyes flashing.

"Who did this?" Zev asked, his rumbling voice was so wild Dyna knew his wolf was fully awake.

She didn't want to explain her encounter with Dalton. Cassiel was not aware of the customs of the Magos Empire, but Zev was, and he would hunt down the young mage to protect her. That was not something she would add to his conscience.

"It's nothing." Dyna tugged her arm away. "Two young men wished to make my acquaintance."

Which proved to be the wrong thing to say when a snarl tore out of Zev's throat and Cassiel grew murderous. The statement was far more suggestive than she had intended.

"When did this happen?" the prince demanded. "Outside the pub?"

Zev lifted her wrist to his nose and inhaled deeply, capturing Dalton's scent off her skin. He marched for the town.

"Zev." Dyna grabbed his arm. She didn't have the strength to stop him, but he immediately halted, his first instinct always to prevent her from any harm. His eyes, pinned on Landcaster in the distance, glowed in the night. His wolf had returned in full force and itched to eliminate any threat. She felt it in the way his limbs vibrated with the need to shift. "They were only boys."

"Age does not excuse it," Cassiel said, as if he too wanted to search for them.

"We must go," she reminded them. "It's not safe here, as you said."

Zev rubbed his face, forcing himself to turn away. "Aye, that's best."

"Can you shift?" the prince asked him.

Zev flexed his hands and claws grew from his fingers, fur sprouting along his arms. He nodded.

"Good. I suggest you take to your wolf and we travel all night. We need to put as much distance between us and this town as possible."

"But you could not keep up on foot."

Cassiel looked up at the sky where a strong gust was dragging in a veil of clouds. His large wings unfurled behind him, feathers fluttering in the breeze. "It is a good night to fly." His gaze fell on Dyna, and he eyed her from head to toe. "You hardly weigh much. I can bear the weight."

Bear the weight? Did he mean to *carry* her?

Reading the shock on her face, he arched a brow. "Is it the height you fear?"

Her stomach dropped at the reminder. Both times Cassiel had flown with her were out of necessity. He had deliberately avoided her whenever possible, but now he offered of his own will to carry her? The thought of being that close to him, of embracing him all night, sent an unexplainable feeling through her.

"It's quite high," she squeaked.

Amusement swam in eyes from a face that never smiled. "I will not drop you."

"Flying would be much faster," her cousin added as he slipped off his tunic.

Dyna clasped her hands together, ignoring the rush of nerves plunging through her. "Very well."

Zev went behind a cluster of bushes to finish undressing and sauntered out as a wolf. Once their packs were strapped to his back with some rope Cassiel produced, they were ready.

Cassiel told him, "We shall meet in Elms Nook. It is a woodland seventy-five miles east from here."

Her cousin could run that much distance in a night, but she wasn't sure about the prince. He didn't appear concerned about it.

Zev nuzzled her shoulder then took off into the forest, the chains jangling in his wake. Dyna prayed he would be all right.

"Keep the coat," Cassiel said. "You will need it."

He fixed it over her shoulders and made sure the length covered her legs. The long coat fell past her feet, gathering on the ground and deflecting most of the frosty air. His graceful fingers fastened each button and buckled the belts. She peered up at him as he worked, not sure what to make of this unexpected consideration.

Once the coat enveloped her, he lifted the collar around her neck. The edge of his hand grazed her chin, leaving a faint tingle where he had touched her and she couldn't help shivering. Cassiel took a step back, rubbing his hand like he wanted to remove the sensation.

The oversized coat may be more than a means to guard her against the cold, but also a way to guard him against her.

The prince studied her, his brow furrowing. "We will have to see about you learning how to defend yourself." The way he said it sounded like a thought he unintentionally spoke aloud. "Ready?"

Dyna nodded, something fluttering in her chest. Not looking away from him, she gathered her nerve and closed the gap between them again. He stood quietly, considering, or perhaps waiting for her to decide. She slowly latched her arms around his neck. He inhaled a low breath, and his hands hesitantly, lightly, settled on her waist. There were many layers between them, yet heat radiated where they joined.

"I'm ready," she whispered.

Cassiel crouched, and her heart jolted when he swept her off her feet. She easily fit into the crook of his arms. There was strength in them and security in the manner he held her. Wings spreading wide, his muscles flexed beneath her, legs bracing. He looked up, and a rare excitement rose to his face.

"Hold fast." The words were soft against her cheek and her only warning.

They shot into the sky.

Dyna inhaled sharply at the whip of icy wind. She dug her fingers into Cassiel's back or tried to. His firm shoulders moved fluidly under her hands in a steady rhythm as they climbed higher. He was more lean than muscular, containing his own kind of strength. Of course, he needed to be strong to control such massive wings. They gracefully beat, riding the night wind.

He took her further than the treetops he had kept to before. Landcaster quickly grew smaller until it was nothing but a smudge on land. The tail end of the Zafiro Mountains rose in the distance, standing mighty and proud in their witness until they too grew smaller. She was amazed by how far she had gone from home.

Wonder pushed down her fear, and she settled against Cassiel, seeing the world from a new perspective. He carried them on swift wings, no falter brought on by her extra weight. This was his natural ability, a part of who he was, and it peeled away a section of his carefully placed mask. Beneath the cool exterior, she glimpsed a side of him he hid so well—the pure joy it brought him to fly.

At the sight of her smile, a cocky smirk surfaced on his face. "Shall we rise above the clouds?"

"Impossible."

A touch of mirth glinted in his eyes, and Dyna immediately regretted challenging him. His arms tightened around her, pulling her flush against his long frame. She could almost feel his heart and the elation beating with it. Or was it her own?

The wind rushed to meet them as they picked up speed, whipping her hair into her eyes. Dyna clung tight to him, but she trusted Cassiel not to drop her. Even with the hundreds of feet of distance between her and the ground, she knew there was no safer place than in his arms.

He flew higher, icy air stinging her face, and she noticed the canopy of rapidly incoming clouds. They dove into the barrier before she could gasp, and a blanket of mist coated them. There was nothing but a thick, grey shroud and she struggled to breathe in the thin air. As soon as she thought there would be no end, they broke through.

They had entered a soft plain swathed in brilliant moonlight. Nearly a full pearl, the gleaming moon reigned among the immense throne of clouds, a queen in its own right. The view was stunning.

Dyna glanced at Cassiel and saw he was pleased with whatever he gleaned from her obvious awe. The moonlight cast him in a glow, his black wings shimmering like they were covered in a layer of frost. For once, his gaze was warm and searching. He didn't fully smile, but it surprised her to see the makings of one in the corners of his mouth. This was a gift, she realized. An intimate piece of his life he chose to share with her.

"Possibility is limited by perception," he said thoughtfully, as if the thought was a new revelation.

What was their first encounter, but an impossibility made a reality? Days ago, she could not have fathomed his existence, and yet here he was. A descendant from the Heavens, showing her far more than she could have imagined. That was the true gift.

"May it not be limited by our belief," was her reply as she admired the divine creation of him. "But by our imagination."

The Celestial prince looked above, and she read the question there. The velvet sky was endless. Sparkling. A beautiful deep dark blue that gazed at them in return. She too wondered what lay beyond.

Dyna stretched out a hand, needing to touch it. Cassiel granted her wish. With the soft beat of wings, they soared past the impossible and aimed for the stars.

CHAPTER 24

Von

Brisk wind and conflicted thought accompanied Von out of Landcaster. The future was uncertain, taking from him any sense of normalcy. This day had set in motion something ominous. There was no stopping the force that was Tarn. He was an imminent avalanche that would bury all in his path if unleashed.

Von veered off the road and climbed sloping hills until he came to an empty valley west of the farm town, the tall grass rustling in the night breeze. He reached out and pressed his palm on an invisible, solid surface. Cold and slithering, it glowed faintly at his touch, rippling like water. The ripples spread and curved, revealing a massive, translucent dome.

He pushed against it. The slippery entity resisted at first, then it stuck to his fingers, enveloping his hand and arm. It coursed over the rest of his body, making him shudder. Once the spell determined he was permitted to enter, he passed through its threshold, and the camp appeared.

At the center loomed Tarn's great tent, rising like a black peak among the hundreds of smaller tents circling it at a set distance. Torches spread throughout the camp, speared into the mud. Raiders mingled at small fires, laughing, drinking, and eating out of steaming bowls. Each wore all black and was well-armed.

On the north end of the camp stood the cook's tent. Smoke filtered out of the opening on top, carrying the scent of dinner. Von strode for it, nodding to the Raiders as he passed. They leaped to their feet, returned salutes, then made themselves scarce. Regardless of how many years they served under him, they maintained a layer of fear. Von didn't go out of his way to intimidate them, but they had seen how brutal he could be to maintain obedience. He needed to be hard on them so the master wouldn't be.

Von entered the cook's tent and found a towering Minotaur inside. At nine feet tall, Sorren filled most of the heightened space. He sported an auburn pelt beneath his stained apron. Only one horn extended on the left of his head, a sawed-off stump rose where his second horn used to be. Gold earrings glinted on his long, floppy ears, and another hung from his snout.

Sorren acknowledged Von with a grunt as he stirred an enormous cauldron over a fire that sizzled and popped. The stuffy space carried the smell of stew, hinted with stale sweat and herbs. Behind the creature was a table stacked with dirty dishes and vegetable scraps. To the right was another table where Von found his subordinates. They raised their heads from their meals when he entered and stood to attention.

Each commanded a different faction among Tarn's Raiders, and Von commanded them all. Captain Elon, who led the spies, was indifferent as always. There was no evidence of his confrontation with the Rangers on his person. Next to him was Lieutenant Abenon, a dark-skinned man with a nest of black curls, and two scimitar blades strapped to his back. The Mirage Desert native led the Raiders.

The remaining member of the group, a bearded old mage by the name of Benton, looked annoyed as usual. The cooking fire sparked against the red crystal on his gnarled staff. He oversaw anything to do with magic.

"I found the Maiden," Von announced.

Elon remained apathetic, Abenon grinned, and Benton's mouth thinned in a tight line.

"The local authorities have discovered our presence," Von continued. "Lieutenant, inform the men. We move out in an hour."

"Aye, Commander." Abenon rushed out of the tent.

"Benton," Von called to the mage next. "Your son encountered the Maiden. Use him to cast a location spell on her."

"No." The old mage jerked a step back, causing the brass bangles around his bony ankles to clank. His fingers gripped his staff tightly. "Why are you helping Tarn with this? You know the abominable thing he wants. If he gets his hands on the Unending, we will never have our freedom. Nor will anyone in this world."

Von couldn't argue. The mage was right. With the Unending, nothing could ever oppose the master. But what choice did he have? What choice did any of them have?

Benton was the only one who verbally opposed him. Of the two-hundred men in camp, less than an eighth were slaves either by coercion or by debt. The rest followed Tarn devotedly.

"I say we band together and kill him," the mage raged, his wild expression urging them to join him. "Set me free. I'll do it."

Von scowled. Such treasonous words could lop off all their heads. By duty alone, he should slit the mage's throat there and then. "You dare say that in front of me? You've grown too bold, Benton. It is against the law to harm your master."

"He is not *my* master."

Von nodded to Benton's bangles that marked him as a slave. "Those say otherwise."

The mage glared down at his feet. "These manacles may bind me to this camp, but they will cease to work if I destroy the Crystal Core in his tent. It is the only thing preventing me from killing him!"

"You cannot go near it, you fool," Von said as he slowly reached for a particular knife sheathed on the back of his belt.

"If you will not join me, then I will take you down with him." The mage's dark eyes glowed red in tandem with the crystal of his staff. "I may not be able to enter his tent, but this camp is set on the ground. You seem to have forgotten to which guild I pertain." Benton slammed his staff into the dirt, and the earth trembled violently. The tent shook, and the pots rattled, dishes crashing. "What is to stop me from burying you all alive?"

Elon joined Von's side and raised his glowing blue palms. "Cease or this will not end well for you."

"I do not fear you, pointy-eared toff!" Benton spat. "You elves utter your incantations. I'll kill you before you speak a single word—"

Von hurled the knife and it pierced Benton's shoulder, knocking him down. The mage screamed as a brilliant wave of roaring red power peeled out of him and whooshed into the hilt of the knife. The tremors immediately stopped.

Benton panted, sweat gleaming on his insipid face. "You siphoned my Essence?"

Von crouched by him and yanked out the knife. Studded in the pommel was an amber bead glowing with the power it had consumed. Within it was a tiny black plant with three heart-shaped leaves. "Black clovers," he said, examining the bead. "Nasty little buggers."

Benton's eyes bulged wide. "Where did you get that?"

"Where is not important. I've siphoned your Essence within an inch of your life. Rebel against the master again, and I will take all of it."

"He would never allow it. I am worth more than you."

"He has no need for rebellious slaves. There are mages aplenty but his patience is limited." Von cleaned the blade on Benton's robes, then stood and tucked it away. "This is not the only clover we have, but you only have two sons. Know your place, or they will suffer the consequences with you."

"Touch them and you die!" Weak sputters of magic sparked at Benton's fingertips, but that was all he mustered.

Dalton rushed into the tent with his older brother, Clayton. The boys gaped at their father and Von. They must have sensed magic in the quake, and who had caused it. Both ran to Benton's side.

Clayton shot Von a glare and he pressed on the wound. His palm glowed yellow with his Essence as he healed Benton. He had the same narrow face and nose of his father, along with the defiant twist of his mouth. Neither he nor Dalton asked what happened. This was not the first time Von had to subdue the old mage.

"Rest, Benton," Von said, giving him a casual smile as he deliberately laid a hand on Dalton's shoulder. "Once you've regained your strength, prepare the location spell."

Benton's face turned purple, but this time he didn't refuse. Clayton helped him up, and the mages shuffled out without another word.

Von sighed and rubbed his face. He hated making such threats, but it was necessary to keep them alive. If Benton had revolted while Tarn was present, this bluster would have ended differently. The old mage must have known it as well. His antics never started when the master was around.

"Track the Maiden meanwhile," Von told Elon. "Keep your distance and find out what you can about them. Take Novo and Len with you. Leave Bouvier behind. I have another task for him."

Elon nodded and soundlessly slipped outside.

The tables rattled as Sorren moved stiffly around the tent. With each of his heavy steps, his thick slave bangles clanked against his hooves.

"Let me." Von waved him away and helped pick up the dishes off the floor.

The Minotaur's deep voice rumbled in the tent, "So, it is happening."

"Aye, it has begun," Von said, letting his informal brogue accent seep through. He didn't need to hold up airs around his friend.

"Benton's right. Why do you refuse to fight? I'd stand with you."

Von busied himself by tossing the broken dishes in an empty barrel. Discussing it would only lead to arguments with Sorren and Yavi, as it had several times before.

Many years ago, Von had sworn an oath to serve the Morken family many, so perpetual enslavement to Lord Morken's eldest son was not much of a difference. The terms of his life-debt were binding law on the earth and in the Heavens. Ironic thing it was, since he constantly committed crimes to fulfill his obligation.

"We're slaves. We have to obey whether or not we agree with it."

Sorren dumped two bowls of mutton stew on the table, the contents spilling on the surface. "I never agreed to be that man's slave," he growled. "Nor did Benton. Did you?"

Von looked away. He bid Sorren thanks for the food and left the stuffy tent. The activity outside was bustling as the men broke down the camp and loaded wagons.

Abenon marched through the camp, barking commands. "Drop those tents! Load the horses! Pick up the pace, you daft, lazy swine!"

Von chuckled and shook his head. He headed for his tent beside a cluster of thick shrubs and trees set further from the others. Other than Elon, no one dared go near his tent, so it surprised him when Len slinked out from behind the trees. The lass stopped at the sight of him, and he caught the brief flicker of alarm before her expression smoothed. Len lifted the hood of her black cloak over her equally long black hair.

"What are you doing?" Von asked, glancing in the direction she came. Had she been in his tent?

Len widened her dark eyes innocently and canted her head as though she didn't understand. The dusky skin of her soft features marked her as a foreigner as much as the *X* brand on her cheek marked her as a slave from Versai. Tarn had purchased her from the slave traders when she was a child, but after ten years—although Von had never heard her speak—he knew she understood Urnian when it was convenient for her.

"Report to Elon."

Len ducked her head and darted away, moving swiftly through the shadowy corners of the camp. Another figure joined her, and they vanished into the dark together. She and Novo had taken to their spy training well. Elon may have taught them a little *too* well.

Von glanced around before continuing to his tent. The flaps of the entry moved gently in the soft breeze, carrying the scent of canvas oil and wild grass. It was nearly dark inside, only a single candle flickering atop a storage chest placed between two cots. To the right stood a small wooden table and one chair.

"Yavi?" Von sensed her presence behind him before her arms wrapped around his torso, her cheek pressing against his spine. He placed the bowls on the table. "I've brought you supper. Eat quickly. The camp is moving."

Her arms tightened. "I heard."

"Did the tremor frighten you? It was only Benton having a fit."

"I'm all right." Something in her voice proved against it.

"What is it?"

"I ... I have something to tell you," she said, the airy words quivering.

He turned around to find Yavi's hazel eyes puffy and red, tears glinting on her lashes. He immediately assumed the worst. "Has someone learned of us?"

She closed her eyes and shook her head. "No one knows."

Von exhaled, letting his worry wash away. Yavi was his secret—a sweet betrayal that could take both their lives. It was against slave edict for life-servants to have life-mates or family. They lived only to serve the master, but she had become his reason for living.

He gently cupped her slender face in his hands, adoring the light sprinkle of freckles on the bridge of her nose. Long auburn tresses of wet hair stuck to her temples from how long she had cried. He wiped her wet cheeks, delicately brushing a thumb over her lips. They were as pink as the dawn and soft as satin. His favorite part of her face.

"Who must I kill for causing my lovely wife to weep?"

He intended it as a playful question, but he meant every word. The men knew not to touch her. They had seen what he had done to the last one who tried.

Her exquisite mouth tweaked in a faint smile. "No one today, my love."

Von glanced over her kirtle to her bare feet.

"I'm not hurt," Yavi reassured him. Her fingers brushed the strap of the cylindrical case on his shoulder. "You've brought me another scroll ..." she trailed off when she noticed the stains on his coat. "Is this blood?"

"Aye."

"Von ..."

"It was necessary." He took her hand. "What troubles you?"

Yavi searched his face. There was so much passing over hers that he couldn't guess what she was thinking, only that she was afraid. She closed her eyes and embraced him tightly. "You'll send me away from you soon."

Von sighed and wrapped his arms around her, resting his chin on her head. "We've discussed this. I need to find a way to gain your freedom before Tarn no longer has need of you."

They were quiet, fearing that would be sooner than they were ready for.

"Was Len here?" Von asked.

"Oh, um, yes."

"Why?"

"She comes to see me occasionally." Yavi pulled away, giving him an edgy smile. At his frown, she huffed. "She's becoming a woman. Who else is she to discuss such things with?"

Von grimaced, not wanting any further explanation. He'd always thought of Len as a child, but she was a couple of years older than the lads. Other than Yavi, there were no other women in the camp. "She speaks to you?"

"In a way."

"Hmm. Well, come and eat. You missed breakfast this morn." He guided Yavi to sit at the table, but she took one whiff of the mutton stew and ran out of the tent. She heaved and gagged over some shrubs, trying her hardest not to spew. Von held back from going to her, wary of anyone who might be watching. "Yavi?"

"Oh, don't fret about it." She waved him off, breathing in deep gulps of air. "I must have eaten something that didn't agree with me."

"Then let it out. I'll ask Sorren if he has anything to settle your stomach."

"No," she blurted. "I'm fine. No need for fuss. Will you take the food out of the tent, please? I can't stand the smell."

Von frowned but did as she asked. Only then did Yavi go into their tent again and lay down in a cot. "Will you stay with me for a while?"

He pretended to grouse, although there was little he would deny her. "How could I refuse such a fair lady?"

She laughed and held out a hand to him. Von laid down beside her and she curled against his chest. He traced patterns on her back, inhaling the floral scent of her hair. He could spare a few minutes before he needed to resume his role as commander.

"Why must the camp move so soon?" Yavi asked. "We've only arrived yesterday."

"We encountered Rangers."

"Oh." She studied his frown. "But there is something else, isn't there?"

Von sighed. If he had never gone to Landcaster, would it have made a difference? "We found the Maiden."

Yavi's eyes widened. "God of Urn, you found her?"

"Aye, her name is Dyna. She is only a wee lamb. Too innocent and much too trusting. Tarn will tear her apart should he get his hands on her."

It had been five years since Tarn received the divination about the 'Maiden with the key'. Von had hoped it was all a ruse, and that they would never reach Mount Ida where the Unending laid. That hope shattered when he met Dyna. Now she was in danger, and he couldn't protect her this time, not from his master.

"He hasn't captured her yet?"

"No, we are to observe her and her companions for now."

Yavi squealed with delight. "Companions? She's gathered the Guardians already?"

Von chuckled at her excitement. "There are two young men with her, but I'm uncertain if they are the foretold Guardians. Elon has gone to confirm."

"What do they look like?"

"One is a werewolf—"

"The moon dweller!"

"Aye …" Which Von found rather concerning. A werewolf meant trouble. He supposed they would be fine, as long as they didn't confront him at night. "The other didn't seem as capable. Too refined and pretty."

"Pretty?" Yavi giggled. "You mustn't assume. One never knows what a divination truly means. They tend to be particular in that manner."

Von tightened his hold around her. He had refused to believe the Faery Seer, for she had given him a divination of his own. Prophetic words he had ignored but couldn't forget. *"Only whence she burns will she be free …"*

"Von? What is it?"

He debated whether he should tell her his greatest fear. The promised future he had refused to believe. But it was coming. He sensed it barreling toward him faster than he could run. "I had hoped it had all been a lie."

"The fae folk cannot lie, love."

It was Yavi's smile that kept him from telling the truth. If he were to reveal the Seer's words, it would frighten her as much as it did him.

"Aye, but they have a knack for telling half-truths," he said. "Never trust the fae. They will no sooner ensorcell you to dance forever on Faery Hill than to help you."

"Well, it's a good thing the fae live in Arthal, is it not? They are a thousand leagues from here."

It was a mild comfort. While most of the fae courts were in Arthal, some could be found in Urn. Not the Seer, though. She was confined to her eerie cave. Those seeking to know their future went to her.

"And now Tarn's divination is coming to pass," Yavi said excitedly. "Come, tell it again."

"I have repeated it to you many times already. You have it memorized by now. I must return."

"Not yet. I want to hear you say it." Yavi's fingers slid up his coat, undoing the buttons one by one. She slipped her hands beneath his shirt, and he inhaled a breath as they inched over the ridges of his stomach to his chest. She kissed the corner of his mouth and her soft lips moved across his jaw to his ear. The sensation sent a spark of heat through him.

"Hmm… it's not fair to use your wiles, woman." Von gripped her hips, reminding himself he had work to do. But they had so little time together, every minute was more precious than gold. He couldn't bring himself to go—or stop. His hands continued roaming down her back.

"Von, tell me," she murmured.

He tugged the sleeve of her dress down her shoulder, running his nose along her collarbone, whispering against her skin: "'Seek the Maiden with emeralds for sight and tresses of fire, for she holds the key to the Unending thou desires. Beware the Guardians who come to shield her from thee. She will be protected by one of divine blood and a dweller of the moon howling to break free. Thus follows a warrior bestowing his vow, and a sorceress grants her sorcery. A familiar face vies for vengeance, and a creature with the strength of ten eradicates the forgery. Great peril in the venture thou art pursuing. Be not swayed by love, lest it be thy undoing.'"

"'Be not swayed by *love*, lest it be thy undoing,'" Yavi's voice spiked when Von kissed the pulse on her neck. "There is a possibility he will fail."

"The lass won't entice him."

"The foretelling didn't say it would be the Maiden who he loves. It could be anyone, even a man."

Von laughed at the ridiculousness of it.

"It's possible. I have never seen him with a woman."

His laughter died away. "Tarn has not touched a woman since we left Troll Bridge. He lost his love-mate in the Horde of trolls that overran our old town."

"Oh ... You've not once told me he had someone."

"It was a long time ago, and he was a different man then. We both were."

"Azure Knights, hailed from Old Tanzanite Keep, sworn to protect the land of Azurite for your liege lord." Yavi smiled at him with admiration.

Von thought of Lord Morken and his cold demeanor that Tarn inherited. He had served the Earl of Old Tanzanite Keep when they once lived in the northern end of the kingdom. That was before the Azure King gave Lord Morken peerage of the isthmus. There, everything changed.

"We are knights no more. Tarn cares nothing for honor, nor fealty, and certainly not for love. To him, it's a weakness. More so since he's been warned by the Seer. His only goal is the Unending. He will never let himself be swayed."

Yavi dropped her head against his chest. "Then will we never escape him?"

Von lifted her chin. "You have my word. I'll free you from his chains. I swear it."

Even if it meant letting her go and never seeing her again. Whatever it may cost him, he would return the freedom that was stolen from her. It would be the last and only priceless gift he could give.

Yavi rose on one arm and leaned over him. The silken tresses of her hair curtained around them, brushing his face. She smelled of wildflowers and fresh air after rainfall. He wished he could encase it somehow. To take it with him wherever he went so he wouldn't forget it.

For all of their hopes and dreams, he knew he could only save one of them. He'd have to stay behind so she could escape. The hourglass of their time together had turned over, and tiny grains of moments like these spilled toward the day he would have to say farewell.

Yavi held his gaze as she stripped away his coat, letting it drop to the ground. The bandolier went next. He lifted his arms as she pulled off his tunic. Desire burned in the liquid hazel of her eyes. Her gaze dragged across his abdomen to his chest, full of need and wicked intent.

Duty could wait a while longer.

Von pulled the laces of her bodice loose until the dress slipped off in a pool of fabric, leaving her bare and perfect for him. The sight lit everything within him ablaze.

No matter how many times he had her, it wasn't enough. It could never be enough.

If he could live forever in a single moment, it would be right here with the woman who truly owned every part of him. Where nothing and no one else mattered. But this was merely a stolen moment that wouldn't fully be theirs until they were both freed.

"There must be someone out there who can fill that man's heart the way you have filled mine." Yavi pressed her lips over a scar on his chest. "I hope and I pray for it."

Secretly, he did too.

CHAPTER 25

With a furious cry, Dyna swung a fist at Cassiel's face. He easily careened to the right. She stumbled past him with the momentum of the missed blow, and her knees hit the grass. She paused there to catch her breath. They had been practicing for two days. Why couldn't she hit him?

"Get up," Cassiel commanded.

Dyna released a frustrated huff and rose to her feet. She brushed the sweaty strands from her forehead as she faced the prince again. Wings arched behind him, he stood confident in the meadow where they had set up camp for the evening. His sword remained sheathed, nor did he bother to hold up his defenses. He wore a loose white shirt, which hung slightly open, giving a tantalizing glimpse of his chest. It kept drawing her gaze.

Cassiel beckoned her forward. "Again."

She attacked and he deflected every punch without effort. Each time they touched, a gentle zap of energy passed between them, rushing through her until it fluttered in her stomach like a tickle of feathers.

The zaps occurred only with skin contact. She suspected it was the reason Cassiel had avoided her before. He didn't anymore. Not since the night he carried her through the sky. If it bothered him now, he gave no sign.

"Move your feet," he instructed. "Hold up your fists."

Pivoting on her heel, Dyna swung again, but her foot caught the ground unsteadily and she missed.

"Focus."

She was trying, but his intense stare was distracting.

"You need to learn this, so *that* does not happen again," the prince said, glaring at the discolored bruise on her forearm. It had formed into the shape of Dalton's hand.

She tugged on the sleeves she had rolled up to her elbows and covered the tender spot. Lady Samira had warned they would discover her, but Dyna didn't think it would happen so soon. What were the chances of meeting a mage in the first town they reached? If an adult mage had found her, she would have been spirited away to Magos, never to be seen again.

She missed another strike and tripped into Cassiel. He frowned down at her, standing a foot or so taller than her short height. Her heart spiked, very aware of the inches between them. He took her wrists, long fingers wrapping around them, sending a gentle current down her arms.

Why did that keep happening? What caused it?

He set her back on her feet. "That is enough for today."

"No, let's continue." Dyna shook out her tingly hands, ignoring the blush heating her face. She wanted to keep sparring. When Dalton had grabbed her, all she could do was squirm and yell. She didn't want to feel so helpless again. "If I can learn to harness Essence, I can learn how to defend myself."

She went for a surprise kick, but Cassiel sidestepped and swept the other leg out from under her. She hit the ground with a wheezing gasp.

He shook his head, his expression nothing short of disappointed. "This may be a waste of time."

Zev chuckled, enjoying the view from where he sat on a large flat rock by a brook. "She only lacks proper instruction. It's not enough to tell her to strike your palms."

Cassiel crossed his arms. "If you have a better method, then, by all means, do step in."

Zev strolled over and helped her up. "First, protect your face, Dyna. You leave too many openings. Second, mind your feet so you don't trip over them."

"All right." She got into position as she looked at her scuffed shoes. The soles had quickly worn down, allowing rocks to dig into her heels. They weren't made for travel and wouldn't last much longer.

"Set them apart, parallel to your shoulders, and bend your knees. When you swing, use the force of your entire body. Your punch will land with greater force when it hits less than the full range of your arm." Zev demonstrated, and she imitated his position.

Cassiel eyed her stance critically. "She does not exactly inspire confidence."

Zev turned her so she faced the prince again. "Never take your eyes off your opponent. Anticipate his movements so you can avoid them."

Dyna raised her fists and braced herself. She studied Cassiel's posture, the shift in his expression, muscles tensing.

"Ready?" He lunged without waiting for a reply. She ducked under his arm and swung. He rapidly deviated backward. Her knuckles skimmed past his jaw, scarcely missing it. Both blinked at each other, then she broke into a wide grin. It wasn't a hit, but that was as close as she ever made it past his defenses.

Zev patted her head. "Well done."

"Mere luck," Cassiel said.

"You let your guard down."

The prince shrugged in mild admittance, but he was studying her with a furrowed brow. "She is small. Against a man determined to hurt her ..."

She wouldn't stand a chance. With only two days of instruction, Dyna felt no more capable of fighting now than she did in Landcaster.

"She needs a weapon."

"No," Zev frowned at Cassiel.

"She needs to learn—"

"*No* weapons." An edge had risen to her cousin's voice, but it was not anger. He looked uncertain, worried. "Dyna, I'll always protect you, but one day I might not be there. If you're ever cornered by a man, aim for his more *sensitive* areas." He moved to Cassiel's side and motioned at his body parts. "Eyes, throat, kidneys, and groin. One punch or kick there will take him down long enough for you to escape."

Cassiel's responding glower nearly made her giggle. He turned away and headed for the brook. "I will not participate in such a demeaning demonstration."

Zev chuckled, calling after him. "She cannot spar with me. It's not practical against my strength."

"Let's rest," Dyna said, hiding a grin. "I'll see to our dinner."

She headed for their camp set up a few yards away near the forest. Zev went to the brook. He laughed again at whatever Cassiel said as they refilled their waterskins. Dyna was happy to hear it. The tension between her cousin and the prince was dwindling as they traveled together. She hoped it meant Cassiel was finding them tolerable.

Dyna smiled and stirred scraps of vegetables in the boiling pot hanging over the campfire. They didn't have much to eat, but broth would do good in the chill. It would pair perfectly with bread. She had been craving the taste of fresh rolls, still steaming when cracked open. She'd have to ask Zev to include it in their provisions once they reach Corron.

The meadow had quieted with the gentle lilting of Cassiel's flute. Dyna glanced at the brook and found Zev blankly staring at the water flow, wearing a familiar uneasy expression. Tomorrow was the full moon. They had yet to tell Cassiel about Zev's Other form. He hadn't noticed the chains yet, nor had Zev attempted to mention them.

Dyna sighed and took out an empty burlap sack from their pack, heading to the blackberry bushes on the edge of the forest. She picked berries while she debated telling Cassiel about the Other, but it wasn't her place. Zev couldn't bring himself to tell the prince what his chains were for, and she couldn't either. They both worried about the same thing. What would Cassiel think of him after tomorrow?

The bag slipped from her berry-stained fingers. She lowered on her hands and knees to search for it in the tall grass when she heard a threatening hiss. A brown snake slithered out of the underbrush with a black pattern etched onto the scales coursing down its back, and two minuscule horns extended from its head. She immediately recognized the venomous snake. It hissed, flicking out its long black tongue, and her heart rammed in her chest, panic gripping her. If the snake bit her, she would march through Death's Gate within seconds.

She nearly jumped out of her skin when a quiet voice spoke to her from beyond the trees. "My lady, please do not move."

Dyna stifled a whimper, fearing the presence and the imminent death in front of her. She didn't dare look away from the snake's glistening black eyes. Its hisses grew more aggressive and it reared back, baring its fangs. A scream tore out of her mouth as it lunged, but an arrow whizzed through the bushes and pierced the snake's skull inches from her face.

She heard the flutter of wings before Cassiel dropped beside her. "What is it? What happened?"

"Dyna!" Zev reached her next. "Are you all right?"

She stared at the dead snake pinned to the ground and pointed a trembling finger at the trees. "Someone is in the forest. He spoke to me."

Zev inhaled the air. His wolf eyes flashed, and he growled. "Who goes there?"

Cassiel unsheathed *Lahav Esh*. Luminous white flames sprung to life along the blade, and the sight of it sent a spike of apprehension through her. His wings were exposed, but he didn't attempt to hide them. He must have come to the same conclusion she did. Whoever was in the forest had already seen him.

"Forgive me, I did not intend to frighten her," the voice said. The stranger had an elegant accent, the *Rs* of his words smoothed over. It hinted he came from a different part of Urn. "I could not stand by while she was to be bitten. The venom of an ecru snake is fatal."

Zev yanked her away from the dead snake. "He killed it?"

Dyna nodded and said to the dense trees, "I owe you my life, sir."

Cassiel glowered at her. "Do not acknowledge that."

"I'm required by law to do so."

"I relieve you of your debt, my lady," the stranger said. "By my honor, I mean you no harm."

"Then make yourself known," Cassiel called out.

The foliage rustled, and he pulled Dyna backward as a figure emerged. Zev coiled, ready to spring at the slightest provocation.

The stranger wore a tattered cloak of deep evergreen, its color having camouflaged him well within the leaves. With the hood over his face, his mouth was the only visible feature. He stepped into the light, followed by a stunning white stallion. Its velvety coat took on the sheen of the evening sky.

Cassiel pointed the sword at them. "Stay where you are."

The horse neighed wildly and reared against its reins. The stranger stroked the horse's silky mane and calmed it in a soft language Dyna didn't understand. *"Atse neib esemlac, Osom'reh,"* he soothed, running a hand down the muzzle. *"Neidan et aramitsal."*

The soft words were soothing, even putting her at ease. The beautiful steed settled, snorting softly.

The stranger reached in his cloak and handed his horse something to eat. Beneath it, she glimpsed old leather armor. Dirt layered his torn, white trousers and his leather boots were worn thin. He carried a fine quiver on his back and in his hand, an elegant longbow etched with a filigree of gold. Strapped to his waist was a fine sword with an obsidian hilt, and a scabbard gilded with golden leaves. The weapons and thoroughbred stallion seemed out of place on the poor man.

"Who do we address, sir?" Dyna asked.

The stranger removed his hood, and she gaped at the striking elf before them. His irises were an unusual shade of turquoise and pointed ears peeked out from his long blond hair flowing down his shoulders. His curious gaze moved past *Lahav Esh* and observed Cassiel's black wings, then Zev's yellow eyes. He didn't appear intimidated by who they were.

When he looked at her, she received a warm smile. He laid one arm across his chest and bowed. "I am Rawn of House Norrlen, General of the Armies of the Greenwood Kingdom. My lady, I have come to seek an audience with you."

CHAPTER 26

Dynalya

The Elvish horse ate oats from Dyna's palm without a fuss, nuzzling her shoulder and face every so often. Upon seeing Lord Norrlen's kind smile, she had decided she immediately liked him and welcomed them to their camp. He was grateful for the bowl of broth she had offered and sipped it quietly in content. He must have been famished.

Zev and Cassiel carefully watched him from where he sat on the opposite end of their campfire. They said, if the elf was to speak with her, then he must give up his weapons. Which he did so willingly.

"Fair is fond of you," Lord Norrlen told her, breaking the silence.

"Nice to meet you, sir Fair," she said to the horse, petting his velvety flank. Fair nickered, snorting into her hair and making her giggle. "Earlier, you called him by another name."

"*Osom'reh*," Rawn said, easily switching to the soothing Elvish language. "His name in my tongue. Fair is a near equal translation in Urnian."

"Dyna," Cassiel called. Rarely did he speak her name, and she detected the aggravation in his tone. Arms crossed, his steel-cut eyes held hers. He tilted his head slightly, indicating she should move away from Rawn.

Zev also watched her with gleaming yellow eyes. He rested on his knees, his muscles taut, ready to attack at the sign of any threat. His wolf hovered just under the surface of the sharp angles of his scruffy face. He didn't like that she stood so close to the stranger. Dyna didn't want to unsettle them further, so she returned to sit between them.

By Cassiel's feet lay Rawn's sword. On the pommel was the crest of a blooming *Dynalya*, her name's origin, and the insignia of the Greenwood Kingdom.

When Rawn finished, he looked at her and said, "Thank you for the meal, my lady. May the God of Urn bless you for it."

She blushed. "Oh, I am no gentry, Lord Norrlen. No need to refer to me as a Lady. My name is Dynalya, but you may call me Dyna."

"If you do not mind me saying so, I would prefer to regard you in such respect."

She smiled shyly and consented to the title.

"I heard your companions call you Dyna, but I was not aware it was a sobriquet. The *Dynalya* is an invaluable flower that only grows within the Vale. Their petals are as red as your hair; the name suits you." Rawn said her full name in an accent foreign to her ears, but it sounded all the more beautiful.

Zev's eyes narrowed. "You've heard us? When?"

Rawn paused, glancing between him and Cassiel before saying, "I was in Landcaster whilst I overheard you call her by name and speak of a map to Mount Ida."

Cassiel and Zev leaped to their feet. The prince whipped out his sword and fur rippled across Zev's arms, his claws extending.

"Wait." Dyna latched onto their forearms. "Let him speak. Anyone could have overheard us."

"Is he the one you revealed our plans to?" Cassiel asked without looking away from Rawn.

"No, not him."

"You have followed us since Landcaster?" Zev snarled, his canines flashing. "That means you've tracked us for two days. I should have heard you or caught your scent."

Rawn held their hard gazes, his expression calm and impassive. "After leaving town, I witnessed you shapeshift into a wolf, Zev, and Prince Cassiel taking to the skies."

Zev's eyes widened at the use of his name because he had not given it. Dyna was more surprised that Rawn didn't react to his ability to shapeshift at will.

"I was left to track you at a distance and did not reach your camp until today. Tracking you was without difficulty. I needed only to spot Prince Cassiel in the sky at night." Rawn looked at him next. "I have not seen a Celestial with attributes such as yours."

"The elves are bound by Rael's Accords," Cassiel said tersely.

"Yes, you need not be concerned."

"How do you know of my title?"

"Like the werewolves, we also have keen hearing. I did not need to be within proximity to listen to your conversations. Forgive the impropriety. I desired to reveal my presence; however, I was uncertain how I could, short of eliciting distrust as I have done so now."

"My trust is limited even with a proper introduction, Lord Norrlen. If that is indeed who you say you are."

Dyna frowned. "You don't believe him?"

"The Norrlen family is well known," Cassiel told them. "They are famed soldiers that have served within the Vale of the Elves for several thousand years. But I'm not inclined to believe him to be of House Norrlen, let alone the Army General of King Leif, the ruler of Greenwood."

"I understand your misgivings," Rawn said. "I would have preferred to meet your acquaintance under more agreeable circumstances."

Dyna studied Rawn. He didn't appear much older than thirty years, but he carried himself with elegant conduct. His measured manner was of another time. "Lord Norrlen, may I ask your age?"

"I am two-hundred-and-seventy-three-summers old."

Her mouth fell open. "Is that why your speech is odd?"

Zev nudged her for the brazen question.

Rawn smiled, not at all offended. "One could say so."

"It is hardly worth noting," Cassiel said, sheathing his sword.

"Do Celestials live longer than elves?"

"Not anymore." He lifted a hand, fingers a whisper away from brushing her lips as if to stop the new series of questions brewing at the revelation. She wanted to know more, but his proximity momentarily stalled her thoughts. He peeled his eyes away from hers and said to Rawn, "The more important question is, why are you here?"

"I suppose it begins with the contention in the Vale."

"Do your kind never tire of war? There is always a word of the Green Elves fighting with the Red Elves."

Dyna canted her head in confusion. Rawn didn't look green.

"Referring to elves by color has come about to differentiate which kingdom we belong to," Rawn informed her. "The Vale was once a single kingdom before it divided in two during the year three-hundred-and-seven, at the end of the Elfheim Age. Greenwood was established in the southeast and Red Highland in the southwest. Unfortunately, the Vale falls into warfare every few hundred years, and that time is upon us once again." He paused, expression growing grim. "The Red Highland King seeks the Dragon's Eye."

"A dragon's eye?" Dyna asked in intrigue. "Why would he want that?"

"Not an eye. He is referring to the tale of the Twin Dragon Blades," Cassiel said.

"Oh." That was not a tale she had heard before.

Rawn nodded. "Two swords were forged some millennia ago from the fires of Bái Lóng, the white dragon deity of the Xián Jīng Dynasty. These swords had such unimaginable power so terrifying, the emperor of Xián Jīng ordered them to be destroyed. Unfortunately, they were indestructible. He then sent forth his most trusted envoys to conceal the swords on opposite corners of the world. One of these swords was named the Dragon's Fang, and the other was the Dragon's Eye."

Dyna pictured the magnificent swords, coated in dragon scales, fire reflecting off the deadly blades. What sort of magic did they possess?

"Red Highland seeking the Dragon's Eye signifies a threat of war for Greenwood," Lord Norrlen continued. "My king bestowed upon me the task to find the Dragon's Fang, for it is the only sword that can challenge the Dragon's Eye. I traveled to Xián Jīng immediately and spent years searching for the confidential accounts of the concealment mission of the twin blades, and additional years translating them to Urnian. In the last scroll, there was an inscription stating the Dragon's Fang rests on land not found."

Now it all made sense to Dyna. "So, you are now searching for Mount Ida. It's an island that no one can find."

Rawn sighed, looking past them to the west wistfully. "It is the only location the sword could be. I've searched the entire world hither and yon for Mount Ida, to no avail. It has not been without difficulty, for Red Highland has learned of my mission. They have sent several assassins to impede me and have placed a bounty upon my head. I have kept in hiding to evade them, hindering my journey further. I cannot return to Greenwood until I have located the sword, and time has been merciless in its passing. I long to be home again. I have not seen my wife since the birth of our son nigh a score ago."

Her mouth fell open. "You've been searching for Mount Ida for twenty years?"

"I have neglected my family for far too long whilst in search of the Dragon's Fang," Rawn said, his brows furrowing. "I have done so for my king and country, but I'm eager to return to them. Therefore, at the notice that you had a map to Mount Ida, I followed. Please forgive my transgression, on my honor it was not with ill intent."

He shifted on his knees and bowed his head, his blond hair curtaining around his face. "I beseech you. Please allow me to join your company. I have traveled to all continents of this world, and I have reached all regions of Urn. I can guide you to Mount Ida in safety. You have my word, whither thou goest on this quest, I pledge to guard your steps and shield your life, to the end of the world and back."

The promise in his words settled over Dyna. This is what they needed, someone to guide them on their journey.

"No," Cassiel said.

"But we need a Guidelander. He knows the country."

"*No.*" He repeated, his face set in stone. "How are we to know if there is any truth to his story? It would be foolish to invite a stranger into our midst."

She got to her feet. "But he saved my life, Cassiel."

"People will do anything to gain your trust."

She may not know much about the world, but oaths from the elves were a pact of honor. "Well, I believe him."

"That is because you are a stupid human," Cassiel snapped.

She winced. For the first time, the insult stung as if he had slapped her.

His scowl faded. "Dyna, I—"

"This matter concerns us all," she said, looking away. "We should have a vote. I say he stays."

Cassiel rubbed his forehead. "I say no."

They turned to Zev. He glanced back and forth between them, then at Lord Norrlen, who awaited the verdict.

"Zev," she pleaded, but he shook his head.

"I'm sorry, Lord Norrlen." He took Rawn's sword and handed it back to him. "You're a risk. I cannot allow that around her."

Rawn exhaled a long breath and rose. "I was enchanted to meet you, my lady. I shall not forget your kindness."

She heard the faint sadness in his voice. "You're leaving?"

"I must respect the decision of your companions. They heed for your safety. Be wary. Danger may lurk herein."

Cassiel and Zev looked at him questioningly.

"It is but a word of warning. Eyes are everywhere, and I do not believe I am the only one in Elms Nook." Rawn took the reins of his horse and tipped his head in farewell. "I bid you a good evening." He mounted Fair's saddle and cantered away for the forest.

Dyna watched him slip into the trees without looking back. "I know there are risks and dangers out here, but he was telling us the truth. He only wants to return to his ... family." Her voice pitched on the word.

Zev reached out to her, but she moved away. "While Lord Norrlen was forthcoming, we know nothing about him. Cassiel is right to oppose it."

"Of course I'm right."

She glared at him.

He scowled back. "This is for your own good."

"I'm not a child, Cassiel. You'll not decide what is for my own good."

Dyna headed for the brook, ignoring their calls to return. Their concerns were valid, but she merely wished to help Lord Norrlen while he still had the chance to see his family again. She had lost her own, and no matter what she did, she could never have them back.

CHAPTER 27

The road to Corron was long and uneventful, if not fairly awkward. Cassiel trailed behind Zev and Dyna, straining to hear their whispered argument. Anything they said was made indistinguishable by the crunch of gravel beneath their boots. Their pace quickened whenever he neared, quieting whatever they were discussing. They had no interest in speaking to him today.

He glowered at the evening sky, wondering if it had to do with yesterday. Dyna had not spoken to him since then. How could she not see they couldn't trust the elf?

She must be angry with him, though. Cassiel had to admit he was too harsh. The hurt look on her face wouldn't leave him. She wouldn't even look his way now. The day had dragged without her excited chatter that he had unknowingly become used to.

"It's time to make camp," Zev announced.

He led them off the road and into the forest for half a mile until they found a small clearing. While the others made camp, Cassiel worked on gathering brushwood for kindling. He took out a flint rock and a small rod of steel from his pocket and beat them over the sticks. The sparks quickly caught the kindling on fire.

Dyna set out a handful of vegetables and herbs for soup. Cassiel hesitated before taking a potato and peeling it for her. She muttered a faint thank you. He supposed that was a good sign and helped her with the rest, but the tension didn't go away. They remained in uncomfortable silence as they waited for their meal to cook, and it continued while they ate.

As the sun lowered and the wind grew colder, so did the mood. At one point, Zev glanced at the darkening sky and stood, but Dyna tugged on his arm, arguing again in hushed whispers.

Cassiel crossed his arms, fed up with this. "What is it? If you have a quarrel with me, out with it then."

They both stopped to look at him over the campfire. Zev wore a guarded expression, while Dyna wouldn't meet his gaze.

"This has nothing to do with you," Zev said.

"I disagree." They were hiding something, and Cassiel sensed it was dire.

"I don't have time to explain."

"*Make* time."

Dyna sighed. "We said we would work to trust one another. This is one of those moments, Zev."

She riffled through his rucksack and pulled out an extensive set of thick, coarse chains. They clinked as they piled on the ground at her feet, manacles hanging on each end. Cassiel stared at them, feeling like an idiot for not questioning what had been causing that racket in Zev's pack.

His mind raced with the history of his people chained and caged. He was far away from either Celestial Realm, and no one knew where he was. He warily rose to his feet, reaching for the hilt of his sword. "What are the chains for?"

Zev took in a deep breath and looked him in the eye. "I have two forms. The wolf and the Other."

Cassiel knew as much. What did that have to do with the chains? Zev looked up at the sky again, and he made the connection then. Tonight, there was a full moon.

He straightened from his defense, relieved but also alarmed. "You will chain yourself."

"I must, or the Other will go on a rampage. I cannot control it."

A cold flush washed through Cassiel as he recalled the massacre in the glade.

"That is all I have time to tell you." Zev turned away. "Let's go, Dyna."

Cassiel glanced back and forth between them. "Go where?"

"In the forest," she said. "I have to chain him to a tree."

He glared at Zev. "You have her do such a barbaric thing?"

"I have to," she cut in defensively. "Zev can't touch the chains. They're made of silver."

He looked down at the ugly mound of metal. Now that he saw them, the chains were an exact match for the odd scars marking Zev's body.

Dyna riffled through her satchel and pulled out a vial. The one with the murky substance she fed Zev when he had been poisoned with silver.

"What is that?" Cassiel asked.

"Wolfsbane. It helps to subdue the Other." Dyna gathered the chains and headed with Zev toward the woods.

Cassiel rubbed his face and exhaled heavily. "I shall accompany you."

He took a stick from the fire to use as a torch and walked ahead before he could question the decision. He was morbid enough to want to see what the Other looked like, and he needed to be sure it wouldn't harm Dyna while being restrained.

No one spoke. Their steps crunched over fallen leaves and their breaths clouded in the chilly air. As the forest darkened with the descent of the sun, the shrubs chirped with crickets and mice, an owl hooting overhead—an audience to their somber march.

Zev stopped in front of an old elm tree, with a strong trunk and thick protruding roots. "This one."

Dyna dropped the chains there and set down the vial by her feet. Her hands shook as she untangled the mass and gathered the pair of manacles. She wound the long chains around the tree once. Then she stood in front of Zev, not looking at him.

"It's necessary," he said.

"It's unbearable." She strangled the chains tight. "But I gave you my word."

Zev held out his hands as a prisoner would. She unlatched a manacle and enclosed it over his right wrist. It clamped shut with a loud clang. He cried out and fell to his knees. His skin sizzled against the metal, smoke rising from beneath.

Dyna's face crumbled. "I'm so sorry."

Cassiel cringed, trying not to inhale the smell of scorched skin. Zev endured this each month?

"The next one," Zev said through his clenched teeth. He lifted his free, limp hand. Once she attached it to his wrist, he would be secured to the tree. "Hurry, the moon is coming."

She quickly unlocked the second manacle, but Zev's head jerked up and he looked past her, his eyes blazing yellow.

"What is it?" Dyna spun around.

Cassiel scanned the dark woods. All three of them holding still and silent. Nothing moved or made a sound, but goosebumps prickled across his arms.

"Something is there," he said under his breath. He dropped the torch in the mud and whipped out his sword, white flames flaring to life.

A black streak burst through the trees and tackled Dyna to the ground. Her scream rang in the woods. Cassiel stood frozen in place at the sight of the wolf on top of her, teeth bared in her face. Dyna didn't move, her wide terrified eyes fixed on it.

"No, Tasnia!" Zev shouted. "Look at me!"

The wolf did and growled viciously, drool seeping through its teeth.

"I know you're angry," Zev said, holding out his chained hand to the wolf pleadingly. "You want revenge for Owyn and the others, but my cousin had nothing to do with it. Please don't hurt her. Take my life instead. It's yours."

"No," Dyna whimpered.

The wolf's rabid growls raised the hairs on Cassiel's arms. She was going to kill her.

"Tasnia," Zev called to her. "Please."

Cassiel tightened his grip on his sword's hilt. If he could only get close enough. He took a step, but the wolf snapped her teeth inches from Dyna's neck, halting him in place.

"I tore them limb from limb," Zev said, his tone turning cold and goading. Tasnia's glowing eyes cut to him, lips pulling over her glistening teeth. "I gutted them, like the animals they were. I turned Owyn into a mangled piece of flesh, and when he couldn't do more than beg, I snapped his neck. And I *enjoyed* it."

Tasnia launched at him with a feral snarl. Zev fell back under her weight. He deflected her bites, his clawed hands fighting to keep her jaws at bay. Cassiel grabbed Dyna and yanked her away from them. A silver light filled the clearing as a full white sphere shone in the night sky.

"Take her away from here!" Zev shouted at Cassiel. Fear, desperation, and pain swam on his face. It was all he managed to say.

His eyes rolled, and he flopped on the ground, convulsing violently. He screamed as his bones broke and reformed. His back snapped and bent, muscles writhing and stretching under his skin. Sharp claws grew from his fingers and toes. Black fur sprouted all over his shuddering body, a long tail extending behind him. His face twisted and stretched, reforming into a drooling snout full of sharp teeth.

Zev was gone.

In his place, a huge hybrid of a man and wolf stood on two legs and howled at the sky.

The Other.

Tasnia didn't run. Even as the beast grabbed the wolf by the neck and lifted her, she didn't struggle. She simply hung in its clawed hand as though accepting her fate. Her gasping breaths grew weaker and weaker as the Other squeezed, and Cassiel flinched at the crunch of bone. The wolf fell limp, then was tossed aside into the bushes.

The Other's glowing eyes focused on him next. With only one chained hand, nothing was keeping it restrained.

Run, instinct commanded, but fear rooted Cassiel to the ground. He could not move or tear his sight away from the monstrosity now hunting him.

He didn't realize Dyna had left his side until he spotted her behind the Other with the second manacle. She inched toward it, but the chains clinked. The beast spun to her and roared. She screamed, the chains slipping from her trembling hands. It swiped at her, and the blow threw her across the clearing. She smashed against a boulder with an awful *crack*. Blood gushed from her hip to her thigh where her dress was slashed apart. The Other bound for her, drool seeping from its sharp teeth.

Dyna shook her head. "No, Zev!"

It lunged and bit into her shoulder. Her piercing scream rang in the forest. Blood gushed down her back, soaking her clothes. The Other began dragging her away.

Move!

The thought launched Cassiel from his stupor, and he sprinted for them. He soared into the air, releasing a furious bellow. The beast turned as he rammed his boot hard in its face. The kick stunned the Other enough to release her from its jaws, and Cassiel snatched Dyna from the ground, carrying her into the air.

She clung to him, her hands shaking. "We have to chain him to the tree. The wolfsbane, I dropped it somewhere. But if you can get it—"

"Are you mad?" he said. "I am not going anywhere near that thing."

"If Zev runs off, he may kill someone. We must restrain him!"

The Other circled the ground below, watching them through hungry eyes. The chains dragged behind it, still attached to one of its front paws. Cassiel didn't care if the beast ran off as long as it left.

Dyna brushed his cheek. He jolted at the touch and met her sad gaze. Tears glistened like pearls on her lashes.

"Please," she pleaded, her voice breaking. "Please help him."

She was placing her faith in him as she had done in Hilos. As much as he didn't want to get involved, he couldn't refuse her when she looked at him like that.

"He only needs to be chained to the tree with the other manacle."

As if it were that simple.

The beast lunged at them. Cassiel dodged the snapping teeth by a hairsbreadth. He flew higher and placed Dyna on the tallest branch of a tree. The Other made another leap. Cassiel used the opening to fly down and grab the other end of the chains.

He remained grounded, facing off with the beast. It prowled forward, iridescent eyes catching the moonlight. Cassiel forced himself to take a breath, his body buzzing with adrenaline. The chains rattled in his quivering hands as the creature circled him.

He opened the manacle. All he had to do was chain the Other to the tree. How difficult could that be?

The Other pounced. Cassiel sprinted forward and slid on the ground, coming out from behind. It snarled and spun for him again. He flew into the air, and using all his strength, he slung the chains, lassoing them around the Other's body. He wrenched it backward with the force of his wings, knocking it off its feet.

Cassiel stalled for a second, surprised that it had worked, then dragged the heavy beast to the tree. But the Other quickly untangled itself from the chains and lunged at him. He threw himself back as claws tore through his shirt. Cassiel landed heavily on the ground and he slapped at his chest, feeling damn fortunate to find it intact.

Realizing he had fallen where Dyna had dropped the wolfsbane, he dared look away from the beast for a second to search through the carpet of leaves. His fingers closed over a familiar round shape.

"Cassiel!" Dyna screamed.

He dodged a snap of teeth by a fraction, leaving the Other to crash headfirst into the tree. The beast staggered over the roots, dazed by the blow. Cassiel raised the jar of wolfsbane and when the beast roared, he tossed the contents down its gullet. A horrid keening ripped through the forest. It fell back and thrashed, howling in agony.

Cassiel grabbed one end of the chains and flew around the tree rapidly, ensnaring them around the Other several times, then clamped the manacle around its free wrist. The beast thrashed against the restraints, growling and snapping its jaws at him.

He stumbled away, watching to see if the chains would hold. They didn't budge. The Other yowled as its fur smoked beneath the chains. With a howl of defeat, it slumped against the tree.

Cassiel leaned on his knees as he breathed heavily, catching his breath. He shook his head at the creature he had subdued. It held no resemblance to Zev. "He's gone."

"No," Dyna's whimpered, tears streaming down her face.

"That thing is not your cousin," Cassiel said.

"He will be himself again in the morning." She began climbing down the tree, blood pouring from her leg. She cried out from the strain on her wounded shoulder and her bloody hands slipped from the branch she hung from. Cassiel launched up and caught her, bringing her to the ground.

Once he set Dyna down, she took slow steps toward the beast. "Zev, it's me. You know me, don't you?"

"What are you doing?" Cassiel said. "Get away from it!"

Dyna shook her head, sobbing. "I know you're still in there. You can defeat this. Please, please try."

The Other stopped whining and focused on her.

"That's right, it's me." She raised her bloody hand to caress its snout, but the Other went into a frenzy and lunged at her.

"Get back!" Cassiel yanked her away.

"Zev is in there. He heard me."

"He nearly tore you apart!"

Blood flowed from the deep gashes on her shoulder and waist. Her shredded dress barely hung on her frame by strips. Zev had tried to kill her. Cassiel saw Dyna's horror the moment she realized that. Her breath came in rapid bursts, her body shaking.

"Breathe …" he said steadily.

She couldn't. Her eyes rolled, and she toppled forward.

"Dyna!" Cassiel caught her and patted her face. It was no use. She had lost too much blood.

He swept her into his arms and flew back to camp. Soon the flickering orange flames of their campfire appeared ahead, and he swooped down, laying her on the grass by the campfire. Cassiel grabbed Dyna's satchel and flipped it upside down. Azeran's journal, her notebook, and dried plants fell out. There were no bandages, and the ceramic jars weren't labeled. He wasn't familiar with their uses, much less the plants. Like a fool, he hadn't bothered to remember anything she had said about them.

"Damn it all!"

She was the Herb Master. He didn't know what to do. The lack of bandages was beside the matter. He had to stop the bleeding.

Cassiel lifted the soaked kirtle to examine her mauled shoulder. The shredded fabric fell away in his fingers, revealing her bare body. Dark red trails spilled from the punctures in her shoulder where Zev had bitten her. He parted her torn skirt to find the same was true of the serrated gashes running from her waist to her thigh. Cassiel pressed his hands over the wounds, applying pressure. Her warm blood seeped through his fingers. Dyna's pulse was faint and too slow.

He could feel her life was slipping away.

Cassiel lowered his head. "I do not know how to save you. I cannot stop this."

He pressed on her wounds harder, desperate to keep her from losing any more blood—

Blood.

His blood could save her! But he couldn't give it to her. It was illegal, and he was a cursed half-breed. His blood might not even work. Cassiel's hands shook as he wrestled with his morality and Celestial law. To break such a monumental law of giving divine blood to a human called for exile. They would take his wings and he would never set foot in the Four Celestial Realms again.

Dyna's pulse faded beneath his fingertips, drowning him in desperation. He looked at her pallid face, wishing she would wake and give him that carefree smile of hers he thought he didn't like. If she died when there was a possibility of saving her, he truly would live to regret it.

Cassiel rummaged through their rucksack, tossing out items until he found the carving knife. He winced as he slashed both of his palms. Taking a shuddering breath, he placed them over her wounds.

The moment white light flashed beneath his hands, he knew instantly he had made a grave mistake.

Power shot through his body like a bolt of lightning, filling every crevice of his being with incredible heat. It weaved through muscle and bone with a force that, had he not been kneeling, would have knocked him down. The burning power continued its course from him to Dyna, and light burst from her in a brilliant ray.

Her heart hammered like the rapid flutter of a hummingbird inside of his chest. His hands throbbed with electric warmth where they connected. There was a tugging and a merging inside of him as his life force stitched with hers. Violent waves of pleasure rushed through his veins, blood pounding in his ears, stealing his breath. When he thought it would consume him whole, the sensation waned and his racing heart slowed. In tandem with Dyna's.

The realization of what he had done weighed on his shoulders with the weight of the world. He had only meant to give her his blood, but in his panic, he *exchanged* blood with her instead. Because of it, Cassiel knew one thing with a terrifying certainty that shook him to his soul.

He had Blood Bonded with Dynalya Astron.

CHAPTER 28

assiel had studied many subjects during his lessons, but the governess of the castle completely disregarded the topic of Blood Bonding. *"You will find no one willing to bond with you, Your Highness. Therefore, it is pointless to discuss the subject."* He hadn't argued because he agreed.

No one wanted a Nephilim for a life-mate.

Cassiel snatched back his shaking hands and drenched them in icy water from a waterskin. The deep lacerations tingled as they knitted closed. He stared in dismay at his unblemished palms. There was no washing Dyna's blood out of his system.

The brisk wind blowing through the trees chilled the sweat on his back, and a shiver passed through him as a howl echoed in the distance. He looked up at the moon among the glimmering stars.

"Elyōn ... what have I done?" the whispered words shook on his lips.

He had been a child the last time he spoke to the God of Life. To expect any guidance was trivial, for it never came when he needed it. Perhaps he wasn't worthy of receiving any. He was a mistake—a thing that was not meant to exist.

Cassiel closed his eyes, using all his will to wish away the last hour. But an undeniable mesmeric force hummed between him and Dyna. Shame bore down on him like a judgment from the Heavens.

Celestials reserved the Blood Bond for those who'd found their life-mate, for the act of exchanging blood intertwined their lives forever. It could never be undone. Not until he walked through Death's Gate, which wouldn't be for many centuries after she had long passed. He dropped his head in his hands, groaning as he pulled at his hair.

On the impulse to save her life, he had unintentionally married her. Was that all it took to gain a wife?

He thought the bonding act was complex and required something more meaningful. But he had not attended Celestial weddings before, so he'd never seen the bonding performed. Nor had he cared to learn. From what little he heard of it, there were oaths said during the ceremony, then some corporeal and psychological changes followed as the bond was established. He couldn't recall the details in his jumbled thoughts. But there was one thing he knew—Blood Bonds didn't forge any feelings of affection.

Dyna would resent him for this.

Cassiel looked down at his newly bound wife and grimaced at the sight of her naked body prickled with cold. He moved to cover her with a blanket, but he noticed her injuries had not healed. Did his blood not work?

Her breathing was steady and the deep lacerations no longer bled. He took her wrist and felt her strong pulse. His blood *must* have worked. Well, this was the first he'd ever healed someone. He wasn't sure what to expect. His healing was instant, but perhaps his impure blood took longer to heal others.

By the moonlight, he noticed something else. Rows of old jagged scars coursed from Dyna's collarbone to her chest. Claw marks. This had happened to her before. From the depth and width of the scars, the attack had been life-threatening, yet she survived.

Cassiel sighed and covered her. "You will live this time too. I suppose that is all that matters."

After setting a pot of water to warm over the fire, he ripped his ruined tunic into large strips. He removed the rest of Dyna's torn clothing, careful to avert his eyes when possible. He left the petticoat, as the only damage was a slash in the bloodied skirt.

Gently, Cassiel washed her with the heated water. The metallic scent of blood was so strong he almost tasted it. Then he bandaged her thigh, waist, and shoulder with pieces of his tunic.

Whenever he brushed her skin, a tingle moved up his arm in response. The line of energy felt similar to Soul Searching, but this was ten times more substantial. It had to be part of their ... new connection.

Cassiel tucked the blanket around Dyna once more. Crusted blood caked her tresses and brows, speckling her lips. He cleaned her face, then worked on washing her hair, running the soft strands between his fingers.

Of all the most ridiculous mistakes, he bound himself to a human. Cassiel straightened at the reminder.

Dyna was *human*.

She didn't have to abide by Celestial customs. She had not consented to marry him so their marriage was invalid. But annulments never occurred among the Celestials. Blood Bonds were sacred. Perpetual. If his father learned about this, he might compel her to honor it.

Then he must never know. No one must know.

Cassiel cursed and kneaded his temples. It would be impossible to hide this for long. He'd be forced to confess if his father attempted to wed him to another. Once bonded, he could never exchange his blood with anyone else. Doing so was adultery. That infidelity would not only defile a Blood Bond, it would also bring self-suffering and spurning.

Even if that didn't happen, Dyna would feel the change between them. While she wouldn't understand it at first, he would have to explain what it was, eventually. Angst stirred in him. He didn't want to see her disgust when she learned she was tied to him.

No.

He would let no one obligate her to honor the bond.

Not to him.

He refused to let her live the life his mother had. If they forced Dyna to stay in Hilos, the hatred of his people would break her. Imagining it made his fists clench. If he could protect her from anything at all, it would always be from that.

Perplexed with himself, he studied the soft curves of Dyna's face. The fire's glow highlighted her silken mouth and nose. He lightly brushed a stray strand of hair from her cheek, his fingers tingling.

What was it about this human that gave him the need to keep her safe?

Perhaps it was because she was trying so hard to do what she could on her own, and he wanted to help where she fell woefully short. Or because, as silly as she was, he found her incredibly brave to venture out into the unknown world to fight a demon.

Dyna whimpered in her sleep. She murmured indiscernible words, growing more agitated as teardrops formed in the corner of her eyes. Cassiel touched his chest at the trickle of fear weaving through him. It wasn't his fear—it was hers.

Filtering through the bond between them.

As her whimpers grew, so did the panic he felt from her until it grew frantic. Cassiel reached out to wake her, but hesitated to touch her battered body. He found a spot on her ankle and wrapped his fingers around its delicate circumference. The bond vibrated with warm energy, fading the fright that had twisted through him.

Dyna's cries quieted, and she woke, blinking sleepily at the night sky. He attempted to stealthily remove his hand, but she noticed him.

"Cassiel?" She moaned, pressing on her forehead. "What happened? Where is Zev?" She sat upright, causing the blanket to drop and expose her. He snapped his face away. Dyna screeched, rushing to cover herself. "Where are my clothes?"

"I had to remove your dress to mend your wounds," Cassiel said, forcing his voice to remain even. He motioned at the pile of bloody rags near him. "That is all that is left of it, and I found no change of clothing for you."

"Oh ... I lost my clothing in Hilos."

Cassiel sighed, lacking the energy to be annoyed. He was busy trying to get the image of her breasts out of his head.

"Did you rip your tunic for me?"

She must have noticed the color of her bandages, and that he was bare-chested as well.

"Garments are replaceable, you are not." Cassiel cringed for saying such a thing. What was wrong with him?

There was another short pause, followed by the sound of Dyna shifting around a bit. "I'm covered. You may turn around now."

He didn't dare. It was fortunate the dark hid his hot face because he was sure it had turned bright red. His wings twitched at her stare digging into his back.

"You have saved my life once again. I'll forever be within your debt."

He groaned. Instead of being upset with him, she was grateful. That only made him feel more ashamed. "Enough with that nonsense. This is the last we speak of debts."

"Thank you, Cassiel. You're a good person."

The flush seeped down his neck. "I'm not."

"You are."

"I'm *not*." He motioned sharply through the air to end the debate.

"What happened to your hand?"

Cassiel glanced down at his palms. Leftover blood that had dried all over his wrists and arms.

"Are you wounded? I'll tend to it."

"It is nothing."

Cassiel quickly washed off the blood, then removed a clean tunic from his pack and slipped it on. He wrapped his wings around himself, wanting to disappear from her sight. They sat like that for a moment, with his back to her and the crackling fire. Their shadows swayed together in the tall grass.

He wanted to ask how Dyna was feeling. She didn't seem to be in any pain. Had she healed yet?

A howl rang over the treetops.

"The beast has been doing that for a while," he said.

"Zev is not a beast. He will be himself in the morning."

Cassiel glowered at her shadow. "I should never have given you my knife, Dyna." He turned around. She glowered at him from the mound of blankets wrapped around her up to her neck. He lifted the rags of her bloody kirtle. "Zev almost tore you apart. If he is not a beast, why is he chained like one?"

Dyna looked away, her eyes welling. "Because I promised Zev that I would chain him. If I didn't, he would have ended his life."

Cassiel's growing irritation deflated with the whoosh of breath that left him. There was nothing to say to that. He tossed the rags in the fire, and they watched the flames devour them.

"Zev's father was a good man," Dyna said softly. "He was my father's younger brother. Both were prominent Herb Masters, but the village was too small, so Uncle Belzev traveled for work in nearby towns. One day, he announced that he had wed, and he moved away to live with his bride. My father never met her and my uncle never spoke of her. Years later, he returned to North Star with a baby in his arms. Only then did he tell my father he'd been living in Lykos Peak with a werewolf who'd taken him for a mate. But he left because she rejected their child. She didn't want a half-breed pup."

Cassiel's chest tightened. Another howl resonated in the distance with all the lament he felt in her story.

"My father took them in and Zev grew up into a sweet boy. He was three autumns old when I was born. He has always watched over me as an older brother would. As a child, I didn't realize that Zev was special. I thought his ability to shapeshift into a wolf was normal. I hadn't noticed he only shifted in front of our family. When a villager witnessed him change, fear spread and the council banished Zev from ever returning to North Star. He didn't understand why the villagers called him a beast and threw stones at him. He was only a little boy. It broke his heart to be unwanted."

The slurs Malakel spat at Cassiel during their childhood rang in his ears. *Dirty half-breed. Cursed Nephilim. Abomination.*

Dyna curled over her knees, resting her chin on her arms as she gazed at the campfire. "They returned to Lykos Peak so Zev could be with his kind. We held reunions in a meadow outside of the village for years until the Shadow killed my family. Uncle Belzev no longer came, but Zev and I continued to meet. As he aged, he became more disheartened. The Pack saw him as abnormal, so they shunned him, and his mother couldn't love him. Despite Zev's breed, I think she resented him because Belzev had chosen him over her."

The brunt of resentment and jealousy was all too familiar to Cassiel. It drove Queen Mirah mad when his father chose his mother. His childhood was laden with her hatred. *You are nothing.*

"Matters became more difficult when Zev reached maturity at thirteen." Dyna's soft voice dropped to a whisper. "The day he had his first full moon shift, the Other appeared."

Cassiel suppressed a shudder. "What is it?"

"It's his second form; a manifestation that comes from being half human and half wolf. Powerful and aggressive. Werewolves don't rear pups born of mixed blood because they fear it."

"The change looked painful," Cassiel said, remembering how Zev floundered as another force bent and stretched him like dough.

"It is. When he shifts into a wolf, it hurts, but it's quick and his mass stays the same. But when he shifts into the Other, the bones in his body break and force him to enlarge into a new form."

"Where did he get the chains?"

Dyna rubbed the old scars on her collarbone, staring blankly past him. "His father had them made after ..."

"He attacked you."

"He didn't mean to. He wasn't in his right mind."

"Do not dismiss it. Those wounds had been enough to kill you."

"Belzev treated me with Essence Healing."

Cassiel frowned, but he didn't argue on the matter of her family's use of magic. Something significant had to have saved her from such grave wounds. "And the Pack turned a blind eye to it?"

"The alpha was forced to allow them to live in Lykos Peak because Belzev had saved the Pack from an epidemic. They were indebted."

Cassiel shook his head. "But how did your uncle live in werewolf territory? The full moon forces all werewolves to relinquish control to their wolves. Their first instinct would be to hunt."

A sad smile tugged on a corner of Dyna's lips. "Uncle Belzev built their home on the outskirts of Lykos Peak near a cluster of ash trees. They hate the scent. He planted wolfsbane around the house for good measure, which is toxic to them. The Pack never hunted him, but I suspect fear of the Other kept them at bay."

"The chains are enough to hold him?"

"Silver is the bane of werewolves. Belzev used the chains to contain the Other during the full moon, and he created a diluted elixir out of wolfsbane to help subdue it. The elixir made Zev ill, but his father said he would no longer need it once he learned to control the Other. With training, he did eventually learn to delay the change from coming nearly all night. He always reverted to the Other, but it fortified Uncle Belzev's belief that he could control it." Dyna paused and pointed her face up at the sky, twinkling with a sheet of stars.

Cassiel inhaled a shallow breath at the depth of sorrow that washed through him. "But he could not."

Tears rolled down Dyna's cheeks, gathering at the end of her chin. Her voice wobbled as she spoke, "One autumn night, on Zev's eighteenth day of his birth, Uncle Belzev decided he was ready to be unchained. Zev woke the next morning to find his home covered in blood, and his father torn apart. Can you imagine how he must have felt to realize he had killed him with his own hands?"

Cassiel couldn't answer.

He envisioned the carnage with Zev kneeling in the middle of it, lost and broken after seeing what he had done. All of that horror and pain placed a weight on Cassiel's chest.

"His mother wanted him dead," Dyna said. "The alpha banished him instead. But Zev didn't want to live anymore. He wandered into the forest to die. I found him days later in the meadow, delirious from starvation and deranged from the Madness. I promised Zev that I would chain him myself. I had to, so he would live. Three years have passed, and I have chained him ever since." At the end of her story, she laid her head in her arms. Her shoulders shook as she soundlessly wept.

Anguish and grief stirred inside of Cassiel. He wasn't sure how much of it was his or if it was all hers coming through the bond. The grief was heavy, distressing, and it engulfed him in a way that left him disoriented. He wanted to take that feeling away from her, if only to stop it from affecting him.

Now he understood why Zev was on the verge of falling into the Madness.

Guilt had broken him, but he smiled and laughed for Dyna's sake. He played that role for her. The deep-rooted instinct to protect his family was the only thing keeping him alive.

Not once had Cassiel stopped to consider the people he traveled with. Zev's childhood in Lykos wasn't much different from his in Hilos. They both received scorn and repugnance for being half-breeds. He realized with horror that he had treated Zev the same way. He wasn't any better than Malakel. Self-disgust twisted Cassiel's stomach.

But this method of restraining the Other form was too dangerous. She had to stop.

"The best thing is to let him go," Cassiel said. "You cannot be responsible for his chains any longer."

Dyna wiped her face with a blanket. "I must. I made a promise. I'm the only one he can count on or he'll become feral."

Tension pulsed in Cassiel's temples. "Chaining him will eventually get you killed. You nearly died today. *Again*. Why must you constantly risk your life?"

"For my family."

He stared at her in disbelief. "What?"

"Some people value wealth, land, and prosperity. I value my family. They are all I have, and one thing I've learned is that family is something we must hold on to."

That made little sense to him, for he had nothing of the sort with his own. The entire concept was foreign. All he had from his family was disillusionment.

Cassiel scowled at the fire. "Family hurts you far worse than anyone else ever could. Relying on others, expecting anything of them, only leads to disappointment."

"Even so. There is nothing on earth or in the Heavens that would keep me from helping those that I love."

Gods, she was incomprehensible.

Cassiel's fists clenched on his lap so tight his nails cut into his skin. "I do not understand you. When you and I touch, I see your soul. I see your heart. If anyone has truly suffered, it has been you. Yet hatred and selfishness have not corrupted you."

Dyna gasped. "What? You can see my—"

"I do not understand it!" he snapped. "Why are you not consumed by wrath for what happened to you, and those you care for? You have reason to hate your fate and curse the world. Why have you not run away and hidden from all that burdens you?"

Why did she keep fighting to live her life to the fullest when he had long given up on living his?

Dyna pressed on her chest, and those glimmering eyes of hers burrowed through him, seeing past the wall of stone he had built steadily around himself. Through the bond, she was feeling all of his spite and rage. It was infuriating, maddening, and humiliating.

Cassiel wanted to fly away from her. Far away in any unknown direction until he could no longer feel her presence inside of him.

"Anger," she said, holding his gaze. "Hate. They were with me for a while, but I chose not to let them stay. It was difficult, but I had no use for them."

Cassiel shook his head, still not seeing how that was possible. "I need them …" The whispered confession slipped from his mouth as though another had spoken them.

Anger kept him alive. Hate made him strong. Without them, he had nothing.

"I understand." Her soft reply burned through him, blurring his vision.

"No," he said tightly. "You do *not*."

She wasn't a cursed half-breed. She wasn't born as the object of disgust and ridicule for others to spit on. How would she ever understand?

Dyna rose and came to kneel beside him. Cassiel searched her face, trying to understand. He tried to perceive something, anything, dark or flawed she had not shown him. The only thing imperfect was the fractures around her heart.

The way she was looking at him was as bizarre as she was. He didn't want her sympathy. He didn't need—

Dyna laid a warm hand on his cheek and a hum of energy passed through their physical connection, moving through him. By her surprised expression, she experienced it too.

For a moment, Cassiel thought she had discovered what had happened between them. He had the frantic urge to escape, but it ebbed as the bond filled him with gentle peace. The sensation wrapped around him with a warmth that made his rigid shoulders sag, and he inexplicably leaned into her palm. He was slow to recognize the feeling of comfort.

Why was she comforting him when she was the one in need of it? Her strange nature countered all he believed about humans, or was it this human that was different?

Dyna treated him like his lowly existence didn't bother her, like the thing he was didn't sicken her. His mind struggled to accept that she didn't reject him, but he sensed it through the bond. She had no aversion to him, even after the cold way he treated her when she never once deserved it.

Why spare him any kindness? He'd given her more than enough reason to spurn him.

Cassiel's second sight triggered, and her mesmerizing soul opened to him in a surge of vibrant colors. He didn't know how such a beautiful thing could exist, or how he had the privilege to see it.

Dyna went very still, having guessed he was Soul Searching. But she didn't move away. She held his gaze as her soul drew him in. Cassiel's eyes drifted shut and let himself fall. All that he was dissolved. All that troubled him lifted. And he faded into its endless depths.

While he became lost there, he thought he might find himself there too.

CHAPTER 29

Zev

Fire burned through every facet of Zev's sanity. A dry cry left his mouth, growing into screams as the searing agony consumed him. The chains were like bindings of hot iron. Smoke and steam billowed from where the silver touched him. He tried to move, but the chains had ensnared his naked body tightly against the elm tree, the heavy shackles clamped around each wrist. To become so tangled during the night, the Other must have fought desperately to free itself.

Zev ground his teeth, trying to push the agony out of his mind. Clouds of his ragged breath hovered in the morning chill. The cold did little to ease his burning skin. The chains and his teeth rattled from his uncontrollable trembling. There wasn't anything else to do but wait for Dyna to release him.

An elm leaf drifted down and landed on the ground by his face. He memorized the vivid orange color, smell, and jagged shape, trying to think of anything but the burning and ringing in his ears.

The Madness was whispering to him again, always whispering. *Forget the pain. Forget the past. Forget the chains. Give in.*

Zev growled and willed the mad thoughts away, the distraction leaving him vulnerable to the pain again. It consumed him to the point of delirium. His cries rang in the clearing, filling the forest with his agony and grief.

He had to endure it. He deserved the torture.

The chains were a punishment for his greatest sin, and the scars left behind were a testament. A son who murdered his father had no right to anything else.

Zev's vision distorted and darkened, hovering on the edge. His senses dulled as he became numb. Dyna had never taken this long to free him, and the tight chains had well burned through his skin. His body has reached its limit.

He was dying.

The thought should have frightened him, but he was ready to go. He wanted to leave this world and go to another place where all this pain ceased to exist.

A dark shape slipped from the trees. It approached him under the shadow of the morning clouds, its movements agile and soundless. A black cloak shrouded its form, a hood obscuring its face.

Death had come to collect his soul.

It reached his side but made no move to take him. Why was it only staring at him? Was it waiting for permission?

Zev rasped, "I'm ... ready to pass through ... the Gate ..."

Death didn't respond.

"Please ..." he begged. "Finish it."

After a pause, Death's cloak moved aside to reveal a black-gloved hand holding a dagger. Morning light shone on the sharp edge and the red gilded hilt. The weapon seemed familiar, but he couldn't remember where he'd seen it.

"Zev!" a faint voice filtered through his muffled hearing. "Zev!"

Death vanished in a gust of wind as a glowing form came through the shrubs. A Seraph swathed in light. The being rushed to his side, and her face became clearer.

"Zev, I'm here!" Dyna's cool hands took his sweaty face, and his senses slammed back into place. All of it hitting him with the suffering and stench of his burning flesh.

Dyna fumbled with a key hanging on a piece of twine. She jammed it into a manacle, and he heard the distinct click of his freedom before the manacles clanked in the dirt. She tried to be gentle in removing the chains, but Zev screamed with each piece of his melted skin tearing away with them. She recited apologies like a prayer, tears streaming down her face. The vile chains formed a pile by her feet, strips of his decaying flesh sticking to the thick links. The silver left burns crisscrossing from his neck to chest, all around his back, continuing down his legs.

Dyna quickly laid a blanket around his waist and brought a waterskin to his lips. The icy water smoldered down his dry throat.

"Please, let me heal you."

"No," he said, his voice but a raw whisper. "Don't."

"Why do you do this to yourself? These burns can become infected."

"No!" Zev pulled away. The injuries and the disfigurement were a penance he must wear. His own eyes welled at the sound of her soft crying. "I'm sorry."

He looked at her again, finding she still faintly glowed. Her disheveled red locks shrouded her bowed head and one of his tunics hung on her thin frame, falling off a narrow shoulder smeared with dried blood. Her bloodied petticoat was shredded, torn by what must have been his claws.

Zev winced as he forced himself to sit up. "Dyna, what happened?"

She couldn't have escaped without any significant injury, but he didn't see any on her. Her dried blood smelled odd. It was mixed with another sweeter scent he had smelled before.

"Is that Cassiel's blood?" Zev asked in disbelief.

Dyna nodded. "He helped me restrain you ... and I think he healed me."

Zev's eyes grew wide as he looked her over. For Cassiel to have done that meant only one thing—he had no choice.

"How bad was it? Tell me the truth."

She wouldn't look at him.

He reached out to her, and she recoiled. At the phantom of fear on her face, misery swallowed him. How many more of his family must the Other kill before his end?

Zev pulled at his hair as the Madness screeched in his thoughts, *Bringer of ruination. Seed of misfortune. You reek of death!*

His wolf snarled within the confines of his consciousness, and fur sprouted along his body as it dominated over him.

"No, no, I'm all right. I'm alive! Don't listen to its lies!" Dyna wrapped her arms around him. She murmured reassurances until the mad whispers faded.

Her scent had changed. It was slight, lingering under the surface. She smelled ethereal.

Like Cassiel.

"Forgive me," he pleaded. "Please."

Dyna shook her head. "There is nothing to forgive, Zev. It wasn't you."

But it was him. The Other would always be a part of him. The mad whispers returned, beckoning and alluring. Zev craved to accept what it offered him. He didn't want to live like this anymore.

Dyna held him as he bitterly wept, all of his pain spilling from him in shuddering cries. She didn't let go even after he was empty and exhausted. They sat together in silence for a long while, letting life pass them by.

When it became late morning, Zev spotted the carcass of a wolf tossed halfway in the bushes, flies buzzing above it. He didn't need to ask to know he had killed her too.

"Who was she?" Dyna asked.

"Tasnia, Luna of the Lykos Pack. Owyn's mate." Zev crossed his arms over his bent knees and laid his head over them. "She came for me."

Tasnia had been one of the few werewolves who had been kind to him. And he repaid her by taking away her mate. He'd seen the beginnings of wild Madness in her last night, along with rage, sorrow, and betrayal. He should have known she would come after him after what he had done to her mate.

"It was more than that," Dyna said. "When the Other appeared, she didn't run. Nor did she fight."

Zev closed his eyes. Tasnia must have tracked him at a distance, waiting exactly for last night so he would kill her. She chose to end her life as a wolf rather than let the Madness take her, simultaneously inflicting her revenge. The guilt of her death at his hands and Owyn's last words would always remain with him.

You're no wolf. You're a demon.

Dyna took his arm. "Come, let's return to camp."

Zev staggered to his feet, stumbling against the elm tree, barely able to stand. Dyna leveled beside him so he could lean on her, and they wobbled away, only pausing so she could grab the cursed chains and lug them along. It was a slow trek through the forest as he dragged one foot in front of the other.

They eventually left the tree line and entered the clearing where they had camped. The Celestial prince sat by a roaring fire in the middle of a grass field glistening with a layer of morning dew. To Zev's surprise, he rushed over to help them. Cassiel took the chains from Dyna and brought Zev's arm over his shoulders. He withstood most of the weight, half-carrying him the rest of the way to camp.

Zev hissed and winced as they helped him lay flat on the wet grass. He closed his weary eyes against the glare of the sun. Profound fatigue fell over him, pulling him under.

"Let me heal you," Dyna pleaded again.

Zev didn't want to argue with her about it anymore. He rolled over, giving them his back. Cassiel cursed under his breath at the sight of the burns there.

"I cannot look at you this way," she said, her voice quivering. "Please."

The sound of her crying was as painful as his wounds, so he didn't protest again. She kneeled and held both of her hands above his body. Warmth fell over him as vivid green Essence radiated from her fingertips. Static charged the air, prickling along his skin. The light grew and enveloped him in a cocoon.

Cassiel inhaled a sharp breath.

Gradually, the strain on Zev's body eased as his pain melted like snow in the spring. Lying still, he watched the wounds go through the stages of healing as if time sped past within the green light. The burns closed and scabbed, then the scabs fell away to leave behind distended pink scars. The last wound over Zev's heart scarred, and her Essence faded.

"There," Dyna murmured faintly, then she collapsed.

"Dyna!" Cassiel exclaimed. "She's unconscious."

Zev sighed and rolled over.

The prince held her limp body on his lap, her head lolled against his chest. "What happened? What was that?"

"She will be all right," Zev garbled. "She needs rest."

"You both do."

Zev mumbled an incoherent reply and his bloodshot eyes slid closed as sleep took him.

The smell of porridge drew Zev from his dreams. It burbled in a small pot hanging over the campfire. Dyna slept soundly in the grass beside him under a pile of blankets. Cassiel sat with them, his distant gaze fixed on her face. He held a black wing extended above her, providing shade against the sun shining high in the clear blue sky.

"How long did we sleep?" Zev asked, his throat still rough and dry.

"Half the day."

Zev moaned as he pushed himself upright. His muscles were stiff and sore.

Cassiel didn't comment on what had occurred last night. He was studying Dyna worriedly.

"She will wake soon," Zev said as he went to his pack to change into clean clothing and strap on his boots.

"When?"

He didn't know. It could be a day or a week. Hopefully not much longer. She had exhausted herself completely to mend him.

Cassiel glanced at him, examining the new scars that layered his arms and legs. "That light she invoked, that was Essence Healing?"

"Yes."

"But you remain scarred."

Zev rubbed the chain-link imprinted on his elbow. "Essence Healing uses life-force energy to mend wounds and illness. Similar to your divine blood, but not as powerful, nor is it a definitive cure. Dyna cannot use it to self-heal, and it doesn't cure disease. It reaches within the body to locate injuries and increase the body's rate of natural repair."

"She mentioned healing magic requires a lot of power."

"Depending on the extent of the wound, it can spend her Essence and render her unconscious until she recovers."

"Hence why she has not awoken."

"It would happen to my father occasionally. He was also an Herb Master of Azeran's line ..." Zev trailed off. He hadn't meant to speak of him.

"From where I stand, I do not believe it was your fault," Cassiel muttered. "He left you unchained."

Zev inhaled a deep breath. "She told you?"

"She did."

He turned away, staring down at the discolored, warped tissue on his wrists. Cassiel hadn't demanded answers because Dyna had already given them.

"I wish she hadn't. You despise me enough as it is."

A slight flush colored the prince's face. "I do not despise you. I did not know how to define you. I have learned that people are all the same, no matter where they originate. They reject and fear what does not fit in their societal conformities."

Cassiel plucked one of his fallen feathers nestled in the grass and spun the shaft between his fingertips. "Celestials deem themselves as a pure and sacred race. They are intolerant of anything unnatural. They hated me for being half-human, and I hated them for their bigotry. I swore that I would never be like them, but I—" He sighed and tossed the feather in the fire where it burst in a spark. "I have done the same to you. That was wrong."

Zev raised his eyebrows. "Are you apologizing?"

Cassiel cleared his throat again, fidgeting with the ivory buttons on his tunic. "I am admitting failure in my conduct."

Zev smirked, running a hand through his matted hair. That may be as close to an apology as he would get. "I should not have kept my condition from you. It's difficult to speak about."

"I understand that more than most. But if you had kept it from me last night, and I had not followed you into the woods, Dyna surely would have been killed."

Zev flinched.

"Do you not remember?"

"I have no memories of when the Other overtakes me."

"You were determined to kill us." The wind blew against them, drifting Cassiel's scent toward Zev. It was subtle, but the prince smelled like Dyna.

"You gave her your blood."

Cassiel's flush reignited, filling his face. "She was dying and I-I did not know what else to do."

"You saved her life yet again. I know what this means."

Cassiel's eyes widened. "You do?"

"It is illegal for Celestials to give their divine blood to humans. You could be found in contempt."

"Oh, right ..."

Zev was not sure if the prince looked relieved or frightened by that. "It's a grave law you've broken for her sake. Whatever repercussions may come against you, I'll speak on your behalf and explain to your father what happened."

"That is unnecessary," he said uneasily.

"Thank you, Cassiel. She wouldn't be alive if not for you."

He cringed, the flush moving down his neck. "Please do not thank me."

Zev tilted his head, trying to read him. "Why? It's truly a debt I'll never cease to pay."

Cassiel sighed. "I only ask that you not speak a word of this. That will be thanks enough."

Zev readily agreed. In exchange for saving her life, he would have said yes to anything.

Zev didn't sleep much that night, neither did Cassiel. They sat with Dyna, waiting and hoping she'd wake. The more they waited, the more anxious they became. She was too still, her breathing too quiet. Zev constantly listened for her heartbeat, and Cassiel checked her pulse.

After half a day with no change, they both tried to occupy themselves with menial tasks around camp like organizing their supplies, and scourging for food. At one point, Zev made the time to properly bury Tasnia. He owed it to her and Owyn.

At dawn the next day, both breathed a sigh of relief when Dyna's eyes, at last, fluttered open. Her complexion had lost its color, face gaunt, and hair dull. Her vitality had been drained, Zev thought as she gave them a wan smile. It went into him. He had to resign himself on the matter. Her health would improve once she recovered her Essence.

Zev insisted she eat, so the prince served them tea and manna bread from the last of his rations. As they ate, they discussed if they should continue traveling.

"You need another night of rest," Zev said, trying not to grind his teeth at the sight of the purple shadows around her eyes.

Dyna shook her head as she sipped from her cup. She huddled under a mound of blankets, not able to stop shivering.

Cassiel frowned at her. "We will not reach Corron before nightfall. Might as well sleep."

"I don't wish to waste any more time," she said.

Zev reluctantly gathered their packs and they went in search of the main road. Once it was found, they kept to the forest, using the barrier of tall shrubs between them and the road to conceal them from view.

After a mile, Dyna seemed to gather more energy. She hummed to herself, picking sprigs along the way. Kneeling by a shrub, she tucked a lock of scarlet hair behind an ear and chewed on her lip as she wrote something in her notebook.

Whenever she stopped, so did the prince. When she continued, so did he. Zev studied their peculiar movements. They moved in an odd synchronization, subconsciously mirroring each other. Periodically, they glanced at one another when the other was not looking.

Dyna stretched on her toes to scrape a loose piece of bark off a tree, and her petticoat swished aside, the slit exposing her thigh. Cassiel reddened and looked away, meeting Zev's amused smirk.

"What?" he asked defensively.

Zev arched a brow. "You're acting strange."

"Oh, am I?" Cassiel hiked his pack over his shoulder, moving past him. "Given last night's events, I think that can be forgiven."

"Right." Zev fell into step next to him. "Sorry."

"I am a fool for not figuring it out sooner, even with the chains."

"What did you think they were for?"

"Well, uh ..." Cassiel scratched at his chin.

"You thought we would chain you up and bleed you dry." Zev crossed his arms. "You truly do assume the worst of people."

"There is always the threat of poachers hunting my kind."

"Does she look like a poacher?" Zev nodded in Dyna's direction. She tapped a graphite pencil on her notebook, lost in thought as she studied another plant.

"Well, no," Cassiel said indignantly. "But most would not resist the chance to capture a Celestial."

Zev clapped the prince's shoulder, almost knocking him over under its weight. "I don't need chains if I wanted to restrain you. It wouldn't take much to break one of your wings to keep you from flying away."

Cassiel narrowed his eyes.

Zev laughed and strolled ahead, listening to him grumble under his breath.

"Don't pay him any mind, Cassiel. He's only teasing," Dyna said.

"I preferred it when he growled at me."

She laughed. "You lie."

"How dare you accuse a prince of lying," Cassiel replied good-naturedly, making her laugh again.

Surprised, Zev paused and turned around. Dyna and the prince walked casually together, much closer than he had allowed before.

"About last night, I wish to thank you for what you did," she said.

"You have nothing to thank me for."

"We both know that's not true." Dyna stopped and took Cassiel's hands in hers. They both jumped suddenly and looked down at their intertwined fingers, neither letting go. "This feeling, this is what you call Soul Searching? It feels different from before."

Cassiel stilled. He swallowed, looking away from her questioning gaze. When he noticed Zev watching, panic briefly crossed his features. He snatched his hands back. "We best hurry if we are to make any ground. Corron still lies forty miles ahead."

The prince rushed onward and left them behind. Zev frowned, not sure what to make of the odd reaction. Dyna gave him a confused smile.

As they walked, Zev couldn't shake the odd sense his cousin wasn't the same. Besides her scent, there was something else about her. Something new he couldn't quite describe. Last night she had changed.

And he suspected it wasn't all his doing.

CHAPTER 30

Von

Von listened to the evening wind whistle outside of Tarn's tent. It shook the ceiling, tinkling the charms hanging from the supporting beams. There were several in variety: wooden ornaments, dried herbs, lustrous beads, strips of paper written with calligraphic symbols, and crystals. Von had gathered them all during their travels across the world, each made to guard the master or some other purpose that served him.

A large blood-red crystal hung in the center from a clasp in the shape of talons. The Crystal Core. It's what subdued every reluctant slave made to wear the brass bangles. The crystal's magic kept them trapped within a certain distance of the camp and away from the crystal itself. It also inflicted unpleasant punishment should they try to harm their ward.

Charred outlines of runes marked the oiled canvas of the tent where a Druid had embedded them. The spells were over a decade old, but the charge of their power moved within the space, prickling against his skin.

Von's footsteps sank into the furs spread on the ground as he walked around the room to light the candles set upon iron stands. Chests full of glinting gold rested beside a tall four-poster bed made of a luxurious dark wood. Silk black sheets and fluffed pillows layered the plush down mattress.

It was an extravagant bed for someone who never slept in it.

The master took six drops of Witch's Brew in his wine each night so he wouldn't need rest. Tarn had too many enemies to risk such things. Von could count on one hand how many times he'd seen him sleep. The first time was the night they survived the Horde, and the second …

Tarn sat at the dining table with Yavi. He watched her intently as she studied the Sacred Scroll acquired in Landcaster. The jagged scar running across his face appeared more prominent and unsightlier in the candlelight.

Von would never forget how Tarn's face had split in two with skin and muscle splayed open. But the screams that echoed in his memories didn't belong to the master. They belonged to the Xián Jīng assassin that had given him that scar.

He moved on to the candle stands set beside the desk. Thick tomes were set neatly upon it, flanking a map of Azure. He lit the last candle and brought it to the table where Yavi worked among a clutter of missives, documents, and Sacred Scrolls.

Her quill tinkled lightly in the inkwell, then she continued writing on a separate piece of paper. The low light glowed off her face in the darkened tent, illuminating the auburn tresses that fell in soft waves along her shoulders. She sat a little straighter, her eyes glimmering a little happier as she worked. Translating Sacred Scrolls was the only time she was allowed to read and write. Such education was a rare thing among women, especially to Yavi's degree.

Von followed the swirl of the wet ink as it formed neat letters. When she finished the last sentence, Tarn snatched the page, leaving a splatter of ink on the table.

"It should not have taken you this long," he said, his pale eyes zigzagging as he quickly read.

Yavi returned the quill to the inkwell and lowered her gaze. "This scroll was lengthier than the others. Some words of the old tongue are not found in present Urnian. I translated it as well as interpreted."

"Meaning your work is rubbish. What good are you if you cannot do what I acquired you for?"

She clasped her trembling hands and hid them on her lap. "I'll do better, Master."

"It might serve me better to sell you and be done with it."

It took all of Von's will not to react. Apprehension swam through his veins. "It would be difficult to find another slave that can read ancient Urnian, Master," he commented casually. "In addition to the twelve languages that she speaks, reads, and writes. She serves you well when we travel abroad."

Tarn's cool eyes narrowed on him past the edge of the page. "You will only give your opinion when I ask for it."

Von deferentially bowed his head.

Tarn continued reading and motioned dismissively in Yavi's direction. "Go."

She stood and gave him a quick bow before turning to leave. Her gaze, radiating with worry, fleetingly met Von's then she slipped out of the tent. An amethyst crystal hanging above glowed and slowly spun, shooting purple rays of light on the canvas walls. The Forewarning Crystal announced any presence within a twenty-foot radius around the tent, so they'd always know if someone was near. The lights ceased once Yavi moved outside of it.

Von prayed the master's threat was empty. He knew one day he'd have to separate from Yavi, but not like this. Not when she could be sold and taken to a place he couldn't reach.

Tarn tossed the page aside. "Another worthless scroll. This one speaks of the beginnings of the world. You revealed my presence in Azure for this?"

"Forgive me, Master."

"Each one you have brought me has been useless."

"Shall I cease the search for the Sacred Scroll of the Unending?"

"No." Tarn lifted his tankard and swirled the wine inside. "It's out there somewhere. Rozin Ida discovered it nearly three-hundred years ago. I'll find it as well."

"Will you keep the slave woman until then, or shall I find a trader?" Von kept the question indifferent, cold. He never referred to Yavi by name in front of Tarn, never showing he cared much of anything for her.

Inside, his chest compressed under a boulder of tension meant to crush him. He quickly shoved the feeling away, aware of the Mood Rune that could pick up any strong feeling in the tent.

His question went unacknowledged.

"I am beginning to suspect it may be on Mount Ida," Tarn said to himself.

It was possible. The Unending Scroll had led the infamous pirate to the hidden island, to begin with. It was there that Captain Ida obtained invincible power. Now they were searching for it.

But would Tarn sell Yavi? Von clamped his mouth tight to keep himself from asking again, lest he risks exposing them.

He picked up the page she had written and blew on the semi-wet ink before tucking it into a leather folder. It was thick with pages she had previously translated over the years. Most were parables or teachings on the meaning of life and the dimensions of The Seven Gates. None of which were of any use to them. He took the folder and the scroll to the desk and returned them to a coffer filled with the other Sacred Scrolls he'd collected.

None had been fairly earned.

Killing for the words of the God of Urn left a foul stain on Von's conscience. A black blot no amount of scrubbing could wash away. The holy law dictated that sins committed during servitude belonged to the master. So why did he feel the weight of them?

"Bring me the study on the Moonstone," Tarn said.

Von searched through the tomes. He pulled out one with a blue leather-bound covering and the title embossed in silver that read *Magos Artifacts of the Orbis Era.* He delivered it to the table. Tarn opened the book and flipped the pages to a detailed illustration of the Lūna Medallion. It was plated with silver and inlaid with diamonds, weaving around an iridescent stone at its center. The medallion had harnessed the powers of Azeran Astron and nearly won him the Magos Empire, but it was the Moonstone that Tarn needed to succeed in his plan.

The illustration looked too real. Tarn brushed his fingers over the page as if wishing he could pluck it free.

Would he lose interest in Dyna if he had it? With the Moonstone, Tarn could reach Mount Ida in a blink of an eye. It opened portals to anywhere the wielder wished and only required the light of the moon to evoke its power. Even a human could use it. Von could send Yavi back home to her family where she belonged. But finding the stone was another matter.

"Still no leads?"

"No, Master. Bouvier maintains that the Lūna Medallion disappeared at the end of the War of the Guilds, but he will not cease searching for it." Their fourth spy was resourceful in tracking rare artifacts and valuable information. It had taken much of the load off of Von's shoulders since Bouvier had joined them a year ago.

A section of the scar running through Tarn's brow creased. "Where is he now?"

"I sent him to Corron yesterday to track down the broker the merchant had mentioned."

"Ah, that's right. You suspect the merchant may have told him of my whereabouts." Tarn held up his tankard, and Von served him more wine.

"If he does, Bouvier has been ordered to eliminate any concern."

Tarn planted an elbow on the table, resting his chin on a fist. He flicked another page in the book, pensive at whatever passage he read there. "I remember a time when you resisted such things."

"I live to serve you."

"Do you?"

"Yes."

The rune for truth, which looked like the outline of a horizontal hourglass, glowed blue for honesty. Had Von lied, it would have turned red.

"When is Elon to return?"

It had been three days. Von was running out of excuses. The elf didn't normally take so long to return with information. "He'll arrive soon."

Tarn looked up from the book, pale eyes beginning to frost. "That is what you said yesterday."

"It shouldn't be much longer."

Von glanced at the small glass orb the size of his fist that rested on the table beside Tarn. On the polished surface appeared a glowing map of the region and a speck of green light that represented Dyna's location in the east. The tracking spell Benton had placed on her guided them well enough. But somehow, she had gotten far ahead of them. They were a day's travel behind her.

Tarn shut the book. "See to the camp's breakdown. It's dark enough to move."

Von suppressed another sigh. "Yes, Master."

It relieved him to be excused, but it was another form of punishment. Since Landcaster, the camp moved each night. His scouts had reported sightings of bounty hunters, Rangers, and the Azure Guard on the main roads. So, the camp was constantly on the move, traveling by night to avoid detection. The men had gotten little sleep because of it.

Generally, when the authorities discovered Tarn's presence, they were quick to leave for another part of the country or to another continent. But now his master's sole focus was the Maiden.

Great peril in the venture thou art pursuing.

The Seer's warning was too vague to mean anything. It could mean the pursuit of the Unending would put Tarn at risk—he was already at risk with the Azure Guard searching for him—or it could mean demise. But for whom?

It would all be over soon.

Von was about to leave when the Forewarning Crystal spun, announcing another presence. Finally. Elon had come to give his report.

But Geon called from outside instead, "Commander Von, I've returned with word from Corron."

Von frowned. "It must be a message from Bouvier, Master."

"Good."

He parted the tent flap aside, letting in the brisk wind. Geon's ruddy face stood out in the night. The lad saluted and handed Von a folded note along with two wooden cylindrical cases. He dismissed Geon, then returned to the dining table to set the cases down and unfolded the note.

Tarn arched an eyebrow. "Well?"

"After a thorough questioning, Bouvier concluded the broker knew nothing of your presence in Azure," Von said as he read it. "The man deals in antiquities. He had a couple of Sacred Scrolls, which Bouvier relieved him of."

"Hmm." Tarn removed the lid from one of the wooden cases and slid out a brittle piece of rolled-up parchment. He carefully unfurled it and took out the second scroll. Both were ancient and filled with a faded script.

"The broker admitted he was to purchase another scroll from Beryl Coast," Von added. "It's a city on the north-eastern coast of Azure. The temple ruins there are under excavation."

"Send word that Bouvier is to go to Beryl Coast and investigate further. Call the slave woman back here to work on these."

The Forewarning Crystal announced more company before he could answer.

"I have returned," Elon called out.

It was about bloody time.

Two shadows slipped in through the tent's entrance. Elon and Novo were indistinguishable beneath their black cloaks, both wearing masks that hid the bottom halves of their faces.

Von waited for a smaller form to enter behind them, but the amethyst had stopped spinning. "Where's Len?"

Novo's dark eyes flitted to his captain.

Elon lowered his mask. "I assigned her to stay behind. She knows how to remain out of sight."

Von frowned. Why leave the girl behind when Novo would have been better suited?

If it bothered Tarn, it wasn't obvious. He inadvertently raised Len, training her himself before she became one of his spies. The girl was hardly seventeen, but she was his best after Von and Elon. And fiercely loyal. In a way, the Raiders thought of her as Tarn's adoptive daughter. They were careful around her in case they should anger him. Elon had no such aversions. He implemented her as he would anyone under his command.

Tarn flicked a hand. "Report."

Elon described the journal where the map to Mount Ida was kept. Even from a distance, he could confirm it was enchanted, and it was sired to the Maiden.

The news invited an interminable pause. So, it wouldn't be enough to steal the map. They had to take Dyna too. Von suspected as much, but he had wished to spare her. How did she come about a magic map?

"What of her company?" he asked.

"She is accompanied by two young men," Elon said. "They are the first Guardians mentioned in the divination."

"We assumed her cousin was the dweller of the moon, but you're telling me the other is the Guardian of divine blood?"

Elon nodded. "He's a Celestial."

Von's thoughts stalled for a moment, failing to comprehend. Dyna's prince didn't have wings.

"You heard right," the second spy spoke up, pulling down his mask and hood and revealing a young man with long brown curls tied at the nape of his neck. Novo's mustache curled as he flashed them a grin. "The bloke has himself a pair of *black* wings. He uses some sort of magic coat to hide them."

Black wings? That couldn't be right. Celestials were described to have the same uniform features: white wings, blond hair, and blue eyes. Dyna's prince didn't match that description. Perhaps he wasn't a Celestial, but he had other abilities Von hadn't realized at first, like the ability to fly.

"Is that how they got so far ahead of us?" Von asked.

Elon nodded. "He flew her away from Landcaster."

"They are much more than they appear to be, Commander," Novo added. "Especially the other one."

"What do you mean? Something happened with the werewolf?"

"But he's not a werewolf, is he?" Novo exchanged a look with the captain.

"He is a Lycan," Elon replied.

The truth rune cast a daunting blue hue within the tent and Von was, once again, stunned into silence.

"I saw his bloody Other form meself," Novo said, his face half shadowed in the eerie light. "They had to use silver chains to restrain it."

Von cursed under his breath. Lycans were far more dangerous than werewolves. They were more violent, stronger, and they could shift during the day.

Tarn lazily swirled the wine in his cup. "He didn't sense you?"

"I invoked a cloaking spell," Elon said.

Novo smirked. "Aye, we moved about freely without being noticed. But it would have been wise to finish him while you had him right in front of you, Captain. He was weakened."

Von scowled at Elon. "You exposed yourself? Then they must know we are tracking them."

"They do not."

"The Lycan was too delirious from the silver," Novo explained. "He thought Captain Elon was Death himself coming to take his soul through The Seven Gates."

Then Novo was right. It would have been the opportune chance to eliminate a Guardian, especially one so dangerous. Why hadn't Elon taken it?

Von sighed and rubbed his face. "And what of the other one? You're certain about what he is?"

A Guardian with divine blood was what had convinced him the Seer was a fraud. Celestials had been extinct for five hundred years.

Elon nodded. "The Lycan had wounded the Maiden, and the Celestial healed her with his blood."

Von stared at him, too shocked to speak. They were up against a being of the Heavens?

"He's a Nephilim." Tarn leaned forward in his chair, a shadow of interest rising on his face. "Half-Celestial, half-human. There were rumors of such a breed created during The Decimation. Evidently, the extinction of Celestials was false."

The Seer must enjoy playing games. *One never knows what a divination truly means.* What other half-truths had the pixie hidden in her words?

"Where are they headed now?" Tarn asked.

"Corron," Elon answered.

"They plan to take a caravan to the Port of Azure and aboard a ship for Dwarf Shoe," Novo said. "They will arrive in Corron by midday tomorrow."

Tarn's face gave nothing away, but Von had long learned to sense when his master was forming a plan. The city was where they would make their move. Trepidation grasped him like tree roots, burying him under a mound of adrenaline. It was the feeling he always had before a fight.

Death would collect souls soon.

"Good work. Pull back and send for Len," Von ordered.

Novo nodded and slinked out of the tent.

Elon lingered. "Another Guardian may have appeared."

Tarn's pale blue eyes snapped to him. "Another?"

"Who?" Von asked.

"Rawn Norrlen. A Green Elf."

It surprised Von that Elon reported this so calmly. The old scar on the back of his hand appeared waxy under the candlelight. Removal of the tattoo signified disgrace and banishment. No one knew why Elon was exiled, but he must no longer feel loyal enough to care about an enemy of Red Highland. Either that, or he had well-established restraint.

"Lord Norrlen requested to join the Maiden's company. He was denied."

"Then why do you suspect he may be a Guardian?"

"The Norrlen House is known in the Vale for its deeds in serving the throne. He is a soldier of great renown we should not underestimate."

"Rawn Norrlen," Tarn mulled. "Where have I heard that name?"

"He led the Battle of Fen Muir that won Greenwood the recent war against Red Highland." Elon held Von's stare, and what he said next sunk a chill through him. "Rawn gave the Maiden an oath of protection, and an oath from an elf is binding."

Thus, follows a warrior bestowing his vow.

The divination was rapidly coming together. More Guardians would soon follow.

"Then we shall not wait for him to keep his oath." Tarn's eyes were two orbs of ice as he looked at Von. "Bring her to me."

Before he could answer, there was a clamor of voices outside the tent and Abenon shouted for the men to take up arms.

Geon burst through the tent. "Commander, the Azure Guard has found us! We're under attack!"

CHAPTER 31

Von

How had they been discovered? That was impossible. They had cloaked the camp. But Von heard the clash of steel, the shrill of neighing horses, and the cries of his men as they fought or died. He ran out of the tent, then he saw it. The shimmering protective barrier that usually hid the camp had disintegrated, leaving them exposed for all to see.

Benton. Damn him! Neither the old bastard nor his sons were anywhere in sight.

"Commander," Geon caught up with him.

"Find Yavi. Protect her."

"Aye." Geon split off in the opposite direction.

Von sprinted for the sounds of the melee with Elon at his side. They came upon a battle, or what could only be a massacre. Azure Guards and Rangers on horseback rode into the burning camp, cutting down Raiders where they stood. Their swords gleamed in the torch fires that had caught on the grass and fallen tents. Smoke and the stench of charred canvas filled the air. His men scrambled to arms, most falling before they could defend themselves from the ambush. The enemy outnumbered them three to one.

"Let's even up the odds," Von snarled.

Elon drew out his blade and laid his hand on the flat side, bringing it to his mouth. *"Nev emah'cucse narg naidraug led ot'nemaruj, edeneita im adamall,"* he murmured to it softly like waking a lover from sleep. Power crackled around him, and the atmosphere grew thin. The wind churned, debris swirling at his feet as he extracted Essence from the trees and earth. He continued chanting, his voice growing into a haunting echo. *"Nev at'reipsed. Nev leif, recen'va sim sogimene. Nev ye ratroc, Anadoug Luza."*

Vivid blue vines sprouted from Elon's hands, twisting around the hilt of his sword. Light flared and coiled up his arms, setting the blade alight.

"Down!" Von roared. The Raiders all dropped on his command.

Elon brandished his sword in a graceful swing, and a blue ray ruptured from the blade. It sliced through the air, passing over his men, and cleaved through the unprepared Rangers in one fell swoop. Bodies split in a volley of limbs and heads, turning the field into a crimson sea.

Von gritted his teeth, his stomach churning at the gruesome devastation. The Blue Scythe, the elves called it. A deadly and powerful spell. It cut down the unit of Rangers, but their victory was short-lived. A company of Azure Guards and a calvary of Rangers waited on the far end of the field.

Elon breathed heavily, sweat shining on his face. The spell had cost him. He couldn't perform it again without losing the stamina he needed for the fight. The enemy knew it too.

The lead Azure Guard on a white horse drew his sword. "Lay down your arms and give us Tarn!"

Von took out his knives as Abenon and the Raiders lined up behind him and Elon. "You'll find no cowards here!" he shouted back. "If you want him, then come and get him!"

Without hesitation, the lead Guard bellowed for an attack. The cavalry reared and charged across the field. Beneath Von's feet, the ground vibrated, and the night thundered with the pounding of hooves. His men braced themselves, readying their weapons, faces a mix of dread and wild adrenaline. Their fear permeated the air.

"Should you fall?" Von recited.

"March through the Gates!" the Raiders recited as one.

"Go with your God!"

"AND MAY HE RECEIVE ME!" they shouted in a war cry.

"Aye, may He receive me," Von repeated under his breath. He exhaled deeply, gripping his knives and his nerves as he watched the stampede of horses come for them. His heart thudded in his chest with the beat of the charge, his blood running cold. Gods, he didn't see any hope of surviving this. They were at a disadvantage on lower ground, and most of his men would be trampled to death. "If you can manage any more spells, now is the time," he told the captain.

In reply, Elon raised his gaze to the moon and held out a beseeching hand to it, his voice slipping into an eerie resonance once more. *"Anul ed sol soleic, at'serp em ut redop, nev Aivull Ed Soyar."*

Static pressed against Von's skin, everything in him growing rigid. Clouds roiled overhead, cracking with thunder and flashes of light. The cavalry reached them when a rain of lightning speared the terrain between them in blazing columns. *Boom! Boom! BOOM!*

The blasts wrenched Rangers and horses into the air, their frightened screams vanishing with them into the smoke. Von's ears rang from the proximity of the blasts. He could only hear his pounding heart and ragged breathing. It lasted for a brief moment, then all sound snapped back into place. The wet thud of falling flesh and bone crashed around them. The twisted body of a Guard slammed onto the ground at his feet.

The Raiders broke into a cheer. Von raised a fist over his shoulder, and they fell silent at the signal. While that attack spell had been powerful, it couldn't have taken out a full cavalry. Smoke choked the field, obscuring their view. There was absolute silence. He peered into it, listening. Waiting.

Elon tensed. "They are coming."

"Ready!" Von warned the men.

He felt the beginnings of a rumble before he heard it. The rumble grew louder and louder until it was upon them. Azure Guards burst through the haze and Von and the Raiders clashed into them in a clang of steel.

Elon skewered a Guard through the gut and spun to behead another with a quick slash. He moved with lethal dexterity and precision, his sword severing every life it met. Abenon dove into the fray with his scimitars, leaving behind a trail of bodies.

Von ducked out of the way of a blade, inches from taking his head. He pivoted around the Guard and flung a knife at an incoming Ranger, impaling him through the throat. Another Guard paired up with two more and all three circled him. Fire glinted on their polished badges engraved with the Azure sigil. They eyed him steadily as they moved into a practiced formation. They were men of skill, given authority by the king to uphold the law. By all rights, good men. A shame they had to die here.

Von removed two knives from his bandolier and flipped them in his palms. The Guards attacked, and he let the knives fly. Two went down. He grabbed a fallen sword and whirled on the third Guard. It settled into his hand with familiarity. His limbs moved on memory, past training surging through him. The blade swept through the air and sliced across the Guard's stomach. Von turned away as he fell.

More came.

He no longer felt the weight of the weapon. It was an extension of him as it carved through muscle and sinew, the movements as easy as breathing. Evade—slash—parry—strike.

Mud and blood coated his face as he hacked his way through the ranks. A Ranger charged at him on a horse, rapier waiving, as Von drew his blade from a dead Guard. He hefted up the sword and hurled it like a spear, sending it straight through the man's chest.

Elon chanted another spell. The scattered flames around the camp rose in a huge inferno. Like a tsunami at sea, it rolled over a screaming unit of Rangers and Guards, carrying them away. The fire caught on crates and tents, lighting up the camp.

Burning grass and the metallic stench of blood overtook Von's nose, smoke stinging his eyes. The forest caught fire as the winds spread the flames. Orange and red bled across the sky. The sight of it reminded him of his greatest fear.

Von ran through the ignited camp. He reached his tent only to find it had collapsed in the mayhem.

"Yavi!" he shouted over the din.

A distant scream reached his ears.

On the other side of the camp, Von spotted a laughing Guard standing over a Raider. Geon, bleeding from a gash on his cheek. He took a kick to the gut and he cried out, curling into himself.

"Leave him alone!" Yavi shrieked. Another Guard struggled to hold her back as she fought for all she was worth.

The Ranger aimed another kick, but Geon snatched his leg and tripped him. Then he rolled for his fallen sword and leaped to his feet. "Put her down! Fight me!"

Von had ordered the lad to protect Yavi, and he would do so until his last breath. He sprinted for them, cutting down anyone who stepped into his path.

The Guard only laughed and easily disarmed Geon, knocking him to his knees. He grinned as he lifted his weapon above the boy's head. Von dove between them and blocked the blade with a knife. He stabbed the startled man through the neck and whirled on the other, attempting to drag Yavi away.

"Why do you fight?" the Ranger growled at her. "I've come to free you."

"She does not want to go with you," Von said as he took out another knife. "Let her go, and I'll not kill you."

The Guard looked back and forth between him and Yavi's scathing glare. "All of you are loyal to him, even the slaves. You're traitors to the King!"

He used Yavi like a shield and dragged her backward toward the steep hill, ending in a roaring valley of flame.

"Stop." Von quickly closed in on him with Geon armed on his left.

"Stand back!" the Guard shouted.

"Release her first."

"Do as I say or I will kill her!" He pressed the edge of his sword against her throat until a trickle of red leaked down.

Panic. Pure panic.

Von's hands shook and his legs went numb. He couldn't think straight. They were too close to the fire, too damn close. Flames licked the sky. It reached out for their heels, hungry and waiting. Mere inches away. All he could see was the orange cast and feel the stifling heat on his face.

Only whence she burns will she be free.

Only whence she burns.

She burns.

Burns.

"Von." Yavi's delicate throat bobbed, sweat gleaming on her pallid face. She never looked away from him as her tears fell. There was nothing but unadulterated will in her eyes. And permission.

"Release her," he grated. "I'll not say it again."

The Guard pointed the sword at him. "Back off!"

Yavi jabbed her elbow into the man's ribs, creating an opening. Von threw a knife and it went straight through the Guard's skull, between his eyebrows. His horrified expression froze, and he tipped backward.

Taking Yavi with him.

Her scream pierced Von's heart. "No!"

He sprang to the edge. By some miracle, she clung to the tall grass, the greedy valley of flames waiting to embrace her. Von and Geon grasped her wrists and hoisted her up. Yavi collapsed against him in gasping sobs. They sunk to their knees together, and she buried her face in his neck, stifling her hoarse cries. He clutched her to him. His racing pulse throbbed in his ears.

Was it finished? Had this been enough to thwart the Seer's divination?

"Commander." Geon clapped his shoulder. "It's over. We won."

Scarcely.

The screams had quieted, and the smoke lifted. Fires flickered among the mounds of bodies dressed in black and blue.

Von pulled Yavi to her feet and made their way to the gathered crowd. The Raiders jeered at the single surviving member of the Azure Guard. The man kneeled among his dead comrades, calm and poised. Short gray hair framed his stern face, lined with a trimmed beard. Two Raiders fought over his elegant blue coat. A badge with his rank decorated the lapel. They had caught the colonel who had called for the attack.

Abenon spat on the ground. "Kill the bastard, or I will."

Elon turned to Von for his order. They all glanced up at where Tarn stood on a hill against the background of smog in the moonlight. Von grabbed the man's arm and hauled him to his feet. The colonel didn't resist as he was marched up the hill and forced to kneel before the master.

Tarn faced them, holding a sword that wasn't his. The pommel was engraved with the Azure sigil. Blood dripped from the blade, beading on the grass by his boots. Lifeless Guards laid scattered behind him. This must have been the true intention of the battle. A second ambush on their target while the other units distracted the Raiders.

The colonel looked at his dead men and clenched his jaw, remorse and anger contorting his expression. There had been too many for a normal man to kill alone, but Tarn was not a normal man.

He tossed the sword aside and crouched down, fixing his cool eyes on the colonel. "What is your name?"

The man raised his chin and rumbled, "I am Colonel Jasia Moreland of the Azure Guard."

"How did you find me?"

"The King knows you're here, Tarn Morken. All of Azure's finest are scouring the land for you. You may have defeated us here, but no matter where you run or whichever hole you crawl into, this will finish with you hanging by the end of a rope."

Tarn lifted his gaze to the smoke-smothered sky. The gleam of the fire highlighted the sharp edges of his face, leaving the rest draped in black. "There is only one place where this will end. After years of searching, I am at last one step closer to finding it. I've long decided that the rivers will flow red and the world will burn at my feet before I allow anyone to impede me."

In a move so quick, Von nearly missed it, Tarn lashed out at the colonel's throat. The man flopped on the ground, gurgling and clawing at his neck where his windpipe had been crushed. His face shifted from red to purple, vessels bursting in his bulging eyes. Legs thrashed as he wheezed desperately for air.

Von looked away, but he couldn't ignore the sounds. Torturous seconds seemed to stretch into minutes until the frantic spasms slowly weakened. Then, with one last painful gurgle, all went quiet. The colonel lay face down in the grass, mouth gaping open with his curled hands stretching for something out of reach. Another body was added to the masses. And it served as a glaring reminder of his master's capabilities.

Tarn tucked his hands in his coat and strode away for his tent. "Bring me the Maiden. Kill the wolf and bleed the other dry."

Von closed his eyes and bowed. "Yes, Master."

Von's gray horse nickered uneasily as he strapped the saddle in place, hooves pawing at the ground. "Easy, Coal."

He fit the bridle and tossed the reins around the saddle's pommel. Coal was an easy, obedient horse, one who had learned to pick up on moods and mirrored them. Von was rarely ever nervous, but unease settled over him since Tarn gave the order to go after Dyna. He shook it off. This task would be no different from the many others.

The Raiders had packed up camp and were nearly ready to move out. The dead were left where they fell. It was wrong, but there was no time to bury them. The fire would only draw more attention.

Abenon's voice echoed in another field opposite of where the skirmish took place. He swore and barked orders at the twenty Raiders chosen for the capture of the Maiden, relaying all the information gathered by the spies.

"After this next mission we will reach Mount Ida," Abenon said, trotting his horse back and forth in front of the unit. "All that stands in our way is a dog and a fowl. Any of you bollocks botch this, I'll leave your corpses to the crows. Capture the Maiden and you'll be shitting gold for the rest of your lives!"

The Raiders cheered at that. Bloodlust shone on their crimson smeared faces. Their victory against the Azure Guard had intoxicated them with confidence, and they were ready for another fight. He wondered if they realized how close they had come to death. Without the aid of magic, they most certainly would have lost their lives.

"He has a penchant for flair," Elon said, and Von nearly flinched at his sudden appearance. It was unnerving how soundlessly the elf moved, as if he traveled through the shadows. "Are you certain you do not wish for me to accompany you, Commander?"

"I need you here," Von said, knowing the elf would be their only hope if the Azure Guard returned with more men. Next time they may not be so lucky. "You are in command while I'm gone. Make your way east and wait for me by the Kazer Bluffs. They open to an inlet out of Loch Loden. I will take that course once I have the Maiden. Meet me there at midday the day after tomorrow." He paused, then added, "Take Len with you."

It was best to be prepared, and she was their best with a bow.

"Did you find Benton?"

The elf's expression didn't change save for a slight tightening of his jaw. "The mages were in their tent. Sleeping."

That was a load of pish. Not for one moment did Von believe Benton had slept through the fight. This must have been another attempt to free himself. "Keep him confined. I know he led the Azure Guard to us. Not one word of this until it's been confirmed."

Elon nodded and vanished into the night as quickly as he appeared.

Von kept Benton's betrayal from Tarn for Dalton and Clayton's sake. They didn't deserve to be strung up because of their father. When he returned, he planned to have a *conversation* with that old bastard.

"Commander," Geon called. He trotted over on a brown mare. "May I join the unit?"

Von mounted his horse. "Stay here."

"I want to come. I'll not let you down."

"I said no." Von glowered at him. The lad nearly joined the dead not a mere hour ago. They were heading to another battle and surely there would be more losses, but not on his end if he could help it.

"Let him go," Yavi said as she approached. She stopped under the cover of the trees, close to his horse and out of view of the remaining Raiders readying the wagons. "He was in Corron with Bouvier. He's learned his way around the streets."

Geon nodded eagerly. "I know the best way in and out of the city. With my help, the Azure Guard won't see us coming."

Von had to admit that would be useful.

He groaned. "Fine, but only so you can relay a message to Bouvier. You'll stay out of any confrontation with the Guardians. Go on, report to Abenon."

"Thank you, Commander." Geon cantered off to join the others as the men mounted their horses.

"You shouldn't encourage him, Yavi. It'll be dangerous," Von said. He signaled to Abenon, giving the order to move out. The ground rumbled with the beat of hooves as the Raiders galloped northeast for Corron. They would ride all night and should arrive midday after Dyna, if not sooner.

"Aye, it will be," Yavi said, watching their departure. Her kirtle and hair fluttered in the strong wind like a stream.

"You're worried about the Maiden."

"That man is sending you to kidnap another person, and to snuff out the lives of two more," she said. "These people could mean our freedom."

Von had not let himself think about that. His duty was to the master. The holy law decreed it. Betraying Tarn was the same as betraying the God of Urn.

Yavi scowled at the black tent in the distance. "Imagine, what future could you have had if you hadn't been so selfless fifteen years ago? Tarn was at your mercy. He should be *your* life-servant."

Von sighed. "His father was my liege. How could I keep him as my servant?"

"He had no qualms on his end," she snapped.

That betrayal still stung. Tarn had been his friend, or perhaps he had been a fool to think so.

When Azurite fell to the Horde, the carnage in the field outside of the town was much the same as this one. Covered in dismembered bodies of both human and troll. The gray-scaled beasts reeked of swamp and carrion, their corpses left to rot in the summer heat during the day-long attack. Von and Tarn were the only surviving knights on their last breath as they fought their way through the Horde.

Tarn lost his weapon and the trolls descended on him. Teeth crushed through bone, tearing through flesh as they ate him alive. Von didn't think twice about saving him or relieving him of his life-debt. But when Tarn came to his aid immediately after, the same courtesy was not returned.

Von had wondered many times afterward if saving Tarn had changed the course of the world as it had changed the course of his life. They both should have perished that day.

"Do you regret it?" Yavi asked.

"What's done is done."

"He must not have the Unending, Von. What do you think he will do with that power?" She motioned to the bloody field. "How many more need to die? How many more must you kill for him?"

Von had lost count of all the lives taken at his hands. He wiped a stray tear from her cheek. "I don't have any say in this."

"You do. I wish you'd see that." Her welled eyes looked up at him, pleading for him to make the right choice. But what was the right choice? Spare innocents or uphold his holy duty as a life-servant?

He didn't know what was right anymore.

"I fear this task won't be as easy as you're used to," Yavi murmured against his calloused palm. "Beware the Guardians, the Seer said. They won't let you take her without a fight."

"Well, they would be poor Guardians if they didn't fight, eh?"

She shook her head. "I'm not jesting. I have an awful feeling."

He smiled, if only to hide that he felt the same. "I'll come back to you. I always do."

"You better, Von Conaghan. Don't leave me alone in this world." *Not with that man.* She didn't need to say it. He heard it as clear as he'd heard the fear in her voice.

"How could I when I love you more than my own life?"

Yavi smiled through her tears as she approached the horse. "How much?"

Von stooped down, pulling her close. "This much," he whispered and dispelled any further protest with a kiss.

CHAPTER 32

Dynalya

Dyna stood on a knoll overlooking a vast green moorland dappled with wild heather. Wispy clouds moved idly across the morning sky, chased by their shadows sweeping beneath them. The weather was tolerable for a change.

Behind her, Cassiel and Zev conversed comfortably as they put away their bedrolls and packed their bags. Her cousin's laughter rebounded off the short crag that had sheltered them for the night. The sound lightened her heart, but her smile wavered when she rubbed her right shoulder where his teeth had severed through. Cassiel's blood had left no evidence of the injuries she sustained that night. She would have thought it only a nightmare, but a faint luminance exuded from her skin.

Dyna glanced at Cassiel. The silver buttons of his dark blue vest hung undone, leaving his white tunic to flutter in the wind. The sun gleamed over the sleek plumage of his wings, curving like half-moons to his heels. His black hair fell over his face as he put out their dying campfire. A soft, haloed glow outlined his head. She thought his radiance was something she had imagined, but she realized it was the divine blood that flowed within him, and now within her.

His gray eyes met hers, and something fluttered in the pit of her stomach. Seeing him, being around him, sent a vibration through her. Since the full moon, his presence hovered on her skin as a tangible entity. No matter where Cassiel was, her awareness followed him, even when she didn't intend it.

And when they touched, a flare of warmth ignited her very soul, tethering her to him in a way she didn't comprehend.

What did it mean?

Zev dropped an arm around her shoulders and peered down at her with concern. "All right?"

She managed a smile. "Yes."

He frowned. "You're pale. Come, have a sip of water at least." Zev guided her to sit on a boulder. He handed her a waterskin from his pack and watched her drink. Dyna's hand trembled when she handed it back. "Are you feeling faint?"

"Oh no, I'm fine." She fidgeted with the frayed hem of the brown tunic she borrowed from him.

Zev crouched and rested a hand over hers, dwarfing it. "It was wrong to have you chain me, Dyna. It's awful and dangerous. I almost killed you once before. If not for Cassiel ... Forgive me."

"Oh, Zev. I know you would never consciously hurt me."

"I've decided that you will no longer bear the responsibility of my chains. I'll not put you in such danger again."

"But I made a promise."

"Which is now void. I relieve you of your debt."

The heavy burden she had carried for so long lifted, only to be replaced by guilt. "I must keep my promise, Zev. It's my turn to save you now."

She would have frozen to death on the Zafiro Mountains if not for him. He had never asked her for anything in return, but this she would do.

"I relieve you of your debt," Zev said firmly.

"No, I won't let you."

He slumped on his heels, sighing heavily. "Dyna, please."

"You need me. You can't chain yourself."

"I will do it," Cassiel said, where he stood on top of the crag above them. He looked out at the horizon where the dirt road wove through the hills. In the distance were other travelers making their way to Corron.

Zev faced him, his eyes widening. "You will?"

"For the duration of our journey, I will see to your chains."

Such a gracious offer nearly brought her to tears. She never would have expected that from him. "Thank you …"

"Yes, thank you, Cassiel."

The prince shrugged. He hopped down and pulled out his enchanted coat from his rucksack. His wings vanished as he slipped it on.

Zev curiously eyed Cassiel's flat back. "How does it work?"

"Stardust."

"What's Stardust?"

"Exactly as it sounds." Cassiel hiked his pack onto a shoulder and headed east.

"It's a spell made from the stars," Dyna explained to Zev as they followed. "It creates unlimited space on anything it touches. Azeran said that at the commencement of the world, fallen stars burned through the atmosphere like rays of fire and crashed into the oceans, creating land and life. One such star fell in the region that became Magos. It's believed this is how the Spatial Gate was created, and that it introduced Essence into the world. Mages from the First Age crushed the star and turned it into a spatial spell in its mineral state. They learned to use it to conjure pockets of limitless space wherever there is none."

Cassiel glanced at her fleetingly, arching an eyebrow. She almost thought he looked impressed. "Precisely."

"And Celestials use this to travel?" Zev asked.

Cassiel nodded. "A dash of Stardust on the inside of our clothing gives us the capacity to hide our wings."

"How did the Celestials obtain Stardust?"

"Before the Decimation, Hilos traded freely with the outside world. Our feathers significantly enhanced magic and were therefore prized by the Magos Empire. The Archmage that lived during the Calx Age traded ten-thousand pounds of Stardust for five thousand pounds of Celestial feathers. Each of the Four Celestial Realms possesses a vat of the remaining Stardust. My uncle gifted me with a vial to spell my clothing. It allowed me to conceal my wings and pass as a human during my travels."

"Did you bring more enchanted clothes?"

"No, my father confiscated them upon my return to Hilos. He prefers I travel by night out of sight. I hardly managed to hide this coat. There was no way to attain more Stardust without arousing his suspicion. It is well guarded."

"Why?" Dyna asked.

"We reserve Stardust for those who must travel to the Four Realms on rare occasions. Importers and emissaries, for example. Whenever a Celestial leaves the safety of the Realms, it is a great danger to us all. One mistake would unveil the secret of our existence and threaten our survival once more."

"But you've traveled several times between Hilos and Hermon Ridge," Zev said.

"Being a prince has its merits. My father and uncle trust me to avoid exposing myself."

"But if by some unfortunate chance, you did?"

He hesitated before saying, "Then, I would have no choice."

Dyna felt a sudden bout of nausea. "No choice?"

The sickness worsened as Cassiel pressed a hand to his stomach. The dread filtering through her mirrored the dread in his gray eyes before they hardened. "I bear the responsibility of keeping our existence a secret to any extent necessary."

She didn't need further explanation. He may have spared her in Hilos, but he would never extend such benevolence to anyone else again.

"Perhaps you may find a mage merchant that sells Stardust," she said.

"Unlikely. It is rare and far too expensive." Cassiel quickened his pace and moved ahead, effectively ending the conversation.

As of yesterday, he had returned to his curt manner. She supposed it stemmed from the law he broke by giving her his blood. Zev had explained how serious that was. Dyna sighed. Since their meeting, she'd only caused him a series of inconveniences. He must find her a nuisance.

Cassiel halted and turned back to look at her, his expression softening as he searched her face. "Come along. We are not too far from Corron now."

They trekked for several miles, passing stone markers at each intersection. The dirt road changed to cobblestone as they neared the city, and it became more crowded as others joined them. Many had traveled from afar, some on foot, others on horseback, or by caravan.

It amazed Dyna how different they were from the people in her village. The crowd was a wildflower garden of color. Men and women with skin like sunflower hearts. Their hair and eyes were an assortment of different shades and textures she had no names for. Some wore caftans fluttering like the petals of poppies and marigolds, others in elegant dresses flowing in shades of bluebells and lilies. The local men wore imposing armor in the livery of their lords. Field laborers in weathered clothing pulled along carts of fruit and vegetables.

Eventually, the road led to a wide bridge suspended over a great lake. The wind whipped Dyna's hair in her face, carrying the scent of mossy water. Several fishing boats idled on the clear blue surface and birds screeched as they circled overhead.

Beyond the shoreline, the city of Corron was nestled within steep hills layered in pine trees. The stone structures with their red roofs spread throughout the land and up the hills like stairs to the sky. A bell tolled somewhere in the distance, announcing the midday hour. Dyna stopped by the parapet to marvel at the sight of the immense lake.

"Loch Loden," Cassiel said as he paused beside her. He pointed to a patch of forest on the north of the lake outside the city. "Beyond the woodland is an inlet that streams past the Kazer Bluffs to the Saxe Fjord which opens to the Saxe Sea."

Dyna smiled, glad that he was speaking to her again. "Is that how we will reach the port?"

"No, it is safer to take the road. Hurry along. We are almost at the gate." He ushered her onward, keeping to her right side, and Zev blocked the crowd on her left.

The bridge was the only way into Corron. It was packed with people slowly inching toward the entrance. Standing guard at the gate were several men wearing navy regimental coats, black trousers, and boots. Brass buttons shone on their lapels, gold stitching trimming the cuffs and pockets. A badge of the Azure sigil was pinned on the right side of their chests. Each was armed with a sword sheathed at their waists.

"Who are they?" Dyna asked.

"The Azure Guard," Zev said as they watched a pair of uniformed men inspect wagons and carts before allowing them through. "They keep the King's peace. Something must have happened to bring so many together."

"They are searching for someone," Cassiel said warily.

A nervous jitter grew in Dyna with each step they took closer to the gate. Zev and Cassiel visibly stiffened. But why should they worry? The Guards weren't looking for them.

When it was their turn to enter, the Guards only glanced at them before waving them through and her apprehension melted away. Zev exhaled and Cassiel's shoulders loosened. They passed through the city gates where more Guards were handing out notices. She received one, finding it held the sketch of a man.

His face was all angles, expression indifferent, cold. His eyes were outlined and devoid of color, leaving them to appear piercing. A distinct, long scar ran diagonally across his face from his right brow to the left side of his chin. She found him attractive despite the disfigurement. He was perhaps ten years older than Zev, but those hard eyes made him seem older.

Large black script was stamped across the top of the page.

WANTED BY THE CROWN
REWARD OF 10,000 GOLD PIECES
DEAD OR ALIVE

Ten-thousand gold pieces? Dyna couldn't imagine having that amount of money. She had five russets in her pocket, which was the common currency. Five hundred russets were the equivalent of one silver coin, and fifty silvers equaled one gold piece. Why was this man worth so much?

The notice listed his crimes; theft, obstruction, murder, and several others. Under the man's sketch was his name: *Tarn Morken.*

"He sounds a most dangerous man," she said.

"Oh, aye," the Guard agreed. "Pray you'll not cross paths with him. But don't you fret none, miss. The Azure Guard will soon have him in irons."

Zev frowned at the sketch. "You believe he may have come this way?"

"Rangers spotted him in Landcaster. His only path is east. We have men patrolling each village, town, and city from here to Hallows Nest. Including every seaport in the kingdom. I reckon he'll be noosed and hooded in The Blue Capitol before winter's end."

"Noosed and hooded?" Dyna repeated.

"He's destined for the gallows, miss, if the King is in a merciful mood. If not, Tarn will meet the royal executioner to be drawn and quartered. Then he will be beheaded," he added with a shrug.

She gasped in horror, reaching for her neck. Cassiel glowered at the Guard and Zev quickly steered her along.

She soon forgot about the wanted man's fate as they followed the crowd into the marketplace. A blend of exotic spices and the smell of fried fish filled her nose. A chorus of accents from all over the country blended in a hum. Stalls lined the streets, merchants selling and auctioning a panoply of wares. Their hawking shouts blurred together in a roar.

Colorful banners and canopies hung between the buildings. Flags fluttered from the rooftops, displaying the King's colors—deep navy with Azure's golden sigil of a woven seven-pointed star.

Tiny pink sprites flitted overhead, zipping through the air like curious dragonflies. Dyna gaped at the sight of an enormous Ogre with blue-tinted skin and a mace resting against his shoulder. It stomped by, causing the ground to tremble under his heavy steps. Inhumanly beautiful women with flowers and leaves in their moss-green hair rolled past in their chariots pulled by steeds of smoke.

"It is impolite to gawp," Cassiel told her, and she promptly closed her mouth.

"There were only humans in Landcaster."

"You will find the deeper we travel through Urn, the more variety of folk you will see."

She looked in every which way, trying to take it all in. "This is amazing."

He rolled his eyes but a smirk rested on his mouth. "This is another filthy market."

When they reached an intersection, Zev brought her to a stop so he could read the several signs nailed to a lamppost, each pointing in a different direction. "I think the inns are ahead."

"We need to find the merchant traders to secure a ride to the Port of Azure," Cassiel said. "I'm not keen on traveling the rest of this journey on foot."

"Shouldn't we secure lodging first?"

"It's midday. Most likely any rooms that can be let, have been."

"We may still find something available if we hurry," Dyna told them, trying not to show her disappointment. She wanted to look around, but they had other obligations. Tomorrow morning would be better suited to explore and replenish their provisions.

They merged into the current of people that carried them further through the marketplace. The narrow streets became more crowded as they went. Crammed bodies shoved and elbowed past her, and she lost hold of Zev's arm. The small opening between them quickly filled with more people, leaving her to fall behind.

She tried to slip through, but the mass of bodies swallowed her up. Unfamiliar faces drowned her in a blur of color. Pushed and jostled helplessly along, she struggled to find her footing. Another sudden thrust from behind knocked her down. Someone grabbed her elbow before she hit the ground, jolting her with a batch of fiery energy. A band constricted in her chest when she heard a familiar voice and the threatening curse it spat. The mass quickly parted.

"Did you trip over your own feet again?"

Dyna groaned as her face heated, hardly able to meet Cassiel's cool gaze. "I tripped over half the population of Corron."

He hauled her to his side. "What am I to do with you?"

His arm clamped around her waist and pulled her protectively against him. She blushed under the stares of those watching. Cassiel ignored them. He guided her along until they reached a wide road where the crowd had thinned. There, she found her cousin waiting by a wagon.

Zev exhaled in relief when he spotted them. "Dyna, stay close to us. Any man here is likely to throw you over his shoulder and whisk you away if you're not careful."

An awful shudder crawled down her back. The fates forbid.

Cassiel took her hand, eliciting more ripples of energy. "I will not let that happen."

Dyna's stomach pitched by the fierce way he looked at her. An electrical current danced between them. His fingers slipped away before she could study the feeling further.

"Good sirs! Miss!" A woman waved at them from the doorway of her shop. The tall windows displayed an assortment of stunning dresses, like the scarlet one she wore. Her round face was a rich cedar color, complete with a motherly smile. She popped her hands on her hips as she sighed at Dyna. "I do hope you mean to tend to this one. She is honey wine to those in dire thirst for it."

Cassiel's expression darkened. "Your pardon?"

The woman strolled over to them in a huff, black ringlets bouncing on her head. The sunlight shone on the lace trim of her dress, embroidered with gold flowers along the collar and sleeves. A gold chain circled her curvaceous waist, dangling down the front.

"I speak the truth, milord," she said, switching to a more respectable title once she noted Cassiel's air of nobility. Dyna saw it too in the way he held himself, in the authoritative raise of his chin and cold assertive glare. "She will attract the wrong attention in that *garb*."

All eyes landed on Dyna, and she tried not to fidget as they inspected her. The oversized tunic sagged off her shoulders and her torn petticoat exposed her thigh. She flushed, tugging on the tunic's hem to hide it.

"And what attention would that be, wild-cat?" Zev asked irately.

The woman's eyes flashed lime-green, the pupils thinning into black slits. That's when Dyna noticed her pointed ears were dusted with soft fur.

"Don't you growl at me, wolf. I only mean to give you a fair warning." She looked Dyna over, tsking sympathetically. "Shame on you lot for leaving her to trod about in her undergarments. It's only asking for trouble."

"It's not their fault, madam," Dyna said. "I was unprepared for our journey and my only kirtle was ruined."

The woman smiled and patted her cheek. "Well then, I suppose that means you need a new wardrobe. My name is Namir. Come to my shop, and I'll see that you leave it looking as a Lady should."

"Thank you, but we haven't the time." Or the funds, by the look of Namir's dress.

Cassiel sighed and rubbed his forehead. "She is right. What you are wearing is not suitable."

"I agree," Zev said under his breath, "but I don't have the coin to afford her shop."

"I will bear the cost." Cassiel dropped three gold coins in Namir's palm. "Whatever she needs."

Namir's long fingers grasped the payment with a wide smile. "With pleasure, milord."

Zev shook his head. "I can't ask that of you, Cassiel."

"Think nothing of it. I insist. Go on, Dyna, and be quick about it."

"But—"

Namir wrapped an arm around her and whisked her away. "Now, now, lass, you mustn't refuse the offer of a gentleman," she said in her ear. "Especially one as attractive as that one."

"Oh, well, I—I um …"

Namir laughed, guiding her through the ornate door of her shop. "Ah, so he's the one you fancy! I was wondering which of the two it might be."

Heat rushed to Dyna's cheeks. "Fancy?"

"They're both quite handsome," Namir said, peeking out the store's front window at them. "But *that* one is finer than a spool of silk! A bit stiff, but at least he's wealthy. Take it from me, one can't be too fussy when finding a good husband that'll treat her well. Be sure to marry that one in a trice."

Dyna's blush filled her face. She peered out the window at Cassiel and Zev, who appeared to be having a mild argument. Undoubtedly, about the purchase of her clothes. The prince caught her looking, and she quickly ducked away.

"There is nothing of the sort between us, madam. He's … an acquaintance."

Could she call him a friend?

"Silly girl," Namir sang as she ambled further into the shop, her heels clacking on the wooden floorboards. She waved her arms at the exquisite pieces on display, their colorful fabrics shimmering under the chandelier hanging from the ceiling. "Men don't buy dresses for *acquaintances*."

Dyna had no reply for that. If anything, it sent a nervous quivering through her.

"Now," Namir clapped, turning to her with a grin. "Let us begin, shall we?"

CHAPTER 33

Dynalya

Tue to the madam's word, Dyna left the shop looking like a Lady. An emerald dress with tapered sleeves fit her perfectly. The satin material flowed around her like water, much lighter than her wool kirtle had been. "To match your eyes," Namir had said when she chose it.

Zev stood from the bench outside the shop when he saw her, a grin lighting up his face. "You look lovely, Dyna."

She smiled and took the sides of her skirts, dipping in a curtsy. She looked for Cassiel, but he was nowhere in sight.

"Here is all that I've picked out for her," Namir told Zev, handing him a large bundle wrapped in brown paper and twine. "Everything she should need. Some more suitable for travel."

"Thank you."

"Yes, thank you, madam," Dyna said.

"It was my pleasure." Namir winked playfully. "Should you pass through Corron again, come see me." With that, she slunk back into her shop.

"All you need now is a cloak, but it'll be at my expense." Zev made a grand show of bowing and offering his hand. "May I escort you milady?"

Dyna giggled and played along, placing her fingers in his palm. "Why thank you, milord. You're far too kind."

"Think nothing of it, I *insist*," he said, mimicking Cassiel's cool manner. He curled her hand around the crook of his elbow and ushered her along the street.

All banter aside, she admittedly felt self-conscious that Cassiel offered to pay for her new clothing, but also grateful. "It was very kind of him."

"Unusually courteous, one might say."

"Stop it." Dyna playfully smacked Zev's arm. "Where has he gone? I must thank him."

"He wandered off somewhere hereabouts. We'll find him." Zev veered toward a merchant stall selling capes and cloaks. He riffled through them, frowning thoughtfully. "See anything you like?"

"Hmm." Dyna lifted a capelet about her size, but her thoughts continued drifting to Cassiel. She searched for him in the bustling crowd. Why would he wander off when they had been in a hurry to seek lodging?

Her gaze landed on a stall draped with a black canopy. From its bearings hung dried herbs, crystals, and clinking glass chimes. An old woman sat behind the counter. She was pale and wrinkly as a dried date. Deep purple robes enveloped her small hunched frame. She wore a matching turban over her white hair and a dirty sash tied over her eyes. The old woman must be blind but appeared to look right at Dyna, as she beckoned her forth with a knobby finger.

Under thrall, Dyna crossed the street to her.

"Good evening, deary," the old woman said. She spoke with the Azure accent but underneath, lingered the faint hint of another. "May I interest you in a charm for luck, or perhaps a potion to capture the heart of your unrequited love? I have amulets, enchanted baubles, and the like."

On the counter were neat rows of glass jars containing shimmering powders and bubbling liquids. In bowls, she had desiccated newts, ground-up beetles, and foul-smelling herbs.

Followed by baskets of polished bone carved in the shape of people, and flat stones painted red with curses. These were the wares of a witch.

Dyna took a step back. "Oh, um, no thank you, madam."

"Nothing to your liking? What are you seeking on this fine day? I have a great many things, some too dreadful or too rare to leave out on display. Who knows, I may have what you desire."

She gave the question some consideration. The mention of rare items surfaced a thought. "Do you perhaps have Stardust?"

The woman's lips thinned. "I don't sell mage magic, deary. Stardust is much too costly to acquire and I am but a poor, poor gypsy."

The sun caught on the edge of a pendant that peeked out from a fold of her robes, glinting on what looked to be a diamond. Somehow, she must have sensed Dyna looking because she quickly tucked it away.

The old woman held open a wrinkly palm, long yellowed nails curling at the end of her fingers. "For a russet, I'll read your fortune. Yours seems to be an interesting one."

Dyna hesitated, but she wanted to know what the woman may see in her future that was so uncertain. She took her hand. The moment they touched, a zap clashed against her Essence. It was the same sensation she felt when Dalton had grabbed her.

The old woman inhaled a sharp breath. Her wrinkly face creased with shock, her mouth falling open. She reached up and pulled down the sash to reveal a stunning pair of eyes the color of lilac petals.

A realization washed through Dyna's mind. The old woman was not a witch at all. The meeting of their Essence and the unique eye color revealed one unquestionable fact: the old woman was a sorceress.

They gawked at each other in silence. Dyna could hardly believe it. Mages were one thing, but seeing a sorceress outside of the Magos Empire was incredible. Impossible even, yet here she was.

Dyna wanted to embrace the old woman and tell her she knew of the dreadful ways practiced in Magos. But she only managed one breathless word, "Oh …"

Zev approached the stall. "What are you doing, Dyna? I told you to stay close."

The old woman gasped and leaned back as she took in his size and many scars. Her eyes lingered on his muscular arms and broad chest before rising to his face.

He scratched at the stubble on his cheek, unnerved by her stare. "Um, we should go."

"She was reading my fortune," Dyna said. "For a russet, she'll read yours too. Go on."

He too hesitated, then held out his hand. The old woman tentatively reached out. She tapped his fingertip and immediately recoiled as if he'd burned her.

"What did you see?" he asked warily.

Her wide eyes bounced between them. Had she sensed what he was?

Cassiel appeared beside them and glared at the wares, pulling Dyna back. "Nothing good will come in any dealings with a witch."

"She's not a witch."

He frowned at her, but then did a double-take. Whatever he was going to say was forgotten, his gaze slowly traveling down her dress then back up.

The old woman smirked. "My, aren't you a pompous lord?" She snatched his hand, and the color drained from her face. "God of Urn."

Cassiel ripped his hand away, wiping it on his coat in disgust. He scowled at the others. "Stop dallying. We must go before the taverns are full." He stalked away into the throng.

Zev placed two copper coins on the counter. He turned to leave when the old woman grabbed Dyna's wrist and wiggled her fingers over her. An electric tickle sprouted from her scalp and floated to her toes with a shudder.

Zev yanked her away. "What have you done?"

The old woman shrugged. "A little spell."

Dyna's heart jolted. "You cast a spell on me?"

A menacing growl rumbled in Zev's throat, his wolf eyes surfacing as fur rippled along his arms. The old woman gasped and quickly jumped out of her stool. But she didn't run. She glared at Zev as a stream of palpable energy crackled in the air, and purple electricity sparked at her fingertips.

Zev leaned on the counter, his sharp claws splintering into the wooden surface, baring his teeth. "Undo whatever you've done to her. Now!"

The old woman snapped her fingers. The world came to a standstill, and the buzz of the market vanished. Dyna whirled around, finding people like statues. Some were mid-stride on the street, merchants with their hands cupped around their mouths. Birds were suspended in the air; tarps and canopies caught mid-flutter in no perceivable wind. Her cousin's face was stalled in a wild glare.

"Zev?" Dyna waved a hand over his eyes, then tried to shake him when he didn't respond. "Zev! What is this?"

It was as though life had stopped and left her outside of it.

"This is a rift in the Time Gate," the old woman said, her Magos accent ringing true. Unlike Lord Norrlen's soft *R*s, hers were accentuated, seasoning her speech. "Time is a peculiar thing. Try as I may, I cannot manage it to go forward or *backward*." She glowered at their surroundings. "But I've learned how to make it stop."

"You did this?"

The old woman's image blurred and rippled in a veil of purple light, then it dissolved to reveal a young woman. Dyna's mouth dropped open. She wasn't one to fuss over her looks, not having the time to care about vanity, but the sorceress's beauty immediately intimidated her.

White hair cascaded down her back in a river of starlight. She had graceful features; alabaster skin, lashes, and brows like threads of silver, with soft pink lips, and too perfect cheekbones. Tight, black leather britches and a matching redingote hugged the curves of her long legs and slender waist. A medallion inlaid with diamonds, and a pearlescent stone in the center gleamed on her full chest. It was the very medallion seen among the pages of Azeran's journal.

"You're of the Lunar Guild," Dyna whispered.

The day darkened, and thunderclouds rolled across the sky. The sorceress's crystalline eyes glowed vibrant lilac as electricity spiraled around her, weaving through her locks. An invisible charge hung in the air with a violent energy that clashed against Dyna's Essence.

She'd never felt such magic. So wild and untamed. In such abundance, it was primed to tear her apart.

"This is my only warning," the sorceress hissed. "If you tell anyone of my whereabouts, I will hunt you down and leave you trapped in a time rift. Where you will remain until your bones turn to dust. I've spent far too many years in hiding to be caught now."

Dyna took a staggering step back. "I—I would never speak of it. You have my word."

"I'll hold you to that." Then the sorceress snapped her fingers, and the world flashed a blinding white.

Dyna blinked frantically to clear her spotty vision. Life returned with an onslaught of market clamor and the bustle of movement around her.

"Witch! What spell did you … use?" Zev trailed off, his shout falling to a confused utterance.

The sorceress and her belongings had vanished. There was nothing but a vacant spot in the line of merchant stalls, as though she was never there.

For the first time in her life, Dyna heard Zev curse. He practically dragged her away in the direction Cassiel had gone, muttering the orison against dark entities.

She struggled to keep up with his rapid pace. "Zev—"

"God of Urn, Dyna. Only you would find a witch."

She stopped herself from correcting him. The sorceress warned her to remain quiet, but Dyna didn't fault her for it. She had to protect herself to maintain her freedom outside of Magos.

"I should have known what she was. She smelled of wild magic."

"You can smell magic?" This was the first time he'd mentioned it.

Zev's brow furrowed. "When you use Essence, it smells like a spring mist in a meadow. Her Essence smelled of ... lightning."

Lightning had a smell?

But that was exactly how Dyna would describe the power of the sorceress. It was like the crackle of lightning before a violent thunderstorm.

"At least I have her scent in case she is a threat. How are you? The spell, did it hurt?"

"No, I'm fine."

There was no telling what the sorceress had done to her. Dyna didn't feel any different, but she had the funny sense that they would meet again.

CHAPTER 34

Lucenna

The invisibility spell hid Lucenna perfectly. She stood in the street, unseen by everyone in the market. She watched as the wild strapping man ushered the redheaded girl away. Dyna, he had called her. And she was a sorceress. Proven by the flicker of Essence Lucenna had felt from her.

That was as startling as being discovered.

Lucenna waved a hand over her invisible merchant stall. It lifted into the air, shrinking in size to a miniature figurine before it whizzed toward her. She opened the flap of the black satchel hanging from her shoulder, and the stall flew inside. She slipped into a nearby alley and leaned against the brick wall to catch her breath.

The time spell had required a lot of power, and it had spent a significant amount of her Essence. It was foolish to use such a spell, but she panicked. That was the first occurrence someone had discovered what she was, and her first instinct had been to defend herself. She decided at the last second to let Dyna go with a warning. But now her spell may have alerted any Enforcers within Azure to her presence.

Their sole purpose was to capture escaped sorceresses and return them to the Magos Empire. They had been hunting her for years. She had to be careful not to attract them, or worse yet—her father. Although Lucien would have warned her if any were in the area. She evaded capture for so long because she had his help.

Lucien would scold her thoroughly if he knew she put herself at risk. He probably already knew. He was her twin brother, after all. Lucien could always sense when she used large bouts of Essence or whenever her emotions roiled her magic.

And she had done both.

On cue, a familiar tick throbbed in Lucenna's temples steadily. She groaned and frowned down at her satchel. White light streamed from the edges of the opening, pulsating in a matching rhythm. It was coming from her orb, but she didn't want to answer it. She already knew what he would say.

Lucenna pushed his inquiry aside, assuring him she was all right through their sibling link. That would only placate her overprotective brother for so long.

She hurried down the alleyway, keeping the invisibility spell in place. She navigated the maze of alleys guided by black smears of paint marking the way at each corner. The markings blended in well with the dirty brick walls. It was not noticeable to anyone not knowing to look for them. They were painted by the ferryman who smuggled people and contraband in and out of Corron.

She reached the dead-end of an alley deep in the bowels of the city. There was an opening in the brick wall, big enough for someone to slip through. Lucenna went in and came out on the side of a steep hill thick with trees. A thin, worn trail cut through the carpet of dead leaves and moss. Careful not to slip on the muddy slope, she made her way down the hill to a secluded lakeshore shrouded in overgrown reeds. The rowboat was not there. The ferryman must be working.

With an impatient sigh, Lucenna sat on a log to wait. Her eyes watered from the sun shimmering on the surface of the lake as the water lapped on the bank. She curled her nose at the stench of the muck and mire, trying not to breathe it in. Her heel bounced as she watched the patch of woodland hiding a secluded stream that veered off Loch Loden. That was where the ferryman would come.

Where was he?

Her temples ticked again with Lucien's call. He wouldn't stop until he knew she was safe, and if she didn't answer, he would use other means to contact her. Lucenna rolled her eyes and reached in her bag. It was bottomless, enchanted to hold an endless number of items. Stardust really was useful.

She pictured her orb and a glass ball the size of a small melon appeared in her palm. It throbbed with dazzling light, fog swirling inside like trapped smoke. After undoing her invisibility spell, she tapped the surface, and the fog ebbed, revealing her brother's image.

Long, pearl-white hair framed Lucien's sculpted face. A knot formed between his white brows as he studied her and her surroundings. He was in his bedroom by the view of his large bed behind him and the floor to ceiling bookshelves. Beside him rested his staff made of ash wood, carved around a jagged cerulean crystal that matched the color of his robes. Sunlight from his bedroom window shone in his lipid lilac eyes.

Seeing she was safe, he arched an eyebrow. "Lucenna."

She imitated his stern expression and serious tenor, "Lucien."

"I thought your purpose in Corron was to earn coin. Care to explain why you meddled with the Time Gate?"

Lucenna balked. "You sensed from the Magos Empire that I stopped time?"

He smirked. "I did not, but thank you for confirming."

She glowered at him. How did he always do that?

"I may not know which spells you invoked, but I can sense how much magic you wielded. Accessing the Time Gate exerts the most out of you. That kind of magic leaves a significant trace in the air. There were no Enforcers in that district, but they will surely be on their way now."

She cringed sheepishly. "And Father?"

"Fortunately, he was called to Castle Ophyr to tend to guild matters."

Meaning their father was in Magos, so he had not sensed her magic, but news of it would reach him, no doubt.

Lucien searched her face worriedly. "Lu, you mustn't continue to tamper with time. You cannot change the past—"

"That wasn't my intention this time," she said.

"Then what happened? You cast more than one spell."

Lucenna fidgeted with the medallion, recalling her encounter in the market. "I met a sorceress."

His eyes widened. "There should be no other sorceress in Azure, or the rest of Urn for that matter."

She had thought the same thing when she met Dyna.

The Liberation smuggled women and children out of the Magos Empire, but they ceased to release them in Urn as the Enforcers caught most. Because of this, they resorted to sending refugees on ships across the sea to the free nation of Carthage instead.

"I would have assumed her to be of the Sun Guild because of her red hair, but her Essence was diminutive, hardly worth anything." Lucenna shrugged. "And she spoke with a native Azure accent."

"Ah, I see," Lucien said excitedly. "She must be free-born, a descendant of one of the many sorceresses The Liberation has freed. Low Essence indicates mixed bloodlines. She's not a citizen of Magos."

Lucenna smirked. "That would explain why she was sauntering about without a care, and she's already been discovered. When I took her hand, I sensed another mage tracking her Essence with a location spell."

Lucien grew alarmed. "By touching her, that spell can lead the mage to you."

"I know, but you needn't worry. I cloaked her and severed his spell."

"Good. Yet that doesn't explain why you meddled with the Time Gate."

Lucenna balanced the glass orb between her palms, contemplating how to explain herself. She might have been too harsh with Dyna, but she had to take precautions. "The girl discovered what I was. I stopped time to deliver a warning."

Her brother frowned. "You threatened her."

"A little."

"Hmm and did you check to see if she was not in a dire situation herself?"

That was the first thing she had checked. Dyna didn't appear abused or downtrodden, and her companions cared for her well-being. They weren't mages, but they weren't human either.

The robust man contained magic in him. Dyna had called him Zev. Lucenna couldn't help staring at him. Rough, brawny men were not seen in Magos. But there was something dangerous about him, and it had convulsed her magic in a warning. She'd only dared to touch him with a fingertip, and it was enough to get a glimpse of a terrifying wolf-like beast snarling back at her.

As for the striking young man, that one was a Celestial. When she took his hand, her Essence collided with the magic from his concealed wings and the divine blood coursing through his veins. How could that be? Celestials no longer roamed the Mortal Realm, and their characteristics were described to look much different.

"Was she all right?" Lucien asked when she took too long to answer.

"Yes, I believe so."

Her twin brother sighed and rubbed his forehead. "Lu, while I'm elated to hear of other sorceresses living free, you cannot risk yourself so carelessly. Cease to disguise yourself as a fortune teller for a meager pittance."

Lucenna couldn't read fortunes, but it was easy to deceive those searching for promises of wealth and love for a russet. "There is only so much I can scrounge."

"I'll send you gold."

She made a face. "To do that must open a portal and Father would sense it."

"Through the bank, then."

"He would notice the missing funds, Lucien. Leave it be or he will quickly discover that you're helping me and have you convicted for treason. I won't have anyone else die for me."

His brow pinched, and he looked away. "You do me an injustice to carry all the blame when it belongs solely to me. I introduced you and Mother to The Liberation. I was the one who filled your heads with hope for the future."

Lucenna let her bangs fall over her eyes so he wouldn't see them mist. "I accepted this mission because hope is all we can vie for. I have not given up. And I won't."

"You've searched for nigh on four years. What if we are not meant to find it?"

Lucenna laid a hand over the Lūna Medallion hanging from her neck, stroking the edges of the inlaid diamonds and carved runes. Her fingers passed through the illusion spell that reflected an image of the Moonstone at its center. The real stone had been missing for centuries, stolen and hidden away in a place that only existed in fairy tales. "There are other options."

Lucien's eyes narrowed. "Black clovers are *not* the answer."

"The Liberation begs to differ."

"Those plants are rooted in dark magic, Lucenna. Have you not learned your lesson?"

"Oh, you mean because my actions led to Mother's demise?" she hissed.

"No." He slammed a hand on his desk. "I mean, they are dangerous."

Lucenna glared at him. "I'm alone, Lucien. I can only do so much with what I know. The Guilds have no genuine power. The Archmage has taken it all. As long as he has the Tellur Medallion, the Liberation has no chance against the empire. The Sōl Medallion vanished and this," she lifted the Lūna Medallion, "is useless without the

Moonstone! Every passing day that I don't find it, more of our people die under the laws of the Mage Code. So, tell me, how else do you expect us to attain our freedom if not with dark magic? With compliance and diplomacy? Yes, because that has served you so well before."

As soon as the words left her mouth, she regretted them. Her brother didn't react. His face was an impassive mask.

"Lucien—"

"Leave Corron at once," he said stiffly. "It's not safe."

She lowered her head. "I will."

"Contact me when you've moved to a secure place." His image faded from the orb, and it returned to clear glass.

Lucenna groaned and let it sink back in her satchel. She should not have said something so cruel.

A thin strip of sunlight streamed in through the leaves and caught on the pink diamond ring on her fourth finger. It reminded her of another ring Lucien had once planned for a girl he loved. A ring he could never give.

None of it had been out of compliance.

She picked up a rock and hurled it at a tree with a furious scream. For each rock she threw, Lucenna imagined smashing the Archmage's skull in. She desired nothing more than to obliterate him for all he had taken from her family, and everyone oppressed under his heel.

Breathing heavily, she dropped her head against the battered tree bark, feeling no more significant than the mud splattered on her boots.

Who was she to overthrow an empire?

The gentle sound of oars cutting through water drew her attention to the woodland. The ferryman came into view. He rowed his boat through the lake, carrying a handful of men toward the shrouded shore.

They were all dressed in black and took orders from another man with honey brown hair wearing a black leather coat. He was too far to hear what he was saying, but she was curious enough to pry. Lucenna cast an amplification spell to listen in on the conversation, and the man's brogue voice came clear as if he'd spoken in her ear.

"I've lost her location," he said, frowning down at something in his hand. "Spread out. Search for her. When you find her, report to me immediately."

Find who?

"Don't confront them. Don't attract attention. Tomorrow we engage."

The men nodded with serious expressions. "Yes, Commander."

He was a commander? He didn't appear to be part of any regiment, and they wore no livery or crest of their liege lord.

The men noticed her one by one as the boat neared the shore. A man with dark skin and black curls nudged the leader, motioning at her with his chin. "Commander Von, there's a witness."

Magic pulsed at her fingertips, ready to attack should any of them approach. The commander studied her. His eyes landed on the medallion, and she quickly tucked it away.

"Leave her be." He turned away. "She knows nothing."

The boat reached the bank, and the men disembarked, their boots splashing in the water. Lucenna stepped far aside, not making any eye contact as she waited for them to pass. The men varied in size and age. The youngest appeared no older than fifteen. To her relief, they marched by without a word and headed for the trail.

The ferryman stepped out of his boat next. He was a stocky man, his face bronzed and hair bleached from his daily work in the sun. Commander Von handed him a bag clinking with coins.

The ferryman accepted it with an askance expression. "This is four times the fare, sir," he whispered, though it was clear in her ear. She looked away, feigning disinterest.

"Aye," the commander said, matching his volume. "Payment for services rendered and for the remainder of my men waiting to be ferried. The rest is for your discretion."

"I heard what you were on about. I won't abet in any abductions."

"You misunderstand. I have come for my dear sister."

"You need twenty armed men to retrieve her?"

"They are not for her but for those who have spirited her away from my father's home in the dead of night."

"Oh," the ferryman said, his tone easing out of suspicion. "Well ... I don't want any trouble."

"Aye, and you shan't have it. We'll need passage again in the morn."

"Very well. Good day to you."

Commander Von climbed onto the shore and brushed his hair out of his sea-green eyes, glancing at Lucenna. He gave her a slight nod in greeting as he moved on. Part of her wanted to cast a truth spell on him and probe into his matters further. What he said sounded true, but she also sensed lies.

"Leaving so soon?" the ferryman asked her. He turned his boat around so the bow pointed outward.

"Yes, I tended to my business here."

"Fine that. Come aboard." He sat at his place by the stern with his back to her, lifting his oar.

Lucenna took a step toward the shore when the commander whispered behind her, "I'm sorry, lass."

A blow burst in the back of her skull, stealing all feeling in her legs. The world skewed, and the ground rushed to meet her.

Then—black.

CHAPTER 35

Cassiel

Cassiel sat by a large fountain, watching the spray of water trickle over the tiers. Tiny sprites swam around in the basin, peeking at him from beneath the lily pads with marble-like black eyes. They leaped and dove out, their teal forms arcing through the air before splashing into the pools again.

By luck, he had found a public courtyard away from the commotion of the market and the suffocating crowd. It set him on edge to be around so many humans. Here it was much quieter, the tall shrubs of the well-kept garden reducing the racket and stink of the city. A perfect place to think.

Dyna.

Gods, she made him restless. He tried to ignore it, but the more he did, the more he was aware of her. Often, he found himself studying her little quirks. Like the way she bounced on her toes when she was anxious or excited, and how she bit her lip in concentration or how her eyes brightened with wonder when she experienced new things. Inexplicably, he found it endearing. It unnerved him to think that way about anyone. Let alone a human.

She also impressed him. How was she able to find happiness within her tragic life when he couldn't? The more he questioned himself about her, the more frustrated he became. It was a waste of energy to ask things he couldn't answer.

The bond hummed in Cassiel's chest, alerting him Dyna was near before she and Zev emerged from one of the four streets leading to the courtyard. Her eyes found his and he took a moment to peruse her new appearance. She had braided sections of her hair in a crown along her hairline, pulling the tresses back from her slender neck. Silver embroidery shimmered on the long bell sleeves of her emerald satin dress. It hugged Dyna's waist and bust, drawing attention to curves he hadn't allowed himself to notice before.

Cassiel twisted his fingers tightly around the drawstring of the burlap sack on his lap. "Took you long enough," he said, conveying annoyance he didn't feel.

Zev frowned. "I would have rather you'd waited. It was difficult to locate your scent among so many. Where did you go?"

"I went to find the merchant traders. I secured our spots on the next caravan leaving the city tomorrow afternoon ..." Cassiel trailed off at grim expressions. "What happened?"

Zev rubbed his face. "The witch may have cast a spell on Dyna."

Cassiel quickly stood. "What spell?"

"Didn't say. One moment she was there, then she vanished."

"I told you nothing good would come of it!" Cassiel took Dyna's arms and looked her over for any injuries or changes. "Did it hurt?"

"No," she said, her eyes widening.

"Did she utter any incantations? Did she say anything at all?"

Dyna looked away. "No."

"Perhaps it was only an act to frighten you. Witches speak their curses. But why did you stop to talk to a witch?"

"I wondered if perhaps she sold Stardust ..."

Cassiel stared at her. She had tried to find Stardust for him? Why? He didn't ask her to do that.

"We should go before we have no lodging for the night," Zev told them.

They continued deeper in Corron and came upon the first tavern. The taproom was rowdy with patrons, their titter, and chatter filling Cassiel's ears. The heavy scent of grease and sweat mingled in the air. They shouldn't bother with this place. All the rooms were surely let.

"I'll inquire about room and board," Zev said before Cassiel could say so, and he wrestled his way through the swarm.

"Prince Cassiel." Dyna's soft voice was almost lost in the clamor. She kept her gaze trained on the floor. "I'm sorry to have inconvenienced you. Your coin would have been better suited to replace your tunic."

He frowned. "I am not upset about that."

"But I *have* upset you."

He didn't know how to answer her without it being a lie. He was not angry with her, but with himself.

Dyna lifted her head and the lanterns above lit her hair in a soft crimson glow. "I placed you in a burdensome position by healing me."

A flush surged up his neck to his face. "It is not a matter of concern," he said too sharply.

"All right ..."

A nervous flutter wormed between them. He was not sure if it came from him or her, or both.

After a long silence, Cassiel cleared his throat and handed her the burlap sack he carried. "Here, this is for you."

"For me?" Dyna peered inside. It contained a set of knee-high leather boots. The soft leather was a rich sienna color with brass flourishes. "You bought me shoes?"

Cassiel shrugged like he hadn't searched for the best peddler in the city. "Your slippers will not last much longer on our journey."

He reached in his coat and handed her another paper package. A small smile pulled on the edges of her mouth when she opened it and pulled out a silvery caplet made of crushed velvet. The bond hummed with her happiness, but also sadness.

"I don't know how to thank you."

"There is no need. It does not compare to your old cloak. Hopefully, it will do." He'd tried to find something similar but, no one in Corron sold anything near its quality. "How did you get a hold of an enchanted cloak?"

"It once belonged to my father and his father before him."

Cassiel looked away at his twinge of shame for having thrown it in the dirt. He made her abandon it in Lykos.

Dyna looked up at him suddenly, her brow furrowing. She took his hand. "It's all right."

A lump formed in his throat. Had she felt him? He let their hands linger together for a moment longer than he should have before tugging his away. "How, uh, how is your shoulder?"

"It's perfect."

"Good."

Dyna faced forward, this time with a genuine smile. She moved closer to the foyer, bouncing on her toes to look over the crowd for Zev. Cassiel stayed by the door, leaning on the wall with his arms crossed as he watched her, ignoring the tingle her touch left on his skin.

Their Blood Bond was establishing much quicker than he had thought. Dyna's presence and her emotions coursed through him constantly. Her short bursts of confusion could only mean she felt him too.

He tried to control his own emotions, but having them out on display filled him with a jumble of them. It was bad enough that he had hers to deal with too. He attempted to put space between them, to shoulder her aside as he had before, but when he did, her responding sadness flooded him with guilt.

It was exasperating. He didn't have time for trivial things such as feelings, but he couldn't shake off the chaotic ones raging inside of him. It was a mixture of anxiety for breaking another Celestial law, an exhilaration that his blood worked, and disgrace for what he had done to her.

Dyna was his Blood Bonded.

The significance wasn't lost on him.

Saving her had also answered a question he had always wondered about his impure blood. He could heal others. That must mean his blood was divine enough to slay the Shadow, so she didn't need to risk her life crossing Urn. He could keep her safe.

Cassiel pressed on his temples. But what of the map?

He finally had a chance to reach Mount Ida. He needed Dyna to get there. Was it worth risking her life for his aim? A darker thought rose above the rest: he may not find what he searched for on that island.

"Redheads are always the ripe ones, yeah?"

Cassiel glanced at a table set by the wide windows near the entry where a group of four men sat and drank. They were laughing, spouting vulgarities—and leering at Dyna.

"Fine tartlet, that one," said a bearded man in a cocked hat. "I wouldn't mind having a go with her in the heather."

A dark-skinned man with a red rag tied around his head laughed and tossed back a swig. "That one looks highborn, Garik. She'd never pay a gobshite bastard like you any mind."

Garik laughed and said to a skinny man with a nest of ginger hair beside him, "That's what this smug twat said about the last trollop to warm me bed."

A larger man, burly and flat-nosed, cackled loudly. "Aye, you're always rutting the lassies. How do you manage it with your ugly arse?"

"Why, it's simple. Women like men who tell them the truth. To that sweet thing there, I'll say, 'Miss, I'm a seafaring man needing a place to berth my ship, and the dock between your thighs looks a lovely place to moor.'"

Rage blazed through Cassiel as their infuriating laughter rang in his head. Namir was wrong. Good clothing didn't divert the wrong attention. Men were vile, regardless of how one was dressed.

They quieted with his approach, and he loomed over Garik. "Attempt it, and you will have no ship to berth."

The men stared at him for a second, then burst with hysterical laughter. They laughed so hard tears welled in their eyes, one smacking the table.

Garik's mouth twisted in a mocking sneer. "You shouldn't spit out threats you can't keep, *boy*."

Cassiel clenched his fists. The insufferable man might learn he was very capable of keeping threats.

"Cassiel." Dyna came to his side. She hadn't heard their conversation but must have sensed his fury. It was burning through him, heating his head. Her wary gaze flickered to the snickering men leering at her. She took his arm and tried to pull him away. "Let's wait by the door."

Garik smirked and took a drink. "Ah, so she is with you, then. My apologies. You've done well for yourself, boy. Fine tartlet she is. Too fine for the likes of you. I can see why you wouldn't want to share."

Cassiel ground his teeth. He itched to wipe that nasty grin off the whoremonger's face.

"Come along," Dyna pulled on him harder, and he allowed her to turn him around. "We don't want any trouble," she said to the men. "Good day."

"Aye, good day it is, love," Garik replied as his eyes dragged up her body. "Might we make it a good night as well? I bet you taste quite sweet."

"Mind your damn tongue," Cassiel snapped.

"Believe me, boy, one night with me and she won't mind my tongue at all."

His companions roared with laughter.

Cassiel slammed his fist into Garik's face, the blow tossing him out of his seat. Garik scrambled to his feet and tackled him backward into a table, sending tankards and plates crashing to the floor. He got a punch in before Cassiel hit him with an uppercut, then kicked him back. He rolled off the table, blocked the man's next swing, and delivered a powerful hook to his gut. Gasping, Garik dropped to his knees. Cassiel grabbed his coat and lost himself to the feel of his fist bashing the man's face bloody—in the feel of bone cracking against bone.

Dyna screamed his name.

It was the only warning before Cassiel turned to the large man coming at him with a dagger. Zev dove between them in a rapid blur. He caught the knife-wielding hand and crushed it in his fist. Cassiel winced at the resulting sound that he could only describe as branches snapping in half. The man's agonizing scream cut off when Zev's shoulder rammed into his ribs, throwing him over his back, and sending him crashing through a window.

Bystanders gasped and backed away from Zev. He growled at Garik's remaining companions, his eyes flashing yellow. They quickly grabbed Garik's arms and wasted no time dragging him out of the tavern.

Cassiel wiped his blooded lip. "Thank you."

Zev nodded. "Care to explain?"

"I would rather not."

Zev would most likely rip out their throats if he heard what they said about Dyna. Cassiel found her shocked face in the crowd and she rushed to his side.

"Are you all right?" she asked.

"I'm fine, all things considered."

She wiped the droplet of blood on his nose. "You're bleeding."

"It has healed," he murmured. "We must go before the Azure Guard arrives." He pulled out a small pouch of gold coins from his pocket and tossed it to the innkeeper who gaped in dismay at the broken window. "For the damages."

Then he strode out the establishment, feeling rather smug. Dyna and Zev followed him from tavern to tavern across Corron in search of lodging. Twilight fell when they stopped at the remaining inn embedded in the hills. Mold tainted the poor stone structure. The crooked roof tiles appeared to hold on by mere will alone. A corroded wooden sign squeaked on its loose hinges as it flapped in the wind above the door. Ironically, etched on it were the words *The Last Resort*.

The hum of activity from within proved the establishment was in full service. They found the taproom was lively but not crowded, and most of the patrons were men of the Azure Guard. Cassiel told the others to wait by the door and made his way to the bar.

"Evening," he called to the innkeeper. The wizened man grunted a nod as he wiped down the counter. "Do you have any accommodations available?"

"I have just the one, milord," the old innkeeper replied in a thick Urnian accent.

"One? I need three beds for the night."

"Do ye now? Pardon me for not meeting yer expectations, milord. I have only one room left, but it is quite posh and might be up to yer refined tastes. It's on the second floor with lots of space, a big bed, and complemented with a private bath. Including a view of Loch Loden if it be to yer fancy." The innkeeper's dull sarcasm promised the opposite. He glanced past him to Zev and Dyna. "With extra guests, it'll cost two silvers for the night."

Cassiel glowered at the ridiculous amount. "A room here is worth ten russets, if that."

The innkeeper forced a smile that showed this was not the first time he had argued about it. "Anyone having made their way to my inn means there is no other lodging in Corron to be let. High demand makes for high rates. Pay the fare or sleep on the streets. It makes no difference to me."

Cassiel ground his teeth. Generally, he wouldn't let someone exploit him, but he couldn't expose Dyna to the dangers of the city at night. "You have no other quarters?"

"Yer welcome to the stable or here in the taproom."

Cassiel sighed and let two coins clatter on the counter.

The innkeeper grinned and handed him a single iron key. "Welcome to the *Last Resort*, milord. Will ye be having food and drink as well?"

His mouth watered at the mention of food, and he tossed him another coin. "Yes, three meals. Two with no meat, and water to drink."

The innkeeper chuckled. "Aye, take a seat. I'll have it brought out to ye."

Cassiel waved to Zev and Dyna, pointing to a round table on the far end of the room, and they made their way to it. Breadcrumbs and spilled ale littered the surface.

"They will serve us soon enough," Cassiel said as they sat down. He slid the key across the table to Dyna. "There was only one room available. You take it. Zev and I will sleep down here."

She looked to Zev and slightly shook her head, her eyes wide and pleading.

He took the key instead. "I'll stay with her tonight."

"What?" Cassiel frowned. That was inappropriate, no matter if they were blood-related.

Zev shrugged. "She's afraid to be alone at night."

He glanced at Dyna and her cheeks bloomed pink. Afraid to be alone? No, it was more than that. Whenever night fell, she grew more skittish, always watching their surroundings as if she expected something to jump out.

She squirmed under his stare, fidgeting with her sleeve. "Perhaps we can all share the room? We have already slept together outside under the stars. This would be the same."

Cassiel balked at the thought and cleared his throat, pulling at his collar. "That is not the same at all."

"Is it better than the alternative?" Zev asked. "Dyna will not sleep alone. She can't."

"I'm sorry, Zev," she muttered. "I should have grown out of it by now."

He patted her back. "It's not your fault."

Dyna closed her eyes, and her brow tightened. A distant fear trickled through the bond, settling over Cassiel. Cold, sharp claws grasped him, filling him with deep-set desperation and terror. She lived with this fear?

They both flinched at the sound of a heavy thud on the table. A passing barmaid had set down a flagon and mugs. Another placed three steaming bowls down with a basket of black bread before running off to serve more patrons. At the smell of the food, Cassiel forgot their conversation. He inhaled the scent of his meal and barely hid a moan. They had served him wild rice topped with buttered mushrooms and herbs.

"It smells delicious!" Dyna said.

"It does." Zev grinned at his plate. Steam swirled above the sizzling lamb's leg, nestled in potatoes and carrots. The brown skin was crisp and glistened with oil and rosemary. She laughed as he ate it with relish.

Cassiel was halfway through his meal by the time Zev had devoured his, nothing left but the bones sucked dry. "Are you satiated?"

Zev pouted. "Not at all."

"Then, by all means, order another meal. I paid the innkeeper far more than our stay here is worth."

Rubbing his hands together, Zev left to do that. Cassiel poured himself a drink as he glanced at Dyna. She nibbled on a roll of bread, lost in thought until she sensed his stare and looked up.

"All right?" he asked.

"Yes, and you?"

"Me?"

"Why did you fight that man?"

Did she not know why?

Dyna tilted her head, her knowing green eyes searching his. Oh. She had understood the vile words Garik said, but she hadn't understood why he fought him. Cassiel didn't either. He had been so angry that he wanted to hit the man and keep hitting him until he couldn't lift his arms. But with each beating of his fist, his fury had melted into a blind rage, and Garik's face had merged into his brother's and everyone else who so reviled him. His knuckles were then cracking against their bones, returning all the hate he had endured.

"Cassiel?"

"It is of no concern." He inhaled a deep breath and sighed, shaking his head. Seeking a distraction, he took a sip from his mug and nearly spat it out at the sweet fermented taste. "Excuse me, what is *this*?" Cassiel asked the barmaid passing by as he indicated the flagon with revulsion.

She frowned, as though confused by what he was asking. "That is mead, milord. Our finest."

"I requested water."

"Oh. Father thought it a jest."

"It was not," he replied tersely.

"Sorry, sir. I'll see to it." She curtsied and hurried off.

"I don't care for mead either," Dyna said. "I'm not fond of the taste."

It wasn't the taste that bothered him. His head was pounding from the little he sipped. Celestials didn't drink. Allegedly, it sullied their sanctity, but he suspected it was because they couldn't hold it.

Strangely, his bond with Dyna also became muddled. Was it because of the mead?

Zev returned with the same meal and ate heartily between chugs of the drink. He seemed to enjoy it well enough so Cassiel tried it again. Letting the mead linger on his tongue, he found it crisp with hints of honey and other spices. His face flushed as the mead quickly worked its way through him, leaving him lightheaded. The Blood Bond faded further. It was thin. Wrong.

He didn't like it.

The part of him that wanted nothing to do with the bond was relieved to be free of it, but the rest of him detested the feeling. It left him apprehensive and sore, as though the bond itself was warning him that something was wrong with Dyna. A fading or broken bond meant death, but she was right in front of him, alive and well. He had to fight the urge to reach across the table and take her hand to ease his worry.

Cassiel shook his head to rid himself of those thoughts and continued filling his mug. Between him and Zev, they drank two more flagons of mead. By the end, he was swaying in his chair, floating on a cloud of euphoria powerful enough to dull even his worries.

He lazily rested his chin on a hand, peering at Dyna through his double vision. "Why do you fear to be alone?"

"Leave her be," Zev slurred. "She has suffered things you couldn't imagine." He offered Dyna a lethargic grin and gave her head a clumsy pat.

Cassiel snorted into his mug. "Haven't we all?"

"You're a condescending bird…" Zev mumbled. He lifted the flagon, waving it at him. "Here. Have another drink. May it mend your terrible manner. It's much needed."

"Do not—" Cassiel lifted a hand to point at Zev, only to knock his mug over. The contents spilled across the table and Dyna scooted her chair away before it poured on her lap.

Zev snickered. "You've made a mess, Your Highness!"

Dyna shook her head. "You're both drunk."

"Oh, aye, and I like it!"

Cassiel smirked. "I suppose I do as well."

"I thought it was against Celestial faith to drink. Your brother would have a fit." Zev sat straight in his chair with a stern expression and spoke in Prince Malakel's self-important voice, "You have dishonored the Soaraway family!"

Cassiel leaned back in his chair and laughed at how well Zev mimicked him. But his laughter died away, and he dropped his head in his hands, feeling sick. Not because of the mead, but because it occurred to him Malakel was right. He was always dishonoring his family.

Be it from drinking or existing.

You are irrelevant. A blight. When you are gone, no one will ever care to remember you.

With a bitter curl of his lip, Cassiel poured himself another drink.

Cheers.

Dynalya

With great effort, Dyna steered her inebriated companions through the crowded taproom and up the stairway. It took three times as long because they kept tripping over their useless feet, laughing and stumbling into each other. She was exhausted by the time they reached the second floor. Her steps faltered at the dark hallway, the hanging lanterns casting eerie shadows on the walls. The window at the end of the hall was black with the night outside.

Dyna followed behind Zev and Cassiel as they staggered along to their room. She unlocked the door with shaking fingers, and the hinges creaked as it slowly opened.

Darkness waited inside.

She stopped short at the threshold, her heart pounding as goosebumps crept up her arms. Cassiel and Zev wobbled into the room, dropping their rucksacks on the floor with heavy thuds. Both headed for the small bed set near the door. They flopped on it together, and the wood base groaned under their weight. They complained about the other being in the way, elbowing and kicking to claim space.

A lantern rested on the nightstand next to the bed. She took a deep breath, ran inside the room, and quickly lit it. As soon as a soft light illuminated the space, it loosened the threads of fear that never left her.

The room was a decent size. The bed was set against the wall and across from it were large double windows with the shutters closed. Beside it was a matching armoire with brass knobs. A folded screen divided the space, hiding the chamber pot and bath. She opened the shutters to let in the moonlight, but an adjacent building blocked most of the view, leaving only a sliver of the lake below.

The room soon filled with a symphony of soft snores. Zev slept facedown, hanging half over the bed with his messy hair stuck to his face, leaving only his scrunched lip visible. The prince slept on his back at an angle with his legs resting over Zev's butt. Dyna stifled a giggle, wishing to have a portrait of the spectacle they made. She was glad to have witnessed Cassiel laugh and banter with Zev. It was nice to see for once, even if he was drunk.

After pulling off their boots, she covered them with a spare sheet, then she picked up the paper bundle of her new clothes and went behind the folded screen where a copper bathtub filled with water waited. She blushed at the thought of bathing in the same room as Zev and Cassiel. But they wouldn't wake anytime soon, and the screen was solid enough for privacy. Dyna carefully removed the emerald dress and hung it over the screen. She stroked the beautiful stitching of flowers and vines along the hem. Never had she worn something so fine.

She stepped into the tub and sank into the tepid water, sighing as it soothed her sore feet. Her head rested against the edge of the basin as she smiled to herself. It had been a good day. Cassiel could be condescending and cold, but sometimes it was interrupted by snippets of kindness. The obvious embarrassment at catching himself made it all the more charming.

Dyna stayed in the bath until the water grew cold. Once dried, she picked out a new chemise made of soft linen. The armoire contained spare blankets she used to make herself a spot near the bed. She laid down on her back and watched the shadows of the lantern sway on the ceiling.

It reminded her of her bedroom back in North Star. Was her grandmother in good health? How was Lyra doing? Was she all right? Grandmother Leyla must be so angry with her and terribly worried. Dyna sighed, wishing she could see them.

Zev mumbled something indiscernible and rolled over, the movement causing Cassiel to slide off the bed. Dyna scuttled out of the way before he dropped heavily where she'd been lying. He groaned in complaint. His sticky eyes blinked open, and he sat up to pick at the buttons of his coat, but his fingers wouldn't coordinate.

"Here, let me." She laughed softly and unbuttoned it for him.

He shrugged it off and his wings spread wide, the black feathers casting patterns on the wall. Cassiel peeled off his tunic next. She quickly looked away but couldn't help stealing a peek at his sculpted body. His arms stretched behind his head, his biceps tightening as the warm glow of the lantern fell over the dips and planes of his firm torso, defining every muscle. Face on fire, Dyna pulled her gaze down.

Cassiel yawned and laid out on her makeshift bed, wings settling on his back like a sleek blanket. She remained sitting beside him, not sure what to do. He took her bedding, and there was no room on the bed with Zev.

"Why do you fear being alone?" he asked again, his soft words heavily slurring.

An embarrassed flush rose to her face. "Only when it's dark."

"You fear the dark?"

She looked up at the writhing shapes swarming on the ceiling. "It's not the dark I fear, but the things that may lurk within it."

Cassiel squinted through one eye, then rolled onto his side and lifted a wing as though to invite her in. She fought the blush rushing to her cheeks. Surely, that was not his intention—

He grabbed her arm and yanked. She fell with a yelp against him, and he covered her with his wing. It was warm, soft as silk—and much too close for her comfort.

Dyna's heart caught in her throat. "C-Cassiel."

"There." He sighed in content, his breath trickling her neck, still damp from her wet hair. It sent a nervous shiver through her. He brought an arm around her waist and drew her closer, holding her hot cheek against his bare chest. "It is odd … why do you put me at ease?"

Dyna was too startled to speak. She tried to calm the wild gallop of her heart and failed miserably.

"So long as I am with you, there is nothing to fear," he mumbled, his words thick and slow on his tongue as sleep pulled him. "I will protect you from the dark and the shadows. My blood proved I can."

Discomfort replaced itself with astonishment and Dyna leaned her head back to look at him. "What do you mean?"

"I will slay your demon."

"What?" she breathed. "Your father said that your people could do no such thing anymore. That your sanctity had diminished."

"It is true, but only for those who have taken human lives. I have not."

She widened her eyes. "Why are you telling me this now?"

He closed his eyes. "For once, I realize I am not as sullied as they led me to believe. I have the ability to do something that many others cannot do. Perhaps there is a reason for my being here, in this world."

He peered at her through his lashes, and again she saw the makings of a smile on the edges of his mouth. A feeling rose in her chest, light and airy. Wistful. Another wave of bewilderment hit her to find it was Cassiel's hope. How was she able to feel that? It was new, but raw and so frail, as if he feared wanting it.

And Dyna realized then it was because others told him he didn't have the right to a thing such as hope. They didn't allow him any happiness. All because he was half-human. Her eyes welled in anger and she regretted not throwing that fig at Malakel's face.

But Cassiel barely survived the Other. The Shadow would be too much for him. Too vicious and merciless. She couldn't ask him to fight it for her.

"There is a reason for your existence," she said. "But not to fight the Shadow."

"But I can—"

"No, it's too dangerous."

He blinked at her sleepily, frowning. "Do you not wish to return home?"

"More than anything, but I can't involve you in this. I don't want you to get hurt."

Cassiel scoffed and shook his head. "You are the most incredulous person I have ever come across, maddening even." He brushed the hair from her face and his fingers faintly trailed down her cheek, leaving behind a tingling trail on her skin. "But I find I do not mind it in the least." The way he was looking at her made her heart do all sorts of flips. "Your eyes are beautiful," he mumbled as his own slid closed again, his breaths deepening. "They remind me of …"

"Of what?" Dyna whispered when he fell silent.

His only response was a faint snore.

She smiled, well aware of her heated face. He liked her eyes? What had gotten into him? He had never said such things to her before.

Cassiel held her captive beneath his arm so there was nothing to do other than watch him sleep. His features were smooth of any irritation, long dark lashes kissing his cheeks. He looked serene, happy even.

It wasn't often he let her get this close. Reaching out tentatively, Dyna brushed her fingers along his sleek feathers. She traced the outer edge of his wing, carefully, lightly, moving over the margins to where it met his back. Her hand brushed over his shoulder, layered in muscle, and up to his neck, fingertips stroking his smooth jaw. A current pulsed where they touched, fluttering in her stomach.

What was this energy between them? Did it have to do with feeling his emotions? Was she truly feeling him? Whatever this energy was, it didn't feel wrong.

Ignoring her blush, Dyna closed her eyes and settled on his chest. She listened to his steady heartbeat as hers slowed to match his rhythm.

At times, it was a difficult thing to believe Cassiel was real. He was starlight, and wonder, and questions without answers. But she was willing to wait to uncover them.

His soft breathing lulled her, chasing away all her fears. One day she would have to face the shadows, but at this moment in his arms, it was the furthest thing from her mind.

She slipped into a peaceful sleep with his soft feathers against her cheek, and his scent lingering in her dreams.

CHAPTER 37

Lucenna

Lucenna woke up in a strange place with a foul headache. She moaned, pressing the heels of her palms against her pulsing skull. It was as equally unbearable as the hard bed she laid in. Someone had graciously provided her with a coarse blanket and an itchy straw mattress, but alarm washed through her at finding herself in an unfamiliar house. It was small and dark, the fireplace providing some light. The window shutters were closed, but she sensed that night had fallen.

Three little girls peeped at her from behind the footboard with wide curious eyes, whispering to each other.

"She's pretty."

"I like her hair."

"Is she to be our new mama?" the youngest one asked.

Lucenna glowered at them, and they giggled.

"Father," the oldest one called over her shoulder. "She's awake."

There was shuffling from the other side of the room. The ferryman rose from his table and approached.

He handed her a cup of water. "How are you feeling, lass?"

"What happened?" She sat up. Her vision spun, and she gripped the bedpost to keep from keeling over.

"You lost your footing on the shore and hit your head. The man helped me carry you up the hill to my home."

"The man?" she hissed, recalling Commander Von's last words before he struck her. "He's the one who rendered me unconscious!"

"Did he?" The ferryman frowned skeptically. He hadn't seen it. His back had been turned.

Lucenna stood, swaying on her feet. "I need to leave Corron immediately."

"Rest. You can't go out now. The Azure Guard patrols increase at night."

"I cannot be here. Please take me out of this city. I must leave tonight."

He sighed. "Forgive me, lass. I cannot risk it. If I'm detained, who will care for my daughters?"

She glanced at his little girls quietly listening. A layer of freckles sprinkled their cheeks. Their unkempt blonde hair was tied back in braids, and they wore clothes too small.

"I work from sunup to sundown," he said, exhaustion and sadness weighing on him. "I hardly have time to spend with them. I walk out that door with a prayer to the Gods to protect them for me while I'm gone, but I know better than to ferry the waters at night."

"There's no help for it then, I'll find my own way out." She had to risk using more magic. With an invisibility spell, she could sneak out the front gates. But how close was the nearest Enforcer? Lucien would know.

"There are your belongings," the ferryman said, pointing by her feet. He had set her satchel against the bedpost. A sack laid on top of it.

"What is this?"

"Is it not yours? The man said it was."

Lucenna grabbed the sack, hearing the jostle of coins inside. It was full of gold. Why would the commander give her gold? She smacked a hand over her chest where the weight of the Lūna Medallion once rested. It was gone.

"No!" she screamed, making the girls flinch. "Where is it! Where is my medallion!"

Rage and anguish surged her Essence forward in an aggressive wave. Its effervescent glow radiated out of her skin, casting a purple hue in the room. Electricity crackled around her, charging the air as an unnatural wind howled through the ferryman's house, creating a violent vortex. His daughters screamed and cowered behind him as furniture crashed across the room. Essence spilled from her in a thick mist, crawling across the floor and up the walls.

"What medallion? I didn't see one!" he shouted desperately, clinging to his children. "I swear it! Please don't hurt my family!"

Lucenna quickly reined in her emotions, dissipating her magic in a puff of smoke. She slumped back on the bed, dropping her head. "Be at ease. I mean you no harm."

Commander Von.

He must have stolen it. He paid her far more than the value of the medallion was worth, but not what it was worth to her. Lucenna scowled at the glittering coins scattered across the room. She didn't want his filthy money.

Oh, but he would pay.

At dawn the next day, the residential street outside the ferryman's house was quiet. A few people ambled about, heading to their daily business. Rosy sunlight gleamed on the high rooftops at an angle and cast the homes in the shade. Lucenna breathed in the crisp air, preparing herself for the day.

"Are you sure about this, lass?" the ferryman asked from his doorway. He held the sack of gold unsurely.

"Yes, take it as a pardon and my thanks for your help. As well as your silence." She held his gaze. "We never met."

He nodded. "As you say."

"You must leave this place." She was sure the Enforcers would come, and they would track her to his home first. "Tell no one of your newfound wealth lest they try to rob you. There is enough gold there to live comfortably for the rest of your life." She glanced past him at his sleeping daughters curled in the bed together. "Buy an estate. Hire housemaids to mind it, and a nursemaid to mind the needs of your children. Pay well for their education and teach them to be strong. In this world, women need to be."

The man stared at the sack of coins. His weary eyes welled as he pictured the image she painted, and the things he might have dreamed of. He gave her a watery smile. "Aye, I think you're right. Thank you, truly. Permit me to ferry you out of Corron so I don't feel as though I have swindled you."

"There's no need. If the gold unsettles you so, accept it as payment for your boat."

"You want my boat? But I was to ferry the man and his lot this morn."

She gave him a dark smile. "I'll see to it. He and I have a matter to settle."

He chuckled nervously. "Ah, then I suppose this is farewell?"

"Yes. And take my word for it—*go*. You do not want to be here when they come searching for me."

The man didn't know who *they* were, but he nodded from the severity in her tone. As soon as he closed the door, Lucenna cast an invisibility spell over herself. She walked along the street of wattle and daub houses, her heels clacking on the cobblestone to a steady rhythm.

She gathered her Essence, excited to at last wield magic freely. Lucien confirmed the Enforcers were two days out. There was enough time to enact her plan.

She wouldn't leave without the Lūna Medallion. It was a family heirloom, the making of a legacy she tried to live up to, and it represented the hope of every sorceress in the Magos Empire.

Commander Von made the greatest mistake of his life the day he crossed her.

Lucenna closed her eyes and breathed in deeply. Her consciousness slipped into the *Essentia Dimensio* where Essence became alive. It brought her to a pitch-black environment devoid of anything, but its energy hummed through her in welcome.

Her Essence appeared as a vivid sphere of purple lightning that convulsed and swirled before her. She flicked her hand up and the sphere zoomed high above into the empty blackness, exploding in a rain of light. Streaks of purple spread outward, expanding like a net in the dark for her target. But it thinned and lost color the further it went out until her Essence completely faded away.

Someone else had already cloaked Commander Von.

Lucenna clenched her fists. He had the services of a mage! But none of the men with him had been one. She would have sensed it.

Well, it didn't matter. The Moonstone may be missing, but the medallion was created by one of the most powerful mages in history. His Essence had eternally infused inside, and it was not hidden from her.

She cast out another tracking spell, searching for the Essence that closely resembled her own. This time her power moved surely through the *Essentia Dimensio,* and it landed in the distance on two glowing bulbs of light. One was the radiant mauve Essence trapped in the Lūna Medallion, and the other was green.

It took her a moment to figure out the green light was Dyna's Essence. It was odd that the tracking spell targeted her, and that she was within immediate proximity of the medallion. Was that a coincidence?

There was no time to waste thinking about it.

Lucenna hooked her spell onto the medallion and opened her eyes to the real world. A trail of translucent purple fire, visible only to whoever she wished, appeared at her feet and snaked down the quiet street. Leading her exactly where she needed to go.

CHAPTER 38

Dynalya

Dyna hardly listened as Zev rattled off the list of provisions they needed to purchase for their journey. She followed him to a merchant selling grain, and he asked for a pound of this or that, his voice muffled in the buzz of her thoughts. Cassiel lingered a few feet away, but his presence pressed against her back. She could feel his eyes on her as she felt his agitation.

Her elbow was still sore from where it had slammed on the floor when he pushed her off him that morning. It startled her awake as much as his feeling of horror and shame had also hit her. He then bolted from the room without a word.

Dyna fisted the sleeves of her dress, crushing the soft linen in her fingers. There was pressure on her chest and a mist in her eyes.

She was sure now that she could feel his emotions. Why? How?

It was too much and too confusing. None of it made sense. But she would rather focus on that than the humiliation she felt when Cassiel pushed her away like she was a vile thing.

"There, a couple of pounds of oats," Zev announced to them as he added the sack to his pack. "What next?"

"Produce," she mumbled.

He led the way into the crowd with a cheerful whistle. "It's a nice day, isn't it?" When no one answered, he frowned at them and nudged Cassiel. "Did you not sleep well? You were gone when I awoke this morn."

Dyna stiffened at the sudden bout of Cassiel's tension that gripped her.

He glanced at her uneasily. "I needed some air."

Zev chuckled and whacked his shoulder. "You drank yourself into a tizzy last night."

"I will never partake again."

She tried to ignore the sick feeling that indication brought.

The bustle of voices in the market grew louder as the sun rose higher, and the crowd thickened. They reached a street lined in carts of pumpkins, squash, radishes, and carrots along with every fruit and vegetable in season. Zev's pack grew bulkier with each purchase added to it. He asked them to make selections, but for once, Dyna wasn't in the mood.

Distracted, she bumped into Zev when he halted in the middle of the street. His sharp yellow eyes scanned the throng.

Cassiel moved closer to her, eyeing the sea of faces. "What is it?"

Zev frowned. "I had a sudden feeling we were being followed, but it must be nothing. I am unaccustomed to being around so many people"

"Yes, it is making me edgy as well."

Zev shook his shoulders to get rid of the feeling and continued onward. "We're almost done here."

"Can we explore the rest of the market?" Dyna asked. "We didn't have the chance to do so yesterday."

"Cassiel, do you mind?" Zev asked him.

Dyna made a face. Since when were they so friendly that they asked each other for permission? Why was she so annoyed when this was what she wanted?

Cassiel shrugged. "I suppose."

Zev smiled at her. "Go, he'll accompany you while I continue buying the provisions. That should give you some time to look around."

Dyna exchanged a startled look with Cassiel, then glanced away. "You're not coming with us?" she asked Zev.

"No, there are a few more items we need."

"I will go buy the provisions," Cassiel blurted. "You stay with her."

Zev chuckled. "Oh no, I'll buy the food. I cannot live off pomegranates and seeds. I'm going to the butcher for salted meat."

Dyna kept her gaze on the ground, waiting for Cassiel to protest further. He didn't want to be alone with her any more than she did.

He sighed and handed her cousin some coins. "See if you can find a farmer that sells rice milk. And hurry or we will miss the caravan."

"Aye, I'll meet you here in an hour." Zev patted her head. "Take care of her," he told Cassiel, then merged into the crowd.

She and Cassiel stood in the middle of the street, looking at anything but each other. She fidgeted with the tapered sleeves of the sapphire dress she wore, the sun catching on the hem decorated with embroidered roses. Yesterday, it had thrilled her to receive the dresses. They had been gifts, evidence that he cared. Now she only wanted to give them back.

Silly girl. Men don't buy dresses for acquaintances.

Ridiculous. Namir had filled her head with scandalous suggestions and illusions.

But Cassiel had given her his blood and defended her against that man. He held her all night, reassuring her of her fears. He was there for her. Why do any of it if he didn't mean it?

Dyna wanted to ask but couldn't bring herself to. She waited for him to say something. To explain, to give an apology, or even to call her stupid for making assumptions. Anything to relieve the air full of things left unspoken.

He said nothing.

She really was a stupid human.

Fighting the embarrassing urge to cry, Dyna wandered away. She stopped in front of a stall at random. It only sold weapons, though. Before she could move on, Cassiel lined up beside her.

She lifted a crossbow, feigning interest. The thing was crude and heavy, with a bolt sitting in the groove. The weapons merchant finished a sale and ambled over to them. He was a willowy man in a showy taffeta waistcoat and gold rings on his bony fingers.

He gave her a haughty simper. "Poison is a better-suited weapon for a woman. That crossbow is too much for you, love."

"You will refer to her with respect," Cassiel's cool voice drifted over her.

"Of course, milord. Your pardon, miss."

They remained side by side, both stiff and unmoving. Dyna held the crossbow awkwardly, not knowing what else to do with it or with herself. She fiddled with the string, then with a lever.

The merchant chuckled nervously. "Careful. Don't pull the trigger."

She raised it, trying to get a feel for how it was supposed to shoot. The merchant jumped out of the way.

"Keep the stock steady," Cassiel said. He lifted the bottom of the crossbow until it butted with her shoulder and helped her aim at the wall. The current of his touch trickled down her arm. She stepped back, putting deliberate space between them. He shifted on his feet and cleared his throat.

"Do they fit well?" Cassiel eventually asked, glancing at her boots. "I assumed your size."

She nodded, fiddling with a spring on the weapon, eliciting a click. "Yes, thank you."

"The pleasure is all mine." After a long silence, he muttered under his breath. "Last night, I-I was sozzled."

A flush worked its way up her face. "Oh, yes, I know."

"I did not mean to—"

"Please leave it be," she rushed out, deciding she preferred not to discuss it after all.

"I should not have—"

"It's fine!" The crossbow slipped from her hands. She lunged to catch it at the same time he did. They caught it between them with their noses a hairsbreadth apart. Cassiel didn't shove her away this time. Neither of them moved, locked in a stare—until the crossbow went off. The merchant yelped and ducked a split moment before the bolt pierced the wall above his head.

"Ah," he squeaked. "Y-you nearly got me there."

"Why is this thing loaded?" Cassiel snapped at him. He took the crossbow from her and laid it on the counter.

"I am so sorry!" Dyna told the stunned merchant, appalled that she had almost killed him. "Please forgive me."

"Have your husband make a purchase, and all will be forgiven."

A blush blazed in her cheeks. This was the second time someone made that sort of assumption. "He's not—"

Cassiel slammed his hand on the counter, his face beet red, getting ready to shout at the man.

"He will," Dyna cut him off before they made a further spectacle.

But at realizing she confirmed them as life-mates, she thought she might faint from mortification. She kept her head low, not daring to look at him.

Her fingers brushed over two matching knives. They had beautifully embossed detailing on the blade and luminescent opal hilts, one white and the other black. She lifted one against the sun, admiring the changing colors in whichever way it caught the light.

After an uncomfortable pause, Dyna put the knife down and made herself break the silence. "Forgive me for having caused you such trouble."

"It is much anticipated now," Cassiel retorted.

It was an answer she should have expected, but she wasn't prepared for how much it would hurt. She moved away from the stall to look for Zev.

"Wait." Cassiel caught her hand, stopping her in the middle of the street. "That was uncalled for."

She kept her back to him. "I had nearly forgotten how uncouth you can be."

He sighed. "Uncouth and a degenerate, it seems. We … we should discuss last night. Will you look at me? Please?"

He gently tugged her hand, an invitation instead of a demand. Dyna shook her head. If she looked at him, he would know everything she thought about it. Maybe he already knew. She could feel him somehow, that must mean he could feel her too. His uncertainty, worry, and frustration came to her in overwhelming waves, melding with her own.

Cassiel lifted her chin. They were silent as they locked eyes, letting the sounds of their surroundings fill the void between them. "Dyna, I—"

A baker across the street hollered that he had fresh loaves for sale. A crowd gathered around the bakery, allured by the smell of baking bread. And it was the perfect excuse to get away from him.

"I … I'll buy loaves for our journey," she said and pulled her hand free.

"Wait—" Cassiel moved to follow, but the merchant called out to him.

"Milord! You agreed to make a purchase."

Dyna took advantage of the distraction and quickly escaped across the street to the baker's shop. She needed some space from him to untangle her thoughts and right her head. She was relieved when Cassiel went to keep his word.

The shop was crowded. She squeezed in and got in line. The delicious smell of bread gave her a small thing to look forward to. She closed her eyes, taking a deep breath, and it helped a little to ease the nervousness that had taken over her.

Dyna couldn't explain herself or her jumbled feelings. She only knew that Cassiel caused them. The truth was, he had always affected her. Not as much as recently, but there was something about him that had connected with her since he caught her out of the sky. Since the moment she touched his cheek. That first electrical current between them had changed something in her. It was as though every part of her craved to be around him. *Needed* to be around him. He was constantly on her mind, his presence always on her skin, his very being alit her soul. But it was all one-sided. She needed to forget that and him so they could go back to being no more than strangers on a journey together.

When it was her turn in line, Dyna requested half a dozen rolls, and the baker's wife bagged her order. Leaving the bakery, she bit into a roll and steam billowed out as she moaned happily. She had missed the taste of fresh bread.

"Is it good?" someone asked with a chuckle.

Dyna looked up at the man she nearly bumped into and a chunk of bread lodged in her throat when she gasped. She coughed, hitting her chest to dislodge it. "Commander Von!"

He laughed and patted her back. "Pardon, I didn't mean to startle you."

"This is unexpected." She smiled, even while everything in her immediately tensed in alarm. The last time she had seen Von, she had told him about Mount Ida. "What has brought you here? You disappeared in Landcaster."

"Aye, I had been in a hurry to be on my way, but I came looking for you. It so happens that I have an old acquaintance that is well-traveled. He has offered to be your Guidelander."

"Oh, is that so?" she said airily.

"Forgive me, I had not thought of him at the time." His deliverance was smooth with sufficient sincerity on his face, but she wasn't convinced.

"Well, I must discuss it with Cassiel." Dyna mentioned him as an excuse, and to let Von know she wasn't unaccompanied.

She rose on her toes, barely glimpsing Cassiel's head above the crowd. He would know what to do about this. The commander following her from Landcaster couldn't be good.

Von grabbed her arm. "If you would like to employ the Guidelander, you must come with me now. He is not a patient man." His tone was a little more insistent, his smile a little more forced.

Dyna jerked her arm away and steeled her expression. "In that case, I'm no longer interested. If you'll excuse me, have a good day."

She gave him a stiff nod and turned to go. She needed to tell Cassiel and Zev right away. They needed to leave—

A calloused hand clamped over her mouth and wrenched her from the street into an alley. Her startled cry cut off as the ground vanished from beneath her feet and Von tossed her on his shoulder. He sprinted away, taking her further and further from the light of the market—and Cassiel.

Fear arrested her heart, squeezing it tight until only her unheard screams echoed in her ears.

CHAPTER 39

Cassiel

The merchant haggled Cassiel for all the coin he could get for the pair of matching opal knives. He wanted to believe he chose them because the edges were fine, and not because Dyna had liked them, but he had seen how she had admired the knives. They would fit perfectly in her small hands. She may not have strength, but he could teach her how to defend herself with a weapon. God of Urn knew she had an uncanny knack for attracting trouble. A part of him hoped the gift might restore the bridge he had knocked down between them.

Well, if he could ever face Dyna again.

It had been a shock like no other to wake with her soft, diminutive form pressed against him. With his hand on the curve of her waist, feeling her warm skin through the thin fabric of her chemise, his body had immediately ... responded.

Horrified, he had shoved Dyna off, startling her awake when she flopped on the cold floor. The hurt and confusion had been clear in her eyes as it churned through him. He hadn't known what else to do or say, so he ran out of the room like a coward.

All the emotions he left her with had swelled through him all morning. She wouldn't even look at him. He hated it, but he didn't know how to talk to her. When he tried, he couldn't get a proper apology out. He kept thinking about the feel of her, and the humiliating things he said last night.

Cassiel groaned and rubbed his face. He had confessed that he found her eyes beautiful. *Gods.* Perhaps he could pretend he remembered nothing at all.

He was tucking the knives into his boots when a rush of fear throttled him in the gut. It was sudden, jarring—and it had come through the bond.

Cassiel launched into the crowd, shoving past protesting people to get to the bakery, but he slammed through the door only to meet startled strangers and the angry baker.

Running back outside to the street, he scanned the faces around him. "Dyna! Where have you gone?"

No one answered. Cassiel's worry grew into panic as her terror filled him. He pushed and thrust through the mass of people, searching for her. Dyna didn't appear, no matter how many times he shouted her name. He checked the bakery again, but she wasn't there. She wasn't anywhere.

Zev would finish him

"Serves you right for leaving her unprotected," a female voice hissed in his ear.

He jumped back, searching for whoever spoke. "Who said that?"

"You'll need my help to find her. I can cast a tracking spell for a small fee."

"What?" Cassiel spun around. "Where are you? Show yourself!"

A young woman materialized a foot away from him. He stumbled backward against the bakery. She was almost the same height as him in her heeled boots, dressed in black leather, her long white hair drifting in the mild wind.

"Witch ..." Cassiel said under his breath.

Her strange lilac eyes flashed with magic. "Pompous lord."

Then he realized who she was. "You're the witch from the market. What did you do to her?"

She hissed, "Don't insult me. I have done nothing to her. Now stop wasting my time or *hers*. She doesn't have much of it left."

"What do you mean?" he demanded. "Where is Dyna?"

"They took her."

His insides dropped through him, sinking into the ground. "Who took her? Tell me!"

"Fool, you have no one to blame but yourself."

Cassiel glared at her. "How do I know you are telling me the truth? This could be a trap."

Her eyes narrowed, electricity crackling at her fingertips. "If I wanted to trap you, it wouldn't take more than a snap of my fingers. I know what you are, *Cassiel*. Named after the first Celestial king of Hilos. It's well known in history, yet you walk around letting others call it out. You're fortunate no one has noticed you yet. Idiot."

He blanched, tensing in alarm. Was this witch under the Accords? He couldn't trust her, but Dyna's fear flooded through his chest, drowning him.

"Now if you want to find her, it will cost you," she said.

"How much?" he asked tightly.

"One tracking spell for one feather."

He scowled. "No."

She crossed her arms. "You do not wish to find her?"

"Of course I do, but it is illegal for my kind to trade or sell."

"I see. Well, best of luck to you both." The young woman shrugged and walked away.

"I cannot give it to you," he snapped.

She kept walking, and he couldn't help but feel that he would never see Dyna again if he didn't stop her.

"Wait," he whispered sharply. "Fine, but no one can see."

The woman motioned at the alley. Cassiel rushed in and she followed, hurrying further out of sight of the market. Making sure they weren't being watched, he reached into the collar of his coat and winced as he plucked a feather.

He thrust it at her. "Now tell me where she is."

She took the black feather, and its profile glowed gold. Her lilac eyes widened. "Incredible …"

Cassiel pressed a fist to his chest as more of Dyna's fear seized him. "Cast the spell!"

The witch tucked her new prize inside her bag. "It's done. Follow the trail. It's only visible to you, and it will disappear once you find her. Now go. You best hurry."

Then she vanished from sight.

Follow the trail? What trail? He didn't understand what she meant until he spotted it. Down the alley appeared a path outlined in translucent purple flames—the tracking spell she had promised. He sprinted down the illuminated path. The sound of his footsteps echoed off the brick walls. It led him around a turn into a wide alley centered between endless rows of tall buildings.

Cassiel didn't want to think of what he would tell Zev if he failed to find Dyna. None of this would have happened if he had kept her with him. But she had wanted to get away from him, and he let her because he lost his nerve. At the moment, he had cared more about saving face than her safety.

The witch was right. He was a fool.

Cassiel skidded around another turn when the tracking spell faded. Ahead of him at the far end of the alley was Dyna. But his relief was short-lived.

She shrieked and kicked, thrashing helplessly against a man in a black coat. He gripped both her wrists in his hand, ignoring her as he spoke to another hidden beneath a gray-blue cloak. The group of men accompanying them laughed at her efforts.

Cassiel clenched his fists, rage blazing through him as he sprinted for them. "Dyna!"

All eyes fell on him.

"Cassiel!" At the sight of him, she fought harder against her captor. "Let me go, Von!"

She freed an arm and swung it back into his groin. He doubled over in a gasping grunt and she broke away, but a man with dark skin snatched a handful of her red locks before she could escape. Her painful cry twisted through Cassiel. Filling him with fury, helplessness, and desperation to reach her.

Dyna raked her nails across the man's face, and he cursed, releasing his grasp, only for Von to recover, and whip an arm around her waist. Shrieking, she punched and kicked, using her heels to bash his shins, doing everything she could to escape, but he held onto her well this time. Cassiel skid to a halt when the other men formed a wall between them as they armed themselves with daggers and swords.

"Release her!" he snarled at Von. Whoever the man was, he was leading these brigands.

Von looked at him over the heads of his men with an unreadable expression. "I leave this to you, Abenon."

The man with bloody scratches on his cheek grinned. "With pleasure, Commander."

"No!" Dyna fought to reach him.

Von hoisted her onto his shoulder and shoved the youngest of them toward the man in the cloak who was already leaving. "Go with Bouvier, lad."

"No, I'm with you," the boy said firmly. They ran together down another alley with her screaming Cassiel's name.

"I'm coming for you!" he shouted after her. "I swear it!"

He had to say it for her and himself. He *will* get her back.

Dyna's cry soon faded. He had the frantic urge to fly after her, but he couldn't do so without revealing the existence of Celestials to more humans. And he hated himself for it.

Cassiel grit his teeth as he faced off with the men. "Who are you? What do you want?"

They only laughed as they circled him. He turned in place to keep them all in his view. Whoever they were, they undoubtedly planned to kill him.

His mind raced as he staked his surroundings. The alleyway was wide enough for combat, but not wide enough ambush him all at once. There were too many. The chances of surviving were slim unless Zev joined him soon.

Lord Jophiel had trained him well, but in all the years Cassiel had traveled alone between the Celestial Realms, not once was he faced with the dilemma of taking lives for the sake of his own. He steeled his resolve with his uncle's voice. *"The moment your life is in danger, there are only two choices to make: you fight or you die. I have prepared you for both, but I'll tell you one thing—dying is easy."*

It went against the law of the Heavens to kill humans. There would be no redemption for this, but he had made his choice.

Dyna needed him.

"Go now if you want to live," he warned. "If you stay, I will not hesitate. The first one forward will be the first one down."

Abenon snorted and wiped a streak of blood from the cut on his cheek. "Are you the Celestial? Do you have a pair of shiny black wings under that coat?"

It was as if they had dumped a pail of icy water over his head. The witch and now all these humans knew what he was? This encounter was not random.

"Should you fall," Abenon said to his men.

"March through the Gates," they replied in unison.

"Aye," Abenon grinned. "And may He receive you. Now take him down, but don't kill him. Not until we drain him of every drop of his precious blood."

A cold shudder went through Cassiel. He truly had no choice.

Lahav Esh hummed as he drew it from the sheath. Brilliant white flames burst to life along the blade, and the heat warped the air. The men took a step back, holding up their hands against the blazing light. His pulse throbbed with the rhythm of the convulsing flames. His fist shook around the hilt of his divine weapon, knowing its one true purpose was to protect humans, not slaughter them.

"Should the flames touch you, they will consume you whole to your very soul," Cassiel said.

No one in the Mortal Realm had the power to destroy a soul, but he hoped the lie would frighten the Raiders enough to withdraw. They stared at him and his sword, calculating, considering, confidence wavering.

"Without a soul, you would never pass through The Seven Gates," one of them nervously muttered.

Abenon snarled at his men. "He lies. Now get him!"

Two men hefted their daggers and attacked from opposite directions. Cassiel moved on instinct, pivoting as his sword blazed through the break between them. He split one from his guts to his sternum and twisted around to run the second man through. The Raider gasped, blood gurgling from his mouth as he caught fire.

Cassiel pulled out his sword, backing away. The men screamed as the flames devoured their entire bodies in a white bloom. In seconds, the fire left behind nothing but a burst of ash, like black snow, scattering across the ground and sticking to the sweat on his skin. He gasped at the sudden pain searing inside of his chest as he felt *Elyōn* damn him for all eternity. A profound sorrow fell over Cassiel, filling him with the urge to drop to his knees and weep. No one had ever spoken of this part.

"Bloody hell," a Raider said. They stared at him, some with shock, others with fear.

"Lieutenant," another Raider called to Abenon. "The captain failed to warn us of this."

Warn them? They were not speaking of Von who they had called commander. How many more were involved in this?

"What of it?" the lieutenant snapped. "We outnumber him, you useless bastards."

"Tell me where she is and no one else needs to die," Cassiel said. He didn't want to kill them. They needed only to get out of his way. "Please."

But Abenon signaled, and four Raiders attacked. Cassiel rode on pure adrenaline, holy fire roaring as steel clashed against flaming steel. He moved further into the alley, parrying and pivoting from the onslaught of attacks.

Cassiel broke through their defenses, his sword splitting through opponents one by one, their screams echoing against the walls. Smoke pillars billowed in the air as their bodies became puffs of ash in his wake. His fear had drowned in a cloud of wrath at their persistence. They were forcing their deaths on his hands.

A Raider came at him. They crossed swords, bringing them face to face. The flames, inches from the Raider's nose, shone in his petrified eyes.

Cassiel shoved him back, giving him the chance to escape. "Tell me where they took her and no one else needs to die," he repeated. It was an offer. A plea.

But the Raider attacked again. Cassiel evaded the incoming blade and impaled him through. The man clutched Cassiel's coat, gurgling his last breaths before the flames consumed him. He ripped out his sword, letting the burning body drop.

"No one else needs to die!" Cassiel roared in fury and exasperation. He was already damned, but he could feel how each life he took sullied him further, painting his soul black.

He only had a split second to duck as two more Raiders swung their swords for his neck. The blades met in a violent clash above his head, clanging like a broken bell. He dropped *Lahav Esh* and simultaneously drew out the knives from his boots, impaling his two attackers in their stomachs. Cassiel sliced through muscle and bone as he ripped the knives upward out of their chests.

"No one else ..." A spatter of warm blood hit his cheek as the two bodies fell.

There was a stillness in him.

A glorious emptiness.

All he felt was the slick hilt of his weapons.

"Fine," Cassiel grated. "You want to die? Then I will kill you all."

He sheathed the knives and took up his sword, letting the flames catch on the clothing of the fallen, as he faced the remaining men.

Eight dead. Twelve alive. Twelve obstacles between him and Dyna. There was nothing in his mind now but a severe determination to cut them down out of his way.

The Raiders hung back, floating ash sticking to their sweaty faces. Their wide eyes flickered from the charred remains of their comrades and him.

"Cravens," Abenon barked at them. "Must I grab you by the bollocks? Get him." No one moved. "Damn the lot of you. Master Tarn will hear of this!"

Master Tarn?

The lieutenant waved his men aside and unsheathed his twin scimitar blades, their curved edges glinting menacingly in the white firelight. He held them with obvious skill, and Cassiel braced himself.

Abenon grinned. "Once you're dead, I'll be the one to keep your sword."

He came like a whirlwind. Cassiel attuned his defenses to keep up with the rapid dual blades, but he struggled to parry Abenon's attacks. It forced him back, the twin scimitars a millimeter from overtaking him. The men jeered and laughed, their confidence renewing. But the lieutenant wasn't aiming to kill. He aimed to disarm him.

They didn't want to spill his blood yet, not until they had something to contain it.

Abenon delivered a spin kick to Cassiel's face, hurtling him into another Raider. Bulky arms wrapped around him from behind. They compressed so painfully tight it forced him to lose hold of his weapon.

"I got him!" a rough voice snarled in his ear. The greasy Raider smelled of weeks old sweat. The stench made Cassiel's stomach heave.

He flexed his wings with a furious cry. They burst free of his coat with such force it sent the Raider airborne. The man smashed into a wall across the alley and fell into a broken, bloodied pile. The Raiders marveled at Cassiel's wings with their mouths slacked, greed filling their eager faces.

"What'd I tell you?" Abenon grinned. "Do this and you daft twats will be up to your necks in gold. Don't let him fly away!"

They charged at him.

Cassiel grabbed his sword and flew into the air out of range. The Raiders hurled knives at him. He blocked the onslaught, but there were too many at once. Pain pierced his right wing and he didn't realize he was falling until he hit the ground hard. The impact stole the air from him. His sword had fallen out of reach, so he reached for an abandoned knife.

When the first Raider grabbed him, Cassiel shoved the blade up through his jaw, but he lost the knife when the others fell on him. He curled inward, tucking his arms around his head to protect his face from their pummeling blows and kicks. A brutal scream tore through his throat when heels stomped on his wings. The tendons snapped beneath their soles, blinding him with agony.

The attacks stopped. Cassiel opened his eyes to see his flaming sword come down on him. Abenon blocked the swing with a scimitar, bringing *Lahav Esh* to a stop an inch from Cassiel's head. He shrunk back from the severe heat, but the fire quickly died out, leaving the blade to smoke.

The Raider who held it glowered. "It's wrecked."

Cassiel closed his eyes in brief relief. Humans couldn't use Celestial weapons.

Abenon shoved the Raider away. "If you remove his head, his blood will spill all over the ground, you idiot."

Another Raider hooked an arm around Cassiel's neck and squeezed. He wheezed for air, his fingers clawing at the thick leather of the man's coat. He tried to get his wings to move, but they twitched on his back, broken and useless. For a second, he feared he'd lost his ability to self-heal, but then his injuries tingled and numbed.

"Horace," Abenon snapped at the Raider choking Cassiel. "What are you doing?"

"He killed Locke, Pip, and the others," Horace said through his teeth. "He turned them to ash. They will never pass through The

Seven Gates. Let me kill him, Lieutenant. I want to watch the life drain out of him before I break his neck. I can do it without spilling his blood."

"No, we will take him *alive*. Now bring me some rope."

"Commander Von said Master Tarn wanted him bled dry."

"Aye, but not here."

Those names. Cassiel knew he'd heard them before, but the thought slithered away as all strength left his limbs, and his vision darkened.

Dyna. For all of his efforts, he couldn't save her.

Horace jerked and released his chokehold. Cassiel gasped for air but lost it again when the Raider's full weight collapsed on top of him. From his back jutted three arrows.

The men swore and backed away. The quiet was eerie as the sound of soft footsteps approached and a stranger in a tattered green cloak came into view. He held a loaded bow with two arrows aimed at the Raiders.

"Gods." Abenon motioned at his nine companions. "Well? Kill him."

The stranger shot the arrows, killing one. He dropped his bow and whipped out a luminous sword from beneath his cloak. It caught the sunlight as it swung to meet the others coming for him. He was a blur of movement, disarming the Raiders in one swing and slashing through their bodies in the next. The men hit the floor at his feet. He flicked his sword, removing the blood, and calmly sheathed it before gathering his bow and Cassiel's weapon from the ground.

"Who are you?" Abenon demanded.

The stranger slipped off his hood. Teal eyes looked at them from a face set in sharp calculation.

"He's that elf, Lieutenant," another Raider said. "The famed warrior of the Vale."

Abenon gritted his teeth, spitting another curse.

Rawn removed the body pinning Cassiel down. "Are you wounded?"

"Clearly," he grunted as he sat up. "You followed us?"

"On my honor, I did not. I was in Corron when I heard the commotion."

"You heard us?" But they were deep within the alleys.

Rawn tapped his ear in reply, then yanked out the knife stuck in Cassiel's wing. He winced at the dull pain, but the wound had already stopped bleeding. The Raiders watched in amazement as it healed.

Lieutenant Abenon sneered and readied his scimitar blades. "I rescind my order, men. You can stick the Celestial a few times."

Rawn lifted *Lahav Esh* and handed it to Cassiel. Once the hilt was in his hands, petals of white flames unfurled. They faced the Raiders, ready for another fight, when a familiar growl rumbled behind them.

Cassiel smirked at the sound. "At last."

A shadow leaped over his head and landed in front of them. Sharp teeth flashed from its black jaws, yellow eyes gleaming, muscle rippling beneath its fur. Abenon froze. He stared at the massive wolf in dread, the color draining from his face.

Zev looked at Cassiel over his shoulder questioningly.

He motioned at the men with his chin. "They took Dyna. They kidnapped her."

Zev's frightening snarl reverberated in the alleyway. He stalked forward. Predator locked on its prey.

Cassiel shrugged at the Raiders. "I suggest you run."

They tripped over each other to escape, but Zev leaped, taking them down under his weight. Cassiel cringed at the sound of their horrid screams and the crunch of bone. Blood streamed through the cracks of the ground, trickling past his boots. So, this was what became of those who threatened the werewolf's cousin.

Abenon scrambled away from the attack with one of his bloodied arms hanging uselessly at his side. He snatched up a fallen scimitar and descended on the wolf gutting a man.

"Zev!" Cassiel shouted.

The wolf dodged the strike and pounced on the lieutenant. Abenon's gurgling scream cut off, blood spraying on the alley walls. Cassiel looked away, ignoring the churn of his stomach.

Zev shifted into his naked form and pinned his glowing eyes on him. He shook and heaved with rage. Blood stained his mouth and chest, his rippling body hovering between wolf and man.

A deep, bone-chilling growl rumbled in his throat, "How was Dyna taken? I left her in your care!"

Cassiel dropped his gaze.

Zev snarled at Rawn next. "Why are you here?"

The elf secured his bow across his chest. "I was not involved."

"He had nothing to do with it," Cassiel said. "Someone they called Commander Von took her."

Zev bared his teeth. "Commander Von was the man Dyna met in Landcaster."

Cassiel cursed. That was where he had heard the name. He scowled at the crossroads of four alleys veering off in different directions. The witch's tracking spell had long since faded. "He took her down one of these alleys."

A Raider sitting against the wall cackled. Red streamed out of the fatal gash in his abdomen. "You'll never get her back."

Cassiel crouched in front of him. "*Where* is she?"

The Raider gave him a bloody grin. "Piss off."

"You will tell me. One way or another."

The man spat a clot of blood at Cassiel's cheek. "There is nothing more you can do to me. I'm already dying."

Cassiel wiped his face and with it the last of his morality. *Lahav Esh* scraped off the ground as he lifted it and pressed the burning blade to the man's pant leg. The fire immediately caught. The Raider cried out and smacked at the flames only for them to ensnare his hands, ascending his arms. His wailing screams echoed in the alley.

"God of Urn," Rawn murmured.

"Tell me where Dyna is, and I will end your suffering," Cassiel said, devoid of any sympathy. He didn't care about right or wrong anymore. He only cared about finding her.

The Raider writhed in agony. "Kill me!"

"Tell me where she is."

"My soul!"

"Where?"

"Ferryman! BOAT!"

"What?"

The fire moved up the man's neck to his face, consuming his skin. The stench of his searing flesh and hair burned Cassiel's eyes. He tried to ask more questions, but they were drowned out by the Raider's shrill screams.

Zev grimaced at the sound. "He will draw the Azure Guard to us."

"Enough of this," Rawn said, thrusting a knife into the man's heart, killing him instantly.

"Why did you do that?" Cassiel snapped. "He was revealing where she was!"

Rawn shook his head. "He was speaking nonsense. It was senseless torture. What has overcome you?"

What had overcome him? Desperation so thick he choked on it.

Cassiel balled his fists, his fingernails cutting into his palms as he felt the need to torture something else. After killing so many humans, it was as though he wanted to continue his murderous rampage. They took her, whoever they were. He'd make them suffer for it.

"Zev, you have met the commander before," he said tightly. "Can you track his scent?"

Zev's eyes glowed yellow and his nostrils flared. He sniffed the air in each alleyway, then sank into a crouch to sniff the ground. His brows furrowed.

"What is wrong?" Cassiel asked, afraid of the answer.

The werewolf stood, staring at the alleys in dismay. His fists shook. "I ... can't smell him or Dyna."

"What do you mean?" Cassiel demanded.

"I sense a trace of magic here," Rawn said. "I suspect they used a cloaking spell. He must have the services of a mage. However, unless the mage was present to cloak Lady Dyna, that should not have masked her scent from the ground."

All the air left Cassiel's lungs. "Von carried her."

Zev roared a curse and kicked a broken crate, sending it crashing across the alley. It splintered into a thousand shards of broken hope.

Cassiel's legs wobbled, and he collapsed against the wall. How could he lose Dyna? The bond was intact, which meant she was alive, but she was terrified. Her fear washed through him like an icy wave. He held on to the sensation. It was his only connection to her.

He closed his eyes, and she came to him, smiling that carefree silly smile. She was his bonded. His to protect. She belonged at his side.

Find her.

A power shifted inside of him. It rushed through him in a barreling wave and broke through an internal barrier in his mind. It locked onto the connection he had with Dyna. Her life force pulsed within him, flaring in the pitch darkness of his misery. It pulled him to the east, showing exactly where she was.

His yearning demanded she be found, and the bond had responded.

Cassiel leaped to his feet and sprinted down an eastern alley. The wolf and the elf ran beside him wordlessly. They didn't press him. He wouldn't have known how to answer if they had. How could he explain something he hardly comprehended?

He didn't know what it meant. But for once, since their Blood Bond had been established, it felt right. It felt true.

As if Dyna was meant to be his all along.

Von

The rapid beating of Von and Geon's footfalls echoed through the vacant alleys of Corron. He followed the ferryman's markers that led them to the shrouded hills bordering Loch Loden. They needed to get Dyna to the Kazer Bluffs, where Elon was to wait for them at midday. Which was soon. When the location spell had vanished yesterday, he and the Raiders had spent all night and most of the dawn, searching for Dyna until they found her in the market. They had wasted too much time.

The master was waiting.

His back ached from Dyna's fists constantly beating against it. She weighed nothing, but she had given him so much trouble that they'd had to bind her limbs and gag her with torn strips of Geon's tunic.

Eventually, her beatings had slowed and grown weaker until she laid limp over Von's shoulder. The sound of her soft weeping stirred familiar guilt. A reminder of the last time Tarn ordered him to steal another girl, who fought him until she too gave up and cried in defeat.

Von had stolen Yavi from her father's home in the middle of the night—the true story he had fed the ferryman.

Tarn had ordered her captured for her linguistic skills. She didn't deserve to be stolen from her life and family any more than Dyna did. Yavi's forgiveness was a miracle Von wasn't worthy of, but he spent every day loving her for it.

Von reached the dead-end of the alley containing the gap in the wall. He slowed to a stop and put Dyna down. She teetered on shaky legs. Geon attempted to steady her, but she shoved him off. The binding around Dyna's ankles had loosened enough from her wiggling. She tripped in the attempt to kick it off and fell against the dead-end wall. When she noticed the gap there, she quickly backed away from it. Her wide eyes flickered back and forth as she studied the space between him and Geon. Her legs braced in preparation to run.

"You'll never make it, lass," Von said. "Stop fighting."

She glared at him and reached up with her bound hands to yank down her gag. "I'll never stop fighting you."

He almost smiled at her valor. She reminded him too much of Yavi. He wished he could walk away and let her go. But he couldn't.

"You're a feisty one." He sighed. "I'll give you that—"

She dove for her escape. Von grabbed her arm and spun her around, holding her back flush against his chest. She thrashed and kicked, screeching like an angry cat. He replaced her gag to muffle the noise and snatched his hand away before she bit his fingers.

"Take her legs," Von told Geon as he hooked his grip around her underarms.

"Please be still," Geon pleaded with her.

This was not something Von had planned for him to do, but the lad obediently grabbed Dyna's ankles and hoisted her up parallel to the ground. She jerked her foot free and thrust her heel in his face so hard that he almost dropped her.

"Hold her tight!"

"Sorry, Commander," he said sheepishly, blood leaking from his nose.

Von grimaced. "All right?"

Geon nodded, quickly wiping his nose on his shoulder. He grasped Dyna's ankles again in a tight grip and led the way backward for the hole in the wall.

She squirmed and jerked, screaming through the gag. They lugged her out of the dank alley and onto the forested hill. Only to find it was shrouded in a fog so thick, they could hardly see a few paces in front of them.

"Strange, there'd been no fog this early morn," Geon said as he set Dyna down on her feet.

"Aye, puzzling that." Von frowned at their surroundings. The trip down the steep hill would be dangerous. "Watch where you step. We'll walk from here—"

The lass tore herself from him and ran, but she lost her footing on the precipitous slope. She fell, bounding into the fog out of sight.

"Dyna!" Von and Geon rushed after her. He couldn't see a thing as they staggered and slid down the hill. All they heard was the terrible sound of her crashing through foliage and rebounding off the ground in her descent. There was a sharp grunt, and a dull thud, followed by a dreadful quiet. "Lass, where are you!"

A faint whimper led him through a cloud of mist on a leveled spot of the hill. Dyna had collided into a fallen log that stopped her descent. She lay there, half unconscious, her arms and legs scraped, her dress torn. A thin red trickle leaked from her temple.

Von rushed to her side. He removed the gag and held up her face, checking her eyes. "Are you all right? You took a blow to the head there."

Dyna moaned weakly, "Ow ... that hurt ..."

Von supposed clear speaking was a good sign.

"She's bleeding," Geon said. He tore at the hem of his tunic again and pressed the cloth to her temple.

Dyna glared at them and pushed his hand away. "Why are you doing this? What do you want?"

Von and Geon shared a look. *They* didn't want anything.

"This is my doing, isn't it?" she asked. "For telling you of Mount Ida. I didn't mean to. It was as if you stole the words from my mouth."

Von nodded. "Aye, I suppose I did byways of a truth spell. It wasn't intended for you."

"What are you going to do to me?"

"I'll not harm you, lass. If it were up to me, you would not have seen me again. My actions are at the mercy of my master."

Her eyes widened. "You have a master?"

"I do."

Traces of sympathy hovered in her gaze. "Why does he want me?"

Von hesitated to answer. He couldn't tell her the full truth. "We need you to view your enchanted map."

Dyna gaped at them. "How do you know about that?"

"Our spies have been watching you. We know all there is to know about you and your companions."

Her face tightened with anguish. "Cassiel …"

"I waited until you were separated from them to take you. It was my poor attempt to spare the Celestial. I'm sorry, Dyna." And he meant it.

Her eyes widened in horror at the realization of what he meant, and she shook with heartbreaking sobs. She folded over herself as if to contain the pain. Von laid a hand on her shoulder and she hit him with her bound wrists.

"Get away from me," she shoved him back. "Don't come near me. None of this would have happened if I had not met you!"

He caught her hands. "I'm beginning to believe that no matter the circumstances of that day, our meeting was inevitable."

"What do you mean?"

"It was foretold many years ago that you would come," Geon said. "The Seer from Faery Hill said the Maiden with the key would lead us to Mount Ida. She spoke of six Guardians who would protect you."

Dyna stared at him. "What?"

"The wolf and Celestial are the first. We captured you now before you had the chance to gather them all."

"Geon," Von warned. The lad was telling her too much.

She shook her head, not wanting to believe them. Her erratic fists pummeled against him again. "Let me go! I don't have the map!"

He grabbed her shoulders, forcing her still. "What did you say?"

She glared at him through her tears. "You assumed I had it."

"Geon, check the bag."

The boy removed her confiscated satchel from his shoulder and rummaged through it. "The journal isn't here, Commander."

Von's hold on Dyna tightened, making her wince. "Where is it?"

Boldness settled over her. She sealed her lips shut, raising her chin. Von worked his jaw as he interpreted her smugness. She already feared they captured her Celestial, so that left only one other.

"The Lycan has the map."

"Lycan?" Her brows furrowed at the word.

"A half-breed werewolf."

Dyna scowled. "Go anywhere near him, and he will *eviscerate* you."

"Aye, or perhaps I'll wait for the next full moon when he is shackled in those chains of his."

She gasped, her confidence fading. "You would be so low as to murder him when he can't defend himself? Is that the kind of man you are?"

Von grit his teeth. "You know nothing of what I have done or what I am capable of. Exploiting vulnerabilities is the least of what I'll do. Make no mistake. I serve Master Tarn in all that he desires, including removing those in his way."

"Tarn?" Dyna breathed the name. "Tarn Morken? The man the Azure Guard searches for?"

Von swore at his careless mistake. "Get up. We need to move." He grabbed her forearm and she bit his hand. He tore away with another curse. Dyna kicked at his shins, but her face suddenly contorted at the impact. She let out a whimper, reaching for her leg, which had grown pink and puffy.

"You're hurt." He reached for her foot but she jerked back, hissing at the pain the movement caused her. "I need to remove your boot before the swelling sets in."

She bit her trembling lip and gave him a tight nod. Lowering to a crouch, he carefully took her heel. She braced her hands on the ground, grinding her teeth as he gently slipped the boot off. He frowned at her inflamed foot.

"You've sprained your ankle. Must have happened in the tumble down the hill." Von stood and faced Geon. "We must carry her down. Scout ahead and find the ferryman. Mind your steps."

"Aye, Commander." Geon vanished into the mist.

Von glowered at the teeth indentations on his hand. "You've got a pair of fangs on you, little minx. You may be more trouble than you're worth."

Dyna winced as she shifted against the log for support. "Why does Tarn seek Mount Ida?"

He gave her his back, watching the swirl of fog. "It's an island full of treasure."

Her brief silence told him she didn't believe a word. "He could attain gold without risking his life. To have gone to the fae for divination means he seeks something more."

She was too sharp for her own good.

"Mount Ida is an island of wonder. Of great magic and unknown peril."

"You are headed there as well," he said. "Why?"

Her expression withdrew, and she stared blankly past him. "To dissipate the shadows."

Before he could ask what that meant, a shocked cry rang on the hill. The fog thickened, darkening their surroundings. Dyna gasped and peered nervously into the mist.

"Lad?" Von called out. He armed himself with a knife and took a wary step forward. There was another shout, followed by branches snapping as something crashed through the shrubs. "Geon!"

His skin prickled as he searched the fog swirling around them. He sensed something there, lurking out of sight. His heart rate spiked as a layer of sweat sprouted on his skin. Had the Lycan caught up to him?

They flinched at Geon's scream. His body hurled past Von and slammed into the ground.

"Geon!" He rolled him over onto his back. The boy stirred, moaning. At the sound of approaching footsteps, Von took out another knife.

A woman appeared from the mist with eyes that glowed violet. A curtain of shimmering white hair cascaded around her stunning features etched in fury. It was the young woman he'd stolen the Lūna Medallion from—the woman he didn't stop to think twice about who she was. Which, Von realized, was a grave mistake when she conjured forth a blue sphere of magic in her hand.

He stumbled a step back. God of Urn. It couldn't be.

The sorceress grants her sorcery …

"Release the girl and return what you stole from me at once," she hissed. "I'll not say it again."

Von looked at Dyna. If he could, he would, but Tarn would never accept his failure. "It'll be the end of me if I do."

Purple electricity crackled around the sorceress. "*I* will be the end of you."

A horrid chill crawled down his back at Death's icy hand brushing against his neck. This had been the warning he felt since he left camp, the warning that his time had ended. He had no hope against magic.

No.

He refused to die here and never see Yavi again. He had made a promise that he wouldn't leave her alone in this world, and he aimed to keep it.

Von's boots shifted through the mud as he moved into a stance. The knives flipped in his deft hands, and he regained assurance in their familiar weight. He had killed many with them in odds as risky as this. He had not killed a woman before, but there was nothing he wouldn't do to return to Yavi.

The sorceress narrowed her eyes at his resolve. "You have made your choice."

She flung her sphere of blue magic. Von ducked, and it exploded behind him. She cast a volley of brilliant spells, missing him by a hair as he dodged and dove. Each move brought him nearer until he reached a suitable distance. He launched off a boulder and threw his knives at the sorceress, but with a sweep of her arm, an invisible force knocked them out of the air.

Damn. He must get closer.

A streak of lightning came for him and he careened out of its path, heat singeing his neck. He rolled across the ground and tossed another series of knives, one after the other. She pitched them away with a flick of her hand. It was enough to distract her for a second.

Von sprinted for the sorceress. He dove under her last attack at close range and came upon her startled face as he slashed for her throat.

The knife bounced off an unseen barrier with a loud *clang*.

The collision rippled the air between them, revealing a transparent golden shield. She sneered. With a wave of her hand, a blanket of purple Essence ensnared tight around Von. Sparks of electricity zapped him and he cried out, convulsing violently. He tried to break free, but he couldn't move an inch. The magic had immobilized him. She flicked her fingers upward, and he lifted off the ground a foot above her. By her smirk of victory, he knew this was it.

He had lost.

The sorceress pointed a glowing finger at him, and Von stared into the vivid, purple beam as he held onto the image of his wife. Her smile. Her voice.

I love you more than my own life.

The sorceress tapped his forehead. A blow exploded in his head like she had cleaved his skull through. His vision blackened, and darkness consumed his world.

Then he fell into oblivion.

CHAPTER 41

Dynalya

Commander Von hung suspended in the air by a cloud of purple Essence. Limp and lifeless. With a flick of her wrist, the sorceress released her magic, and he hit the ground with a heavy thud. He didn't move. The boy who'd been watching the skirmish from behind the tree closed his wet eyes and dropped his head against the trunk.

Dyna's vision blurred. She didn't want Von to die. She didn't want anyone to die.

"Are you all right?" the sorceress asked her.

Dyna had to swallow so she could answer. "Did … did you kill him?"

She scoffed. "Do you weep for him?"

"Did you?"

"Not yet." The sorceress curled her lip. "He's under a comatose spell."

Dyna released an exhalation of pent-up breath.

"Will any more of his men come?"

"I'm not sure. They—Cassiel, he—" Dyna covered her mouth, more tears welling in her eyes. He hadn't been able to reach her. Had they captured him? Was he alive? She should have stayed with him instead of being blinded by her selfish feelings. None of it mattered. All she wanted was to be with him now.

The sorceress rose. "He fought them well. You will see him again."

"I will?" Dyna pressed on her heart, clinging to that hope. Something stirred in her, filling her with his presence as if he indeed was coming.

The sorceress flicked her wrist again and the fog dissolved away. Rays of golden sunlight streamed through the trees. They were about midway down the hill. Not close enough to shore, but the surface of Loch Loden was visible through the branches.

"Thank you for helping me," Dyna said. "I need to find my companions."

"I don't have the time to help you there." She waved a dismissive hand at the commander. "I only came to deal with this man."

"I'll not let you get anywhere near him, witch!" Geon stood on shaking legs in front of Von, wielding a knife.

The sorceress rolled her eyes as they sparked with power once more. "Haven't you had enough? Either you move, or I will *make* you move. Choose."

The boy glared. "I won't."

"Very well." She raised a hand and clenched it into a fist. Geon's right leg snapped out from under him with a sickening crack. A bloody jagged piece of bone protruded from his torn shin and he fell to the ground, his mouth splitting wide in a scream. Dyna cringed, horrified.

But Geon forced himself up, sobbing from the agony. He laid over Von, using himself as a shield. "I care not what you do to me! I won't let you touch him."

The sorceress hissed. "*Move.*"

"You must kill me first."

She flicked a hand, hurtling the boy into another tree with a brutal thud. Still, he got up again with a whimper, digging his fingers in the mud as he crawled to Von.

"Gods, you're relentless."

"I won't let you kill him," he said, snot and tears streaming down his face. "If it were me lying there, he would fight for me too."

"Must I break every bone in your body?" the sorceress twirled a finger, and Geon's arm snapped under him. His horrid wails filled the woodland.

"Stop," Dyna cried. "Don't hurt him anymore!"

The sorceress's eyes flashed, her power filling the air with static. "They stole from me."

"Then take what belongs to you and leave."

"You would petition for *men* who intended to spirit you away?" She spat the word in disgust and incredulity as if they were vile creatures not worth the dust under her boot.

Dyna held her harsh gaze. "Yes."

The brave boy was defending his commander. She didn't want to see him tortured because of it.

The sorceress's lips tightened in a thin line. Her glowing eyes locked on Von and Geon with such loathing, it reminded Dyna of the way Captain Gareel had looked at her. With hate. His hate had been rooted in fear for humans. What did the sorceress have to fear from them?

No one was here to stop the sorceress from enacting her will. With a flourish of her hand, Von's body flipped over on his back.

"Don't," Geon begged. "Please!"

Dyna only looked at her, silently pleading.

The sorceress huffed. She flicked a finger and from Von's pocket emerged a silver pendant floating in the air. Diamonds and engraved runes bordered the circumference. Dyna had only glimpsed it in the time rift. Seeing it now, she was certain it matched the one in Azeran's journal. But there was a groove in the center where the Moonstone should be.

The sorceress secured the pendant around her neck and she laid a hand over it, closing her eyes from visible relief.

"The Lūna Medallion," Dyna murmured.

The sorceress spun to her. "What did you say?"

Cassiel's faint voice drifted over the hill. Dyna's heart flooded with joy at the sight of him soaring through the air, his black wings carrying him over the trees. She called his name and his storm-cloud eyes locked on her.

He circled overhead once, not waiting to slow his descent before he tucked in his wings and swooped down. He stumbled on his awkward landing, running the rest of the way to her. Dyna choked back a sob and reached out to him, needing to touch him.

"I found you," Cassiel said, breathless.

He dropped to his knees and removed the bindings from her wrists. His arms closed around her, holding her tight against his chest. The energy hummed between them, gentle and soft.

Tears spilled down her face, and she crumbled against him in shaking sobs. He held her as she cried, and even when she quieted, he didn't let go.

"I feared I would never see you again," she murmured, listening to the rhythm of his heartbeat.

"As did I," he said into her hair, his breath tickling her cheek.

"You can say it. I'm a stupid human."

Cassiel pulled back to look at her. He lifted her face and gently wiped her tears away. "I am the stupid one. I should not have let you out of my sight."

She chuckled faintly. "Stupid Celestial."

A smile lit his face for the first time since they met, and her stomach pitched. He looked at her with a tenderness that left her heart soaring like it had its own pair of wings.

He rested his forehead against hers. "I am glad you are safe."

She closed her eyes and leaned into his embrace. With him here, everything had righted again.

A massive black wolf came tearing down the hill and Cassiel stepped back as it rushed into her arms.

"Zev!" Dyna hugged him tightly. The wolf pressed his head against her shoulder, whining. "Lord Norrlen is here as well?" she exclaimed when the elf slipped from the trees next.

He lowered to one knee beside her. "I am pleased to have found you, Lady Dyna. Are you injured?"

"She is bleeding." Cassiel touched the cut on her temple, making her wince. His gaze hardened into steel when he noticed her other injuries. "Who hurt you?"

"I'm fine," she said, looking him over. His coat was missing, leaving his wings exposed. His torn clothes were bloody from wounds that had already healed. "What happened?"

Cassiel looked away. His balled fists covered in dried blood hung at his sides. His irises dulled to the muddy wisps of smoke blowing in the wind after all that mattered had gone up in flames.

He killed them to save her.

All because she spoke to Von.

Dyna shook her head, covering her face. "This is my fault."

"It is not," he said.

"Do not dwell on it, my lady," Rawn told her. "The circumstances were unavoidable."

Zev shapeshifted into his human form and wrapped her in a hug. "Thank the God of Urn you're safe. How did this happen?"

"Von came for me, but she stopped him with her magic," Dyna said, nodding to the sorceress standing behind them.

They all faced her. She repeatedly glanced between Cassiel's wings and Zev, surprised by his change.

Cassiel glared at her. "*You.*"

"I recognize her scent," Zev said, his nostrils flaring. He stood, and she yelped at the sight of his nudity. She turned her red face away. Rawn offered Zev his cloak and passed Cassiel his coat.

"She's the witch from the market," Cassiel told them as he slipped it on.

"I'm no witch," the sorceress hissed.

"Thank you for coming to her aid," Rawn said.

"I didn't do it for you." She scowled down at Von by her feet. "He stole something from me. I came to retrieve it."

"You *used* me," Cassiel intoned, his expression burning with rage. "To distract the others."

She crossed her arms. "And?"

His face turned all shades of red, his hands curling like he wished to wrap them around her throat. "I have taken lives that were not mine to take. I am damned because of you!"

The sorceress stepped back from his fury.

A weight pressed on Dyna's heart. Burying her into a vast depth of grief that she thought something had broken inside of her.

This was Cassiel's pain.

He had told her last night that for once he didn't see himself as sullied—that his blood was pure enough to help her. She had seen the beginning of happiness in his eyes, but now misery clouded them.

"If you need someone to blame, then blame him," the sorceress said, pointing at Von. "They were coming for her, no matter the circumstances. Would the result have been so different if he had taken her in front of you?"

"Had we all been together, I would have torn him apart before he got his hands on her," Zev growled. His yellow eyes flashed as they pinned on the commander. "Is he dead?" He glanced at Geon, who recoiled against the tree at his back.

Rawn approached to check on Von and the sorceress backed several feet away from him, electricity sparking around her. He kept his hands out, faced down to show he meant no harm. He crouched by the commander and pressed two fingers at his neck.

After a pause, Rawn said, "He lives."

"I placed him under a spell. He won't wake without another." The sorceress crossed her arms and faced Dyna. "How is it you know of the Lūna Medallion?"

"My ancestor wrote its history in his journal. The Medallion is the emblem of the Lunar Guild. An heirloom of the Astron family infused with the power of the moon and stars."

The sorceress's white brows knitted together. "Who was your ancestor?"

"Azeran Astron."

Her mouth fell open, struggling to form the words she eventually spat out. "You are not of the Astron lineage."

Dyna sighed, feeling a bit dejected at the immediate dismissal. "I see the Moonstone is missing, however. I know where to find it."

Her eyes widened further. "What?"

"Dyna," Zev warned.

"No," Cassiel added under his breath. "Speaking of it is how we gained an elf."

Rawn perked at the mention. Dyna gave him a slight smile. Did that mean he might join them after all? He had helped Cassiel, and the sorceress had helped her. Both needed something from Mount Ida, and inexplicably, she trusted them.

"We owe it to her," Dyna said.

Cassiel scowled. "She has already received her payment."

He didn't explain further than that.

"I don't need your help. I'm well aware of its location," the sorceress said. Her white hair flared as she spun around and walked away, heading for the shore. Within the following second, she winked out of view.

"Wait—" Dyna tried to stand but whimpered at the sharp jab of pain in her ankle and throbbing at the base of her skull.

"What's wrong?" Zev crouched by her again. "I smell blood."

She winced and touched her head. Now that she had moved, something wet trickled down her scalp to her neck. The blow against the log must have been worse than she thought.

Rawn approached her. "May I?"

She nodded, and his gentle fingers slipped through her hair, probing the back of her head until she flinched. His hand came away with red smears.

Zev growled, and he bounded for Von.

Dyna saw his wolf claw at the surface in demand to kill. To protect his pack, to protect her. "No, Zev!"

"Commander didn't hurt her!" Geon shouted at the same time.

"It's the truth," she said. "I fell. He didn't mean for it to happen."

"He kidnapped you!" Zev snarled.

"He was only doing as our master bid!" Geon said.

"Who?"

"Von called him Master Tarn," Dyna answered.

Rawn's expression grew alarmed. "My lady, if Tarn is pursuing you, then you are in grave danger."

"What do you mean?" Cassiel demanded.

"Who is he?" Zev asked next.

Rawn gathered Dyna's things into her satchel. "A discussion for another time. We must depart from here forthwith."

"Help me stand, please," Dyna said. Cassiel hoisted her up, and she stumbled against him, whimpering at the painful jolt that ran up her leg.

He hooked her arm around his neck for support. "You cannot walk on that ankle."

"What do we do about him?" Zev asked, his yellow eyes fixing on Geon.

The boy cowed against the tree, sweat dripping down his gaunt face. "I'm sorry we took her. We had to."

Rawn laid a hand on Zev's shoulder. "We have spilled enough blood today."

"Are they all gone?" Geon asked. "The Raiders?"

No one answered him. He dropped his head.

"Cassiel, take me to him," Dyna said. "Please."

She brushed his cheek, and calm energy passed between them, softening the scowl on his face. Geon may be their enemy, but she wanted to help him. A part of her hoped it would ease her guilt over the deaths of his companions, and what stopping them had cost Cassiel.

Cassiel half lifted her, relieving the weight off her sprained ankle. He brought her to the boy who scrambled back.

"It's all right," she said, sinking to the ground next to him.

"What are you doing?" Geon asked cagily.

Dyna only smiled. She closed her eyes and laid her hands on his twisted limbs. A wave of heat unfurled in her chest as her Essence surged forth. The power traveled throughout her body in a steady stream, gathering and taking from her own life. It coursed through her arms to her hands at her command.

A vivid green light enveloped Geon's entire leg and forearm. She sent it deep into his limbs, targeting the torn muscle and bones. The broken pieces moved, and he squeezed his eyes shut, gritting his teeth from the pain. Her body trembled from the strain as Essence freely flowed from her and into this boy she didn't know.

Heal, she ordered, *restore.* Slowly, the bones connected and fused. His torn skin and muscle stitched layer after layer until large pink scars formed. The light receded along with its warmth, leaving her cold and empty. Dyna slumped, completely exhausted.

"There, that'll do," she murmured. "Your leg and arm will be tender for a few weeks. I've mended what I can, but your body must do the rest. Take willows bark for the pain, and comfrey to strengthen your bones. I'm sorry. You will have a limp for the rest of your life."

She didn't have enough Essence to restore his leg to its previous state. Her power only went so far.

Geon gaped at his scarred arm. "God of Urn. Y-you have magic?"

"I was not aware she had such an ability," Rawn said to the others.

Dyna stumbled to her feet, her vision swaying. She managed only one step before plunging head-first. Cassiel quickly caught her and lifted her into his arms. It should have elicited a blush, but she had no energy even for that. Her head lolled against his chest, a weight pulling on her eyelids.

"What has happened?" Rawn asked.

Zev said, "It exerts her to heal."

Dyna blinked sleepily at their concerned faces. "I'm all right."

"Go," the boy grunted as he used the tree to stand. "Captain Elon will come."

Cassiel glared at him. "Who?"

"He's an elf." Geon glanced at Rawn. "Our second in command. You may have taken down twenty Raiders, but Elon is worth a hundred men. You don't want to meet him."

"Why would you help us?" Zev growled.

He met Dyna's weary gaze. "I owe her a debt. I may serve Tarn, but I don't wish her any harm. You must leave. Go!"

At his urgency, they ran down the hill. Dyna didn't have the will to remain awake any longer. Her eyes slid closed as Cassiel's stride rocked her to sleep.

CHAPTER 42

Zev

Zev wanted nothing more than to hunt down those who pursued them. It was not in his nature to run away from any threat, but now it was the only option. They needed to take Dyna far away from this place. He caught Cassiel's eye, and the prince nodded in wordless agreement. As soon as it was dark, they would travel again all night to put space between them and this newfound enemy.

Lord Norrlen took point while Zev guarded the rear. The elf descended nimbly down the shrouded hills. Cassiel followed behind, keeping Dyna tucked close. She didn't stir, no matter how much he jostled her. The gray tint to her pale complexion worried Zev. She may sleep for days this time.

But the most concerning was the man who'd sent his men to capture her. The scent of their blood lingered on the prince. Zev would no sooner forget the cold, unfeeling mask Cassiel wore when he had tortured a Raider to learn Dyna's whereabouts. But he was not a killer, and the act visibly affected him.

Cassiel blamed the sorceress. Zev blamed himself. He had separated from them when they should have stayed together. Otherwise, Von would not have so easily taken her.

So many questions ensnared his mind. Who was Tarn? What interest did he have in Dyna? Why was he wanted by the Azure King?

Rawn brought them to a shallow end of the lake. He parted a crop of reeds and revealed a raft resting on the bank, water lapping against it. The crude thing was mere driftwood tied together by spent rope, hardly large enough to hold two people.

"You used this to cross the loch?" Zev asked skeptically.

Rawn withdrew a long rod of wood from the water, an oar he must have used to steer the raft. "It served me well enough."

"With your horse?" Zev scented the Elvish steed on Rawn's clothing, but it was nowhere to be seen.

"Fair awaits me in a northern wood past the bluffs."

Cassiel shook his head. "That raft will not hold us all."

"Then we swim," Zev said as he dropped their rucksacks on the raft and stripped off the borrowed cloak. Cassiel's mouth pursed in distaste at the water. "You cannot risk flying a second time. Someone may have spotted you already. Dyna ... will have to ride with Lord Norrlen."

Rawn knew how to steer the raft, so that left both Zev and Cassiel to stand guard. He called on his wolf and a dull ache went through him as his muscles and bones fluidly shifted. Zev landed on all four paws and shook out his flank. His nose flared at the scent of blood, ash, and sweat mingling with stagnant water and rotting plant matter.

Zev turned to look at his companions and froze. His wolf eyes were much more sensitive, catching things his usual sight wouldn't. Light haloed around Cassiel, which was no surprise, but Dyna ... light streamed from her as bright as a star in the night.

Like a Celestial.

"All right?" Cassiel asked as he kicked off his boots.

Zev turned away, needing to clear his spotty vision and his head.

"May I take her?" Rawn asked.

Zev growled and bared his teeth. Now more ruled by wild instinct, his wolf would not hand over his cousin to a stranger. Cassiel also took a step back, arms tightening around her. How well could they trust Lord Norrlen, even if he had come to their aid?

Rawn dropped to one knee in the muddy bank before Zev as one would for a lord. He laid a hand over his heart, turquoise eyes looking into his. "I give you my sworn word that I will see you and yours to safety."

It was an oath given unreservedly. Zev had heard oaths given by the elves were a binding promise. Though he was hesitant to believe it, he could hear Rawn's heart beating steadily. It carried no lie, so his wolf consented.

Zev looked at Cassiel and the prince's expression tensed. He visibly warred with the choice before he reluctantly passed Dyna to Rawn, holding on a second longer before releasing his grasp.

"Careful," Cassiel said, his hard tone braced in a warning.

"No harm will come to Lady Dyna." Rawn placed her on the raft and quickly climbed on. "Make haste. We mustn't tarry here any longer."

With the rod, he pushed off the bank. Zev and Cassiel slipped into the murky water and flanked the raft, swimming on either side of it. The passing greenery was quiet, save for the soft churn of water, and the chatter of wildlife in the surrounding trees. Zev listened for any threat, sniffing the air for hidden enemies, but his attention continued to draw back at Dyna.

Her light—what did it mean? Did the prince's blood do more than heal her? In the alley, Zev had no way of locating her scent. They had lost her until Cassiel found her again. On instinct, he said. There would be a time to ask about that later.

They reached the Kazer Bluffs. The cliff face rose high, a dominating presence casting a wide shadow over the loch. From what Zev had studied on the map, the bluffs were near the midway point of the kingdom. It was the last southern landmark before the Azure King's castle in The Blue Capitol.

It was an odd feeling being so far away from all that he knew, but nothing at all compelled him to go back. The journey had been a risk from the beginning, and danger was imminent now that Dyna was a target, but Zev no longer had doubts about the prince. He now knew Cassiel would fiercely protect her after seeing what he'd done to get her back.

The prince remained close to the raft during the long swim. His cool, unwavering gaze remained on her and the elf.

"Ask your questions if you must," Lord Norrlen said as he rowed.

Zev nodded to Cassiel. He would have to speak for them both.

"Why were you in Corron?"

"I went in search of a courier to deliver a letter," Rawn said.

"A letter for whom?"

"For my—" Rawn whipped his head to the left, dodging an arrow that zipped past his nose by a fraction of a second.

Zev snarled, and Cassiel swore. A group of men stood at the peak of the Kazer Bluffs. The sun's low blaze at their backs shadowed their faces. Another sat upon a horse with his cloak fluttering in the breeze. A girl accompanied him, tresses of long black hair streaming from beneath her hood. She nocked another arrow and raised her bow.

They were too far down the loch for any normal archer to hit their target. Zev calculated they were over two-hundred yards away, yet she had nearly taken the elf's head. The current was carrying them farther still.

She aimed, sunlight glinting off the arrowhead. The twang of the bowstring echoed in his ears. The arrow whizzed for them but fell short, spearing the water behind them with a soft plunk. Her skill had reached its limit.

Lord Norrlen removed his bow and drew an arrow from his quiver in one swift movement. He let it loose. All was still, the breeze and rustle of the forest muted as the arrow zipped away. It flew true through the air and found its mark, piercing the archer's chest. She fell flat without so much as a scream. One of the men cried out and he grabbed the fallen body, dragging it away.

Zev shared a stunned look with Cassiel. How had Rawn made such an impressive shot?

The horse rider dismounted in no rush and casually withdrew his sword. It couldn't be for combat when they were so far out of reach, but Rawn dropped his bow and withdrew his weapon. The hooded adversary said something in response. The wind muffled his foreign words, but Zev recognized the Elvish language and realized who confronted them now.

Captain Elon, the boy had said. Their second-in-command who was worth one-hundred men.

The familiar tug of Essence prickled against Zev as it churned in the atmosphere, the way it did when Dyna was gathering her power, but this was different. Stronger. Violent. A vivid blue spark sprouted from the captain's hands and wrapped the blade in a crackling swath of blue magic.

Cassiel's eyes grew wide. "What spell is that?"

"*Anadaug Luza*," Rawn said, his jaw clenching. "The Blue Scythe."

Cassiel threw himself on the raft, rocking it unsteadily as he tried to grab Dyna. "Give her to me!"

"Be calm." Rawn planted his feet and raised his sword, sunlight kissing the edge. Not once did he look away from the hooded figure. Opponent set and match. "Come."

Captain Elon swung his sword and magic exploded from the blade in an arc, speeding for them in a blinding inferno. There was no place to run, no place to hide. They were dead in the water.

Zev's mind went quiet for once. The Madness had no response to this.

Rawn parried the Blue Scythe, and it rebounded off his weapon with a crack of thunder. The spell returned the way it came and crashed into the bluffs with an ear-splitting *boom*. The Raiders shouted and scrambled back as the cliffside crumbled beneath their feet. Large chunks of rock crashed onto the bank of the loch. A massive, smoking crevice marred the Kazer Bluffs as if a giant had taken to it with an ax.

"How ... how did you do that?" Cassiel asked, gawking at Rawn.

"My sword is enchanted to dissipate magic," he said, "or rather, in this case, reflect it."

Captain Elon made no more attempts to attack, leaving the current to carry them away. His faint voice reached Zev, as he imagined it had reached Rawn. "Lord Norrlen, we shall meet again."

Rawn sheathed his sword. He retrieved the rod and steered the raft with no further acknowledgment.

Zev and Cassiel stared at him, then at each other, equally speechless. Whatever the boy had said about Captain Elon, they may have met someone worth so much more.

Von

The night chill was as cruel and unrelenting as the quiet wrath rolling off Tarn's presence. Von braced himself where he stood at the center of the dark camp, stripped to his trousers. Geon shivered beside him, huddling his scrawny arms to his bare chest.

The firelight from the torches staked into the ground shone on the grim faces of the Raiders who had gathered to witness. A requirement during lashings. Benton wore a gleeful smile; Dalton and Clayton stood with him, their umber robes swaying in a passing gust. Elon and Bouvier lingered in the shadows, as still as ghosts.

Geon flinched at the sound of the whip unfurling to the ground behind them.

"I will take the lads lashings, Master," Von said.

"No." The boy stood erect and clenched his shaking fists at his sides, with all the bravery he could muster.

"Kneel," Tarn said, his voice set with a dreadful calm.

Von and Geon lowered to their knees. Dirt coated his palms, layered in sweat. He dug his fingers deep, burying them against the bite of sharp rocks.

"You cost me twenty-two assets. Twenty-two lashings you will receive."

Twenty Raiders plus the Moonstone and the Maiden, Von counted. But the true punishment was for failing at his mission. Failure was never an option. Failure got you killed. But Von would gladly accept this instead. He was ready. His back was thick and tough from the many scars that already layered it. He'd been nineteen summers old during his last lashing, but it was a pain he would never forget.

The snap of the whip cracked through the air.

Leather slashed against Von's back, carving through his flesh as it tore free. He bit his tongue to hold in his cry. The whip snapped again and Geon's scream pierced the wind.

One—for Juvo, a lad from Argyle who loved to drink and sing.

The whip ripped through Von a second time.

Two—for Sygne, an old grouch who whistled like a hundred different birds.

The whip cracked so loudly against Von's spine his ears rang and all sound briefly muffled.

Three—for Xeran, who had been saving every coin that fell in his hands for his mother's freedom.

With each laceration into his back, Von recalled the names and faces of the Raiders who had fallen in Corron. Their loss weighed heavily on him. He was their commander. They had trusted him, and he had taken them to the slaughter.

An icy breeze passed over him, but it did nothing to numb the agony as Tarn slashed his back to shreds. Blood poured and soaked his trousers. He clenched his teeth, his shaking fists grinding deeper into the dirt for something to hold on to. It took all he had not to scream in front of his men. Even during this disgrace, he would not show weakness.

Von focused on the droplets of blood in the dirt, trying to force the torment from his mind. Geon had no such discipline. He screamed and wailed as the whip cut into him. Von grit his teeth. He should have never brought the lad into this life.

Tarn continued to whip them until Geon's arms gave out, and he fell face first into the ground, unconscious. Von's limbs trembled, his vision stinging from the sweat leaking into his eyes. He had little strength in him left.

"You failed me, Von." Tarn's words were like shards of ice. "Never have I been so disgusted with you."

He swallowed through the pain, his throat dry. "Forgive me, Master."

Tarn tossed the bloody whip aside. Von counted his steps as he walked away, waiting until Tarn entered his tent before collapsing. The Raiders gathered around.

"Take them," Elon ordered.

Dalton cast his orange Essence over Geon and lifted him into the air. Olsson, a dark, robust man hoisted Von onto his broad shoulders, and he hung there like a limp sack, with not even the will to feel ashamed. Von drifted in and out as they carried him away.

He jerked back to consciousness at the call of Yavi's name. They had brought him to his tent. There was a rush of running steps and she appeared at Olsson's side, her wet eyes widening in dismay. Von faintly smiled at her. He had not seen Yavi when he first awoke. It mattered not what punishment he had to endure. He was with her again. He was alive.

"Bring them inside."

She held open the tent flaps and Olsson transferred Von to a cot, laying him face down. Dalton lowered Geon onto the other cot before releasing his Essence. The Raiders squeezed into the tent and hovered around them while Elon remained at the entryway.

Yavi hissed at the sight of their wounds. Von imagined the skin had swollen with ridges along the bloody slits crisscrossing on their backs in gruesome trails.

"Gord," she barked at the stout Raider across from her. "Tell Sorren I need a bottle of his strongest rum for the commander. And you—" she pointed at the reedy man next to him, "—bring me a pot of boiled water."

They gaped at her, unused to a slave giving them orders.

"Go!" she barked. They rushed out.

Yavi rummaged in the trunk, then took out clean rags and a jar of salve. The two Raiders returned with their items and set them down beside her.

She pulled the cork out of the brown bottle of rum and held it to Von's lips. "Please drink, Master."

Von almost laughed at the title. She had to refer to him as such in front of others, but it was odd to hear. He drank as much as he could, feeling the liquid heat his stomach and rush to his head. She splashed her hands with rum, then stuck a strip of thick leather between his teeth.

"Hold him," Yavi ordered.

Four Raiders kneeled by Von's cot and grasped his legs and shoulders. He sucked in a deep breath—then she poured the rum over his wounds. Fire coursed across his back in a rising wave of torment. He stifled his screams through the leather, convulsing from the excruciating agony. A couple more Raiders joined in, holding him down.

Yavi dipped a clean rag in the pot of steaming water and gently washed his wounds. Gods, she may as well have flayed him alive. Bloody pools formed on the mat beneath him. Sweat beaded on his face as he gripped the cot, his jaw growing numb from how tight he clenched his teeth. Someone briefly removed the leather strip from Von's mouth to give him another drink of rum. His senses dulled and his eyes drooped closed, but each excruciating stroke of the rag beat sleep away.

When Yavi finished, she took out a big glob of salve from the jar and slathered it over his wounds. After the initial pain, it cooled against his throbbing skin, easing some discomfort. "Dalton, lift him if you please."

The young mage cast his Essence over Von, and the orange hue surrounded his body with a warm, electrifying power that raised him a few feet off the cot. Yavi washed his upper body, arms, and neck. Then, she took the roll of dressings and carefully wrapped them around his torso and back.

"What happened?" Yavi asked the men as she worked, and they all burst out at once in a boisterous muddle. "Captain Elon?" she asked him instead.

"The Guardians of the Maiden defeated them," he reported. He was not one to mince words.

"Commander Von was unconscious when we found him," Olssen's deep tenor filled the tent. "We couldn't wake him."

"No, you would not have been able to do so," Dalton retorted. "He was under a comatose spell. Father had to remove it first."

"He was under a spell?" Yavi repeated, surprise filling her words. "I wasn't aware the current Guardians could use magic."

When the sorceress had touched Von's forehead, she had tossed him into a black void. It had been like falling into an endless sleep with no dreams. Next thing he knew, he was looking up at Tarn's icy glare.

"Then we found the bodies," Gord said faintly, his eyes wide and haunted. "Some had been reduced to ash and others were mauled to death. They ripped out Lieutenant Abenon's throat."

Yavi covered her mouth.

Another Raider beside Gord shuddered. "The Guardians are ruthless. The elf took out Len with a shot from three hundred yards away."

Yavi gasped, and Von jolted in alarm. They had killed Len? How? When? He realized she had not been among the witnesses. Neither had Novo.

"Captain?" he croaked, but it was more of an indiscernible gurgle.

"We met them at the Kazer Bluffs," Elon said. "Rawn Norrlen has joined their company. His skill with a bow is unparalleled."

"Len is dead?" Yavi asked shakily, her eyes glistening with tears.

"No. She wore armor."

"Oh!" Yavi slumped back on her heels, a hand flying to her heart. She glared at the expressionless elf and the laughing men. "I don't find that the least amusing. You're terrible, the lot of you."

Von descended back into the cloud of rum as their voices filtered around him, wondering if Tarn would have cared if Len had died.

Yavi finished wrapping his dressings, and she fastened them in place with a pin, then Dalton lowered him back onto the cot. She gave him a sad smile before she moved on to tend to Geon. The lad didn't wake when she poured the rum over his wounds. Elon left the tent as she cleaned him, then the rest of the Raiders followed one by one. Dalton lifted his friend for her to wrap the dressings around his thin chest, departing once she finished.

"Your mending skills have improved," Von said in a rasp.

"Yes, Master," Yavi replied formally. "I have had much practice as of late." She peeked outside of the tent before she tied the flaps closed and hurried to his side. Tears glistened on her lashes in the candlelight. "I feared you dead when you didn't return. You barely escaped with your life, and that monster punished you for it!"

Her hands fluttered around him, not knowing where to touch. She settled with cupping Von's cheek. It was a blessing to see her again. He had expected to die. If not by the sorceress, then by his master. It would have been a death well deserved. He had failed his task. Tarn killed for less.

"I earned it."

Yavi shook her head. "But how did you fall under a spell?"

"By chance, I found the Lūna Medallion in Corron. It belonged to a sorceress."

Yavi inhaled a soft breath. "The one from the foretelling?"

"Possibly." The woman not only came back for her medallion, but she demanded he also free Dyna. A bystander would not have cared. "If she is, it hinders Tarn's advantage. I could not stand against her power. If not for her, I would have captured the Maiden."

Yavi sighed and cleaned the sweat from his face. "Am I awful for feeling relieved that she escaped?"

"No." Von had to admit he felt the same. Tarn would not get what he wanted yet, and that left the world a little safer. For now. He turned his arm over to show Yavi the bite mark on his hand. "Dyna gave me some trouble of her own."

"Did she now?"

"She reminds me of you."

"I'm fond of her already." Yavi gave him a sad laugh, then laid her head on his shoulder, and soon he felt her tears trickling onto his skin. "I cannot stand this life."

"I *will* take you away from here, Yavi. I promise."

"*We* need to go, Von. *Us*. You and me."

"You know I can't." He sighed heavily. "I'm indentured until I am freed."

She wept bitterly. "That man will never free you."

"Aye, he never will. But you are *my* life-servant. By law, I can free you whenever I wish."

The day he'd kidnapped Yavi, she had fallen in a river when she attempted to escape him. Von saved her from drowning by the skin of his teeth. He hadn't planned to claim her as his life-servant, but when Tarn approached her with the branding iron, Von blurted the words of ownership to spare her that pain. Though, he knew she'd never truly been relinquished to him.

Yavi lifted her head and glared at him. "You fool yourself if you believe Tarn will ever allow that. He sees you as his property. In his eyes, what belongs to you belongs to him." She sat back on knees and closed her eyes. "I hate him, Von. I hate him so much. That bastard cut you to the bone and it will leave horrid scars."

A sudden wave of dread overwhelmed his pain.

Von's mind flashed with a memory of a trip he had taken to Arthal with Tarn. They had gone to visit the Seer. She was stunning in all her terrible beauty, with cheekbones as sharp as glass, and translucent wings that shimmered with the gold dust coating her skin. She'd worn a crown of white blossoms and thorns upon her head. Her long locks were the color of the ocean and tangled with braided knots and strips of silk. Black rings circled her golden irises that seemed to glow, her voice as eerie as the howl of the wind when she spoke Tarn's divination.

Von had stood silent and reproaching, disbelieving the pixie's words. He hadn't wanted to believe her.

When they were finished, Tarn had left the Seer's cave and Von moved to follow, but she grabbed his arm and whispered in his ear: *"Only whence she burns will she be free. Her screams will carry in darkness and in ice to haunt thee. They'll cut through thy ears as the scars on thy back. Breaking and mending that which thee lacks."*

He had not saved Yavi from the divination.

Von looked at his wife, and his vision blurred. The Seer foretold their future years before they had met. She had warned him of what was to come. Tarn's divination was proving true, and that could only mean so would his.

No, he wouldn't let it happen.

What was the purpose of divination if not to be a warning? All he must do was keep Yavi from fire.

Von gathered a bit of strength to bring an arm around her waist and pulled her close. He pressed his face into her bosom so she wouldn't see how much the Seer's words frightened him. He had to hold on to the hope that he could save her from the foretelling. To lose her would be unbearable.

"As miserable as this life is, I thank the God of Urn I lived. You are my only comfort in this world, Yavi."

Her lips took his, tender and soft. The pain was manageable now. He didn't know if it was the drink or the affection of this woman he didn't deserve.

"I love you," Von said as he kissed away her tears. "More than I could ever tell you."

"How much?"

"This much." He pulled her close and found her mouth again, deepening the kiss.

"I will need some of that rum if I have to watch this," a faint voice garbled.

Yavi flung herself away and they stared at Geon with unease. Von had forgotten about the lad.

Geon blinked at them drowsily. "Am I alive?"

"Yes, uh, here." Yavi helped him drink from the bottle as she exchanged a worried glance with Von.

A faint, impish smile surfaced on Geon's face. "Naughty."

"Geon!" Yavi smacked his shoulder, then apologized profusely at his wince. "You won't tell anyone, will you?"

He chuckled. "You're my friend, Yavi. You know I won't."

Von exhaled in relief. "No one must ever learn of this."

"Worry not, Commander. You have my word. Though, if I am being honest, I had my suspicions." At their silence, Geon added sheepishly, "You favor her, sir, and well, you share a tent."

Von grimaced. He thought they were being cautious, but sleeping in the same tent together was too conspicuous, even if it was under the guise of a servant.

"Have I been demoted?" Geon asked.

"Aye."

Yavi hummed sympathetically and patted his leg. "I'm sorry, Geon. I know how hard you worked to be a Raider."

He coughed a weak chuckle. "Being a Raider is not as glorious as I had imagined. I don't have the stomach for it at all. I'll ask the cook to take me as an apprentice."

Von and Yavi laughed.

"You will need as much bravery, if not more, to work with Sorren," she said.

"I can do it."

Von smiled. "Are you certain?"

"Aye. I'd rather work with the Minotaur than risk angering Master Tarn ever again," Geon murmured. The amusing moment passed at the mention of him.

"Did you battle with the Guardians?" Yavi asked him after a pause.

"I wouldn't call it a battle. The sorceress threw me about like a sack of meal and broke my arm when I kept her from killing Von."

"You did?" he said in amazement. "Why would you do that? You couldn't hope to defeat her."

"You've saved my life several times, Commander. I have lost count of how many debts I owe you."

"You're a fine lad."

Geon cracked a weak smile. "I reckon I would have died if not for the Maiden. She kept the sorceress at bay and defended me when the remaining Guardians arrived. Then she ... healed me."

Von stared at him. "Dyna healed you?"

"Aye, she mended my broken leg and arm. With magic."

Yavi gasped and moved closer to inspect him. She picked at the torn clothing by his elbow and knee, tearing them further to see.

Von caught a glimpse of the new pink scars he bore. "If Dyna could use magic, why did she not wield it against me?"

"I don't know, Commander, but I speak the truth. My scars are proof. She's special. Please don't tell the master. He will enslave her once he learns of it."

Von couldn't promise that. As long as Tarn didn't ask, it didn't need to be mentioned. But it was only a matter of time until he learned of her power.

Dalton had accused her of being a sorceress, but Dyna denied it, so Von had readily believed her. He had been so busy moving the camp and tending to other matters that he hadn't stopped to think about it. If she had magic, it now made sense why she could reveal an enchanted map.

Yavi worked on straightening up the tent, and Geon drifted off to sleep again. Von attempted to sleep too, but then he heard the crunch of boots on the gravel outside.

"Commander?" Elon called out.

Von stifled a groan, already knowing what he would say. "Aye?"

"Pardon the intrusion. Tarn requests your presence."

"One moment."

Yavi hissed under her breath. "That man has no sense of mercy. Can he not allow you one night of rest?"

Von motioned at her to be silent. Elon seemed neutral, but they couldn't trust that he wouldn't report her. Slave defiance was severely punishable. If he had been whipped for failing a task, what would Tarn do to Yavi for her derision?

Groaning, he sat on the cot with her help and she pulled out a gray tunic from the trunk to dress him. When she placed his arm around her for support, the movement sent a painful shock through his back. Von clenched his teeth, biting back a curse. He inhaled a sharp breath, and forced himself on to his feet. His vision swam. He nearly toppled over if not for Yavi. His legs wobbled with each step to the entrance.

She quickly untied the knots and opened the flaps. Elon lurked beneath a nearby tree where the moonlight didn't reach. "You will need to assist him there," she said.

Elon came forward and took his arm, carefully placing it over his shoulders. They trudged through the quiet camp and Von winced with each step, his slow feet staggering. Sweat dripped down his temples from the strain. He was grateful the men had taken to staying within their tents tonight, so no one had to see his struggle. The trip was long and grueling. An eternity passed before they reached the large, imposing tent, candlelight streaming through the edges of the flaps.

"Thank you for your patience, Elon," Von said. The elf nodded and slinked into the dark. He stood there a moment, gathering the nerve to go inside.

"Don't waste my time," Tarn's cool voice came from within. "You have done enough of that today."

Von took a shaky breath and entered. Tarn sat at the head of the dining table, with a mound of fabric and leather placed before him.

His pale eyes gleamed like two spheres of ice. His short-sleeved tunic hung on him unbuttoned, exposing the old jagged scars covering his chest and arms like a roadmap of the past. Discolored, uneven crevices marked his ribs where the jaws of a troll had chewed through tendon and bone. That day may have ravaged more than Tarn's body. He was never the same after.

Von forced his aching body to bow. He couldn't detain the low keening in his throat when his wounds split open. Blood leaked out of his dressings, soaking into his tunic.

"I did not think it would be so difficult for you to capture a girl," Tarn said.

Von straightened and breathed deeply through the pain. "We were unprepared."

Tarn's pale eyes narrowed. "I'll not hear your excuses. Elon informed you well."

"Yes, Master, but—"

"And now the Warrior Guardian has joined them." Tarn flung the mound off the table at Von's feet.

What he thought was mere fabric had been Len's cloak wrapped around a small breastplate. It was enchanted to withstand any weapon, yet at the center was a sliver of an opening stained crimson. She was the only one Tarn had provided armor for, and it barely saved her life.

How had Rawn pierced her armor? Especially from three-hundred yards away?

"I hadn't accounted for the elf," Von said tentatively. Or the sorceress. When I took the medallion, I failed to realize who she was."

They glanced over to the left when the rune for Truth & Lies glowed blue with his honesty. Von couldn't speak a lie in this tent, and sometimes it served in his favor.

"She may be the fourth Guardian in the foretelling," he added.

Tarn linked his fingers together and rested his elbows on the table. "Was she powerful?"

Von could not describe the torrent of magic she expelled as weak. "Yes."

"Hmm. She must be why my mages can no longer track the Maiden."

Von lifted his head, recalling the glass orb they had used to track her ceased to work the moment they reached the city. "We had lost the Maiden's location at midday yesterday."

"Benton reported his tracking spell had been severed at that time," Tarn said. "Then a second spell was cast to cloak her. He was quite annoyed that another mage had the power to overthrow him."

Von tightened his jaw so he wouldn't smirk. What would Benton say if he realized it was a sorceress and not a mage who had thwarted him?

Tarn narrowed his eyes. "Yet it would not have mattered if you had brought me the medallion."

Even if Von had, it would have been futile. Upon inspecting the pendant, he had attempted to remove the iridescent stone only for its image to dissolve. "The Lūna Medallion didn't contain the Moonstone, Master."

"*What?*"

"The stone was a glamor spell."

The Mood Rune smoldered red, casting a sinister sheen in the tent. It was a dormant rune that only worked during the rare incidences it detected ample emotion. Tarn was an indifferent man for the most part, careful not to allow himself to feel anything. *"Emotions are a weakness,"* he once said. It took a great deal to make him this livid.

Von swallowed. "Forgive me."

"That is all you can say, isn't it?" Tarn inhaled one deep breath, and it surprised Von when the rune stopped glowing.

"The sorceress must have it. I will get it for you."

Tarn leaned back in his chair and crossed an ankle over his knee. "For your sake, pray to your God that you do."

Von bowed his head, confused by his master's sudden tolerance. "Shall I resume the search for the Maiden?"

"Send the spies."

They would need to rely on Elon's skill to track Dyna now that magic was not an option.

"It shouldn't be difficult to locate them," Von said. "They will at some point need to stop in the Port of Azure."

Tarn's jaw worked at the mention of the seaport city. He walked over to his desk where he had laid out maps of the kingdom. "Let's not make it so easy for the Maiden and her Guardians," he said as he studied them. "It's imperative they don't board a ship. Send a Raider to Corron to place an anonymous bounty on their heads through the Azure Warrant Authority. Make it substantial enough to entice the bounty hunters and ensure the notices circulate throughout the kingdom before they arrive at the port."

Von nodded as blood began dripping from the hem of his tunic. "Yes, Master."

"Fifty dead in the camp raid," Tarn said, watching the red droplets splatter in the dirt. "Another twenty killed by the Guardians. Useless, the lot of them."

Von was careful to keep his expression indifferent, but the Mood Rune gave him away when pulsed dark purple with his remorse. He had trained each of those men as they joined Tarn's regiment over the years. Abenon above all had been a fine lieutenant, having joined when he was a lad. He'd been loyal, but Tarn didn't care about who they were, or that they died for his pursuit of the Unending. They were an expendable casualty.

Tarn's cool gaze bore into him. "Are you useless as well, Von?"

He knew better than to answer.

"Go. You're making a bloody mess."

Von winced through another bow, then stepped out into the autumn chill. He looked up at the stars and questioned the God of Urn. What sin did he commit in a past life to be a slave in this one?

Weariness weighed heavily on his bones. He couldn't make his legs move. He was on the verge of falling unconscious where he stood, but Elon slipped out of the darkness and took hold of him again. Von nodded in gratitude.

Without a word, step by step, they gradually made their way into the night.

CHAPTER 44

It was dark. Nothing but a never-ending black. And Dyna was not alone. Something moved within the darkness, claws scraping on stone. She heard its heavy breathing and felt its eyes. A low, crackling growl sounded within the emptiness. The air left her lungs, ice filling her limbs.

The Shadow was coming.

Terror snatched away her voice. She could not scream or call for help. Cold smoke brushed against her back, wafting through her hair. She covered her mouth and smothered her whimpers. Her legs gave out, and she curled into a ball, squeezing her eyes tight. Claws skittered across the ground, slowly coming closer.

Closer.

A sudden beam filtered through her eyelids. Dyna held up a hand to screen her eyes, light streaming through her fingers. Slowly, she lowered her hand to see a *Hyalus* tree. It glowed so brightly it faded the black to a dull gray.

Dyna sat up and searched for the lurking Shadow, but it was gone. She stumbled to the tree and its glowing branches reached out to her. As soon as she took a branch, it gently wrapped around her hand and the tree's light flared, washing away the darkness in a swathe of white.

She blinked and found herself lying on a blanket by a small campfire. Firelight shimmered on the damp rock ceiling above her. At the sound of soft nickering, she noticed Fair. Lord Norrlen's horse grazed in a dark clearing beyond the cave. She picked up on the familiar voices, muted in conversation. Zev sat by her feet and Cassiel sat by her head, one of his cool hands resting over hers. The touch had been enough to pull her out of that darkness.

Had he known she was having a nightmare? Had she been screaming? No one else had noticed she was awake. They were watching Rawn, who sat on the other side of the campfire. He ground dried red petals in a wooden bowl and tossed in a pinch of yellow powder from one of the many pouches on his belt. A sweet floral scent filled the air.

She had not seen the *Dynalya* flower other than in books, nonetheless, she recognized what he was making. A small pot of water simmered over the fire, the handle hanging from a spit. Rawn removed it to pour it into a wooden cup and mixed the powders.

"What is it?" Cassiel asked stiffly.

"It's a remedial concoction for my head," Dyna murmured as she sat up.

"You're awake." Zev exhaled in relief. "How are you feeling?"

She managed a brittle smile. Weakness had settled over her bones. Her Essence was spent. It may take her longer to recover this time. "I'll be all right."

Rawn passed her the cup. "Drink, my lady. You will feel much improved."

Sweet-smelling steam swirled above the red liquid. She blew on the surface before taking a sip. It reminded her of raspberry leaves with a hint of lemongrass and it warmed her sore throat, her headache immediately fading away.

"Thank you," Dyna said.

Cassiel gave Rawn a curt nod. "Given that you came to our aid, you have my thanks."

"That puts us within your debt," Zev said, observing him.

Rawn inclined his head. "I relieve you of your debt. It is dishonorable to gain favors and life-servants at the cost of saving lives. The elves do not practice such a custom. Slavery is banned in the Vale."

"As it is in Hilos and the Four Realms," Cassiel mentioned. "The Celestials are not so arrogant to believe we may own a life. That is not the will of *Elyōn*."

Dyna made a face at him. He deliberately didn't mention that fact the first time he had saved her life. Cassiel kept his expression casual, but the corner of his mouth quirked.

"Von and Geon must be life-servants," she said.

Rawn shook his head. "'Life-servant' is an understated term. They are slaves. To have your life saved only to lose it to enslavement is reprehensible. As of late, several kingdoms have proposed to end the Life-Debt Law, but most of Urn resists it, unfortunately. Owning lives is a manner of wealth."

"Is there a way for them to gain their freedom?" She kept thinking of Von and his insipid face when the sorceress confronted him. He knew she would defeat him, but Dyna sensed his fear had not been against her magic.

"As of last month, the Azure Kingdom has abolished slavery," Rawn said. "On this land, they are free. They need only acknowledge it."

"You mean they can walk away?" Zev asked.

"The braver ones do, but many fear the repercussion. With the proper legal assertion of their rights, those in bondage can attain their freedom. However, with Tarn as their master, it may not be a simple feat."

"Who is he?" Cassiel asked.

"I have yet to make his acquaintance. I know of him through infamy alone. There are several narratives and rumors about him, all of which depict him as a treacherous man who does not fear recourse for his deeds. His band of Raiders pillage and slay in his name. He has murdered and thieved in several kingdoms, many of which have placed a sizable bounty on his head, dead or alive. Therefore, he never lingers in one place for long."

"He's a cutthroat," Zev concluded.

Rawn nodded. "He has no qualms in killing for what he wants. He will take anything from gold to people."

Dyna gasped. "People? You say it as though he didn't earn their servitude."

"Tarn enslaves those with the skills to serve him and there is a rumor that he searches for Sacred Scrolls."

She frowned. "Why would Tarn want those?"

"He does not strike me as a pious man," Cassiel retorted.

"The scrolls hold more wonders than the makings of the world," Rawn said. "Such things could illicit power, if not great knowledge."

Zev growled. "Why did he come after Dyna?"

"Von overheard us speaking of the map in Landcaster," she said. "They've been spying on us since."

"The Raiders knew about us," Cassiel told Zev. "They know what we are."

"That is Tarn's method," Rawn explained. "He studies his opponents before he advances. I suspect he must seek the treasures of Mount Ida. Now that he has learned of the map, his pursuit of Lady Dyna will not cease until he obtains what he wishes."

Zev's eyes glowed iridescent in the firelight. "I'll end it the next time he comes for her."

"Now that we know about him, we will be ready," Cassiel agreed. "I am assuming he is after the treasure."

"I don't believe it's the treasure he wants," Dyna said.

Rawn nodded. "I agree. He has already gathered abundant wealth from his raids."

A snarl ripped out of Zev's throat. "Then what does he want?"

"Power. Mount Ida contains unimaginable magic. Whatever he seeks, Urn and the rest of the world may be at risk because of it."

Dyna shuddered. "The boy mentioned something strange. He said they had been expecting me for years. That a fae Seer had foretold it."

"The Seer of Faery Hill?" Rawn asked in surprise. She nodded. "The Seer is eminent in Arthal. She has the gift to see the future and fate of others. It is a rare ability many among the fae folk seek to use or control. Because of it, she lives in confinement within the Unseelie Court under the protection of the Night Queen. To request the Seer's services, you must entice the Night Queen with a gift. She is known to prefer human children."

A prickle of goosebumps coursed down Dyna's arms. "God of Urn. Do you think Tarn would have ...?"

"From what little we know of that man, I would not think otherwise," said Zev.

Her eyes stung with tears. That poor child.

"Did they tell you what the foretelling was?" Cassiel asked. He looked skeptical.

She shook her head. "Geon called me the Maiden with the key to Mount Ida. He spoke of six Guardians that would protect me. It seems you and Zev are two of them."

The men stared at her, not sure what to make of it. She didn't understand it either, but she believed it. Her journey since leaving North Star had been too incredible to be a coincidence. Zev had protected her since birth, and Cassiel had guarded her against danger since their first meeting.

"I suppose this is where I shall leave you," Rawn said as he stood and gathered his belongings.

"Are you to leave us again, Lord Norrlen?" Dyna asked him.

He paused, taken aback by the question. "I do not wish to overstay my welcome. I have imposed myself again in your matters."

"Something led you to us the moment Tarn came for me. If the foretelling is true, you must be a Guardian. You gave me an oath of protection, Lord Norrlen. You promised to be my shield and to guide me to the end of the world and back. I aim to hold you to your word. Please, be our Guidelander."

Rawn's eyes widened. "If that is what you wish, my lady, I shall join you with goodwill, should your companions' consent."

Dyna glanced at the others, wary of their reactions. She had expected them to immediately refuse, but neither of them did. They studied Rawn in consideration.

"He saved your life," she reminded Cassiel.

Zev crossed his arms. "He also had a hand in our escape from the loch."

They had not told her about that yet.

Quiet anger simmered on Cassiel's face. "There was a second attempt to take you. Their elf wields magic. I doubt we would have survived it."

Dyna would have to reflect on that snippet of information later, for she couldn't help but notice the use of "their elf". She grinned widely and said, "You mean, *our* elf saved us?"

Cassiel rolled his eyes in indignant admittance.

"He can join us then?"

Cassiel and Zev shared a look, and both nodded once in agreement. "I suppose there is no sense in arguing," the prince said.

She beamed and squeezed both their arms. "I knew you'd see reason."

Rawn sat back on his heels, too bewildered to speak for a moment. "Thank you."

Zev pulled out Azeran's journal from his pack. He opened the pages to a section before offering it to him. Rawn's hands trembled as he accepted the journal. He drew in a deep breath and looked down at the blank pages. Cassiel and Zev chuckled at his confusion.

"The map disappears when it's separated from me," Dyna said. She motioned for him to pass the journal to her, and she whispered, *"Tellūs, lūnam, sōlis."*

Rawn stared at the vivid purple swirl of magic as calligraphic strokes swarmed across the page. When the glowing island of Mount

Ida appeared, emotions crossed his face in rapid succession. Astonishment. Relief. Joy.

He blinked his misted eyes and gave a short laugh of amazement. "My lady, you mentioned Azeran Astron is your ancestor. You have an incredible heritage. To be of his bloodline, you must be powerful. I have only witnessed elves and mages with formidable magical abilities perform Essence Healing as you have done."

Dyna shrugged, feeling timid at the praise. "My abilities end there. I'm human, but I share his blood and Essence. It's the reason I can reveal this map."

Rawn smiled warmly. "You are far more precious than I have foreseen. This excursion would cease to exist without you."

"What do you mean?" Cassiel asked.

"He means, should anything happen to Dyna the map would disappear," Zev said. "Only her Essence can reveal its secrets."

Cassiel sucked in a sharp breath. He looked at her as though he feared she would vanish in a wink. She hadn't brought herself to ask him what his true intentions were for going to Mount Ida.

"I will let nothing happen to you," Cassiel declared so ardently that she blushed. He nervously scratched his neck and clarified, "I mean to say that I will protect you from Tarn."

"Me too," Zev said.

Rawn nodded. "As will I."

Dyna's eyes welled at their promises. For once, she felt to be on the right path to her journey. "Thank you."

"What is one man?" Cassiel said to the flames. "You have far worse enemies."

Rawn glanced from him to her, his smile fading. "My lady?"

Zev tilted his head at her and shrugged. "Will you tell him, or shall I?"

She sighed at the reminder. Lord Norrlen should know her reason to reach the island. She would need every possible ally on this mission. Lyra and the children of North Star depended on it.

Dyna pictured the mountain of bones from her dreams. Pitch-black clouds shrouded the peak, smothering the sky from any source of light. The mountain had always represented her fear and the imminent death of everyone she loved. It was fear that kept her back, knocking her down whenever she had tried to climb it. This time, she was determined to reach the top.

"I have a shadow demon to vanquish."

Cassiel

The land of Azure gleamed with the rising sun. A gradient of pink and purple bled across the sky as the gray of early dawn faded. Arms crossed, Cassiel stood on the edge of the cliff that sheltered their camp below.

He had lost count of the days since their escape from Corron. Other things consumed his thoughts. Struggling to find any sleep, he had gone for a flight before the others awoke, but even flying brought him little joy.

He was not the same. He felt it. He was different. Unclean.

Forsaken.

His mother's flute weighed heavily in his limp hand. He'd hoped music would help, but he had no desire to play it anymore. If he was worthless before, now he was truly nothing. There had to be some good in this. He was no longer the person his father claimed, so the throne wouldn't be forced on him now.

"Cassiel?"

He stiffened.

Dyna's slight form passed through the foliage. Her cheeks were flushed from the climb. She clutched the caplet around her shoulders and her breath swirled in the morning chill.

Her foot dragged as she limped over to him. "There you are."

Cassiel turned away and sat on the edge of the cliff, unable to look at her. His promises had turned to smoke, along with the last shred of purpose he'd found. He couldn't be what she needed anymore.

"You should not be wandering about on that ankle," he muttered. "How did you find me?"

"I'm ... not sure."

His wings twitched at the perplexity in her tone. Had the bond led her to him as it had led him to her in Corron?

She settled beside him. "Are you all right?"

He attempted to lie, but Cassiel broke off at the concern radiating from her. How could he explain the festering inside of him? He couldn't.

"I hear you at night," she whispered. "The nightmares."

He closed his eyes, not wanting to admit it to her or himself how much he wished they'd never left the inn. Lying beside her had given him one night of peaceful sleep. He'd never have that again.

"Cassiel." Dyna placed her hand over one of his clenched fists on his lap. His skin vibrated beneath her touch. "What happened was not your fault."

Cassiel gritted his teeth and rose to his feet, striding away. He *was* at fault, and he could not bear to face it while being around her.

Dyna jumped up, following his clipped pace. "Don't do that. Don't take all the blame."

"What do you know about blame?"

"I know plenty. Von would not have come after us if I had not met him. This is *my* doing."

Cassiel stopped with his back to her. "Do you not see?" he snapped. "I took human lives. Any divinity I had is gone."

"You cannot carry the deaths of those men—"

"I will not discuss *that* with you."

"But they attacked—"

"Enough!"

Dyna winced at his shout, and the hurt he caused her punched him in the gut. Cassiel didn't mean to be so harsh, but he couldn't speak of his deeds. They were to lie in the abominable husk of his existence.

He should apologize. So many times, he owed her one, but he wanted her to leave him alone. To go away so she wouldn't see what she could undoubtedly feel from him.

The heavy silence dragged. Dyna's steps shifted in the dirt behind him and Cassiel thought she had walked away, but then a pebble hit his back.

"What are you—" He ducked as another one bounced off his head. "Stop!"

"Foolish, stubborn-headed, full-of-yourself prince!" Dyna pelted him wherever she could hit him with a handful of pebbles. "Killing them changes nothing!"

He scowled and whirled around, not realizing how close she was, and whacked her with his wings. Dyna stumbled backward and slipped off the edge of the cliff.

"Dyna!" Cassiel lunged for her, catching her flailing wrist. He yanked her into the clutch of his arms, and they fell backward on safe ground in a tangle of limbs. Arms and wings held her securely to his chest as his heart raced from the horror of what almost happened.

She shook against him. At first, he thought she was crying until Dyna burst into a fit of giggles. She sat back on her heels and laughed until tears collected in the corner of her lashes.

Cassiel eyed her warily, fearing she had gone mad. "What is so amusing?"

The first rays of the sun glowed through Dyna's hair as she shook her head, grinning. "To think, all this time you were the answer to my problem. You were a mere forty miles from my village in a kingdom of divine beings no one knew still existed. Even so, it changes nothing."

He finally drew her meaning. "For you still would have crossed Urn on your impossible quest to find an impossible place."

"Corron didn't change who you are, Cassiel. You are the same, ornery Celestial who saved me from a cliff. Twice."

"Stupid human." He smirked and curled a loose lock of scarlet hair behind her ear. Realizing what he had done, Cassiel immediately pulled away, but she took his hand again and held it on her lap.

Dyna gave him a soft smile. "I'm sorry for throwing stones at you."

"I suppose I deserved it." Cassiel looked down at their entwined fingers, liking how well they fit together. He grazed her knuckles with his thumb. "I'm sorry for what happened at the inn."

A lovely blush rose to her cheeks. "It's all right. I understand."

"I meant everything I said that night," he murmured. "I wanted to slay the Shadow for you but ..."

He couldn't. Not anymore.

"It matters not," she said. "I wouldn't have let you risk your life for me. This is something I must do alone. Even if you had told me about your ability, my path leads to Mount Ida."

"You say this because of the Seer's divination?"

Dyna nodded. "Perhaps even Azeran's creation of the map led to my future. I believe it. None of this is pure chance. So, please don't feel as though you have failed me. The Raiders—"

She cut off abruptly at the sharp pang that went through him. Cassiel let their hands break apart.

"Why do you want to go to Mount Ida?" she asked, surprising him with the unexpected question. Cassiel looked out to the western horizon, wondering if he would ever find what he sought. "Is it related to that?"

Her gaze flickered to his mother's sapphire ring. He'd been mindlessly twisting the chain from which it hung around his fingers.

Cassiel tucked the ring away. "Do not ask me, for I will not answer."

"Why?"

He sighed. "It has nothing to do with you."

"It does." Dyna frowned. "You were angry that I was going to Mount Ida. I saw your face when your father brought out those books.

That island means something to you." She laid a hand over her heart. "I feel it. And I feel you. Why is that?"

Damn. She truly could feel his emotions as he felt hers. He couldn't hide it any longer.

"You're nervous." Dyna tilted her head. "Now you're anxious," she added at his inner jolt. "Why do I know that? Why do I feel you?"

Cassiel dropped his head. The weight of the truth bore down on him. "You were also unexpected. I did not know saving your life would bring me here. By all rights, we never should have met, but I see now that you are the key to everything. The key to this entire journey. The key to the map. And the key that changed my life."

"What do you mean?"

Cassiel's wings flexed, reflecting his urge to fly away from her again, but if he didn't confess now, he may never say the words. "I must tell you something. Something unfortunate, but you must know. You have a right to know."

Her alarm coming through the bond shackled around his throat.

"I made a mistake," he rushed out. "Please know it was never my intention. I had only meant to heal you. You will most likely despise me, and rightly so, but—"

"Nothing you say would ever make me despise you," Dyna said. "You're important to me."

That shocked Cassiel enough to meet her gaze.

Important? It was another foreign concept, but he sensed she meant it. The bond hummed with her affection. She shouldn't feel that way toward him, and she wouldn't after he confessed. Whether or not Dyna hated him, everything would once again change.

"You do not know who I am," Cassiel said. "You do not know what I have done. I should tell you so you would understand why I am unworthy of such regard."

"You are worthy."

He scoffed. "I am a half-breed, Dyna."

She frowned. "So?"

"That is all I will ever be. That is all my people see."

"That is not what I see," Dyna said. "I see a grumpy, ludicrous Celestial who is musically talented, intelligent, and unique. Someone courteous when he cares to be, even if it makes him uncomfortable." Dyna laughed when he cringed, and she leaned forward on her knees to take his face in her hands. "I see someone who is trying to find his place in the world when he's been convinced he doesn't have one. Someone who is so much more than he believes. I see you, Cassiel."

Her words had done something to the rock inside of his chest, where his heart used to be. She'd chipped away a piece, leaving him a little lighter. A little less angry. Cassiel sincerely didn't understand this human, but he didn't care anymore.

By the connection of her touch, his second sight unveiled Dyna's soul. His eyes drifted closed, all tension easing out of him.

"What does it look like?" she asked, no doubt realizing what was happening.

"It is difficult to describe," he said. "It is as though all the constellations of the cosmos have gathered in one place."

It was both a beautiful and captivating sight.

But her soul was different since Cassiel had last seen it. Within the dancing storm of emerald light, the glowing white cord of their bond braided with the golden lifeline of his soul. It wove through hers, displaying how deeply tethered their fates were to each other. He may no longer have the sanctity to slay demons, but her heart now beat within him and his within her. That one indisputable fact could never be undone.

When the bond first happened, he desperately wanted to be rid of it. But after coming to accept it, he found himself balanced and established. He had been sinking through life, never knowing which way was up or down.

Until her.

Unknowingly, unintentionally, Dynalya Astron had become his sun, and the incredulity of it faded all of his dread.

Cassiel swept another red strand from her temple, letting his fingers stroke her cheek. He waited for her to recoil, to be sickened that someone such as him had the audacity to presume so much. When she didn't shrink away, he gathered the courage to slide his hands up her arms, leaving goosebumps along her soft skin.

Every touch was a question, a request for permission. Her bright green eyes locked onto his, giving the answer he didn't know he wanted. The energy of their bond entwined them, the tendrils of her presence weaving through his every breath. He slid his hand to the curve of her neck and sunk his fingers through her locks, brushing his fingertips along her nape. The soft skin there rushed with warmth and he felt her pulse leap as her heart raced with his own.

Cassiel fixated on her mouth. On those full lips he wanted to touch. His head spun with uncertainty and desire. He swallowed once. Twice. Then trailed his other hand up Dyna's spine. She trembled, inhaling a quivering breath. Her excitement filtered through the bond, mirroring his. He wrapped his wings around her, and with the slightest pressure, invited her to close the gap between them. She drew closer, and Cassiel leaned toward her, a part of him waiting until the last moment for her to protest.

She did not.

Their noses met in idle hesitation. Did he dare? There were a thousand reasons why he shouldn't.

"What were you going to tell me?" Dyna murmured, her supple mouth caressing the corner of his. The sensation sent a tide of thrill through him. "At the inn, you said my eyes reminded you of something."

Cassiel laughed softly, still a bit embarrassed he had admitted that, and whispered, "They remind me of spring. The type of green that comes after a brutal winter has melted away."

Dyna smiled a small smile, her cheeks pinking. He grazed her mouth. Gentle and careful. Tentative. Could he steal a kiss after he had stolen so much from her? Gods, he desperately wanted to, but it wasn't right. Not when he needed to tell her the truth first.

"Whatever your secrets, it won't change my mind," Dyna said as if she sensed his thoughts. "I'll not turn my back on you."

It was a promise he felt seal over them both.

Cassiel leaned back, holding her gaze. He took Dyna's hands in his and she stilled in anticipation. The world fell away, taking all of his doubts and fears, leaving nothing but the silent autumn air between them and the hushed words on his lips.

"We are Blood Bonded."

Acknowledgments

There is something magical about creating worlds and characters in our imaginations. They become real in your mind and in your heart, at least that is true for me. Writing and reading whisk me off to other worlds, and sometimes it's hard to come back. I have been working on *The Guardians of the Maiden* series for over fifteen years, so I'd like to believe my characters exist in some tangible dimension, even if it's just wishful thinking.

When I first wrote this story, I had no idea the adventure it would take me on. I give great credit to all my friends and family who have supported me and cheered me on along the way.

First and foremost, thank you to my husband, Michael, for putting up with the endless hours I spent writing and helping my dreams come true. You mean the world to me, love.

How can I not thank my sister, Raquel Landell? She has been my number one fan from the beginning. You have been supporting me since this story began many years ago and it was your demand for a next chapter that kept me writing.

Special shout out to Holly Black. If I had not discovered her books so long ago, I may not have developed my love for fantasy and storytelling.

I'll never forget the many beta readers who had the patience to read through my *very* rough drafts. I owe thanks to so many of you:

To Chelsea Couch for setting my writing on the right path. To Lauren Lane, my lovely critique partner who always encouraged me. To Hina Babar, my editor who worked hard to whip this book into shape. To Amandine Elaye, and Noni Siziya for telling me how it is. To Lauren Voeltz, Katie Cunningham, and Jessica Scurlock for their unwavering praise. To Will Kerwick for instructing me on how to wield a blade on the page. To all the amazing people in the Book Readers Anonymous Support Group, to my outstanding ARC Team, and to everyone who helped spread the word about *Divine Blood*.

And last, but certainly not least, a special thank you to my amazing Alpha Team who worked diligently to get the bonus content found in this Limited Edition ready for publication. My amazing Fan Club President, Karley Stafford, the brilliant Sherise Mitchell, forever witty Darby Cupid, meticulous Miranda Lyn, kind Nikki Mitchell, sweet Sophie Critchley, darling Lauren Lane, and my twin at heart, Hina Babar, who never lets me get away with anything.

And thank you to sweet Hadar Garson for taking the time to help me with Celestial terminology. You are the best!

Each and every one of you taught me so much and made me laugh along the way. I am forever grateful to all of you for believing I could do this. You helped make this fictional world real.

Thank you.

I am within your debt.

Beck Michaels

Pronunciation Guide

NAMES:

Dynalya/Dyna: Die-nal-yah / Die-nah

Cassiel: Cass-e-el

Zev: Zeh-v

Von: Vaughn

Tarn: Tar-n

Geon: Gee-on

Elon: Eh-lon

Yavi: Ya-vee

Rawn: Ron

Lucenna: Lu-seh-na

Azeran: Ah-zer-ran

Lyra: Lie-ra

Yoel: Yoh-el

Malakel: Mah-la-kel

Tzuriel: Zu-re-el

Gareel: Gah-reel

Lorian: Lor-re-an

Leyla: Lay-lah

Abenon: Ah-be-non

PLACES:

Ida: eye-dah

Hilos: He-los

Corron: Core-on

Azure: Ah-z-her

Magos: Mah-goes

Argyle: Ar-guy-el

Xian Jing: She-an-ging

Harromag Modos: Ha-ro-mag Moh-dos

Saxe: Sah-x

Kazer: Kay-zer

OTHERS:

Tellūs: Teh-lus

Lūnam: Lu-nahm

Sōlis: Soh-lis

Hyalus: Hi-ya-lus

Essentia Dimensio: Eh-sen-see-ah De-men-see-o

Lahav Esh: La-hav Eh-sh

Kados Lezayen: Ca-dosh Leh-za-yen

KEEP READING FOR
A BONUS CHAPTER

Tarn frowned at the shadows steadily growing in the corners of his darkening tent. Firewood in the iron brazier beside him crackled faintly, the low flame casting an orange glow over the runes marking the tent walls. The end of the branding iron he'd been using as a poker glowed molten with the profile of a noble bird, the ice phoenix. He grabbed the handle and adjusted the charred logs to coax the dying flames, eliciting a spark of embers into the air.

The night was approaching, yet Von and Elon hadn't returned from their mission. It was the most important mission he sent them upon. While they had not failed him before, the stakes were high this time. He was so close to getting everything he wanted, he could feel it. The anticipation made him impatient and sleepy.

Attempting to calm his restlessness, Tarn sat at his table as he took out a vial from his coat pocket and poured the black contents over his goblet of wine. It shimmered with silvery magic as drops of Witch's Brew hit the surface before fading away. He drank the potion each night, chasing away fatigue. Chasing away the memories that filled his dreams.

If ever sleep caught him, there was no control over what he saw in that void. He detested it. Detested the utter vulnerability of being subjected to dreams he didn't want to see or remember. There was only one thing he would allow to occupy his thoughts.

Among the missives on the dining table laid an open book with a detailed illustration of the Lūna Medallion. Tarn traced the iridescent stone in the center, wishing he could tear it off the page. He needed that damn stone. By the luck of the gods, Von had sent word back to camp that he'd found it in Corron. After years of searching, at last, he would have it.

The Unending.

To be mortal was to be inept. Uncertain. Feeble. Many hunted him, and many more aimed to finish him. But the Unending would give him eternal power that would assure his life would no longer be at the threshold of The Gates. Only then would he be able to destroy the wheel that sought to grind him into the earth.

As soon as the Maiden and the Luna Medallion arrived, he'd open a portal to Mount Ida. Tonight. It was all coming together relatively easier than the Seer had led him to believe. Which only made him suspicious. It shouldn't be this easy. Anything worth getting wasn't.

Something wedged within the thick pages of the book caught Tarn's eye. He parted them and took out the curl of flaxen hair tied with a black silk ribbon. The sight of it struck him like a bolt of lightning, and he stiffened in his chair. He'd completely forgotten she had placed it there years ago. The lock gleamed gold in the firelight, exhuming a memory he'd left buried somewhere in the confines of his thoughts.

"What do you want to be remembered for, Tarn? The degree of your deeds, or the intent?"

Her voice twisted his stomach with a fathomless fury and age-old pain he cared not to evoke. He scowled and dropped the lock of hair back in the book, slamming it shut.

The amethyst crystal hanging with the other magical charms from the ceiling spun, casting purple rays of light on the walls. He heard the tread of dragging feet outside before Elon entered the tent, supporting Geon. Covered in mud and blood, the boy limped inside.

Behind them followed Olsson, carrying Von over his broad shoulders.

Tarn clenched his jaw, tension building in his temples at what this sight meant. He watched silently as Olson carefully laid the filthy commander on the silk sheets of his bed in the corner.

Elon faltered when he noticed that and quickly said to the Raider, "Not there."

But Tarn didn't care. It wasn't as if he used the bed. He stalked over and studied Von. There were no visible wounds, but he was lifeless. Von had been with him since the beginning, a vital asset he wasn't prepared to part with yet. "Is he dead?"

"No," Elon replied. "He is under a spell."

Tarn slowly turned to look at him. *A spell?*

"We didn't see what occurred, Master," Olssen said in a deep baritone. "We found Commander Von and the boy outside of the city."

Geon kept his head bowed. Tears had left streaks through the dirt on his face.

"How. Many?" Tarn asked tightly. How many more men did he lose? He'd sent twenty.

"All of them," Elon said, but there was a brief flash of hesitation on his usual indifferent expression.

Tarn narrowed his eyes. "Who else?"

"Len."

He goes still, but not his mind. It heated with wild rage, and the Mood Rune on the wall behind him flared red. His hands twitched with a need to strangle whoever hurt her—and strike down the one who allowed it.

Olssen and Geon took a step away, glancing back and forth between him and the rune.

Tarn gritted his teeth, angry with himself for activating it. *Weak.* The word burned in his mind, taking solace in his indignity. Feel nothing, he ordered himself. Yet the rune only dimmed. "How did it happen?" he asked Elon, needing a distraction.

The elf observed him, sensing danger, but replied truthfully, regardless. "She shot Rawn Norrlen and missed. He did not."

Tarn clenched his fists. So, the Warrior Guardian had joined them after all. Another spoke in the wheel. "He killed her?"

"No."

The heat left his head, but his relief soured with irritation at the elf's terse responses. While he preferred concise information on other matters, this was not one of them. Tarn rubbed his forehead. He needed to focus. He shouldn't care for Len. She was like every other soldier. A tool and a weapon that served his purpose.

"Where is she?"

"Novo took her to the mages for healing," Elon said.

That news instantly made Tarn wary. He didn't trust the shifty mages who were loyal to no one but themselves.

He glanced at Von. "Can you wake him?"

Elon shook his head. "This is mage magic which only a mage can unravel. Should I attempt to break the spell, I may harm him."

Tarn exhaled a sharp breath, his patience worn thin. "Olssen, you are acting Lieutenant until I appoint another. See to the camp breakdown. We leave within the hour."

"Yes, Master." Olssen bowed and left to do as ordered.

"Keep them here," Tarn instructed Elon, indicating Von and Geon, then stepped outside.

The camp was quiet, the chilly air laced with tension. The Raiders loaded the wagons, conversing in whispers among themselves. On the perimeter of the encampment rested the mage's tent. There was no need for him to go. This errand better suited the elf, but he needed to see the condition of his asset.

The stares of the men followed him as he crossed the camp. Benton's tent appeared like any of the others, though it was larger to accommodate the three mages. As Tarn approached, the surrounding atmosphere crackled faintly with an electrifying power that prickled on his skin. Silently, he slipped inside, keeping to the shadows of the entrance, and no one noticed his presence.

The heady metallic scent of blood and pungent herbs immediately hit his nose. White crystals dangling above lit the space with soft light. Novo, Clayton, and Dalton knelt by a cot, and over their heads, Tarn spotted Len, where she lay unconscious. They rushed to unbuckle the breastplate, red spilling from the arrow sticking straight out of the center.

She was so still. She already looked dead.

That afternoon she looked sure and strong in her armor. Now she just looked like a little girl in gaudy metal. Why did he think she had been ready for this?

Benton leaned against his desk, casually grinding greens in a mortar as if there was no haste in saving her. No need to because she was dying. Tarn looked away, accepting it for what it was.

"Len, can you hear me?" Novo called desperately, drawing Tarn's attention back to her. "Len!"

"Calm yourself." Clayton pressed his fingers on her wrist. "Her pulse is weak."

"She has a bloody arrow in her chest, halfwit. Take it out."

"Seeing as I am the healer here, you can shut your gob and let me work or you can piss off," Clayton spat at him.

The mage still worked on her. That was enough to draw a delicate strand of optimism Tarn had no reason to form, and yet—

Clayton's palms flared yellow, and he held them above Len, closing his eyes. His brow tightened in concentration, and Tarn held his breath.

"Get ready, Dal," Clayton said. His younger brother nodded and gripped the shaft at the base of the arrow. "Now."

Dalton yanked out the arrow and tossed it behind him, where it landed by Tarn's feet. Novo took off the breastplate, revealing Len's tunic saturated in blood. Clayton placed his glowing hands on her chest, and her life seeped through his fingers, dripping to the ground.

Seeing it pulled something from Tarn as if his blood spilled with hers. He pushed those thoughts away. To care opened the door to death itself. The Seer had warned him of this. He hadn't allowed himself to feel anything for some time, but he couldn't stop the vile rage slipping out of him.

He grabbed the breastplate where it had been thrown and scowled at the jagged gash in the metal. He'd paid a Druid well for enchanted armor to protect his asset, so why had she been wounded? He plucked the arrow off the floor and studied it closely. Beneath the coating of blood on the arrowhead hid a straight carved line with an angular line pointing downward from the end. The rune for dissipation.

A spell used to break spells.

And it had ruined her. Len now looked as vulnerable as the day he purchased her from the slavers. She'd been a thin child, abused and bruised from the beatings she suffered, flinching at any movement near her. At first, she had been a shadow of himself, of everything he had left behind, but then he put a weapon in her hand and severed that fear. He taught her all manner of ways to kill a man with everything from a blade to a needle, and Len took to his brutal training in stride. She grew swift. Intelligent. Lethal.

His protégé.

Tarn gripped the arrow's shaft in his hand so tightly it splintered in half. This was not a matter of caring, but a matter of pride. Rawn Norrlen would pay dearly for this.

Novo gently brushed away the sweaty strands of hair sticking to Len's pale face. The touch was intimate, a familiarity that Tarn had not noticed before. "Tell me she will survive," the spy told Clayton.

"She's lost a lot of blood."

Novo fixed him with a cold glare. "Answer me."

Clayton frowned. "There's a possibility she may n—"

Novo seized Dalton from behind and whipped out a dagger under his chin. "Up."

Dalton's eyes widened. He raised his hands in surrender and slowly rose to his feet.

Tarn eyed the spy narrowly. The eccentric reaction caught him off guard, but it had also diverted everyone's attention from the one who needed it.

"What are you doing?" Benton barked, magic sparking at his fingertips.

Novo gave the mages a malicious grin. "This is to ensure that you attempt everything in your power to keep her alive. You *will* save her."

The spy's threats were always cheerfully delivered, oddly enough, but an edge had entered his casual tone, and a tremble in his typically steady hand. Where there was once confidence, Tarn now saw fear and desperation, other words for weakness and stupidity.

"Let my brother go," Clayton snarled as he stood up, yellow power snaking up his arms.

Novo pressed the dagger's edge into Dalton's gullet, making him hiss. "Careful now, best to continue the healing, mate."

Benton's eyes glowed garnet along with the crystal in his staff, and a vicious power filled the space. "Remove the knife before I remove your head."

"Enough," Tarn said coolly. They all jumped, at last noticing him. "The mages know if she dies, so will they."

The ominous words invited a long pause with the promise they carried. Benton and Clayton withdrew their magic.

"Ah, brilliant." Novo smiled and clapped Dalton's shoulder playfully, as if it had all been a game in good fun. His skilled fingers flipped the dagger in his palm and tucked it into the sheath strapped to his thigh. The young mage rubbed his sore neck, cursing the spy under his breath.

"Come," Tarn ordered Benton and turned away.

"She will live, you scamp," Tarn overheard Clayton say to Novo as he walked out of the tent. "The breastplate detained the arrow from piercing her heart."

The mass Tarn had not let himself acknowledge lifted off his being, but that could only have been the weight of the power gathered in the tent.

The sound of soft footsteps trailed behind him. His wrist prickled, and he glanced down at his glowing bracelet of amber beads hidden beneath the sleeve of his coat. The black clovers within each bead glowed faintly, absorbing the traces of magic in the air that Benton secretly expelled. The old mage was testing his limits. How bold of him.

"I want him dead," Benton demanded. "I'll bury him alive for the slight."

"You feel slighted?"

"He threatened my son!"

Tarn whirled around and caught the mage's throat. He squeezed tightly, Benton's rapid pulse beating against his palm. Benton's hands sparked with magic, but he cried out when the bangles at his ankles struck him with electricity for attempting to harm their ward.

"You dare wield magic against me?" Tarn growled. The black clovers blazed brightly as they absorbed more of Benton's Essence. He squealed, his eyes bulging as he struggled to breathe. "You must think me a fool, old mage. I know you removed the cloaking spell off the camp that night. If anyone is to die today, it is you."

Panic flashed across Benton's features. He attempted to deny it, but Tarn squeezed tighter, making him wheeze. The mage had allowed the Azure King to ravage his encampment, to slay his men, and almost dismantle everything he stole and killed to gain.

"What do you want to be remembered for?" the voice of Tarn's past asked again. Her golden hair swayed as she turned away from him, walking into the shadowy corridor of a manor long left to ruin.

"Degree or intent is irrelevant. There is no difference," he had answered.

Her silhouette faded into the shadows. *"You're wrong. For there is darkness in us all, the only difference is in which degree."*

Benton's face turned blue, his eyes rolling into his head. Tarn held on long enough for him to feel his life slipping away, to feel how quickly it could be taken, before releasing him. The mage fell to the ground, coughing violently as he gasped for air.

"The moment you cease to be useful is the moment you cease to exist," Tarn said. The cloaking spell surrounding the camp was necessary while the Azure King hunted him, but he planned to get rid of Benton as soon as they found another to replace him.

The mage looked up with hatred burning in his eyes. He'd made no secret about how he truly felt. An animal backed into a corner eventually bit back.

Von must have known who had exposed them to the Azure Guard, yet he didn't report it, most likely to spare the young ones. Foolish and too damn soft.

"Pick yourself up."

Benton stumbled to his feet, and they continued the rest of the way in silence. When they reached his tent, Tarn nodded for him to go in first. The mage warily entered, and his attention immediately sought the Crystal Core dangling from overhead. Tarn waited to see what he would do. The mage had not been allowed anywhere near the crystal before, not when it was the one thing that would set him free of his bonds.

Benton noticed him watching and cleared his rough throat. "How may I be of service?" he asked, his tone slightly sardonic.

Tarn dumped the bloodied breastplate on his table. "Wake him."

Benton glanced at where Elon and Geon waited by the bed. Then he noticed Von. His expression twisted in a gloating sneer as he took in the commander's state. "My, my, what happened here?"

"Do as ordered," Elon said.

Benton smirked. Essence filled his hands, and every defense spell within the tent lit up, filling the air with fierce energy. The mage stiffened, shrinking under their power. If he attempted anything, they would immediately attack him.

Benton resumed and slowly waved his hands over Von. His palms flared brightly, and Von woke with a startled gasp.

"Commander," Geon smiled at him with relief. "You've returned to us."

"Aye," Von garbled. Elon helped him sit up, and he groaned, clutching his head. "Bloody hell."

Tarn stood silent, letting him get his bearings. As soon as Von saw him, he lowered his gaze.

"Go," Tarn clipped, dismissing the mage. He waited for the amethyst crystal to stop spinning, then he asked, "What *happened*?"

His fists clenched as Von explained the events in Corron. They were attacked by the sorceress who retrieved her stolen medallion. She rendered him unconscious, so he'd lost the Maiden as well. Geon confirmed the Guardians slayed the Raider unit.

"Why didn't you eliminate the Celestial and the Lycan?"

Von swallowed. "I ... the Celestial is a descendant of the Heavens, and the Lycan is dangerous. I didn't want to risk—"

"Don't feed me that rubbish," Tarn snapped. "Damn your stubborn pity."

Von would be a fine killer if he didn't let his conscience get in the way. No matter how much Tarn tried to strip it from him, he held on to a piece of it.

Geon kept his head lowered as he clasped his shaking hands on his lap. Good. The boy should be afraid.

"You will be whipped for this."

Von stared at him, not with fear but with disbelief and confusion. He had expected death. That would have been kinder. He should know by now not to expect kindness from him.

The torches lit the clearing outside of Tarn's tent. Disquiet hovered among the Raiders who stood motionless in the night. Geon huddled into himself, bare back shivering against the bitter autumn chill. Scars thickened Von's broad back by a flogging he'd already received years ago. It had reformed him into a dependable soldier—until today.

Tarn unfurled the coiled whip, and leather smacked the ground. The boy flinched.

"I will take the lad's lashings, Master," Von said, righteous as always.

Geon raised his chin, staring straight ahead. "No."

It reminded Tarn of another boy who once stood brave and proud beside him, refusing to forgo his punishment. The boy's face almost seemed to surface over Geon's by the distorted firelight.

Instead, he saw *her.*

The ends of her hair and gown fluttered in the wind as she slipped behind the crowd. A cold sensation washed through him. Tarn looked away, knowing she was not truly there. The last time he had seen his mother, she laid wasting away in her bed, taking her last breath.

Like an entity of darkness, he'd slipped into her room during the dead of night, Death's presence lurking in the air. He staggered to her side, exhausted, drenched in mud, blood, and troll entrails. She offered him a feeble smile of relief, as if she had been waiting for him to come.

"Whether by degree or intent, I'll be remembered for my legacy," he told her. *"Whenever they hear my name, they will tremble in fear, for I will be the storm that rains destruction upon them all. I will wipe their nations off the face of the earth, and from the ashes, I shall bring forth mine."*

"This is a path on which you must walk alone, my phoenix," she replied faintly as her ice-blue eyes slid closed. *"To cleanse the evil from this world, you must become its replacement."*

Then so be it.

"Kneel," Tarn commanded. Von and Geon prostrated in the dirt. He gripped the whip, the leather creaking under his fists. "You cost me twenty-two assets. Twenty-two lashings you will receive."

But this was for the failure that led to Len's near demise. She wouldn't have been hurt if it was not for Von's lack of will. Tarn cracked the whip and internally flinched when the barbs pierced Von's skin, splitting his back open. This was for the Unending he should have gotten. He'd been so close to achieving everything he strived for, only to have it slip through his fingers. The lad screamed when the barbs tore into him next.

This was their doing.

Their punishment.

Their failure.

The Raiders winced with each crack of the whip, some turning away. Flesh peeled and tore, splattering the ground red, grotesque yet somehow beautiful. This was for everything he lost, and everything he would soon gain.

Geon collapsed in the dirt and didn't get up. Tarn stopped, breathing heavily. Sweat layered his skin, and blood speckled his tunic. He lost count of how many lashes he'd given them.

Von shuddered on his hands and knees, his britches soaked with blood, weak and futile, a mirror image of Tarn in his past.

"Never have I been so disgusted with you," Tarn said. He froze at the familiar words unintentionally leaving his mouth. Ones he had heard spat at him most of his life. Why did he remember this now?

"Forgive me, Master ..." Von's reply was a shaking thing. His arms trembled, fighting to remain upright.

It gave Tarn no satisfaction to have rendered him this way. The whipping had gotten out of hand.

He threw the whip down and went into his dark tent. The mood rune blazed to life. It switched between colors interchangeably from crimson, black, blue, and purple, pulsing in tandem with his heartbeat, accusing him of his emotions. He felt each one in full measure after having gone so long of suppressing them. They were candles casting light over that which should remain forgotten.

Tarn peeled off his soiled tunic, and the throbbing light highlighted the crevices of the many scars on his body. Deep indentations marked where teeth had torn through him and lodged in his bones. The phantom sensation of being eaten alive never left him, though it had occurred a lifetime ago.

"Why must one fear death when it's not here?" his mother whispered in his ear. *"When it does appear, you're already dead."*

Tarn took out the lock of hair tucked in the book. It still smelled like her, of lavender and a hint of decay. They had already rendered her into the ground. That would not be him. With a flick of his fingers, he tossed the lock in the fire. The strands blackened and curled as they and everything else about her dissolved away.

This journey began many years ago, with only one goal in mind. Nothing and no one would get in his way. The pursuit had already cost him everything, so he truly had nothing left to lose.

Tarn inhaled deeply and expunged his emotions one by one. Anger, fear, regret, and remorse faded like smoke in his next breath. The rune stopped glowing, and the tent went dark except for the few smoldering embers left in the brazier.

The adventure continues in...

Bonded Fate

Guardians of the Maiden: Book 2

About the Author

BECK MICHAELS is the American author of the enchanting young adult novel *Divine Blood*, the first book in the epic fantasy series *The Guardians of the Maiden*. Beck lives in Indiana with her husband and two children, where she spends her time reading and daydreaming of stories in faraway lands.

WWW.BECKMICHAELS.COM